THE SWEETEST DEVOTION

THE SWEETEST DEVOTION

BRITNEY JULY

THE SWEETEST DEVOTION

Editor: Erica Russikoff

Cover Design: Cassie Chapman at Opulent Designs

Character Art: Yenthe Joline (@yenthejolineart)

ALSO BY BRITNEY JULY

FANATIC LOVE

Deeper

for lovers

Playlist

◄ ► ►|

Wild Side (Extended) • **Normani feat. Cardi B**
Nice & Slow • **Usher**
Deeper • **Summer Walker**
Favors • **Travis Garland feat. Tove Lo + 2 Chainz**
Come Over • **Aaliyah feat. Tank**
The Hills • **The Weeknd**
Company • **Tinashe**
All Her Love • **Donell Jones**
Unthinkable (I'm Ready) • **Alicia Keys**
Beauty • **Dru Hill**
Sneaky Link • **Muni Long**
Consistency • **VEDO**
Blue Jeans • **Lana Del Rey**
Marvin's Room • **Drake**
illicit affairs • **Taylor Swift**
The Beautiful Ones • **Prince & The Revolution**
Big Girls Don't Cry (Personal) • **Fergie**
Tightrope • **ZAYN**

I Belong to Me • **Jessica Simpson**

Kissin' on my Tattoos • **August Alsina**

Fallin • **Coco Jones**

Bad Idea • **Arin Ray feat. Blxst**

Somethin About Ya • **J.Howell**

fake smile • **Ariana Grande**

Vices • **Josh Levi**

Purple Rain • **Prince & The Revolution**

Diamonds and Pearls • **Prince & The New Power Generation**

I wonder if it's possible to have a love affair that lasts forever.

— ANDY WARHOL

I

Kennedy

"Stop pouting."

No matter how many times my mother made this demand, I couldn't stop myself from fidgeting and scowling. My stomach was in knots, my palms were sweating, my skin crawled, and I couldn't concentrate on anything else.

This wasn't what I wanted.

On paper, I had it all with no means to complain. And really, there was very little for me to complain about. Born with a diamond-encrusted spoon in my mouth, brought up among the upper echelon, and having attended a decent school for a time, it wasn't a lie that any problems I may have had would be deduced as "First World Problems."

I had never wanted for anything. Didn't know what it was like to go to bed hungry or worry about choosing between paying rent or a light bill. I had never suffered a day in my life. So why was I currently in the midst of a grave mental breakdown?

It was like something out of a soap opera.

My parents had done the unthinkable: they'd gone behind my back and sold me to the Devil himself. And tonight, they were hosting my engagement party.

All of the who's who of Hampton Hills were filling my

parents' lavish home to celebrate this joyous occasion—only, there was no joy to be had on my part.

My ring was gaudy, ostentatious, tacky—whatever you wanted to call the huge diamond my new fiancé had gotten me. A fifteen-carat cushion-cut ring set in platinum marred the fourth finger on my left hand, regrettably.

None of this was what *I* wanted.

My father was Damon Nichols, co-founder of The Residence Hotel hospitality empire. And in order to solidify his latest contract with Las Vegas casino Cartier, he promised something he couldn't afford. Something I had no say in.

My father had fallen ill, this new deal was potentially his last as chairman of the Nichols & Wagner group he'd built, and outside of a percentage of their joint venture, all the owner of the Cartier Casino wanted was *me*.

I'd spent my whole life living in the lap of luxury, traveling the world and seeing all the exciting places my father had built his hotels in. I would give it all up for the opportunity to choose my future and my partner. Okay, maybe not *every*thing. I loved my purse and shoe collection too much to completely part with it.

Still, this was a disaster.

The guests were down on the first floor, while my mother attempted to coax me out of my old bedroom to make my debut and greet my fiancé.

Stylists had taken care of my hair and makeup as my mother saw to it that a rack of dresses was delivered to the house this morning.

My dress cost ten thousand dollars, and on any other night— that wasn't my engagement party—I would've shined in it. Socializing, taking pictures, laughing at really corny dad jokes— the whole nine yards. But facing the dread that was my first official public appearance with my fiancé, Cain Carter, I was resenting the fact that there wasn't enough material to shrink into the dress.

My flirty tulle mini dress featured a plunging neckline that offered up my busty cleavage, a ballerina-like skirt that accentuated my long legs, and an embroidered star pattern, which made me really stand out.

The sheer tulle material called for a nude bodysuit underneath, but I hadn't bothered. If any of the evening's guests stared hard enough, they'd see right through the dress. For my fiancé's sake, I was nice enough to wear a nude thong underneath.

"You could have it a *lot* worse," my mother said dismissively, as if she were dealing with a child and not her twenty-four-year-old daughter. "He's handsome, doesn't drink or smoke allegedly, and he doesn't have any kids for you to take after. You could be with an old troll."

It was easier for her to say; she wasn't the one being forced to marry a stranger. Her father hadn't manipulated her into marrying against her own choosing as a "dying wish," and for the good of the family business.

It wasn't that I didn't know Cain—well, I didn't—but I didn't want him.

He'd asked me out twice before and I'd turned him down both times. Once, because I was dating my ex, Gaius Jones. And the second time because I simply wasn't interested. There was something about Cain I couldn't put my finger on, something that told me to run the other way. Something...*wrong*.

He came out of nowhere. The long-lost heir to James Carter's fortune. James had been the previous CEO and founder of the Cartier Casino in Las Vegas, a single property that was easily the most successful gambling and entertainment resort in Sin City. When he'd died suddenly at the age of sixty-eight, leaving behind a widow who hadn't borne him any children, many were stunned when Cain came forward as the sole inheritor to Cartier holdings.

His mother was unknown, but through two DNA tests and legal binding from James himself, it was proven without a doubt that Cain was now in charge of the Cartier. No one knew him or where he came from, and that made men like my father uneasy. Cain was a wild card. The youngest billionaire in the owner's box.

He was already on the cover of *Forbes* and *Fortune* before he was twenty-five.

Now at twenty-seven, Cain was the most eligible bachelor on the West Coast. Everyone wanted a piece of him. Extremely private, he'd only been seen once or twice with a woman, some beauty who was linked to a modeling career or some form of entertainment.

And now he was linked to me.

I didn't know much about the Bible, but I knew it was written that one of the most perfect angels turned out to be Satan. And considering Cain, I could believe that. He was young looking, mysterious, and intimidating in his Tom Ford suits, but there was no mistaking the air of wrongness about him.

My father had come across his wealth honestly: school, hard work, and fair deals. Rumor had it, Cain's father had done so through brutal measures: dirty money, blood, and lies. James might have been a cheat, but there was something about Cain that threatened more.

My father was co-owner of a five-diamond hotel kingdom. He was ultra-selective of who he let into his circle. With whom he considered doing business. Knowing all this, Cain still turned him down when my father had first approached him. It was as if the exclusivity didn't even faze him.

Or, business wasn't what *truly* interested him to begin with.

I'd said no when Cain had asked me out previously, and now with my father gravely ill, he'd weaseled his way into finally getting what he wanted. Two birds, one stone. My father got to have his precious joint casino and hotel, and Cain got to have me. Everyone won.

Except *me*.

These types of things weren't exactly unheard of in our upper-crust world. Arranged marriages came with the territory of being an heir to multimillion-dollar companies. I'd seen it happen a few times to girls I knew in passing, who ran in similar circles.

Rings were exchanged, hands were shaken, and business ties were set. Nobody batted an eye.

Still, I never saw this happening to *me*.

"I can't," I let out as I pleaded with my mother. "Don't make me do this."

She pursed her lips where she stood beside me, primping her own appearance in my vanity mirror. "It's a done deal. Your father has never asked you for anything, Kennedy. You think he wanted to get sick like this? You think it's easy for him to watch all that he built from the sidelines as he lies bedridden? All he wants is this project to go through. It's not like we signed you up to marry a monster."

But they had. I couldn't prove it, sure, but one good look at Cain and I just knew he wasn't the hero.

My father and Cain had made their deal, shook on it, and signed contracts. I could say no and lose everything, my family and the trust they'd set up for me since birth. I'd be nameless and penniless. Not to mention homeless. There was no way I could continue living in my penthouse suite at Hampton Hills's local Residence Hotel.

It wasn't fair.

My mother stood from the mirror, turning and facing me. "Now, I do believe we've kept your guests waiting long enough."

These weren't *my* guests. No one I truly cared for was here in attendance. My only friend, my best friend Jadyn, was at her home in Bedford Heights. She called bullshit on this whole thing when news hit me a week ago. She would've come in moral support, but I didn't want her to play a role in this bizarre movie of my life.

I was sure Stephanie and Elyse were downstairs somewhere. They were my parent-approved friends—surface-level associates I only knew through my father's business companions.

My mother didn't wait for me to collect my bearings. She looped her arm through mine and tugged me out of the room. The cool air in the hall did little to alleviate the fever of anxiety swelling my body. I stumbled as my mother dragged me down our marbled staircase where already I could see guests here and there on the first level. One of the dual front doors was open. More people were arriving. The late evening outside was a too-tempting escape route.

There was no time for that as my mother put on her best smile, jerked me upright, and began putting on a show.

She wasn't completely heartless. When news struck of my father's deteriorating health, she'd been delirious with grief and denial. He was the love of her life, and she wasn't ready to part with him. But in Hampton Hills, you didn't let your true emotions show.

"Oh my gosh, you look so beautiful, Kenn!" Elyse gushed as we reached our great room where a bevy of guests were. "I still can't believe you never told us you were seeing Cain Carter."

Elyse and Stephanie were good for light conversation whenever we were at an event together, but I saved all personal details of my life for Jadyn. Someone I could trust not to take a bullhorn and broadcast my innermost thoughts to the media.

"We wanted to keep it between us," I lied through my teeth. "After Gaius and all the social media last time, we figured this was best."

It wasn't a total lie. At the time I'd been seeing Gaius, rising rookie running back for the Long Beach Sharks, the media had been all over us. We were "relationship goals" for many as we were often spotted leaving places like Nobu or amongst a Black Hollywood party. I definitely wanted my next relationship to be more private and intimate—instead, I got something much worse as I took in the large gathering that had come to celebrate my engagement.

Elyse nodded sympathetically. "I don't blame you."

"So sad your dad couldn't be here, Kenn," Stephanie said as she reached out and caressed my goose-bump-littered arm.

No one outside of my family knew my father was sick. To the

public, he was simply away on business, unable to attend this heinous little soiree, but sent his best wishes.

I paid Stephanie no mind as I set eyes on Him.

Standing amid two men clad in expensive suits, nursing champagne-filled glasses, was Cain. He didn't smile. Only nodded as he listened to whatever it was that they were saying. In the little time that I'd known of him, I wasn't sure I'd ever seen him smile. Not even in those off-guard shots I'd seen online of him escorting a date from a restaurant or event.

Cain ran the Cartier Casino in Las Vegas, but he lived here in southern California. There was the off chance he'd be a busy spouse where I'd only have to see him once every few months. Honest wishful thinking, really. He'd finally gotten his hooks in me and I knew he wasn't letting me go.

"It's time," my mother leaned close to whisper in my ear. "Don't mess this up. Your father's counting on you."

With a nudge in my back, my mother sent me forth to go and greet my fiancé.

We hadn't spoken at all since my father summoned me home to his room to tell me the news. Cain hadn't even done the traditional asking on one knee. The morning after my father had told me the worst news of my life, there was a knock at my suite and a courier delivered the ring with a simple note from Cain reading, *Yours, C. Carter*.

The two men ambled off and Cain was now alone. I had his complete attention and that only heightened my sheer terror.

The closer I got to him, the more I wanted to disappear into the crowd around us.

Cain stood back, observing me knowingly and expectantly. His black eyes as cold and hollow as his presence before me.

Dark. Foreboding. Soulless. My fiancé.

I came to a timid stop in front of him, unsure whether to speak or shake hands.

Tall, handsome, with skin as dark and brown as my own, Cain

was aesthetically pleasing to the eye, I wouldn't lie, but the lack of warmth around him was startling. No, I would not touch him.

Cain peered down at me, taking me in. His face was indifferent, almost as if he couldn't care less about this party or our engagement.

"There's our happy couple!" A photographer jumped out of nowhere, armed with a camera to snap our photo. Journalists and bloggers were also in attendance to take note of our magical pairing. Cain was a beloved bachelor, and I was Hampton Hills's princess, known for my fashionable influence when spotted out in LA, my last public relationship with an NFL player, and my being the daughter of one of the most successful Black men in the United States. Someone online had already dubbed our impending nuptials as "the Royal Wedding."

Being a Nichols, it came with the territory. We were the premier family of the West Coast. We caused a spectacle everywhere we went. To the public eye, it was only right that I marry the youngest billionaire in the boys' club. With his dashing good looks and my stunning beauty, we were a match made in a dazzling haze of mergers and acquisitions.

Cain's arm came around me so we could pose for the camera.

I studied his hand where it rested on my hip, taking note of a single long-stemmed rose tattoo stretching the length of his hand, from his wrist to his pinky. The stem held a few thorns and the ink was done in black.

Gazing up at my fiancé, I wondered if he had any other tattoos.

The photographer snapped our photo where I smiled stiffly as my body brushed against Cain's. We raised champagne flutes and toasted to our engagement, posed with my mother, and alone as a duo.

"Can we expect a big wedding?" a journalist from some magazine asked as soon as the photographer had stolen every smile he could get from me.

My mother was behind her, nodding at me, telling me with her eyes that everyone was counting on me.

My voice, nervous, weak, came out of me on autopilot. "Oh, I definitely am going to need a *year* to plan all that I have in mind."

"Ooh, can we expect something local, or remote?" the blonde journalist pressed further, her green eyes bouncing from me to Cain and back. "I *love* destination weddings."

Cain's hand lay heavy on my hip, a boulder keeping me in place. To the journalist, I forced out another smile as I pretended to hold my finger to my lips as if I had a secret. "Wait and see."

She bought it. They all did.

As annoying as pretending was, it saved me from the feat of facing my fiancé one-on-one. But that only lasted so long.

With the party well under way, I was finally alone with Cain and there was no escaping where his dark eyes were locked on me.

He didn't smile. He didn't touch me. He didn't break that empty mask of his. "Do you like your ring?"

His voice was firm, commanding, and surprisingly warm.

"I'm sure it cost you a lot of money," I responded.

Cain looked at my ring before meeting my gaze once more. "That's not what I asked you."

I swallowed. "It's a lovely gesture, thank you."

A muscle in his jaw ticked as he nodded, staring down at me silently. I still hadn't answered his question, and something told me he was practicing his utmost patience just then.

A gust of cool wind cut into our tension as a figure approached Cain. A man in an ill-fitting gray suit went and leaned into Cain's ear, whispering something I couldn't hear. I'd seen this man a few times around Cain, one of the few men he kept close to him who did not look like the regular business type I was used to.

Cain kept his attention on me as he listened to his friend speak. And then, in a coded manner, he patted the man's back twice before dismissing him.

Cain thumbed at his full bottom lip as his eyes ran from my

neckline to my feet. "I have to step out for a phone call. Will you excuse me?"

Of course I would. "Y-Yes."

He blinked at my stutter, but said nothing as he walked around me and disappeared.

I heaved a huge sigh and wiggled my fingers, feeling a weight lift from my shoulders.

My mother was far across the room at the fireplace, entertaining old friends of hers. A Congratulations Kennedy & Cain banner hung from one wall to the other as gold and silver balloons floated in the air. The room was bursting with chatter and soft classical music.

I was glad my mother had forgone an official dinner, and instead opted for alcoholic beverages and appetizers. Men and women in red vests and white dress shirts were buzzing around the room and house, hoisting platters of cucumber sandwiches, gourmet stuffed mushrooms, smoked salmon and rye, and little strawberry shortcake desserts.

There was so much going on, so much noise, so many people, so little time to think before I jumped into action.

"Kennedy!" Influencers and other notables called my name as I made a beeline for the exit.

Trying not to draw too much attention to my panic attack, I stopped when approached, smiled and showed off my ring when needed, and lied about my secret fairy tale romance with Cain.

With my mother distracted, I slipped out of the room and headed back up to the second floor to my room and locked myself in.

In the semi safety that was my old room, I began to pace, weighing my options, questioning the sanity of this whole charade.

I couldn't do this. My father was the one sick, but it was me who felt as if I were dying inside.

My mother would kill me once she got her hands on me, but I

had to get out of here, away from this party, away from this engagement—away from Cain.

Because my mother didn't trust me, I knew there was GPS tracking on my phone. I hated to have to leave without it, but I couldn't make a getaway and leave a trail of breadcrumbs.

I had nowhere to go. But anywhere felt better than here.

My mind was made up. I grabbed my clutch, tossed my cell phone on my canopy bed, and stepped out of my room. People were lingering around, having snuck up to the second floor for quieter conversation. No one paid me any notice as I walked with haste down toward the foyer. In a second, I was out the front door and into the night.

My patent leather nude Christian Louboutin heels didn't fail me as I raced out to the valet without looking back.

2

KEITH

I wiped off a smudge of grease from the hood of the deep green Bronco before standing back and cleaning my hands with the old rag.

"You straight," I spoke up as I tore my eyes from the truck and peered over at my boy Savon.

He adjusted his gold wired frames and took in his ride. "Yeah? I'm not gon' be drivin' and my brakes won't work, right?"

His joke failed to humor me. I took my work seriously when I was customizing or fixing a car. "Like I said, you straight."

"Are *we*, though?" Savon questioned next, studying me with a look of seriousness.

I folded my arms, unsure what he was getting at. He'd been my boy since we were kids. Truth be told, we were like brothers, same mother different father type shit. "Whatchu mean?"

Savon lifted his chin at me. "Ain't seen you in a minute. Dude gotta get his brakes fixed just to see if you still around."

Here we go.

Brushing a hand over my head, I took a breath. I peered around my uncle Rod's garage, at anything but Savon just then. We were the only two inside. Business was slow on this Sunday evening, which wasn't surprising since it usually was.

If it was anybody else, I wouldn't say a thing. But like I said, Von was like a brother. "Things just been kinda different for me after...Leila."

Understanding had Savon making an *O* shape with his mouth as he nodded. Everybody knew my ex; she was glued to my side like a conjoined twin at most functions. Or up under me at my place if I wasn't at hers. "Got you."

Just like everyone knew of our relationship, I was sure those closest to me knew of our split, too. It had been a year and some change and I still was collecting what was left of myself.

"I wasn't really fuckin' with no one," I explained further of my self-exile.

"No, really?" Savon responded sarcastically.

I shook my head. "I was in a pit, man. She had me twisted up."

"Shit, remind me never to fall like you did." Savon's pity was another reason I hadn't shown my face around the city much. My grandmother once took a look at me and said I looked like a dog who'd lost his bone.

It was more than the love, though. It was everything. Ego. Self-esteem. Heartbreak. All in one fell swoop.

I still remembered what she'd said to me that day she broke up with me. Leila had come over, as she so often did, but to my surprise she had an empty box with her. She started grabbing things she'd left over the two years we were together around my spot. She fought against me when I'd tried to get ahold of her to see what was wrong.

"We just moving at different speeds, Keith," she'd sighed, sounding exhausted. "We want different things."

I managed to get her, taking her face in my palms and making her see into my eyes. That's when I saw it. No light. No joy to see me. No spark. A pair of dull brown eyes stared back at me and something told me there was no getting through to her.

But I still tried. "Where's this coming from?"

"Nowhere."

"*Nowhere*?" I'd repeated, even more confused.

Leila shrugged out of my grasp, throwing her hands up and gesturing around us. "You not goin' nowhere. I want bigger and better things. You not enough for me."

Her words had hit me hard in the chest, piercing beneath my skin. I'd frozen, saying nothing more as she gathered the rest of her things and left, tossing her copy of my key on the table by the door and walking out.

A few months later I was scrolling through Instagram and noticed she'd become an IG girl, an influencer who went out more and wore less, and all that other shit Drake was whinin' about. She'd done a complete one-eighty, turning into someone I didn't recognize. It wasn't until I'd seen her under the arm of some hot up-and-coming rapper that I deleted my account all together.

Coming back to now, I went and leaned against a beam in the room, looking out across the spacious garage and shrugging my shoulders. I'd fallen into a dark place after that. In and out of depression and self-loathing. I couldn't blame Leila. I was gonna be thirty in August, and ain't have shit to show for it. My education was a GED. My look was intimidating from my face to my tattoos. I could never go corporate. And my past wasn't the cleanest either.

At the time, when I'd first hooked up with Leila, she hadn't cared about none of that. I wasn't looking for love or nothing too serious, but then I'd gone and fallen hard. Consumed in hearts and feelings, until I felt bled dry when she walked out of my life.

In the minutes, hours, days, and so on since the split, I withdrew from nearly everyone in my life. I kept close to my fam, because I was who they counted on and I owed my mother and grandmother more than I could ever repay. But outside of those two, I was like that GIF of Squidward, a mundane existence of home, the garage, and home again.

Love. Love was for suckers.

I *needed* to snap out of it, and running into Savon was a welcome wakeup call.

"Remind *me* to never fall again," I managed to joke for the first time in forever.

Savon shook his head, pushing his glasses up his nose. "See, you should come out tonight. Have a few drinks with the boys, get you some ass, and let this Leila shit go."

I wasn't one of those men that relied on pussy to solve all his problems. Maybe in my younger days when I was first gettin' some skin. But now, the idea didn't even make my dick twitch.

"Nah, as you can see, I gotta work," I pointed out.

Savon smirked, calling bullshit. "Negro, ain't nobody comin' through here tonight."

Uncle Rod's auto repair shop was the only shop open *and* opened till late on Sundays. It made us a step ahead of the competition. It was going on six in the evening, and we closed at eight. Rod wouldn't care if I did decide to close up early, being the only mechanic and employee on duty that night. But still, I wasn't feeling like hitting the bar or a club. Even though a part of me needed to throw myself out there again.

"Yeah, but not tonight, Von," I said.

"Not even for a drink?" he pressed on.

I did like to drink when I was out, but I wasn't in the mood. My current vice was smoking, and I'd been trying to quit— unsuccessfully—for about a year now. Just talking about my split from Leila had me itching to light up a Marlboro.

"Nah, not tonight," I said again.

Savon shook his head. "So what you getting into after this?"

I lifted and dropped my shoulder. "Probably see about that Lakers game."

Savon sucked his teeth. "They ain't doin' too hot this season."

They weren't, but it still beat a loud club or packed bar. "Next time, Von."

He made a face but didn't push. Instead, he crossed over to me and pulled me into a hug as he patted my back and dapped me up. When he reeled back, he caught my eye. "Stay up, king. You too important to too many people. You ever just wanna vent, play ball, watch a flick or somethin', let me know. We *all* go through it."

My heart softened at his words, because I should've known he'd be there for me. "Thanks."

"And don't think we ain't noticed you haven't been around the center either," Savon went on, getting on me for abandoning my work at the local community center.

I wasn't a role model, far from it, but through my trials, wins, and losses in the streets, I'd taken it upon myself with Savon to volunteer at the center to help young guys out, to steer them in a better direction than what we'd chosen.

I rubbed at the back of my neck. "Yeah, I'ma get back on that. I definitely dropped the ball."

Satisfied, Savon backed off. "A'ight then, stay safe and be careful."

We lived in Bedford Heights, a city in Los Angeles County in southern California. Or LA, if you weren't familiar with the area. From the time we were about twelve or maybe even younger, Savon and I stayed in the streets, and we knew the ins and outs of the havoc that lingered. I kept a piece in my house, so I wasn't worried. I had too many battle scars to be naïve when traveling alone at night as well. The Heights wasn't an entirely bad place, especially in recent years, but there was still trouble if you weren't watching your back.

I went and lifted one of the doors to the garage so Savon could ride out.

"You sure?" he asked me one final time as he drove on by to leave.

For a moment, I considered it, closing up the shop early and dipping out for the night. Breaking my depressing ass routine of home and work.

Glancing at the empty garage where only the sounds of the flat screen in the lobby could be heard if I left the back office door open awaited; I really wasn't missing out on much if I cut out for the night.

Still, I wasn't quite ready to make my return to a social life. "Next time, man."

Savon sighed, shaking his head before driving off into the night.

Instead of going back inside, I hung back, giving into temptation. Succumbing to my nicotine cravings.

I really need to quit.

Recluse or not, these days, I wasn't doing anything that was bad for me anyway. A cigarette was the least of my worries.

3

Kennedy

I DIDN'T KNOW WHERE I WAS GOING. I DIDN'T HAVE A plan. And while I wasn't an expert, I had a feeling this was a major no-no in Running Away 101.

My first instinct was to go home. *Rookie move*, I realized. My penthouse was the first place my mother would look and send security to get me.

It didn't leave me with many options. As I sat behind the wheel of my Lexus, I raced through all the places I could hide out until the coast was clear. It was almost hopeless until Jadyn came to mind.

The last thing I wanted to do was drop by unannounced, but I had no choice.

Once I crossed the city limits from Hampton Hills to Culver City and then into Bedford Heights, I let loose the biggest sigh of relief. *Home free.*

Nothing but twelve miles and at least forty minutes were wedged between me, my parents, and Cain. My parents knew about Jadyn, naturally, but they didn't know where she lived. It provided me refuge, a means of a potential escape from it all.

Well, almost. At some point, I *would* have to go home and

face what was laid out for me. For now, I needed a little time to adjust and get used to the idea.

I suddenly felt too young and trapped. Maybe if I knew the guy, *loved* him, had a choice, then getting married wouldn't faze me.

But I didn't, and I felt a buzz of panic creeping under my skin. I couldn't—

POP!

My car swerved to the right of the road, rumbling as I heard the sound of glass bursting beneath my tires.

Shit. Shit. Shit.

"Not good. Not good," I whined as I pulled over before my car lurched into the ditch.

I was at a bend in the road with nothing but trees and nightfall surrounding me. I had just gotten off the highway and was making my way toward Jadyn's, nowhere near walking distance to shelter from the looks of it, not that my heels would carry me.

The smartest thing I could've done was leave my cell phone at my parents' to avoid being tracked. The *dumbest* thing I could've done was leave my cell phone at my parents' when there was a possibility of an emergency such as the one I was currently in.

I was stranded.

Breathe, Kennedy, breathe, I coached myself to keep the anxiety at bay. Bedford Heights didn't have the best reputation as it was. While I knew all the stuff the movies and shows portrayed about the city was just fictional sensation to sell fear and violence, being out here alone at night did scream *Come hit a lick.*

Still, I climbed out of my car and assessed the damage done to my tires, questioning if I could wheel my way to civilization.

By the gaping hole in my front left wheel, I guessed I couldn't.

My lips trembled and ick rushed over me. Did I deserve this? For running off and not being brave enough to face my problems head-on?

I shook my head at the rhetorical questions. This wasn't my

fault. I didn't ask for my father to betray me like he had. He'd left me no choice but to react this way.

Regardless, I had to do something other than standing around like a sitting duck.

It was a fairly warm night this Sunday evening. A low of sixty-something degrees. Crickets echoed in the distance, and a full moon hung overhead amid the glittery stars in the sky peeking out above the trees.

Before I could contemplate walking up the road, a pair of headlights appeared around the corner, saving me the feat.

I stepped out into the middle of the road and waved my arms wildly to stop the driver, and spare them getting my same fate. A look over my shoulder found the remains of a bottle of liquor laying in the street.

A horn blew and I spun around, seeing the mid-size SUV, a Bronco, stopping a few yards from my vehicle. A man stuck his head out his window, gazing from my car to me. "Car trouble?"

I nodded, suddenly worried as I wished it were a woman who had stopped instead. "Yes. There's broken glass and I blew a tire."

The man got back in his ride and soon opened his door and climbed out. Sensing my trepidation, he approached me with his hands up. "You okay?"

No. Far from it. "I...I didn't get hurt. Thank God."

The man was wearing glasses, and behind his lenses I watched as his eyes fell to my clothes and soon my feet. He appeared perplexed as he pushed his glasses up and returned to my eyes. "You sure you're going the right way?"

"Huh?" I always took the back roads to Jay's to avoid lights.

The man scratched at his head and glanced at my Lexus. He then looked behind me and pointed. "Hampton Hills is that way."

Of course I didn't blend in.

Jadyn liked to boast about how everybody almost knew everybody in Bedford Heights. And while it wasn't a poverty-stricken city, I had a feeling no one was driving around with a hundred-thousand-dollar car or owned a ten-thousand-dollar dress. Or maybe it was my awkwardness, the way I kept my distance from this man that screamed I was from the Hills.

"It doesn't matter now, does it?" The question came out snappier than I intended, but I didn't back down from the tone my voice took on. Where I was from or going didn't matter with my wheel totaled.

The man bobbed his head. "You right. You call anybody?"

And now I felt like an idiot for what I had to confess. "I don't have my phone. I would really appreciate it if you let me use yours."

The man peered at my car once again before reaching into his pocket for his device. "I got you. My boy a mechanic."

I looked at the sky, thanking the Heavens for this godsend.

The man came over. "I'm Savon, by the way."

"Kennedy," I told him.

He looked down the way I'd come and back the way he'd traveled from. "Let me get this glass up before someone else gets in trouble. Here." He clicked on the contact for his friend and handed the phone over as it started dialing out.

I took the phone and raised it to my ear as I went and leaned defeatedly against my Lexus.

The phone dialed out only shortly before it was picked up on the other end.

"What's up wit' it?" a man's voice answered lazily.

"Uh, hello? My name is Kennedy, and I'm using your friend's phone. I'm trying to get ahold of a mechanic."

Over on his end, I heard him mumble, "Shit," and seemingly sit up somewhere. "My fault. He gave you my direct line. But, uh, this is Keith, what seems to be the problem?"

I explained to him my dilemma and my location before hanging up and waiting against my car as Savon cleaned up the last of the glass.

I should've helped him, but heels and this short dress weren't the makings of cleaning up glass from the street.

Savon was wiping dirt and grime off his hands as he came back over to me. "You get ahold of him?"

I handed his phone back. "Yeah, he's on his way."

Savon tucked his phone in his pocket. "You wanna wait with me in my truck until he gets here?"

He extended his hand and the sight of dirt had me cringing.

"I'll wait in my own car, thanks." I didn't stay and hear his response before climbing back into my car and locking the door.

Savon returned to his Bronco. Despite my rejection, he stayed with me until his friend was coming our way fifteen minutes later.

Keith maneuvered his tow truck until he was facing the way he'd come in front of my Lexus, making it easier for him to get my car onto his ramp in the back.

Savon got out of his Bronco, so I followed suit and got out of my Lexus to speak with Keith. A good two hours had passed since I'd left my engagement party. I was positive my mother was livid in her search for me. I could only hope Cain was livid *and* changing his mind about marrying me.

Keith got out of the truck, pulling the brim of his faded black baseball cap low as he came over to us. He wasn't dressed in the cliché jumpsuit like I would've expected, but casually in a denim jacket, T-shirt, and jeans along with a pair of Timbs.

He looked at my car and came back to me. I was five-ten, and with the added boost from my heels, I wasn't far off from reaching his height. I could see him beneath his baseball cap, and instantly I stepped back.

Keith had an angry face—albeit he was incredibly handsome, but still, he had a mean demeanor, making me nervous about approaching him. Nothing about his dark brown eyes and soft brown features said friendly. Where Cain read scary and ominous, this guy was more brooding and annoyed.

"Kennedy?" he asked as he tipped his head by way of a greeting toward me.

"Yes. Thanks for coming to the rescue," I said with an awkward wave.

Keith looked to Savon for only a second before going and rounding my car. He came back to the blown-out tire and without another word he squatted down, taking in my damage.

"Good news?" his deep voice spoke up. "You're only going to need to replace this one tire."

It took me a moment to register what he'd said. The sound of his voice left me startled, because how could a man sound like that? God, his voice was deep. Sooo deep. He sounded tired and disinterested, but his voice held an undeniable vigor.

"You got it from here?" Savon asked, reminding me I wasn't alone with Keith.

Keith peered over his shoulder at his friend and nodded.

"All right then. Offer still stands by the way," Savon said, hinting at a conversation they'd had I wasn't in on. He turned to me, bobbing his head and offering me a gentle smile. "He's the best to do it. You're in good hands."

I supposed a man didn't have to be smiling to be good at his job.

"Thank you," I said, feeling my manners coming back. "For stopping and helping me."

Savon acted as if it was nothing to help me. "Not a problem. Take care."

He got back in his Bronco and took off.

Keith stood from observing my tire and faced me. Mean face or not, he was fun to look at. Along his impressive jaw was a light dusting of facial hair, as if he'd shaved just a couple of days ago. His full lips were in an impassive line as he stood before me, and I wondered if they'd ever curled to smile a day in his life. The sight of those dark eyes told me he wasn't one for smiling.

I stopped staring and focused on my car. There was no hiding now, because whatever the damage cost, I would have to use my debit card, a fucking Bat-Signal to my whereabouts.

"What's the model of this car?" Keith asked as he looked down at my tire again.

I looked at my cobalt blue convertible and felt very stupid. "It's a Lexus."

Keith's eyes cut to me, a *duh* look etched on his face. "I'm aware. What's the exact model?"

Why was he asking me this? When I'd wanted a car of my own as opposed to the car service my family would often use, I simply went into the nearest dealership and pointed to the car and got it.

"A Lexus...? I don't know," I said helplessly.

Keith pinched the bridge of his nose. "Is this car even yours? Or are you driving someone else's?"

Technically, everything I owned wasn't mine because I didn't really have my *own* money, but yes, the Lexus was mine and I didn't know a thing about it outside of what type of gas it took and how it felt to drive with the top down on a sunny day.

"It's mine," I snapped.

Keith shook his head, mumbling something under his breath as he took a step away from my car. "Forget it. Let's get it hooked up and we'll drive back to the garage."

I took in the tow truck behind him, one that could use a wash, and frowned. "You expect me to get in there?"

Keith's eyes narrowed as he looked at me. "How else am I going to transport you from here to there?"

Clearly, we weren't on the same page.

"*This* is Valentino," I said incredulously as I gestured to my dress.

Keith's dark eyes ran down my figure, examining my designer dress and my body in it. He did this boldly and unashamed. "And...?"

"If even a speck of dirt gets on me..." I let the idea trail in the air, hoping he was smart enough to catch on.

An impasse settled between us when I said nothing more and he didn't either.

I was being a diva, I knew, but I wasn't about to ruin this dress.

Keith soon snorted, shaking his head. "Jesus."

My disgust annoyed him, but finding an ounce of chivalry, he alleviated the situation by smoothly peeling his jacket off.

The only way to describe the movement was *fluid*. And for a brief moment, I was distracted as he stood remaining in his burgundy T-shirt and black jeans. His arms. So bulky. So tatted. So delicious looking. He wasn't muscular in that way that said he was a gym rat, but in a way that said he'd earned his brawn through manual labor.

I angled my head, admiring the sleeve on one arm holding vivid imagery. Cursive script could be found as well, but he wasn't close enough so I could read it.

Keith stepped closer and held out the jacket for me. "You can sit on this."

I didn't want to be any more of a nuisance, so I accepted the jacket and put it on. Immediately I was hit with the smell of his cologne, something woodsy, vibrant—male. I didn't know a thing about Keith, but the scent of his cologne fit him to a T.

Mmm.

Snapping to, I went into my car and grabbed my clutch and keys. I passed the fob to Keith before looping my strap over my arm.

He led me over to the passenger side of the tow truck and helped me up the lift as I opened the door. I got in and he shut the door behind me before getting to work on hooking up my car.

Admittedly, the cab of the truck wasn't as filthy as I thought, but I wasn't going to take off his jacket just in case.

Five minutes later, Keith returned to the truck and climbed in behind the wheel. With the door closed, we were immersed in his scent and presence. In a way, it was overwhelming, intoxicating, a rush of blood to the head, but I liked it. Something about him felt warm, like a shot of Cognac—bad, but then it was good.

He glanced my way as he started up the truck. "You straight?"

His informal way of asking if I were okay left me nodding as I buckled in. "Yeah."

Keith didn't speak again as he started driving to the repair shop. There wasn't a chance for an uncomfortable silence. No, a rap song was playing from his stereo. The rapper spoke about violence without emotion toward his deeds, sounding ruthless. A glance at Keith found him bobbing his head to the music as if it wasn't offensive. The screen on the radio said it was a rapper named King Von.

Not wanting to hear more of his rhymes, I leaned forward and pushed a button on the radio that changed the station. Tony! Toni! Toné! was playing on the new station, "(Lay Your Head on my) Pillow." A much better soundtrack for the ride.

Keith kept his eyes on the road, but I noticed the way his fingers curled around the wheel even tighter as he drove with one hand.

"You know, for someone who doesn't want to be in this truck, you sure don't seem to mind touchin' shit." His eyes shot to me as he bluntly called me out, but he didn't change the station, thankfully.

I sat up, wanting to apologize, but my pride had me being petty and silent.

Tony! Toni! Toné! crooned on and I welcomed their harmonies as opposed to the brass and gruff raps from before.

We reached the garage, a place called Rod's Repair, and Keith circled the brown-bricked warehouse looking building and pulled in the back where he let up one of the three garage doors to pull in.

I opened my door and got out of the truck and carefully stepped down from the lift. The smell of oil and gasoline permeated the air, and the sight of a few cars waiting in the garage greeted me as I took a look around. I didn't make a move, afraid of getting dirty, jacket barrier or not.

Keith came around the truck my way and gestured toward a door leading into the main building of the repair shop.

"I'll be sure to get on this in the morning," Keith said to me.

My jaw dropped. "The *morning*?"

Keith nodded. "We're closed now."

It was Sunday, I was sure I was fortunate as it was to have caught him at all, but still.

"I need that car fixed now," I begged.

Keith wasn't moved. "Like I said, I'll make it a priority in the morning."

"I...I don't care if you overcharge me, I just really need that car fixed. I don't even have a phone to call an Uber."

Keith came past me, and I was almost positive I caught him rolling his eyes. "I'm not a cheat. I'll get you a spare set up, in the morning, so you can drive to your nearest Lexus dealer."

He wasn't going to fix my car tonight, leaving me even more stranded.

I followed after him as he entered the main building and led me down a brightly lit hallway to the lobby area. A couple of vending machines were along one wall, offering soda in one and snacks in the other. It all served to remind me I hadn't eaten.

There was a flat-screen TV mounted to the wall in one corner where the chairs and couches were for guests to wait at. A *Law & Order* repeat was on.

"I'm going to make a phone call," Keith announced as he came by me after locking the front doors and switching the OPEN sign to CLOSED.

He left me alone and I contemplated getting a snack. The fact that the vending machine held a bag of Garden Salsa Sun Chips was all the incentive I needed to dig through my bag for cash. I walked over to the reception counter to set my clutch on it as I rummaged around in my wallet for a small bill.

It was an off chance my gaze flickered over to the desk behind the counter, but there was no missing the landline staring back at me.

Why hadn't he used this phone to make his call?

Something told me he was making a personal call, but then an ugly inkling of doubt reared its head. I peered down the corridor Keith had gone, the doubt growing.

My curiosity won the best of me as I grabbed my clutch and stealthily made my way down the hall. I told myself I would just use the excuse of needing to use a phone as well, which was mostly true seeing how I had to get ahold of Jadyn or else I'd be on my own.

The door to the back office Keith had gone in was ajar. I poked my head in, catching him standing with his back to me, wiping at his hands with a paper towel as he stood in front of a desk, using the back office landline.

"I'm going to need someone out here right away ... I ran across a woman who claims she doesn't have her own phone and she's having car trouble ... I don't know, I'm just trying to do the right thing here ..." Keith was saying to whoever was on the line.

Shit. Did he call the cops on me?

Before I could stop myself, I burst into the room, racing over to the desk and pushing my finger down on the hook.

Keith whirled around, his nostrils flaring once he recognized me.

"Did you call the police on me?" I demanded to know.

A thick eyebrow arched as he set the phone back on the base. "The *police*? Why would I do that? I was calling you a cab."

I closed my eyes and winced. *Way to overreact.*

"Oh," I let out.

Keith observed me. "*Should* I call the police?"

I took off his jacket and handed it over. "Ha-ha. I thought you thought I stole my car for a second."

Keith set his jacket aside and shrugged those broad shoulders of his. "Even if I did think that, I wouldn't have turned you in. Then again, maybe it would've been entertainin' watchin' you get arrested assumin' you stole *and* damaged the car."

His idea of entertainment was lacking. "Are you always such a prick?"

He snorted. "Are *you* always such a brat?"

No one had ever spoken to me like that. Even as I broke up with Gaius, he didn't lash out at me. I was in the wrong here, but

I didn't want to admit it. I should've been more cautious when driving to Jadyn's. I should've been more polite when dealing with Savon and Keith. I should've spoken up and told Cain this engagement was against my wishes.

My shoulders sagged as I hung back away from Keith. It wasn't his fault I was in a sour mood.

"I'm sorry," I said softly.

"It's whatever," he responded.

My gaze lifted to him. His face was still angry. His tone was still bored. And his energy was still magnetic.

Now that he was right in front of me, I took in his other arm of tattoos. A half sleeve containing BH in hollow block letters along with a city landscape and palm trees. He had pride and love for his city.

I tore my eyes from his arms, finding myself admiring them more and more the longer I looked. The more I studied his ink, the more I was curious what more he possibly held under his shirt. Sometimes too many tattoos could make a person appear dirty, but Keith's made me want to step closer and trace my finger along them. Become accustomed to them and the feel of his stained skin.

His hands were bare of ink, but notably clean as well. I liked that he kept his nails clipped and clean.

Everything about Keith screamed *roughneck*, but undeniably *man*, too. He reeked of masculinity, from the confident way he assessed my car, to the way he walked, carried himself, and spoke. He was equal parts menacing with his angry look, but also alluring with his aura and build.

It was too quiet, making me look up and meet Keith's gaze. He was watching me.

Yikes.

If he were annoyed at my staring, it didn't show.

"You keep lookin' at me like that, and I'm gonna think you want somethin'," he said, his meaning loud and clear.

My stomach took a dive.

God, that voice. I bit my lip. "And what if I do?"

Keith leaned into my face. "This ain't what you want."

His nearness caused me to suck in a breath as something below my belly clenched.

I was sick of people deciding my wants or needs.

Boldly, I reached out and grabbed his baseball cap and took it off his head. He glowered at me, but made no move to reach for it. His hair was nicely styled in a fade with a neat wave pattern on top, letting me know he brushed his hair religiously.

Smirking, I fanned myself with his cap. "I'll say what I want and don't want."

Keith stared at me silently, as if he was restraining himself.

I was only messing around, but a part of me did want to break that empty mask on his face. Didn't he ever laugh? Or—

Keith picked me up, the abrupt action leaving me stunned and breathless, before setting me on the desk. He came close, his face inches from mine. "Is this what you *think* you want?"

I had only been kidding, but the moment swelled over into something else. Something hazy and heady.

A voice in my head told me to stand up and behave, but the order fell upon deaf ears.

It was the night of my engagement party and I was here with another man. One I didn't know any more than I knew Cain. That didn't stop the devil on my shoulder from goading me. From pointing out the electricity stirring in the air. I didn't know this man, but I *wanted* him.

I was sober as could be, but drunk on him, because his gorgeous face, his hypnotic voice, and his presence had me nodding. "Yes."

Keith's eyes were focused on my lips. His hands were planted on either side of me and I felt caged in, but I didn't want to be free.

He came to my ear. "I think you bumped your head when you ran over that glass."

My breathing seemed to heighten and I couldn't think

straight. I wanted what I wanted, and I couldn't explain it if I tried.

I gave in and touched him, feeling the sleeve of tattoos across his silky skin.

"Kennedy," Keith seemed to warn in my ear. He was ruining my fun and rebellion.

"Prick," I teased as I continued tracing his ink.

He reeled back, staring me in the eye. "Brat."

In another moment he dove close and his mouth hovered over mine. We were sharing the same breath, the same temptation, the same want, the same need.

Something told me if I didn't stop now, there was no going back. And for just a sliver of a minute I hesitated, questioning the rationality of the situation. Could I really do this? Go all the way?

I'm doing this for me, I decided as a quick once-over confirmed that Keith was too good looking to pass up. I hadn't been this wild and reckless since college, and with my parents obviously pulling the strings these days, there was no telling when I'd get the chance to feel alive again. One more flicker of my gaze at Keith and I suddenly didn't care about the consequences of my actions.

He wouldn't be my first, or my last, but this was different. There was a heartbeat below my belly button I didn't know existed until this man looked at me the way he was. A beat so strong it was painful. It only symbolized the carnal need I felt for Keith in this moment.

"It could be fun," I offered with a shy smile.

Still, Keith blinked, standing in front of me uncertain. "You for real?"

There was still time to go back. To do the right thing. But fuck it. "Yes."

A husky chuckle rolled off Keith's breath as he shook his head, soon looking away as if to question things further. And then he came back to me, all trace of humor gone as he studied my face and where I sat waiting for him to make a move.

He licked his lips, an action that was dizzying, reminding me...

I placed my hand over his mouth. "But no kissing."

Ow.

Very swiftly, his teeth sank into my skin as he bit me.

I removed my hand and frowned.

"Fine, I won't kiss you there," he said, almost threateningly.

His rough hand gripped my thigh and I squirmed at the feel of his hot skin on mine. His hand ascended up, disappearing under the skirt of my dress, daring to find treasure. The closer he crept upward, the more he watched for my reaction.

Closing my eyes, I gave in to the fire as I spread my legs open for him without shame.

I let out a whimper when he moved my thong to the side and stroked my clit. It had been so long since I'd been touched and I felt myself turn into pure arousal at the sensation of him.

We were alone in the building, presumably, but I didn't want to take any chances. "Close the door and lock it."

Keith made no move to do such a thing. He kept working his finger against my clit, driving me crazy.

"Keith."

He worked his finger some more, and I was losing my resolve to care.

"Keith."

He kept going, coming close to whisper, "Don't you have any manners?"

"Please," I whined as I felt myself rock against his hand.

Keith's hand was gone as he stepped away to close the door and lock it.

My legs were splayed apart, my chest was rising and falling, and all I could think about was him finishing what he started.

Keith turned and assessed me where I waited for him. He didn't look so moody anymore. The heaviness in his eyes alluded to the desire he felt for this moment as well. I wondered how he'd look when he achieved an orgasm. Would his hard mask crumble? Would he moan out my name? Swear? Become oh-so tender?

I was very curious the more I looked on as he stood away from me.

Keith reached back, gripped the neck of his tee, and in one smooth motion peeled the shirt over his head.

Shit.

I hadn't had sex in what felt like forever, but looking at this man shirtless had me ready to do it *all*. The ridges of his six-pack abs and the solid muscle of his pecs had me pressing my thighs together as all I could do was stare. On one shoulder blade I spotted the word *Progress*, and on the other, I noted the word *Patience*.

Patience was the last thing I felt as I saw all that he'd been hiding under that shirt.

He was done asking. Keith sauntered over to me, lowered himself down to his haunches, and wrapped his arms around my thighs, jerking me to the edge of the desk.

Oh.

As if he was hungry for it, he yanked my thong down and flung it elsewhere. My sex was staring him in the face and his eyes were on me, daring me to stop this while I still could. I couldn't turn back if I wanted to. I was so wet with need.

"UGH!" I let out the ugliest cry at the feel of his tongue doing a slow sweep from my entrance to my clit. My head rolled back and my eyes twitched. His grip on my thighs tightened, I couldn't move if I wanted to. All I could do was endure the painful bliss of his mouth on me.

I loved the way he licked me. Patiently. Eagerly. Thoroughly.

When I was close to it, he stopped, like he knew what was coming.

Keith stood and ran the back of his hand across his mouth, and it was so sexy and primal.

His hands went to his jeans and he undid his belt and zipper and let them fall. His ready erection stared back at me and I suddenly questioned my ability to take it.

The cocky look on Keith's face as he fished out a condom from his wallet had me pumping myself up to not back down. We'd come this far, and I was too worked up, needing my orgasm high.

Leaning forward, I pulled his boxer briefs down and freed his member. Long thickness hung between his legs and it suddenly clicked that a part of his energy was pure BDE. Well-earned at that.

Keith regarded me, his ego lessening. "You sure?"

I pushed the material of my dress to the side, exposing my breasts to him as I soon leaned back on my arms. "Yes."

Keith stared at me, the heat of his gaze burning me to cinder. He stepped up to me and placed the condom on.

There was no time to prepare or adjust. In one thrust he was inside of me, possessing me.

"Oh shit." The words left my lips breathlessly and suddenly as my mouth hung open.

I stared up at Keith as he filled me with all of his length. A slow smile burned across his face, as if he knew what he was doing to me.

He looked down between us, silently watching himself pull out of me and enter me again.

It was too much.

"Oh God," I whimpered.

His eyes were back on me. His strokes were slow and maddening.

I palmed at his handsome face, wanting to kiss him, wanting to get lost in his mouth, but resisting the urge.

There was nothing more personal than full-on sex like what we were doing, but I didn't want to kiss him. Didn't want to give in completely to the passion of our tryst.

A kiss wouldn't have happened anyway. Not with my senses slipping from my grasp as he took me deeper and deeper.

And then, as if he missed the taste, he pulled out of me, leaning down for another lick between my thighs, teetering me closer to the brink.

"Keith," I moaned his name. A whiny plea to let me have it. To give me my orgasm. To let me come.

He entered me again with renewed focus, his hardness consuming me to where he was all I could think about. Him and his mean strokes, owning me.

His sex was selfish, but pleasurable. He was taking what he wanted, but giving me what I needed.

He fucked me until I was numb. Until I couldn't see straight. Until I lost consciousness.

4

KEITH

I pulled up my jeans and eased out a heavy breath. I discarded the condom into the wastebasket beside the desk—which I was taking out as soon as possible because Rod was never finding out about this.

Shit.

The comedown had me putting things into perspective, and I had just fucked up bad.

Her wincing had me looking over. Kennedy was slacked against the desk as her hands gripped the edge. She'd done a lousy job of pulling her dress together to conceal her breasts and right her person.

I stayed where I was, not wanting to touch her again. The feel of her soft skin against my rough palms only emphasized how wrong this was. As if the fact that she was driving a shiny new Lexus wasn't a big indicator. Outside of the car, one look at this girl and I knew she was from money. The diamonds in her ears, the pearls around her neck, the air of sophistication about her— she wasn't from around here.

"Are you okay?" I spoke up, assessing her slow, sluggish movements.

Kennedy looked at me from beneath her lashes and behind the curtain of her hair. My breathing slowed because fuck. She was so goddamn pretty.

She tossed me a sheepish smile. "It's been a while."

Same. I mused over her words. So, she wasn't usually this bold. I wasn't either. Not that I hadn't had my share of one-nighters in the past, but none like this. Nothing compared to this.

I scratched along my neck. I didn't know what to think of Kennedy.

One thing that was painfully obvious, was that she was beautiful. In a way that made me feel dirty for touching her. She had a nice deep brown complexion, heart-shaped face framed with long dark hair, brown almond-shaped eyes, and a set of plump lips I wanted to feel between my teeth.

Pretty or not, she wasn't my type. Not by a long shot. One taste of her, one feel of her, and none of that mattered. It was like something out of an old-school porno. Lowly mechanic serving the desperate and horny housewife. But shit, it felt good. She'd looked at me as if I were scum, until I was deep inside her, making her scream. She demanded I didn't kiss her, as if I wasn't worthy —an act probably reserved for the dude she was marrying.

That was another thing. You couldn't miss the huge rock on her left hand. It was the first thing I noticed when I set eyes on her —well, after her face. That and her attitude. Kennedy had a face that could bring a man to his knees, but then there was that diva shit. She was the coldest woman I'd ever seen. I was sure whoever put that diamond on her finger was going to freeze his dick off fuckin' around with her come their honeymoon.

But *I* hadn't.

I would've never gotten into this predicament with a client, but something about the way Kennedy had looked at me, the way she tempted me, had me acting out of character, against protocol. Despite the red flags, all I wanted to do was fuck that smirk off her face. To give the little rich girl something to talk about.

So I went with the vibe.

The only sounds to be heard were a mix of splish-splash and her moans. And I couldn't get enough of it. She was a new feel, but I loved it. The fit of her smaller body against mine, the feel of her taking me inside her, the dig of her nails into my skin. Once I started, I couldn't stop. Her sex was so pretty, I'd had to kiss it twice.

When the walls closed in and the levees broke, I was more than willing to go down with the ship.

Now here we were. The aftermath.

I took in her dizzy, somewhat disoriented, dazed state. I hadn't really been gentle with her. Once the light was green, I went from zero to a hundred miles per hour without thinking.

"Can you walk?" I wondered out loud as I took in Kennedy's condition.

She snorted. "You weren't *that* good."

I felt a brow arch as I pivoted in her direction.

Instantly, she raised a hand, releasing a cute little laugh. "I'm kidding! But I'll live."

I settled down and grabbed my T-shirt and pulled it on. I needed to get out of here.

"God, where are my panties?" Kennedy sighed as she spun around, searching the floor for the soaked thong I'd thrown aside.

I found my baseball cap and screwed it on at the same time she managed to pick up her discarded underwear. She examined them, as if questioning going commando or not.

Again, I stared at her silently. Aside from her attractiveness, she also appeared young. I could already tell she'd someday be fifty giving the women in their twenties a run for their money.

"Can I see your license? We need a copy of it while we service your car." It was a lie, but she didn't even know the make of her car, so I was sure she wouldn't know what was standard procedure or not. It was clear she was an adult, but I still wanted to check on her age.

Kennedy turned around and leaned over to retrieve her fallen clutch from the floor. The sight of the curves of her ass had me wishing I would've taken her from the back as well. She really had a bomb ass body.

Kennedy dug into her bag and fished out her license and handed it to me.

I took it and read it over.

Of three things I now knew. Her full name was *Kennedy Elizabeth Nichols*, she wasn't an organ donor, and she was definitely grown.

"You just turned twenty-four," I said as I held the card out.

Kennedy narrowed her eyes and snatched her license back. "You could've just asked." She put the card away before regarding me. "So, how old are *you*?"

"Twenty-nine."

Kennedy stuck her hand out. "Uh-huh."

I wasn't sure why, but I dug my license from my wallet and handed it over to confirm my age.

Kennedy quickly scanned it. "Keith *William* Avery. You're six-three, and indeed twenty-nine. Almost thirty soon."

"Almost," I said bitterly as I accepted my license back and stored it away.

Switching gears, I went and grabbed the shopping bag out of the wastebasket and tied it up to take it out.

"Do you have somewhere in the city you need to be? I can drop you off," I offered as I regarded Kennedy.

She smoothed out the material of her designer dress—the "Valentino" dress. "So I had to sleep with you to get a ride?"

Despite my hurry to get out of this, I managed to smile. "Nah, I was tryna get you a cab, remember? Besides, it's the least I could do now."

"I have a friend I was going to go see. She lives off Queen Ave on Magnolia," Kennedy explained. She soon thumbed a finger over her shoulder. "First, can I use the restroom?"

I nodded. "It's right out the way you came. Can't miss it."

She slipped out of the room and I tidied up the office as best as I could. The smell of sex hung in the air, dragging me back to our encounter. That was probably one of the best fucks I'd ever had. If not *the* best. I loved the way she took me, how she kept moaning my name. How I fit inside her like she was built exclusively for me.

Shaking my head, I straightened Rod's desk and focused on getting out of dodge.

Following Kennedy's lead, I made a pit stop in the men's room before going out to the dumpster and tossing the trash. Knowing Unc, he'd probably beat me here in the morning, but I'd do my best to get in early enough to fix Kennedy's car and make sure the coast was clear.

There was a chance Rod wouldn't care about this, but I didn't want to push it. My uncle took his shop seriously. He worked hard to own this place and to build his clientele, and I'd be damned if I fucked it up because I couldn't control my urges.

Kennedy met me by the front door, her movement not as swift as it once was. It stroked my ego knowing she could feel me in every step she took.

It had been way too long.

I took her out to my Tahoe where I opened the passenger door for her, but not without giving her one good warning.

I leaned in to whisper, "Don't touch the station."

Kennedy only grinned up at me. "Play something nice and I won't."

Brat.

I resisted the urge to smack her ass as she turned and got into the SUV. Instead, I settled on curling and uncurling my fingers to release the tension.

Tugging the brim of my baseball cap down, I took a moment to breathe and compose myself before rounding the car and getting in behind the wheel.

Kennedy recited the address where her friend stayed, a familiar area that wasn't too far from Rod's Repair.

I put my Tahoe in gear, backed out of the spot, and soon took off for the exit. Not feeling the silence between us, I reached down and turned up my favorite radio station and let the hip-hop beat fill the ride.

Half a minute later, Kennedy sat up, flinching just a little as if still sore.

She angled her head at the stereo. "This sounds familiar."

I smirked, a little surprised she'd know Westside Connection.

I didn't bother educating her on who was playing, and she didn't kill the mood by switching the station. She even seemed to like it, despite their rhymes being not too far off from King Von's. I credited it to their singsong chorus making their song easier to digest.

Not too long later, I pulled up to a little house on Magnolia Ave, in behind a white Volkswagen. A few lights were on and as I faced Kennedy, I found her heaving a sigh of relief.

She turned to me, taking me in that way she'd done back in the office. Long gone was her fear of getting dirty.

"I guess I'll see you in the morning," Kennedy said. The rise and fall of her chest told me just how affected she was here and now in this car with me, with what we'd done.

When her hooded eyes settled on mine, I shifted my attention to her lips before nodding along. My grip on my steering wheel tightened, keeping me in place in my seat. One-off or not, I really wanted to taste those lips.

"Yeah, I'll get right on it first thing," I said calmly.

Kennedy bobbed her head and undid her seat belt. She grabbed her purse and was out of the car. Once she was on the front walk, she looked back at me over her shoulder, those eyes of hers stilling me in place until she was safely inside the house after knocking a few times.

Blinking, I let the moment go and headed home.

I didn't bother turning on any lights as I made it in. Through the darkness, I found my way to the back where my master bedroom was and collapsed as soon as I felt the edge of my bed. I needed this night to be over already.

I took off my cap and dug my phone out of my pocket to charge. My screen flashed a missed text from Savon.

SAVON

Bougie af, wasn't she?

I didn't even bother responding. He had no idea.

5

Kennedy

My entire body was tender and throbbing as I showered at Jadyn's. Touching every ache brought on a new memory of what happened at the garage. Just thinking about it drove my hand between my thighs to relieve some of the pressure —as if I could do myself any justice after *that*.

I was incredibly sore, standing proved to be just as challenging as walking, yet mentally I was fully charged. I'd never been touched like that, and even if another round would surely break me, I wanted to do it again. Keith hadn't made love to me. He fucked me—hard, without restraint, and without an apology.

In the aftermath, I felt empty. His sex filled me and overwhelmed me as he took me on a journey I would never forget, bursting my expectations until I was seeing stars. The moment we separated I felt his absence and a blanket of coldness I couldn't shake.

For the first time in my life, I had been going through a dry spell. At least, I was, until *that*.

Ruined. Just one taste of him and I felt ruined for other men. Or, I definitely thought he was way better than my ex.

Keith was a stranger to me, but he'd left an imprint I felt in every step I took.

In hindsight, I was glad I hadn't kissed him. I would've left that garage without my soul intact, and I was going to cling to it while I still could before I handed it over to my future husband.

Okay, I was probably being extra dramatic about marrying Cain, but I deserved to be.

Had we been a *real* couple, then perhaps I would've considered my little liaison "adultery," but because my hand was forced, I didn't feel guilty at all. A part of me wanted to go and rub it in his face, but then I considered the darkness surrounding Cain's person and I didn't want to test him.

It all came crashing back to me, the engagement and the truth of what this was. My *last* night of freedom where I'd had a one-night stand with a stranger, but come morning, I'd have to face reality and the rest of my life.

I came out of the bathroom after my shower at Jadyn's place wearing a nightshirt she'd lent me. Typically, we weren't the same size, due to Jay being five-one and all. Still, the shirt hung heavy on me, as she'd gotten it in two sizes too big for occasions like snuggling up on the couch or in bed.

I gathered my clothing and stuffed them in a plastic grocery bag. Mentally, I penciled in the idea of hitting the drycleaners as soon as possible. I may not have wanted to go to my engagement party, but I did love that dress.

Jadyn was out in the living room when I found her. Her house was small and intimate, the perfect size for her since she was single and childless. The most company Jay kept was the stray cats she often fed. She had a penchant for feeding the felines. Even more, when they became regulars, she'd name them. As of now, I recalled there was a Sylvester, a Greyer, a Midnight, and a Lionel. It was wholesome how she'd get excited about each visit from one of her furry friends and send me a photo of one eating from the paper bowls she'd set out her door.

That was one of the things that made me cling to Jadyn when I met her at UCLA. We'd both attempted to join a sorority and ended up being a sisterhood of two when we realized it wasn't for us. Right away I'd admired Jadyn's friendliness and kind heart. In the business world, there weren't many true friendships, and being the daughter of an elite, I never found any bonds with any of the girls and boys from my schooling.

Jadyn was different. She was from Bedford Heights and kept a glass-half-full persona that made me more grateful for what I had. Outside of her positivity, I loved her for her dreams. As I went and sat on the sofa beside her, I took in the blown-up movie posters from directors John Singleton and Gina Prince-Bythewood.

"It's always about *boys* in the hood, why not girls? And why not instead of a girl trying to make it out, she's trying to make it through and just live her ordinary day-to-day life? Girlhood or womanhood is just important a journey to follow than our counterparts," Jadyn had said to me when I'd asked her major or aspirations freshman year. Needless to say, she quickly became my favorite person and someone I looked up to.

I hadn't a clue what I wanted to do with my life. Hence my dropping out of school after my sophomore year.

Currently, Jadyn was going the starving artist route as she worked in collections for her day job while penning the perfect screenplay whenever she could get a minute.

I settled in beside her, making sure the large T-shirt covered me as I tucked my legs underneath myself. It had been over half an hour since I'd slept with Keith and still I felt unsteady, sensitive, and branded.

As if the act were a scarlet letter burned onto my chest, Jadyn was staring at me from her end of the couch, her big dark eyes eagerly awaiting my explanation.

"So..." Jadyn said patiently. "What's got you walking funny? Or should I say *who*?"

My cheeks burned as I began to smile. There were no secrets or judgment between us. "Jay."

She leaned close, a lock of her blonde hair getting in her face.

She'd fallen in love with the shade a month after we met and had been faithful to blonde bundles or frontals ever since. "Well?"

Ugh, there was no hiding the truth. I *was* walking different. "So, I was going to call, but I didn't want to chance my mom tracking my phone."

Jadyn's dark eyebrows teetered down as her brown features appeared confused. "Oh, yeah, you had that engagement announcement and party tonight." Suddenly, she lit up, her eyes tripling in size as she looked at my body and back at my face. "You fucked him, didn't you?"

Disgust bubbled in my belly at the thought. Wrinkling my nose, I quickly shot down that idea. "God, no. I took off. I ditched my phone and I ran out of there. I blew a tire on the way here and had to get a mechanic to tow me in."

Jadyn assessed me for damages as she again was perplexed. "So what happened?"

I sighed, lifting my gaze to the ceiling, searching for CliffsNotes on what I'd done this evening. "The mechanic brought me back to the shop...and one thing led to another and we...you know."

Jadyn blinked. "Damn."

"Yeah," I let out. I'd never been so brazen before in my life. I'd had a couple of meaningless hookups in college, but even then I'd known the guys. And then Gaius happened and I was all things monogamy with him. What happened with Keith was so unlike me, but I didn't regret it. He was *good*.

"This calls for wine!" Jadyn announced as she rushed to her feet to grab a bottle.

I gagged. "Ugh, pass."

"Girl, grow up already," Jadyn said as she often did of my not drinking. I didn't care for wine, beer, liquor, or anything alcoholic. It just wasn't my taste. Occasionally, I'd celebrate an accomplishment with champagne if out at brunch or a party, but at home in my penthouse, I kept it simple with water and my beloved white cranberry-peach juice.

When I'd officially turned twenty-one and was vocal about my distaste for alcohol, my father made it a point to provide sparkling grape juice in champagne flutes at all the parties or dinners he and his company hosted, in my honor.

My mood sank. I did not want to think about him.

Jadyn came back from her kitchen holding a bottle of wine tucked under her arm, a wineglass in one hand, and a bottle of water in the other for me.

I accepted the water and watched as she went about pouring some of her wine.

"Please tell me it was worth it," Jadyn said as she gathered her glass.

It was complicated and messy, due to my fiancé, but God, I'd never had an orgasm like that. Everyone in my life, from the time I was a little girl, treated me like a princess, delicate and fragile. Keith had done no such thing. He'd taken me brusquely. When he came, he'd grabbed a fistful of my hair, tilting my head back as his teeth grazed my neck. I shattered beneath him and thought nothing of him stepping all over the pieces.

He hadn't treated me like a lady, but like a good and hard fuck —and I liked it.

"That was probably the best I've ever had," I admitted.

"And you sure he had a job? The best dick I ever had was unemployed, but then again, he had somethin' to prove and was also hobosexual."

I was trying to be serious, but leave it to Jadyn to make me laugh. "Girl."

She threw a hand out in an innocent gesture. "Just sayin'. It look like he broke you off something good."

He had.

That dick tapped my soul.

I was still in my Valentino dress, wearing another man's ring, making the whole encounter dirty and illicit. I regretted nothing. "*So* good."

Jadyn chuckled. "Did you at least get his name? Or did you just pounce on him as soon as y'all pulled into the garage?"

"Keith," I spoke up. *Keith Avery.* A man with three first names, sexy tattoos, and a handsome face that had briefly broke out into the cutest smile when he'd laughed.

"Now that you've had a taste of the Heights, you ain't never going back to them pencil pushers in the Hills."

It all happened so fast, leaving me wondering if this was just a one-night stand, or if there was potential. I mean, I wouldn't have minded having another go at it with Keith.

If the circumstances were different.

I uncapped my water and took a hearty swig as my shoulders sagged. "Right, because now I have to go and face my maker."

Jadyn frowned. She reached out and squeezed my shoulder. "Right, your 'fiancé.' Was he weird? Was he the reason you ran off, besides the obvious?"

Cain hadn't said or done anything weird, but he was still odd. I'd turned him down and he went behind my back and manipulated my father into handing me over. He didn't even seem apologetic about it.

I set my water on the coffee table. "I ran because I didn't want to be there, because I don't want to be engaged to this man."

Jadyn picked up her cell phone. "What's his name again?"

"Cain Carter," I told her. "He's the newest CEO of the Cartier Casino. He's been on a few blogs, but he's super low key. No one knows a thing about him."

That was what made me uneasy about Cain. The very mystery of who he was and where'd he come from. The illegitimate heir to the late James Carter appeared like a ghost within thin air and he was causing a stir amongst the power circle of all of California and Nevada.

Jadyn began cyberstalking Cain as she sat up and scoured her phone.

"He looks good in a suit," she observed as she took in a photo of Cain standing outside the Cartier Casino.

"*Not* helping," I pointed out.

"You could have it a lot worse. I mean, they set you up with a fine ass fiancé at least," Jadyn said with a pitiful shrug.

On paper, Cain was immaculate, wealthy, attractive, quiet, and reserved, but in reality, I wasn't buying it. "There's something off about him, Jay. Something...*lethal*."

I couldn't prove it, but I just knew.

Jadyn continued to scroll through her phone, disappointment soon covering her face. "He seems squeaky clean online." She flashed me yet another photo of Cain at the Cartier. In it, he was standing with some pop legend, one of the many performers who did residencies at their hotel and club.

Cain was about his business. No drama. No legal issues. No major headlines—outside our recent engagement.

By the looks of it, I would be nothing more than a trophy for Cain. A shiny object fit for his ego and image. Arm candy he got to fuck whenever he wanted.

I paused as I sank back against the sofa cushion.

Maybe, maybe I was writing Cain off too quickly. Keith had seemed scary, but then he wasn't.

God, he wasn't.

"At least you got options," Jadyn tried to reason.

Option #1: Put my foot down against this marriage, be disinherited, and be out on the street.

Option #2: Make nice with my parents and become betrothed to Vegas and LA's hottest eligible bachelor.

Option #3: Drink bleach.

Sure, my final option was purely over-the-top, but it sounded better than my alternatives. Really, I was still holding out I could talk my way out of this. That my parents would see the error in their decision. This alliance could be done without *my* hand in marriage.

"Yeah," I said hopefully.

"I mean, thinking positive, maybe he's not a horrible guy?" Jadyn tried to think on the bright side of things.

"Oh sure, this is a fairy tale all right. The one where the huntsman hands Little Red Riding Hood to the Big Bad Wolf instead of protecting her."

Jadyn laughed and took a sip of her wine. Soon, she pouted. "I want to be someone's Darling Nikki."

Confused, I scrunched up my face. "You want to be…caught self-loving in the lobby?"

Jadyn chuckled. "Okay, maybe not an exhibitionist, but I'd love to be this sexual oasis or goddess. Nikki *owned* her sexuality, and I just know she left a mark. Bet you this Keith guy remembers you."

I would remember this sex for the rest of my days. "What about you? Anything new and exciting in your life?"

Jadyn groaned. "Talking to new men is exhausting. They're either too direct or too dry. There's never any middle."

I cringed, thinking of my time in the dating pool. "Know what my biggest pet peeve is with men?"

Jadyn turned, giving me her full attention. "What?"

"Dick pics," I confessed. "Like, I know it's for reference, but I still can't wrap my head around them sending pictures of their dicks next to household items like remotes and Febreze bottles."

Jadyn cackled as she drank more of her wine. "And you know they're not sanitizing that shit either when they're done. Bet you their families are always wondering why they keep gettin' pink eye."

I was laughing again, loosening up despite my ordeal.

But then, I decided to be realistic and come back to Earth. I shook off Jadyn's words and my pleasure. Keith and I had a simple fling. Nothing more and nothing less. My last hoorah before I spent the rest of my life in a loveless marriage.

In the morning, Jadyn dropped me off at Rod's Repair before heading off to work. She'd let me borrow some jeans she'd been meaning to return to the store. While they hadn't fit her, they clung to me like a glove. Her striped T-shirt she'd given me barely covered my stomach, but at least we were the same shoe size.

Note to self: next time you run away, make sure to pack a change of clothes.

"Go with the flow, and give me *all* the details!" Jadyn demanded after I'd climbed out of her Volkswagen.

Business was alive and well this Monday morning as I turned from Jadyn's exit and faced Rod's Repair. Several vehicles lined the parking lot and inside I could see people waiting around the lobby and some standing at the front counter.

This didn't have to be awkward. This semi-walk of shame could be casual, friendly.

After telling myself to believe that lie, I walked into the shop and threaded my fingers together as I approached the front counter. A female mechanic was ushering an elderly couple toward the back of the shop that led out into the garage area. Nowhere in the vicinity did I see Keith.

The male receptionist was typing away at a laptop when I came over to the counter. "Just a second." His eyes were glued to the screen and I took a moment to look around again for Keith. *Nowhere.*

There was a young mother and two of her kids seated on the chairs against the front windows in the waiting area. *SpongeBob SquarePants* was on and the little ones were engrossed as they looked up at the screen with snacks in their hands. Across from the family was an older man sitting back browsing a magazine.

Another man was standing by the vending machines debating on the options before him. Outside of the echoes of SpongeBob, the shop radio was on, creating a lively atmosphere.

"Can I help you?" The receptionist pulled my attention back toward him.

His name tag read *Jake*. His face said he was friendly, but also busy.

"Uh, yeah, I'm here for the Lexus...?" Why had I said it as a question? Now that I thought about it, I hadn't filled out any paperwork with Keith before we'd hooked up in the back office. I was sure he knew my full name now after bullshitting me about needing to see my license.

Jake's brows furrowed and he glanced down at the paperwork cluttering the desk behind the counter. He grabbed a clipboard and held it up, scanning for something. "Oh, yeah, Nichols, right?"

"Yes, Kennedy Nichols," I said. "Is Keith around?"

Jake shook his head as he was back to the laptop. "Busy, and does not want to be disturbed." His fast fingers danced across the keyboard in seconds. "All right, looks like he got you all set up. Let me pull up the invoice and we—"

"Excuse me?" I cut him off, not understanding what he meant by Keith being too busy to see me. "Where is he?"

Jake looked at me funny. "In the back, working on some reports. You're good to go. All you have to do is pay for the spare."

I didn't care about my Lexus. It sounded like Keith was blowing me off, or maybe he was busy and didn't want to be bothered. Still, he knew I was coming by.

"He's expecting me," I said.

Jake didn't look convinced. "Uh-huh, he fixed the car, and then he went into the back and said he didn't want to be bothered while he was back there."

Jake was only following orders, and judging by his demeanor, he didn't want to break them.

One thing about me, I tended to always get what I wanted. It wasn't often I was told no and it stayed that way.

So, I put on my charming I'm-a-princess-and-you'll-obey-me smile and attitude. "Jake, he knows I'm stopping by. If you let me go see him, I won't tell." I pressed my finger to my glossed lips. "It'll be our little secret. I promise."

Jake frowned, his eyes shooting to the people in the lobby and then toward the mechanics in the garage. He hung his head and shook it. "I didn't see you go back there. It's all on you."

Keith must've had him intimidated, because I was too tempted to laugh at the threat.

Feeling perky, I quickly settled the bill and handed over my debit card. It was a smoke signal for my parents on where I was, but I didn't care in the moment. I'd needed last night away from them and that party. I'd needed to clear my head. And while my head wasn't exactly clear or less anxiety riddled, I was ready to face them, and Cain.

I shoved my receipt in my clutch and made my way down the familiar corridor to the back office. Each step found my heart beating hard in my chest. Here it was, my return to the scene of the crime—quite an illustrious crime at that.

The hard part was over; we'd already seen each other naked. There was no reason for me to be so nervous as I gripped the doorknob and felt relief when I saw that it wasn't locked. I blew out a shaky breath and opened the door.

Dr. Dre's "Still D.R.E." played through the shop's radio system. Keith was in the office bobbing his head to the classic late '90s song. He was caught up writing something in what looked like a ledger before he noticed me.

Today he was wearing glasses, an added bonus, because they only seemed to make him finer. The round gold frames complemented his skin tone and gorgeous face. Usually, I liked men clean shaven, but on Keith, I liked the scruff. I even kinda liked that he looked mean, the male version of Resting Bitch Face —or *Resting Asshole Face*. It worked for him, and facing him again after seeing him less than twenty-four hours ago, I now understood why Jake was intimidated by him. One thing evident about Keith's demeanor and energy, was that he wasn't to be played with.

Suddenly, I wasn't nervous. I almost felt playful when I thought about the way he hadn't done a thing about my changing his radio station in his tow truck.

"Kennedy." Keith placed the pen he'd been using in the spine of the ledger and stood up. Like the other mechanics, he was sporting a dark gray short-sleeved work shirt and matching pants. His name was scrawled in cursive on a patch above his right pec.

He must've changed last night, as he'd been about to close up when I'd called.

Keith kept his distance, staying behind the desk as he took me in. "How are you?"

Formalities, huh? "Good. You?"

He shrugged, his face grim. "I'm okay. But I need to apologize for last night."

Apologize? "What for?"

Keith searched my gaze for something, determination etched across his face. "I crossed the line, in *here*, and I'm sorry."

"What? No, you didn't," I responded. Of all the scenarios I'd considered this morning when I was getting dressed to come here, I hadn't imagined him feeling remorseful.

"You sure?" Keith questioned. He rounded his desk and parked himself in front of it, still a safe space from me. He folded his arms and gestured at me with a tilt of his head. "A young woman from out of town stranded in the road, and here I was supposed to help you, and I ended up taking advantage."

Now was *not* the time for chivalry. "That's not what happened. I flirted with you. I *wanted* you. I had a good time last night, and now, I guess I'm the only one who did."

What a great way for my rebellion to blow up in my face.

"That's not what I said," Keith was quick to say.

Oh.

He was quiet as he began to scratch at his neck. A tic he seemed to have whenever he appeared thoughtful.

"You liked it," I said, needing to hear his confirmation.

Keith stared at me impassively. "I did."

We needed to work on his emotions, but I would take his enjoyment in what we'd done. "Good. So did I. Really, if my life wasn't so complicated right now I'd try to make a thing of this."

"And as flattered as I would be at the offer, I'd say no," Keith said matter-of-factly.

His words startled me. "What?"

Keith sighed and looked elsewhere around the room before coming back to me, lifting and dropping his shoulder lazily. "I was distracted last night, but ordinarily, I don't fuck with OPP."

OPP.

Other People's Pussy.

Crass, but I got his point. He'd noticed my ring. But how could he not with how huge the thing was?

I plucked the ring off my finger. As if it would rid me from the whole engagement. "It's not what it seems...exactly."

Keith folded his arms again, perking a brow as if to call bullshit. "I'll bite."

At least he was hearing me out. "I...I wasn't *asked* to be married in the normal way."

"Then why did you say yes?"

"I didn't," I clarified. "My father's a hotel tycoon. He's been trying to do business with this...*asshole* who runs a casino in Vegas for a while—or, before he got sick."

Sympathy crossed Keith's face. "What's wrong with him?"

I gazed at the floor. "He's got ALS."

"I'm sorry to hear that." Recognition set in Keith's eyes and I knew I didn't have to explain further the fatal disease stealing my father from me.

No matter how messed up things were now, I still felt tears prick my eyes at the looming inevitable. "This asshole turned my father and his co-CEO down a few times, until recently he decided he was all in on a joint hotel/casino."

"What changed his mind?" Keith asked.

I looked up at him. "My father's weakening and he got him where it hurts: me. He's asked me out twice before and I turned him down each time. Now, he said he'd agree to this business deal if he could have my hand in marriage."

Keith frowned. "Are you from a different culture...?"

I managed to snort at that. "No. Or maybe I am, because the culture of business and money can make people do some really fucked-up things."

Before me, Keith lost his resolve. "Kennedy..."

I waved him off, not wanting his pity. This was my life. "So, last night was our big engagement announcement and party. I got overwhelmed and fled. I didn't take my phone because I didn't want to chance my mom tracking me down. Not that I can stay away for too long."

"So what now, you're going to really marry some old geezer?"

"He's not that much older than me. He's very successful and attractive. A lot of women would kill to be in my position."

"So, outside of the whole 'asshole' thing, what's wrong with the guy?" Keith asked curiously.

I stood firm in my stance. "I said no, and that's all that matters. To go around me and force my father's hand is psychotic." And borderline controlling. "I don't know how, but I'm going to put my foot down and get out of this. I know what I want, and what I don't."

Keith nodded. "Amen to that. Taking advantage of your dad now that he's sick is some evil shit. And I know he's not well, but your dad really shouldn't put you in this position either."

It was true, and another point I would bring up when I got back to Hampton Hills. They could do their business whatever way they chose, without me.

Cain Carter could not have me.

I shook off my irritation and focused on Keith. "What about you?"

"What about me?" he asked.

He was attractive, clearly hardworking, and a skilled lover. I hadn't thought to wonder if he were seeing anyone. "Are you single?"

"Of course," he said as if it should've been obvious. "I'm not that type of guy."

I liked this answer, as if the idea of cheating was just completely unacceptable to him. He was almost thirty, and it was clear he wasn't about to be one of those men who forever acted on impulses and behaved like a horny adolescent. Who "did them" and broke hearts.

"So…" I threw out. "I'm not a cheater, and you're single. No harm, no foul."

"No harm, no foul," Keith repeated with a bob of his head.

I liked the sight of him in glasses. The serious look on his handsome face. The way his muscles bulged in his arms when he folded them. The way his tattoos complemented his skin and brawn.

Keith chuckled, a husky lullaby. "You keep looking at me like that, and you're asking for trouble."

I'd never been a rule breaker in my life, but suddenly I was down for all delinquency. "I like trouble."

He tilted his head, studying me with pure amusement behind his glasses. "What you so far away for?" He gestured to the side. "C'mere."

I felt schoolgirl silly just then. Too giddy to stop myself from obeying and crossing over and standing in front of him.

His manliness permeated the air. A heavy potion drawing me in and taking no prisoners. Keith was intoxicating.

A gleam hung in his eyes as he stared down at me. "You like trouble, huh?"

"Y-Yes," I breathed out, anticipating his next move.

His hand came down hard on my butt, sending my sex clenching, and a gasp out of my mouth.

Shit.

Why did that feel good?

What more, Keith slid something in my back pocket. "Well, if you're ever having car trouble, here's my card. Give me a ring or somethin'."

Or something.

"Okay," I said.

Keith looked at the clock on the wall and came back to me. "I'll walk you to your car."

"Oh, so there's the gentleman side you keep hidden away," I taunted.

This remark was rewarded with another smack to my butt.

The whole way out to the garage I contemplated saying something else wise and witty to be smacked again.

"All right, just so we're clear, a spare is only supposed to be temporary," Keith instructed as I climbed in behind my wheel. He hung in the window after I'd rolled it down, staring at me as he gave me the warning. "Make sure you get a new tire soon, and watch where you're drivin'."

I saluted him, being a pest. "Yes, sir."

He appeared to be fighting a smile as he stood back and gave me room to leave.

I pushed the Start button and my Lexus came to life. Almost immediately I was assaulted by the loud rap sounds of 21 Savage. I shot Keith a glare, only to find him not hiding his gorgeous smile.

Nice move, Keith, nice one.

The only reason I went to my parents' house right away was to get my cell phone. I also owed them a cursory acknowledgment that I was alive and well, but I wasn't ready to have it out with them on my engagement.

But they lived in a gated estate and there was no going about it without speaking to them regardless. One step in the door and my mother was already waiting for me in the foyer with her arms folded and disappointment teeming loudly from her person. Everything about her appearance was in place, her hair styled and held back in a clip, her outfit crisp and designer, meaning we had company of some sort over. Not that she was otherwise a slob, but these days, she didn't force it when all she wanted to do was be by my father's side.

"You have some nerve." Her tone was dry and tired. We weren't about to argue; she'd had it with me.

I attempted to go by her to get my phone and forgo this dramatic confrontation. "Can we do this later? I do need to talk to Daddy."

Her cold hand wrapped around my arm and pulled me back around to face her. "He's with a specialist up there right now. So whatever it is you want can wait."

My heart stung in my chest. This kept getting more real by the minute and I wasn't brave enough to pretend I didn't care. "Is he doing okay?"

My mother snorted, letting me go and shaking her head, causing her earrings to sway in her ears. "He's not too happy with you, Kennedy. Cain—"

"Mom," I cut in. "Is he okay with his health?"

She calmed down for just a moment. Her forehead creased as she looked down at the marble flooring. "He wants to walk. He's becoming frustrated with having to slow down and take a break. He's angry and I'm doing all that I can to ease *this* for him."

I hugged myself as I felt angry inside at the illness claiming my father.

"The Residence at Cartier is a dream project for him," my mother went on, bringing up the joint collaboration Nichols & Wagner and Cain were creating here in Los Angeles. "I understand this is abrupt and hard for you, but couldn't you please just try to make things less complicated for your father? Cain is incredibly accomplished for his age and he's respectful and reserved."

"He inherited the casino. He didn't earn it like Daddy and Phil with Nichols & Wagner," I countered.

My mother shook her head. "He was upset when you disappeared on him. He wants to have lunch today to clear the air and smooth things over. So, please, go get dressed and meet with him."

I put my foot down. "I have to get my tire fixed. I'm riding on a spare."

She reached out and took my key fob from me. "I'll have it brought in. Oliver can drive you to the restaurant."

There was no pleading with her.

My hands were tied and I hated it. I didn't want to disappoint my father. I knew how much this deal had meant to him in the years he'd been campaigning for The Residence Hotel and Cartier Casino to create a new property here in California. If he were in better spirits, I knew he'd never put me in this predicament.

Maybe if I begged Cain himself he'd see he was being ridiculous.

"Fine," I said. "I'll go get ready."

My mother's cold palm cupped my cheek, bringing my vision to meet hers. "Just try to at least get to know him."

I wouldn't. I would go to this lunch armed with a mission to convince him to drop this charade.

I dressed business casual in a white blouse, black slacks, and my favorite pair of black heels. I styled my hair, put on a little makeup, and half an hour later I was sliding into the back of our family driver's town car. My phone was charged, finding missed calls and texts from my mother and Jadyn. Not to mention the influx of social media notifications and texts from casual acquaintances congratulating me on my engagement. The latest text from Jadyn was snooping on how things had gone when I'd seen Keith.

Oliver came to a stop and I put my night behind me as I faced the restaurant Cain had picked out. *Etienne's*. The sign out front said it held a wide array of famous French cuisine. By the valet taking people's cars in the lane around me, I just knew this was one of those obscenely fancy restaurants that gave guests large dinner plates with small servings along with decorative sauce on the side. Not my favorite, but Cain didn't know me. *Yet.*

Despite my gut telling me to flee, I got out of the car and went inside. I went over to the hostess and put on my best smile and pretended everything was okay. "Hi, party for Carter?"

She scanned her reservation book and faced me with a bright smile. "Right this way." She turned, preparing to lead me into the dining room, her braided ponytail swinging behind her.

It was almost noon and the restaurant was fairly full as we stepped into the left side of the establishment. The smell of sauce and herbs hung in the air as light classical music set the tone. People around me were eating and enjoying their dates or business meetings. No one took notice of the young woman preparing to share a meal with the Devil.

Right away I noticed where Cain was already seated and waiting. Even more, he wasn't alone. Two of his men were at a table not too far from where Cain was sitting. One was scanning the room casually and the other, the tall and heavy-set one was on the phone.

Run! I told myself as my bravery evaporated.

It was too late.

Cain had spotted me and we were too close to the table to turn around. Where Cain was seated was in a lone corner of the restaurant, as only four tables were in the area around him. Outside of his men seated at a table behind him, no one was in this section.

"Here you are," the hostess said as she stood at the table and bestowed me with another big smile.

I tipped my head at her awkwardly before approaching a chair farthest from Cain at the square-shaped table. He'd stood up and appraised me, being a gentleman and waiting for me to sit before he did again.

I sat down and covered my lap with a tablecloth and tried to wipe my sweaty palms on it. Before, it was easy to form a plan to talk him out of this marriage. Now, being so close, recognizing that algid air around him, I could barely bring myself to look at him.

But I did. He was in another expensive suit—a suit he *did* wear well—as he sat across from me quietly.

"Good morning," I spoke up.

Cain glanced at the watch on his wrist and back to me. "Morning."

"Good morning!" A waiter came and interrupted us. A tall man with gold glasses that reminded me of the wrong person just then. Unlike Keith, our server, whose name tag read *Max*, appeared friendly. "Do you need more time to choose your meals? If so, what can we start you off with to drink?"

Cain had been here longer than me, so he knew what he wanted. "Can you bring a bottle of your best red wine?" He glanced at me. "Do you like red?"

I shook my head. "I don't drink."

Cain returned to Max. "I'll take the wine, and she'll have whatever she likes."

In the end, I chose a simple glass of water with a lemon in it. By the time Max had swung back around with our drinks, I'd scoured the menu twice over in an effort to avoid talking to Cain.

Cain ordered the pan-seared foie gras, something that made my stomach lurch in guilt and disgust. I settled on a halibut dish and a side salad.

And then we were alone, awaiting our meals with nothing else to do but talk.

"Something came up," I started saying, waving my hand dismissively on my departure from our party. "An emergency with my friend."

Cain reached into his jacket. He brandished a small pad of paper and a pen and set it on the table. "Why don't we get to know each other a little more? Starting with you giving me your cell phone number so I can get ahold of you in cases of *emergencies*."

If he was calling me a liar, at least he'd been polite about it.

Reluctantly, I recited my cell number as I squeezed my fists shut under the table.

Cain jotted it down quickly before looking over at me. "You ordered the halibut—are you a big seafood eater?"

"I'm a pescatarian," I told him.

He wrote this down. "I eat meat. Will that be a major problem?" He almost seemed sincere.

I cleared my throat, brushing off falling for his tone. If he were sincere, he would've asked me to marry him face-to-face, or taken my rejection instead of this. "I'm not a fan of foie gras, but typically, meat eaters don't offend me." On a rare occasion, I'd eat chicken with Jadyn.

"Favorite snack?"

"Cotton candy grapes," I answered. "Which is ironic, since I don't like cotton candy or the flavor for candy."

Cain wrote all this down as if he were studying for an important test. One could argue at least he *wanted* to know things about me.

"Aren't you going to ask me questions, Kennedy?" Cain asked as he brought his attention from his pad to me.

I didn't want to get to know him, but if I were stuck in this, I supposed I should've tried to see if he weren't completely terrible. "Why did you bring me into this deal with my dad?"

"I like turning nos into yeses," Cain said simply. "I'm not a fan of asking for things, but if I'm approached on something, I want it worth my while."

"I'm not a piece of stock," I snapped.

My attitude didn't deter Cain. His dark empty eyes took me in, examining me. "No, you're not. Next question."

In another moment, we were joined by his heavier associate.

"Dice, Huffman said he can't pay you in full," the man said as he leaned down toward Cain's ear.

Cain blinked, but no emotion came to his face. "We gave him a lot of...*chips*. Tell him I want *all* that they're worth."

The man accepted this. "And if he can't bring it in?"

Cain traced his finger along the rim of his wineglass, face a blank canvas. "Then I hope infant-size coffins are cheap."

I choked on my air, unable to play off my blatant fear.

There it was. That darkness I'd sensed about him from the moment I first met him. He was a killer. A coldblooded one at that.

We were at a public restaurant, not within earshot but he still spoke of taking a life as if he were debating an Armani suit versus Tom Ford.

Cain peered at me. He lifted his hand, releasing his worker. "Beans? Don't interrupt my meal again."

Beans took a look at me and nodded before returning to his own table.

Cain's gaze was cast on me. "I'm sorry about that. I won't make it a habit to discuss business during dinner or when we're together."

"W-What do you do?" I stammered to ask.

Cain almost grinned it seemed. "I run a casino, Kennedy."

I wasn't that naïve. "And...?"

"And that's all I'm going to say on that," Cain said as he gathered his wine and took a sip.

He wasn't just a casino owner. I should've left well enough alone, but if I was stuck with him, I wasn't going to be kept in the dark. "Do you really have to be so..."

"So what?" he demanded to know curiously.

"*Ruthless*?" I asked. "Are you really going to kill..." I couldn't say what he'd alluded to.

A corner of Cain's mouth quirked up. "It's elementary to believe kindness makes the world go 'round."

"And it's pessimistic to believe it won't help it," I shot back.

That smile twitched again. "Next question."

It was clear he wasn't about to discuss his secular business ventures with me. And just then I didn't want to pry any further. Didn't want to get soot under my nails just talking about it. "Why do they call you *Dice*?"

Cain didn't mind answering this. He leaned over on his hip and dug into his pocket and soon pulled out a set of clear red rolling dice. He set them on the table in front of me. "Wanna give 'em a roll?"

I declined to touch them. "No."

Cain shrugged and put them away. "I'm a gambling man. It's in my blood. The name comes with the territory."

"Were you close with your father?" I dared to ask.

Cain shook away the slight gentleness his face once held. "My father and I met for a very short time."

"Long enough for him to make you heir."

He thudded his finger onto the tabletop. "I deserved it."

Touchy. James Carter was a sore subject. "Will I be meeting your mother, then?"

Cain eased back in his chair. "My mother is deceased."

"Any other family?"

Cain looked over at Beans and the other associate before returning to me. "I don't have any."

The air was thick and uncomfortable. I didn't feel safe. All my suspicions had been confirmed and he sat before me so nonchalant. I couldn't focus, let alone eat. Not even ten minutes later when our food arrived.

The halibut looked so good and delicious, as did the asparagus and potato it came with.

"Why didn't you marry that football player?" Cain wanted to know as he cut into his foie gras. He noticed my watching and frowned just a little. "I won't order this again in front of you."

How nice. A murderer had a conscience for his dates. "I was twenty-two and overwhelmed. It was my first ever real relationship. Guy's a sweetheart, but I wasn't ready to be so wrapped up then."

Gaius was young too, and I guessed I feared he'd somehow get caught up in the fame of being a new and highly admired NFL player. That he'd get bored with me. I loved him, I did, but when things got too heavy, I ran.

"Do you like the Sharks?" I poked at my halibut, wondering if Cain was even into sports.

"No, I prefer the Raiders," he said.

Of course.

"Are you from Las Vegas?" I attempted to eat a piece of my fish, to distract myself. The dish was tasty, but I hadn't a true appetite to enjoy it.

Cain's finger tapped on the table as he pondered over my question. I could tell my line of inquisition wasn't his favorite. His short and simple answers a pure testament.

"No," he said after a long pause.

I moved some asparagus around my plate. "Interesting."

"Is that so?" he challenged.

I gathered my water and took a drink. "It's going to be a fun year getting to know you, Cain. I can just tell." Controlling, and invasive yet secretive? Oh, I pictured a great time ahead.

His finger tapped against the table once more. He shook his head, heaving a sigh as he traced his fingers around the rim of his mouth. "I know what you're doing, holding off the wedding like this. I'm not stupid. Just don't embarrass me."

"Embarrass you?" I felt bold enough to laugh at him. "God, as if you shouldn't be embarrassed already after forcing this on me. Because your ego was bruised."

"Careful," Cain warned.

"Or what?"

Cain went back to his plate. He meticulously cut up his foie gras like the psychopath he was. "Be nice, and I'll make it worth it."

There was nothing in the world he could buy me to make a marriage worth it. To make twisting my father's arm okay.

"You're a bastard," I declared.

Cain shrugged as if it the insult were nothing. "I've been called worse."

Why did he want me? Was this really some power play? A show he could have anything he set his mind to?

"The reason I bring up the athlete is because I'm curious,"

Cain began speaking after a few bites into his meal. "Has he been in contact with you since news broke of the engagement?"

I thought back to getting my phone and sifting through my messages. Gaius had sent me a text.

GAIUS

Wow. I know we haven't spoken in a while, but I'm in shock right now, Kenn. Regardless, I'm happy for you. I'll always have love for you, no matter what. Congrats on the engagement! G.

He'd been heartbroken when I broke up with him. Unlike Cain, Gaius would never force me to do anything I didn't want. He was good to spoil me and treat me like a princess.

"Yes," I admitted. "He congratulated me."

Cain took a drink of his wine, humming at the news. "I'm going to be straightforward on this. If you're seeing someone else, I sincerely hope he's bulletproof."

Time stopped all around me as his threat froze me in my chair. I didn't dare ask him to repeat himself. He'd looked me right in the eye and said it plainly and clearly. He would kill a man I was cheating on him with. Which left me asking, "A-And me?"

Cain frowned. "I'll keep you barefoot and pregnant, and then you'll be too busy to think of someone else."

"I'm on the pill."

"I'll crush every one."

"I'll get an IUD."

"I'll rip it out."

A sob escaped from my mouth as my vision blurred. He was a monster. I couldn't. I couldn't go through with this.

Cain stood up and came and sat in the chair closest to me.

"Stop crying," he demanded, watching me blankly. "I told you not to embarrass me."

His cruelty drove the tears faster down my face.

Cain was so close to me I began to shake as I attempted to clean up. All the while he watched me.

"Where is your ring, Kennedy?" He'd noticed I wasn't wearing it.

Honestly, I should've chucked the thing out the window when I was on the highway.

"I-In my purse at home," I said.

There his finger went tapping the tabletop again. "The next time I see you, I want you wearing it."

It wasn't my style or desired type of ring. "And if I don't, you'll break my fingers?"

He chuckled and examined my hand until I snatched it away. "That would be a pity, wouldn't it?"

"Abuse isn't love," I mumbled.

He reached out and touched my cheek. "You should write Hallmark cards."

I closed my eyes at his sarcasm and bit back another cry. He wouldn't get away with this. "My father will never let you hurt me."

Cain barely registered the comment as he angled his head to regard me. "You mean the one that's bedridden and dying? Stop, you're scaring me."

I glared at Cain, hating him more than I'd ever hated anyone in my entire life.

"Don't pout, Wife," he said dryly.

"I'm not your wife," I ground out.

He smirked, a ghost of a smile on his face. Soon, he was leaning close, his dark eyes boring into me. "In case I haven't made myself clear, you belong to me." He rose from his seat and lifted his hand, signaling for Beans and the other man to get up as he stared down at me. "I intended to be good to you. *You're* making this hard." He straightened out his suit and tossed me a pitying look. "Save your tears. I fucking hate seeing women cry."

Without another word, he walked away with his demons trailing behind.

6

KEITH

As tired as I was Monday night after staying until close at the garage, I knew better. I made sure to drive on over to my mother and grandmother's to stop in for a visit.

Outside of Uncle Rod, my mother and grandmother were the only family I had. My father had died when I was a baby. After that, my mother lost contact with his side of the family. It was unfortunate, but it made me extra grateful for the family I did have.

I had a key to the house, but I always knocked or rang the bell out of respect.

It had barely been a minute since I'd rang the doorbell before my mother was coming and opening the door for me.

"Well, look who's showin' his face," my mother remarked as she stood back, taking me in from head to toe.

These days, I was usually a hermit and made sure to stop by once a month at least. It was trash on my part, seeing how they only stayed a few blocks away from me.

"My fault." I leaned down and engulfed my mother into a hug, pressing my face into the crook of her neck as she hugged me back. Nice and tight. I was her only child, and I had to do better on keepin' in touch with her.

Deep into the house, I could smell the remains of the evening's dinner.

It smelled like brown sugar ham, one of my grandmother's famous recipes next to her renowned potato salad.

"What y'all got goin' on in here?" I said as I made my presence known and stepped further into the house after my mother let me in.

"Is that Keith?" the voice of my grandmother, Betty Jean, filtered through the house as I recognized her location in the dining room.

I made my way to her to greet her with a hug and a kiss. Betty was at the dining room table, with a late-night mug of tea in front of her. Her face lit up at the sight of me and that itself made me smile.

At eighty, Betty was a ray of sunshine in this dark world. Nothing kept her down or angry, a trait I wished I'd inherited. Then, I wouldn't have battled with my depression for over a year. Wouldn't have walked around with that perpetual chip on my shoulder. I was working on it, little by little. I was *here*, not home like I'd usually go after work.

"Hey, Betty." I gave her a hug and planted a kiss on her cheek, which she returned hard and long as she often did. When I was a boy, she was always emphasizing how important it was to "love hard." She hugged you like she didn't want to let go, told you you were handsome or beautiful, smart and funny, and squeezed extra hard on those tough days when you weren't feelin' it.

"Big Man!" Betty professed as I stood away from her embrace. She'd been calling me that since I was a little boy. "*What you doin' bein' so tall, Big Man?*" she'd asked me when I'd gone on a growth spurt that never seemed to be ending when I was six.

"I'm just stoppin' through," I let Betty know. I glanced out the room toward the kitchen where I could see pots and pans still out from their dinner. "Smells like a feast up in here."

"Gon' and get you something." Betty waved me off as my mother came and joined her at the table.

I shook my head. "Nah, I'm cool. I'll heat somethin' up at the crib."

"Boy, if you don't get you a plate," Betty snapped.

Of course. "Yes, ma'am, yes, ma'am."

Betty Jean was not to be played with by any means. The kindest, sweetest soul, but she wasn't a fool. Everybody in the neighborhood had love for her, because of her no-nonsense approach and supportive nature. I didn't have any blood cousins, but the block I grew up on had everyone feelin' like Betty Jean was their adoptive grandmother.

"Want me to help you?" My mother was beginning to rise from her place at the table and I shot her down. For as long as I'd known my mother, she was a hard worker, doing what she could to take care of me, and then Betty Jean when she'd stopped working. At fifty-two, my mother was still a schoolteacher, and because I knew she would be going to bed soon to get up early for her class in the morning, I wasn't about to let her lift a finger for me.

I helped myself to the kitchen and made my own plate of Betty's ham, my mother's collard greens, and a portion of the potato salad it had been too long since I'd had. After grabbing a glass of water, I went back to the dining room and sat across from my mother and adjacent to Betty.

"You're looking good," Betty observed as I ate some of her ham.

After last night, I had started off my morning feeling lousy and like a piece of shit for what had gone down with Kennedy in that office. But then she'd come back, telling me she'd liked it— that she wanted more, and as much as I couldn't wrap my head around it, I did feel better. I was no closer to a hundred percent, or my old self, but I was solid.

"Feeling a little better," I spoke up. I tossed my grandmother a smile. "This ham never disappoints."

She smiled. "Take some home with you."

It wasn't an offer I could refuse, so I didn't.

"You seein' anybody new?" Betty asked.

"Mom!" my mother fussed as she scolded her own mother.

Betty rolled her eyes. "I'm just asking, Sherry, dang."

My mother rolled her eyes and shook her head. To me, she softened up, concerned. "How are you doing, Keith?"

I shrugged as I forked at my greens. "I'm straight."

And unlike the many times before when I was asked this question, I was telling the truth.

My mother and Betty Jean gave me my space when I'd first gone into the dark. Something that I'd needed at the time. I didn't want to be nurtured or talked to. I'd wanted to be alone.

Sometimes, when I was close to the edge, feeling like nothing, I thought of them and came back down to Earth. The thought of them kept air in my lungs and a reason to believe in my heart.

It had been a rough year since my ex.

These two women kept my ass in line. There was a rough patch in my teen years, and by the grace of God, my mother had saved me from succumbing to the streets of Bedford Heights. I could never repay her, and I just hoped my love was enough.

I looked her in her eye. "Thanks for asking."

She nodded. "Rod says you've been putting in a lot of work down at the shop. I hope you're finding time for yourself again."

She wasn't wrong. I *did* need to step outside more. I needed to let the past go. "The year's just starting, but I definitely intend to make the most of it."

I wasn't sure how, but I was going to fully pull myself out of the pit I'd crawled into.

Betty Jean yawned and covered her mouth. "I better turn in. Biiig day tomorrow."

I took a drink of my water and took in my grandmother. "What's tomorrow?"

My mother chuckled. "Something's going on in one of her stories she watches."

Betty Jean took a step back, aghast at my mother's blasé

approach to her soap opera. "David is coming out of his coma, and Pauline is going to find out she's been seein' his twin brother the whole time!"

"Yawn," my mother responded with a dismissive wave of her hand. "Give it up already, woman."

"Do not downplay impeccable storytelling, girl."

All I could do was laugh at their bit. They'd been going back and forth about Betty Jean's stories since as far as I could remember. At a time, I'd definitely dabbled in watching with her. They *could* be addictive with the plotlines and dramatics. I wouldn't front.

Betty Jean went to turn in and my mother remained seated across from me. The soft look in her dark eyes let me know she truly cared for me and wanted what was best for me.

"We worry, Keith, we really do," she said to me.

"I know, and it's my fault for being so caught up over that situation," I admitted.

"Getting your heart broken is no easy feat. Can't control how you handle it. It's important to know she was wrong about you, and obviously wasn't a good fit," my mother insisted.

She and Leila had gotten along, because my mother was always so nice to everyone. A habit she'd gotten from Betty. When I thought about it, I came to the realization that I'd probably taken after my father instead, because I wasn't a happy-go-lucky type of guy.

I was still surprised I turned Kennedy on, because a lot of out-of-towners—especially women—thought I was too serious and intimidating.

"Hey," my mother said gently, capturing my full attention. "What's a word of wisdom I taught you?"

A corner of my mouth curled up at the thought of her instilling in me quotes from the intellectuals and greats. "Marianne Williamson, 'Our deepest fear is not that we are inadequate. Our deepest fear is that we are powerful beyond measure. It is our light, not our darkness that most frightens us.' An innate fear to be great can stunt you, so don't be afraid to dream and achieve big."

My recollection of a lesson she'd taught me brought a smile to my mother's face. "You are a great man, Keith. Don't let anyone tell you otherwise."

I finished my dinner, trying and trying to believe her words to be true.

I owed Savon an appearance, so Wednesday night, after work, we linked up. Of all places, he'd chosen Crazy Legs, the only strip club in Bedford Heights, to grab beers and catch up.

We sat at the bar, taking in the music and scene.

"Cole and Wale need to stop playin' and drop a tape, man," Savon observed as he listened to the music playing in the background.

"Heard you," I agreed as I bobbed my head to the beat.

"You know, I'm not gon' lie to you, bro, I didn't think you'd show," Savon said as he looked at me.

I had that coming. "I'ma be around more. Trust."

He cut the humor as he peered into my eyes behind his lenses. "You better be. We need you down at the center."

Yeah, I definitely was going to get my act together. Growing up in the Heights wasn't easy, and no one knew it more than Von and me. Our Face Cards couldn't be touched after earning our stripes, and most times, the new youth listened when we spoke.

"Anyway," he moved on. "What happened the other night? You never texted me back."

"It's a crazy story, man." I shook my head and grabbed my beer. Normally, I wasn't one to talk—not that I intended to tell it all, but the whole thing was still unbelievable to me.

Crazy Legs was buzzing with conversation, laughter, and music from the speakers. No one was paying us any mind as we hung at the bar.

I ran a hand down my face and stared ahead at the wall of liquor behind the bar. "Me and her...kinda got into it at the garage."

"Excuse me?" I could hear Savon's shock in his tone.

I nodded and kept going. "One thing sorta led to another and we had a good time."

He gripped my shoulder, demanding I look him in the eye as I told him. "*That* girl? Let *you* touch her?"

I couldn't be offended, because I got his meaning through and through. Baby girl was a bougie little bih with an attitude that could grate on anyone's nerves.

"It just...happened." I shrugged. "One minute she's actin' stuck-up, and the next...she's asking for it." I winced at the phrasing. "I mean, she gave me the green light. She was feelin' me. Wouldn't let me kiss her, though."

"Oh," Savon said as he took a swig of his beer. "She one of *those*."

I chuckled. I needed to ask her about that. Kennedy had a face that demanded attention. "Who knows?"

"So she ain't got a man? Shit, with that big ass rock on her finger, I was willin' to bet she was marrying some tech guy," Savon went on.

My face scrunched up at the reality that Kennedy was very much engaged. "No, she's getting married, but...it's complicated."

"Sure." Savon's sarcasm bit at me, making me feel a need to defend Kennedy. I didn't know her. Didn't know if she had fed me bullshit to keep seeing me, but I didn't want to set her out like that.

"Nah, she got rich people problems. Some business deal between her pops and this dude has her being married off to finalize it."

Savon looked at me, squinting his eyes, not understanding the scenario either. "What is she? The princess of Zamunda?"

My shoulders shook as I relaxed and laughed. "I don't know, man. Shit is twisted."

"Jesus." Savon took another sip of his beer. "You don't need that mess."

I stroked at my chin, thinking over the stupidity in getting involved with Kennedy knowing her situation. "I gave her my card when she came to pick up her ride Monday."

I could feel Savon's gaze on me. "So, you *finally* over Leila then?"

Lately, I hadn't been thinking about her. Still, there was an old grocery list stuck to my fridge at home I'd kept to have a reminder of her. Her feminine handwriting was all I had left.

I needed to throw it out.

"Guess so," I stated in the end.

Savon whistled and raised his glass in the air, signifying a toast. "Must've been somethin' mean."

That I couldn't deny.

I liked it a little more than I should've.

"All right, coming to the stage is a lady that needs no introduction. Get all your money out right now. I need big bills for this lady, fellas. Let's give it up for Sabrina!" the DJ announced enthusiastically. His words were met with a riotous cheer from the men bordering the stage and those at the tables and booths beyond.

Whoever this girl was, she was a highly admired dancer.

The lights in the club dimmed as a spotlight centered on the stage, awaiting the arrival of the next dancer to come out.

Music began playing, a smooth R&B song I soon recognized as Ciara's "Body Party" just as the dancer emerged from behind the velvet curtains.

Her hair was dyed cherry-red, even in the dim room you couldn't miss it. That or her hourglass figure. Perky breasts, a tiny waist, a light reflecting off her belly button ring, and what looked like a nice ass behind her. She hadn't yet shed her neon pink lace bra, matching panties, or garter belt. There was plenty still left to the imagination, and it was already raining dollar bills her way for how sexy she was.

She approached the pole stealthily and confidently, circling it as her eyes searched the crowd vacantly. Ciara began singing and Sabrina began moving her body sensually.

My eyes didn't linger long on her figure before I really took in her angelic face. There was something about it, something youthful—*too* youthful that begged the question just how old she was. Sabrina didn't look a day past sixteen, and for that, I turned around on my stool and faced the bar again and propped my arms against the counter.

"What now?" Savon wondered. "Y'all gon' see each other in the future?"

"She would have to call for that," I commented. It had been two days and I hadn't heard a peep. "Until then, not much to be said."

Savon considered this. "Would you turn her down if she did call?"

Common sense told me I should've. I wasn't the type of guy to mess with women in relationships, whether shitty or not. Kennedy's case was rare and special.

There was something bratty about her, entitled even. As if she was used to getting everything handed to her. Leila was a regular girl from around the way, and if I wasn't good enough for *her*, of course I'd never meet Kennedy's standards and expectations.

She wouldn't call.

"We'll cross that bridge if it happens," I said, noncommittal.

Savon accepted this. "So, what if word gets out? What if homie try to press you?"

I wasn't fazed. "Ain't nothin' but a conversation, man to man."

Her fiancé didn't scare me, whether I knew what was up with

him or not. His corny power play in getting her to marry him for business said enough about him.

Still, I didn't need that kind of trouble in my life. I had people counting on me.

It didn't really matter. Because I was certain. This was just a one-off. A moment of carnal need and weakness. Kennedy would not call.

Kennedy

I DIDN'T LEAVE THE HOTEL. I FELL INTO A STATE OF numbness that lasted for days. I didn't eat, barely drank, and did nothing as I stayed in my king-sized bed.

The phone rang entirely the first day, until it died from lack of charging.

After that disastrous lunch with Cain, I had nothing to look forward to. No reason to try. The days filtered in and out as I suffered in my lonesome. There was no escaping this dreadful union. No way out of this mess *I* hadn't made.

Well, it wasn't entirely true. I could walk away from everything: my penthouse, my inheritance, and my family. I wouldn't lie and say leaving my belongings and money behind would be an easy feat, but it was my parents that left me gutted at the thought of leaving them for good. At walking away and never speaking to them. Especially with my father's illness.

I was in an awkward situation and it left me sick to my stomach.

Heavy knocks sounded at my front door. Easily heard due to the static silence in my penthouse.

I guessed it was housekeeping. I'd shooed them away Tuesday

morning when they attempted to come and clean. I'd wanted to be alone.

Now, perhaps they were doing a wellness check.

My phone was dead, but the calendar on the wall said it was Friday. The frosted glass clock nearby said it was just past twelve.

Huh.

The knocking was still going.

I climbed out of bed and padded out of my bedroom to get the front door in my ivory silk pajamas. My hair was still wrapped up under my scarf. Usually, when I was on my game, I didn't allow anyone to see me like this, but I was beyond caring about my appearance at this point.

I reached the front door and didn't bother checking the peephole as I unlocked it. I stood back and pulled the door open, prepared to tell housekeeping to fuck off.

Only, it wasn't housekeeping knocking.

It was Cain.

My morally questionable fiancé.

Like always, he was sporting a suit, this one a three-piece indigo wool suit with a striped silver and navy tie that really did it for him. Cain looked impeccable in a suit. It wasn't a surprise he'd been photographed candidly in style sections of gossip magazines and gossip pages online. He was bringing the suit and tie aesthetic back tenfold. His suits didn't outweigh him. He wore them with confidence and a swagger most men would envy.

On paper, and in a photo, we *did* make sense together stylistically. My style was professional—dresses, blouses, and slacks. A look I'd always adored and obsessed over after growing up watching my father and mother go out to dinner or cocktail parties.

Still, even if we looked good together, it didn't mean we were good *for* each other.

Cain's men were hard to miss, as I spotted Beans and another man flanking the elevator and watching the hall for passersby.

I didn't bother greeting my future husband. Instead, I

glowered at him, wanting him to get the hell on with whatever reason he'd stopped by.

He took his time in front of me, examining me in my state of dress. That morning, when I'd washed my face and brushed my teeth, I momentarily rejoiced that I hadn't developed bags under my eyes or dark circles. My grim mind hadn't taken my appearance yet.

"Can I come in?" Cain asked after a pause.

"If I say no?" I challenged.

"Then we can talk like this," he said simply. He remained standing in my doorway peacefully as he stared at me, face hard to read. "I was out of line the last time we saw each other, and it's unacceptable. I'm sorry."

I couldn't control my impulse to roll my eyes. "I don't want to hear your apology. It means nothing, because we're *still* engaged."

"Fair point," Cain admitted.

Even if he looked and sounded remorseful, I wasn't moved. "So don't bother starting off a cycle of doing wrong and apologizing."

Cain peered into my eyes. "I don't make apologies, Kennedy."

Somehow, that felt fitting for what little I knew of his character. He ruled his business with an iron fist. He didn't apologize for anything. Yet, he gave me that grace. "I should feel so special." My eyes traveled to the plastic takeout bag in his hands. "What's that?"

He extended the bag toward me. "Someone told me you haven't left this hotel in days, and I wasn't sure if that meant you were eating or not. It's a bourbon salmon dish."

I folded my arms. "I don't want it."

Cain did me one better by reaching past me and looping the bag on my doorknob. The food *did* smell good, and it was nice he was considerate of my diet.

Cain wasn't fazed by my attitude as he stood back and moved along with his visit. "Listen, I'm going to Vegas for a while."

"Ah, business? Of the requiring infant-size coffin variety?"

Cain snorted softly. "Of the casino variety."

If I was stuck with this man for the rest of my life, I didn't want to be played for a fool.

"Don't lie to me," I told him. "Just tell it to me straight. If you're going to do something heinous, I'd rather hear that than some lie. If you're going to screw some other woman, you can tell me that too."

Cain's eyes snapped to mine. "I'd never cheat on you."

"Said every man ever," I let out sardonically.

He grimaced. "I'm. Loyal."

The finality and anger laced in his two words said enough. Cain was monogamous. This engagement was a sham, and yet *I'd* already stepped out.

"Okay," I said in the end.

Cain ran his thumb along his bottom lip, studying me some more. "Have you seen your father?"

My heart clenched in my chest and all my emotion bubbled to the surface. "No."

"Every second counts, Kennedy," Cain said gently. "Damon's a tough guy. He's definitely putting on a brave face through this all, but he strikes me as the sentimental type when it comes to you. He didn't...relent to this deal so easily. Despite the circumstances between you and me, you should see and be with your father as much as you can."

His words seized my heart in a grip I couldn't shake. Maybe, in some small way, he could understand the harsh reality of losing a parent. After all, he'd lost two. "You must regret getting to James so late."

Cain averted his gaze and placed his hands in his pockets. "Let's not compare notes."

Or maybe he couldn't relate, as he'd never known his father intimately.

Still, it was nice of him to try to smooth things over between my father and me. This whole situation was daunting considering my father's illness. And asshole or not, Cain had a heart enough to understand that.

I didn't know what to say, because despite the dark side of him I'd seen Monday, there was no denying his thoughtful side.

I grabbed the bag of takeout and examined it. "Thank you."

Cain shrugged. "What's your favorite fish?"

I gave him a small smile. "Salmon, actually. Good call." I supposed it would've been nice to ask him about his taste as well. "What about you? What's your favorite thing to eat?"

Cain was taken by surprise, though he recovered quickly. "Steak."

"How do you like it?"

A dark glow passed through his eyes. "Guess."

Because this was going too keenly for my liking, I got back to basics. How would the Devil like his meal? "Bloody," I decided. "Medium rare."

Cain grinned, wagging his finger at me. "Good guess."

I took a step back, closer into my home, placing a much-needed barrier between us. This was too strange and bizarre. Almost civil, even. "Well, have a nice trip, Cain."

He tipped his head at me, eyes once more solemn and serious. "Remember what I said, don't embarrass me."

"Wouldn't dream of it," I let out dryly.

Cain's vision drifted to where I was wringing my hands before me. "And don't let me catch you without your ring again."

My eyes trailed to my naked ring finger. With or without his gaudy ring, I knew I was tethered to him. Stuck in this lifelong arrangement until death-do-us-part. "Anything else?"

A lopsided frown briefly coasted his full lips. "Go see your father."

Perhaps that was the hardest part of this. The severed tie between my father and me. The way there was no going back after what he'd done in throwing me to this man I didn't know, didn't love, and didn't want.

But there was no denying Cain was right. Every second counted.

After a curt nod from me, Cain turned and made his way toward the elevator. Once there, he glanced back at me, studying me.

I gave a tight-lipped smile before grabbing the takeout, stepping further into my suite and shutting the door behind me.

I tossed the bag in the nearby wastebasket and padded back to bed, ready to resume my depression nap.

8

KEITH

I RECOGNIZED HER INSTANTLY. SAME CHERRY-RED HAIR, same sweet looks—only now as I spotted her in Italo's brightly lit pizza parlor, I could really take in her pretty brown face. She was void of makeup and wearing a baggy sweatshirt and khaki pants. Looking youthful as ever, she was reading a book at a lone table and eating a serving of Italo's ice cream. Not many were in the restaurant, and something told me Sabrina was alone.

I shouldn't have done anything. But seeing how I was about to head to the community center to mentor the city's youth, it only felt right.

After putting in my large order for a few party-size pizzas, three in cheese, three in pepperoni, and three in white vegetable, I hesitantly made my way over to the young girl in the corner of the room.

TLC was playing on the radio throughout Italo's that Friday afternoon. It was eighty degrees outside, and so the cool AC was blasting, keeping us cold as we escaped the heat.

The spine of Sabrina's book was worn, letting me know she'd read it a dozen times and cared deeply for its content. The way she sat engrossed, spoon in her hand with melting ice cream, let me know this tenfold.

I cleared my throat as I stopped a few feet from her, not wanting to crowd or intimidate her.

Sabrina looked up at me, her nicely shaped brows lifting in surprise at my intrusion. It was seeing her up close that I again found myself questioning her age. Perhaps she was legal and just making a living at Crazy Legs. Kennedy—why was I thinking about her?—appeared younger than twenty-four herself.

I had Sabrina's full attention, there was no backing down now. "Must be a good book."

A smirk tugged on her lips, almost as though she couldn't believe I was opening with her book. "I only read it twice a year. Sometimes three."

I whistled, questioning the last time I'd read a book. My mother was good with giving me quotes when I was coming up, but I'd never been a reader.

"What's it called?"

Sabrina fiddled with the paperback. "*Night Changes*."

I dared to step closer, spotting a young-looking Black couple in an embrace on the dark blue cover. "About?"

She perked a brow. "You really wanna know?"

I glanced over my shoulder at the back kitchen, where the staff of Italo's were busy getting my orders together. I had a while when it came to those nine pizzas. Returning to Sabrina, I bobbed my head. "Yeah."

She pursed her lips, appearing doubtful. "It's about a young woman who still lives with her parents. And one hot and sticky summer, this older guy down on his luck moves into their garage and starts fixing things around their house to get on his feet." Sabrina's teeth dug into her lip as she cradled the book and spoke of its plot. "So, the girl is totally infatuated with him. Unlike her gilded world of fancy bullshit, he's *real*. But he's mean and standoffish, and doesn't think he's good enough for her." Sabrina gushed as she looked up at me. "It's like...*Poetic Justice* meets *Dirty Dancing*. I'm obsessed."

Sounded like more than just romantic fairy-tale fluff, but a more modern take on real relationships. Too many of us weren't perfect Mr. Suit and Tie. "How does it end?"

Sabrina didn't hide her smirk as she bookmarked her page. "You gotta read it on your own and find out."

I took a step back, wanting space between us. I didn't want to insult her, but if she was a minor, I didn't want to take a chance and leave her alone either. So, I got down to why I'd come over. "I'm Keith, by the way."

Those teeth of hers bit into her lip once more as she blushed a little. Her energy was light, pleasant, and warm. I could see why she'd be the top dancer at Crazy Legs. Something about her drew you in. Made you feel safe.

"My name's Eden," she said with a coy smile on her face.

Huh. Of course "Sabrina" wasn't her real name.

I tipped my head at her. "Nice to meet you, Eden." Maybe she was a kid, or maybe she wasn't. "So, listen, I'm on my way to the community center to have a little surprise pizza party for the kids. If you, or anyone you know—a brother, cousin, friend, ever need guidance or help, you should stop by," I let her know.

That smile arrested her face as she narrowed her eyes. "Do you say that to all the people who come here?"

"I'm not hittin' on you," I clarified.

Something like disappointment crossed Eden's face as she peered down at her book and shook her head. "Of course a good-looking guy isn't here to hit on me. Being a romantic is a gift and a curse, I tell ya." She lifted and dropped her shoulder. "Okay, though, on the community center. Sounds nice."

"I haven't been in a while, but I usually volunteer to mentor a few of the guys who stop by," I said.

"Aww," Eden responded, resting her chin on her fist. "That's sweet."

It was necessary to stop those in circumstances like mine from taking the path I'd chosen. "Offer always stands."

"I'll think about it," she said, making no promises to stop by.

It was something. I thumbed a finger over my shoulder at the counter. "You enjoy that book. I'ma wait on my order."

Eden watched me back off before going and opening her book again. She ate her ice cream with a grin when something interesting happened in her pages and I couldn't help but smile at the scene.

It was the simple things.

The sounds of bouncing basketballs could be heard as I entered through the gymnasium at the Jackson Community Center on Eleventh and Twelfth Street. Boys from their tweens to their late teens were inside having games at the various hoops littering the gym floor. On the bleachers I found other boys reading books, graphic novels and contemporary works. Some were doing homework. And a few were entertaining girls or boys.

Savon stood at the sidelines with an all too familiar young face. Dominique, a kid who was sixteen goin' on thirty. Hardheaded and headstrong, we often butted heads a lot when I attempted to guide his way. He currently stayed with his single mother and younger sister.

"I've been a man since I was nine," he'd boasted when we first ever chatted.

Dom had a slick mouth that sometimes made me want to knock him upside his head, but because I was once an arrogant little knucklehead, I couldn't fault him too much.

I made my way over to Savon and Dominique. "Hey."

Savon dapped me up, but Dom kept his distance. His eyes were guarded as he took me in. "Look who finally showed up."

I'd dropped the ball. I deserved that. "Yeah, I know, man. I'm sorry for not bein' around. Had some personal struggles to get through."

"Uh-huh," Dominique said, as if he couldn't care less.

I was only going to take so much of his attitude. "I got some pizzas in the truck. Come help me unload them in the cafeteria."

For the quickest second Dom's eyes lit up, but he hid any emotion from bubbling to the surface. I didn't know his mother's financial situation, but I did know he had trouble keeping jobs for himself. He didn't like being told what to do. Had an issue with authority. I knew what it was like to be young, Black, and angry, so I stuck by Dom the most because he worried me the most.

Outside, Savon and Dominique followed me to my truck where I opened up the back where the pizzas were in the trunk.

The smell of Italian spices and herbs mixed with melted cheese and sauce had my stomach rumbling.

"Damn, I'm definitely taking some home," Dominique commented at the sight of all the pizza.

"Be my guest," I insisted.

As Dom dug into my vehicle to grab three boxes, Savon peered at me over his head, nodding at me. He silently grabbed three boxes and went in ahead of us.

I leaned against my ride and watched as Dominique got a good hold of his stack. "So, how you been?"

A grim expression covered Dom's face. He caught on quick. "Man."

"Just curious," I said.

"Why?"

"I been there," I said.

Dom rolled his eyes. "You know, if you wasn't from around here, I'd feel like you was full of shit."

"Language," I corrected.

"There you go," he sighed.

"Dom," I said, sounding serious. "How are you?"

His dark eyes met mine and he dropped his guard, if only a little. "I mean, I'm straight. I'm trying to do what I can to help Mom out."

"You working?" I wanted to know. Outside of working at the garage fixing cars, I had a steady flow of money coming in from those around the neighborhood who wanted me to customize their rides with detailed paint jobs or fresh interiors.

Dominique set the pizzas back into my trunk and leaned against the back of my Tahoe. "I got a job at the grocery store, but they be ridin' me, Keith. I don't like that."

"It's a job," I told him. "Go in, do your work to your fullest capability, and that's it."

Dom clicked his tongue. "I know. I know. My people be settin' me straight, though."

A muscle in my jaw tensed and I had to still myself from reacting. Dominique hung around an older crowd—a crowd of bad influences who did questionable things.

"Dom," I started gently.

He groaned. "Keith, man. These my brothers. It ain't that big of a deal."

I stroked at my jaw, practicing some patience. "Sometimes you can be too blind to see what's wrong for you."

Dominique wasn't hearing me as he thumbed at the material of my trunk.

Disclosing my past wasn't something I liked doing, but for Dominique it was necessary. "Me and Von used to own this neighborhood. Or, at least we *thought* we did. I didn't like school either. Hated teachers telling me what to do or think. Didn't like the law. So, I cut class and did what I wanted."

Despite his tough guy stance, I could tell Dominique was listening as he quietly fingered a path along the pizza boxes.

"Sometimes you're just walkin' around mad, and you don't know why," I said.

"It be like that sometimes," Dominique agreed.

It was the simple truth. "I hated the world and everyone in it, and I just couldn't get a grip on anything. I hung around guys who I felt were like me. Guys, who at the time, I didn't see didn't have my best interest at heart," I confessed. "I got in a lot of fights. I had my mom and my grandma in my ear, and the school in the other. I was pretty hotheaded too. Didn't want to hear a thing."

"What your dad say?" Dominique asked me curiously as he lifted his head up.

I shrugged. "Don't have one. He died before I was born. Can't say if he would've had an influence on me or not, but there was a time my mom couldn't straighten me out."

"So, what happened with you?" Dominique pressed for me to go on.

"I just hung around a bad crowd. Made a lot of stupid choices," I said. "Toted guns, stayed out all night—a lot of reckless shit."

"Were you scared?"

I shook my head, telling the truth. "There used to be this one guy in the neighborhood. From the moment I met him, I knew there was something off about him. One time there was someone picking on a friend of his, trying to jump him, and this guy just takes out a knife and..." I made a slashing gesture through the air as I shook my head at the buck-fifty I'd witnessed. "I just remember catching eye contact and seeing nothing there. No soul. No heart. Nothing. He never messed with me, and I never messed with him. We kinda just had an understanding."

"He still around?"

That was the thing, not many were from my teen years. Some stayed on that path and ended up in prison. Others moved away, and I could only hope bettered themselves like what I was trying to do. "Nah, haven't seen him in a grip. A lot of those guys didn't turn out so well." I looked over into Dom's eyes. "Point is, I had a chip on my shoulder for a long time. Didn't even know why I was so angry, but it took my mom and grandma dragging me out of school and sitting me down to realize I needed help. That I wasn't making good decisions."

"I hear you," Dominique said.

I nodded as I held my fist out. He was a big guy, about as tall as me, almost the same build, and same complexion. Sometimes looking at him felt like I was talking to a mini me. I was sure the kid could handle himself, but only so much.

I wasn't going to lecture him too long and hard. It was Friday. The weekend. Today was about pizza and catching up. "Point is, I don't want to see you end up in a rough patch. The thing about hittin' rock bottom, is sometimes you crack. You only get one shot sometimes, and I want you to make the most of yours."

Dom smiled a little as he quickly jabbed his fist against mine. "Yeah, yeah, yeah. I'ma stick with this job, or I'll try to."

It was a start. And that was all I needed to work with.

I grabbed three boxes of pizza and Dominique grabbed the other three. Together we headed for the back entrance for the center, the warm sun on our backs, and the bright day forging on.

9

Kennedy

I DECIDED TO BE BRAVE.

There was a reason beyond my anger I wasn't facing my father. I was *scared*. When my father first began experiencing symptoms of ALS, I felt powerless. For my whole life we'd had enough money to throw at our problems and make them disappear. This wasn't one of those times.

One minute he was this big, powerful man standing at six-three. A man who went on jogs, hunting trips, and ran his business with a kindness you didn't see often in the world of money and capitalism. And the next, he started losing coordination, having issues with the muscles in his legs, and tripping over himself.

It took nine long agonizing months for them to reach their diagnosis of amyotrophic lateral sclerosis, or ALS. That was three months ago.

My father was faring as best as he could—or as well he could compose himself around us. My mother had loved him for her whole life. This was a shock to her entire system. She wasn't ready to face the outcome of a life without my father.

And neither was I.

I was rightfully angry about my forced engagement and

marriage, but I loved my father and couldn't stomach never speaking to him during what remained of his time here. Because there was a clock ticking away. No one survived ALS. There wasn't a cure. Some lived three to five years, others ten, and some even twenty. My fingers were crossed for twenty.

Friday afternoon a courier had arrived at my suite with a bouquet of white roses and a card from Cain. A very short note of *Go see him. – C. Carter* was all that was written. I wasn't too sure how I felt about Cain, but it wasn't lost on me that he was right in my needing to see my father.

So, Saturday morning I got myself together and drove over to my parents' house. The groundskeeper was tending to the lawn outside. The smooth buzzing of a lawnmower could be heard as soon as I got out of my Lexus. The scent of fresh-cut grass filled the air, mixing well with the fragrance of my father's nearby tulip garden.

Inside, I caught my family's housekeeper, Priscilla, heading down the hall with a basket of laundry.

Everyone was moving, going here and there as they'd always done, making the scene of the Nichols estate appear so normal.

It was when I found myself outside of my father's bedroom that it all came crashing down on my shoulders. The conjoined weight of my anger and fear. The uncertainty of my future hung in the balance and I hated having no control over any of this.

With a deep breath, I knocked a couple of times on the door before inviting myself in. Lying back as comfortably as possible in his four-poster bed, my father was wearing silk pajamas. Something so out of the ordinary for a man of his position. Usually, he was up by five on the dot to start his day.

The curtains were drawn, allowing light into the room as he laid back watching something on the large TV mounted on the wall across the room. There was an empty chair beside his bed, probably belonging to my mother.

My father turned from his program, glancing at me

momentarily before doing a double take. At once, a broad smile curled onto his mouth, stopping and starting my heart violently.

He was happy to see me.

Breathe, Kennedy, breathe.

I coached myself to walk over to his bed. To approach him. To be civil.

As much as I loved my father, I hated him for putting me in this awful position to feel so conflicted.

My father had always been so big and powerful to me, but now here he was, so fragile and small it seemed, before my very eyes.

I wanted to touch him, but I didn't know how.

Instead, I found myself sitting in the vacant chair beside his bed, stealing a peek at the TV before turning back to him.

"Hi, Daddy," I spoke softly, my trembling voice giving way to how broken I was at the state of affairs taking place.

My father chuckled, hearty and strong. He was still here. Grounded with me. "Neddy."

The sound of my childhood nickname warmed my heart and stilled all my trepidation. "Long time, no see."

He nodded, appearing thoughtful. "I assume you're angry."

"You're damn right I am," I said through gritted teeth. "It's not fair!"

My father blinked and faced me, sympathy tugging on his features. "I understand."

"Do you? You put me in a shitty position. And I can't even be really mad because…" I stopped myself, trying to stay strong, trying not to break, trying not to let him see me crack. Now wasn't the time for weakness. He was already suffering enough.

"It…won't hurt my feelings if you say I'm dying," he said.

My eyes hurt as I squeezed them shut to stop the tears. I couldn't handle this. I couldn't face this.

There was no time to be upset or feel betrayed with his insidious illness plaguing our family. It felt selfish. Selfish for him to put the burden on me to help his company. And selfish for me to feel anything but supportive and caring as he battled his disease.

"He's a cunning bastard," my father admitted. Oddly, though, he seemed to smile at the fact. "He must *like* you. A lot."

Or he was a control freak who didn't like taking "no" for an answer. "I'm touched."

"Give it three years. Please," my father seemed to beg.

Confusion took over me as I leaned over, resting my arms on his duvet. "Three years?"

My father nodded. "The marriage isn't contractual. There isn't exactly a legal way to rope your daughter into a binding marriage for a joint business venture. There isn't a divorce clause. Cain simply insisted on my end I state in my will you won't receive your inheritance unless you see three full years of marriage." A frown marred his face as he eyed me. "He wanted five, I said two, and we met in the middle on three."

Divorce. It was still a possibility as long as I suffered through three years of being with Cain. This was news to me.

"I think he believes he can win you over," my father went on. "He's a bastard, Neddy, but he knows what he wants."

Or what he thinks *he wants.*

I wasn't sure what Cain saw in me outside of my looks. I wasn't "wife" material. Beyond my age, I simply wasn't interested in having children. My car was a two-door for God's sake!

Or maybe I was a romantic and wanted to be swept off my feet by the right man. Not some devil in Zegna.

"You put me in a terrible situation," I spoke up, blinking back tears. "And I feel forced to forgive you because of what you're going through, and that's not fair."

My father's gaze shifted elsewhere. "I don't want to leave this earth with you hating me, but I'm thinking of your future."

"You don't think I can take care of myself?" I challenged.

I hadn't a college degree or skill to my name. Even if I would've lived off my inheritance, I would've been fine on my own, or choosing a man of my own taste or caliber.

"Nichols & Wagner is half yours," my father said gently. "I'm leaving you a legacy worth billions, and I wanted your children's children secure. This alliance is for your benefit."

Money. Three years of my freedom would amount to more money than I could dream of.

If only I'd gotten a say in this arrangement.

I leaned over, resting my hand on my father's for a moment before I stood up. "I'm just not sure that's worth stabbing me in the chest. We don't know how long you have, but I hope you really reconsider spending your last days choosing business over your daughter."

With that, my bravado saw me out of the room where I wept all the way out to my car.

Jadyn was the best. She only allowed me to mope for so long before coming all the way to Hampton Hills to see me.

It was almost eighty out, making us strip off our clothes and put on our tiniest bikinis and lay out by the hotel's pool. Jay's blonde hair was piled on top of her head in a neat bun, a pair of oversized sunglasses adorned her face, and the sun was hitting her chestnut brown skin, giving her a dazzling glow.

Jadyn embodied happiness just then, while I was sulking in my lounge chair under my sun hat.

"I feel like your dad means well in his own way, but is too caught up in the business side of things to see that he's actually hurting and betraying you," Jadyn reasoned. "He's probably impressed with Cain's pursuit in some way."

It almost sounded like my father was.

I didn't know what to think of it. Cain had promised me loyalty and apologized for his veiled threats at lunch. He'd suggested our marriage be stipulated in my father's will, binding me to this union for at least three years. As if that would be enough time to fall in love with him. I could, or I could divorce when the time came.

This wasn't forever.

Only permanent for now.

"You should have an affair, you deserve it," Jadyn suddenly blurted out, as if the thought had just hit her.

The idea wasn't so bad. "I haven't told the police, but he kinda threatened to end the life of any man who touches me."

Jadyn sucked in a breath as she lowered her sunglasses to gape at me. "Does it make me toxic if I find that...*sexy*?"

"Yes!" I was quick to let her know.

Jadyn bore no shame as she lay back and laughed. "God, this guy is a piece of work, ain't he?"

Dice. I wondered how good he was with them. If he ever leaned down in his expensive suits and played dice games in alleys.

It seemed pretty gritty for a man of his stature, but something told me he wasn't completely white-collar. The idea didn't fit him anyway.

Cain didn't seem like the type of man who bluffed. He'd nonchalantly spoken of murdering a man's child over "chips" like it was another day at the office.

"I don't know, Jay," I admitted. "He didn't seem to be playing around."

"Typical," Jadyn huffed. "You're supposed to be a good girl and keep it 'nice and tight' for him while he has his fun in Vegas."

Oddly, I scrunched up my nose in Cain's defense. "He said he wouldn't cheat on me."

Jadyn deadpanned as she looked my way, not impressed. "Uh-huh."

Men who were the loudest about being faithful typically did end up being two-timing cheats. Gaius hadn't cheated, but he was only at the beginning of his career. Sometimes I wondered how long we would've managed with his lifestyle of away games and gorgeous groupies. There were things I didn't do in the bedroom. A certified "pillow princess," he liked to joke about my preferences. Maybe he would've gotten bored of me. Perhaps Cain *would*.

"I don't think he's kidding about that," I said.

"Hmmp." Jadyn hummed and rested her chin on her palm. "You should call Keith."

Keith. Ugh. My life was a twisted mess, and a guaranteed release after a round with him sounded like true bliss.

"I-I shouldn't," I stammered to say.

Jadyn wiggled her brows. "You should. I mean, fuck Cain—at least once, but on the real, this whole thing is entrapment. You look stressed out."

"I *am* stressed out, Jay," I countered.

"Nothing relieves my stress like some good ol' fashioned dick," Jadyn concluded. She grabbed her drink that was sitting on the table between us. A virgin Shirley Temple. She fished out a cherry and popped it into her mouth. "You deserve a little yummy on the side for what these assholes in suits are putting you through. Just be extra careful with how you move."

I couldn't have Keith in a romantic setting, not that I was interested with the current state of my life, but a little fun would help make this whole ordeal bearable.

"What's he look like again?" Jadyn pushed for more.

I thought of Keith and bit my lip at his mental image. Even just picturing him caused me to lose my breath and squeeze my thighs together. "He's six-three—*big*, and has all these tattoos on his arms." I blew out a breath, not forgetting the most important detail. "He has the meanest face I've ever seen, but he's really handsome."

Jadyn whistled. "Sounds like a man who doesn't play."

Keith definitely didn't give off the vibe that he did. His aura reeked of grown man energy.

I sighed, feeling silly. "He's probably got someone already."

Jadyn pouted. "Yeah, I wouldn't entertain him then." She tossed me a look. "But if he doesn't?"

"You're so bad." I giggled as I grabbed my phone, half

contemplating going through with it. I'd stored his number under the alias *Auto Repair* as soon as I'd hit a red light after pulling out of the garage last week. At the time, I didn't want to take any chances if I clumsily lost his card.

"Do it," Jadyn encouraged as she instigated from the sideline.

This was ridiculous.

A few hours away from Hampton Hills to just breathe and be reckless was juvenile, but I wanted it. I wanted it badly.

Without thinking too deeply, I gathered my phone, pressed Keith's contact, and dialed his number.

My stomach launched itself to my throat as the phone began dialing out. My anxiety was on a high the moment he picked up.

"Hello?" he asked, his tone was alert, curious. His deep voice in my ear set my blood on fire.

"Keith? This is Kennedy," I spoke up, hoping and praying my voice didn't give away how nervous I was. How shy I felt. I never propositioned men for sex. I was used to it being the other way around. Keith was intimidating, but I would not let my fear deter me. I needed to relive that feeling of total liberation from last Sunday.

"Oh, what's up?" he drawled on his end.

I bit my lip. "You said I could hit you whenever I needed something."

"And?" he pressed. I could hear the grin in his voice, letting me know I wouldn't have to spell it out for him.

"I need my oil changed," I whispered.

Ah!

Jadyn swatted me for that remark, doing her best to cover her mouth and not be heard laughing.

Keith chuckled. *God, that chuckle.* "You silly. Let me, uh, drop a pin and you can pull up on me."

His fingers were magically fast, as not a minute later my phone pinged with a text from him listing his home address.

His *home* address.

Shit, this was real.

There was no backing down now.

I swallowed, trying to get my bearings. "Guess I'll be seeing you shortly."

"Guess so."

We hung up and I took in a mouth full of air, unable to believe I'd planned a sneaky hookup.

Jadyn looked on at me like a proud mother. "Well, let me get out of your hair. Sounds like you're about to be busy."

"Did I really just do that?" I had to ask.

Truthfully, I was boring. Not usually this bold and outgoing.

"Yep," Jadyn responded as she sat up and began gathering her things. "And don't you back out, either. Do something for you. Have some fun. And report back."

Do something for me. Easier said than done. The alternative to this was staying in line and in my place. A reality that left me feeling a little more than pissed-off.

But to go and hook up with another man?

I didn't think I would do it. Even after I was showered and pulling up to his address an hour and a half later.

Keith didn't live too far from where Jay stayed. Maybe a few blocks away at the most.

His home was small, intimate. It was all one story and a bright baby blue coloring to the stucco walls. His green healthy lawn was cut and his bushes by his front step were evenly trimmed. I tried to imagine Keith outside, being domestic and tending to his home and I found myself smiling.

Yeah, he was a man's man, good with his hands.

"You came all the way here," I said to myself. "Might as well see it through."

I opened my door, set one heeled foot on the ground, and then the other. Slowly, I got out of my car, shut the door, and turned and faced the house. It was still sunny out, a cheerful day where I could hear children playing nearby and teenagers shooting basketball. There was something idyllic about this street, about this area where Keith lived. A stark difference from my impersonable suite at the Residence.

I went up the front walk and advanced to the front door. Keith must've heard me pull up or was nearby, because before I could step onto the front step and ring the bell, the front door opened and he appeared in the doorway.

T-shirt. Joggers. Tattoos. Baseball cap.

Keith.

I didn't dress up for him. That wasn't what this was about. To keep it casual and under wraps, I dressed like I was out for errands in my pale pink cigarette trousers, white cami, and matching white heels. If Keith thought my look was too serious and plain, he didn't let it show as a corner of his lips curled up.

"Took you long enough," he let out as he stepped to the side and made room for me to enter into the unknown.

A shy smile had me blushing as I stepped inside. Just moving past Keith I was hit with a dose of his cologne. Magnetic. Subtle. Spicy yet woodsy.

My mouth watered at how attracted I was to Keith.

His front entryway was a long hallway with polished wooden floors and no pictures on the walls, just a large mirror by the door for last-minute checks on appearance.

I spun around as I heard Keith shut the door behind us. "Are you going to give me a tour?"

He bit the corner of his mouth, thinking to himself. "Sure, I'll show you all four walls of my bedroom."

I laughed. "Oh yeah?"

Keith studied me; humor gone from his face. "Hungry?"

While I admired his hospitality, I wasn't thinking about food. "No."

He took a step closer. "Thirsty?"

I didn't need liquid courage to see this through, I was ready. "No."

Keith looked past me and back. "What do you want to see first?"

He was giving me what I wanted, a proper tour, but suddenly I couldn't have cared less about making it to the bedroom, I was so ready to jump his bones.

"Your room," I answered softly.

He took my hand and the lead, going and taking us through the house toward the back where his master bedroom was. The few glimpses I got of the other rooms said he was the basic man, lacking true eye for decorations.

His bedroom held a little personality and color as I admired his large bed with navy blue bedding. The cool theme of wood and blue stuck out as I noted the blue furry rug on the floor by his gray ottoman. The room led out into a private patio, and I thought I saw a—

"You have a hot tub?" I asked as I trailed my eyes from the corner of the tub to Keith.

He nodded, appearing confused. "Don't you?"

"The hotel does. I don't in my penthouse," I admitted. At my parents' estate, there was an outdoor pool and a hot tub set up. I envied not having access to my own pool and tub.

Keith removed his cap and ran his hand over his waves. "Got it for a good little deal and set it up a summer ago."

"Cool." I tugged on Keith's gray T-shirt. "Maybe we can put it to use."

He smirked, taking a step back. "In a little bit. First, we gotta settle something."

He sounded like he was talking business and I didn't get it. "Huh?"

"The last time we were together, I did you a favor, and I'd like for you to return it," Keith explained.

It took me a minute to get what he was saying. What he was after. It was the way his eyes traveled to the apex of my thighs before coming back to mine that clarified it. Oral sex.

"I don't do that," I let him know.

He furrowed his brows and shook his head. "Good luck with that marriage."

"Fuck you," I shot back.

"We'll get to that." He grinned. "After you do me a favor."

I scoffed. "I don't get on my knees for anyone."

Keith shrugged and chanced a step closer. "Doesn't gotta be on your knees, you can do it on your stomach lying down. I'm not picky."

"I do not do that."

He leaned close, stopping at my ear, the grin on his face evident as he spoke. "You will for me."

This wasn't going how I'd intended.

Keith reeled back. He read my face and sighed. "Or maybe we'll keep oral off the table."

"Completely?" I asked.

"Completely," he agreed. "I won't touch you, and you won't touch me."

Okay, that wasn't what I expected to hear.

"But you're good at it." I pouted.

There was that devilish grin again. "I know."

I just wasn't a fan of giving oral. Gaius let me get away with a few times a year, but he'd always gone down on me, even when I didn't return the favor.

It was clear Keith wasn't about to go without an even exchange.

"Fine," I gave in, going and setting my clutch on the dresser behind him.

Keith watched me carefully. "It's fine if it's not your thing, Kennedy."

I glared at him. "But if I don't do it, you won't do it."

"Because it's fair," he stated.

He was a man with needs, and he wouldn't oblige mine unless he got his.

If I wasn't familiar with his skilled mouth and tongue, I would've turned and walked out the door. He was giving me an ultimatum without giving me an ultimatum.

Keith Avery was an asshole, but he had a sweet, considerate side. The worst kind of man. Toxic.

And I wanted to bring him to his knees.

"Okay, take off your shirt," I instructed as I stepped out of my heels.

Keith didn't budge. "You don't have to do this."

I cut him a fierce look. "But I want you to do it to me, so here we are."

I got down on my knees in front of him, and to my surprise, he sank down with me to where we were eye to eye.

"I'll know if you're doing a lousy job on purpose," he said.

I was going to make his toes curl.

"Anything else?" I perked a brow, showing my annoyance.

Once more, Keith shook his head, rising to his full height above me. He pulled his tee over his head and flung it to the side.

Angry or not, he did look good enough to eat.

My fingers curled around the waistband of his joggers. Keeping my eyes on his, I pulled them and his boxer briefs down until he was free.

Keith was already erect and well endowed, but I didn't let his size scare me as I went and stroked him for good measure.

He stood watching me, making the act hot. Suddenly, I wanted to please him, to make him feel good and...

"You'll tell me when you're close, right?" I wanted to know, unsure if I was prepared to go all the way with this.

Keith shook his head.

Oh.

Gently, his rough hand caressed my jaw, lifting my head to meet his eyes. "Won't you be a good girl and swallow for me?"

His thumb rolled over my bottom lip and I felt myself nod as I looked into his dark eyes, pressing my thighs together. My sex was throbbing at his tender touch and his attention.

Keith released me and I leaned forward and took his erect member into my mouth. It was too big to fit all the way, proving to be a challenge on my end on how I would break him.

I used my hands to assist my mouth, bobbing up and down, all the while keeping my eyes on his.

His skin was smooth, velvet on my tongue, and the more I tasted him, the more I liked it. He closed his eyes and his hands found my head, his fingers grazing my scalp. *He* liked it too.

I took him out of my mouth and flicked my tongue along the tip, catching his salty early release, seeing how he'd react.

"Oh, shit," he let out.

Grinning, I gave myself a mental pat on the back.

I put him back in my mouth, taking him as deep as I could, until I felt my eyes water. I took him out. Out and in. In and out. Sucking long and hard, warm and wet. Keith's breathing was becoming jagged and he was groaning as his hands tugged on my hair.

"Kennedy." His voice was light, vulnerable, weak.

Yes. Not so big and bad now, are you?

He came without warning. First a trickle, and then he was full-on unloading down my throat. He held on to me until he'd finished, and I had never felt so dirty, so used, so turned on in my life. There in some strange man's house, being a good girl for him, on my knees in my Alexander McQueen pants while my fiancé was God knows where.

Keith stepped back and stepped out of his joggers completely before pulling me up to my feet.

I grinned pompously up at him. "Not so lousy, was it?"

He narrowed his eyes. "My turn."

In record timing he helped me out of my clothing, leaving them in a pile on the floor. Keith laid me down, covering my nude body with his. Skin on skin, soft to hard, it felt intimate this time. He stared down into my eyes and I feared he'd kiss me. Steal my soul right from under me. Sensing my rules, his eyes trailed to my body instead as he began his descent.

His pressed a gentle kiss to my jaw, my neck, my chest. He took my left nipple into his mouth and sucked tenderly as he took my right nipple between his finger and thumb and tugged.

"Oh," I whined at the sensation. My hips bucked up, ready and needy for attention.

Keith looked down between our bodies, chuckling. "In time."

"Please," I begged.

He moved on to my right nipple. "No." He took my nub into his mouth and mimicked what he'd done to my left.

I bit down on my lip, trying to contain myself. It all felt so good. The anticipation. The feel of his weight on me. The way his smart mouth was also delicate.

Two fingers threatened to enter me and I moved to meet them, only to have them disappear.

"You liked it," Keith noted of my arousal at what I'd done to him.

I refused to respond. Yes, I'd liked going down on him, seeing his handsome face contort in ecstasy, seeing him weaken at my will.

"Say it," Keith urged, plunging his fingers inside of me. They didn't compare to *him*, but I was greedy and would take what he would give me.

"I liked it!" I called out.

"Good."

Keith planted kisses down my stomach until he reached his goal. The moment his tongue touched my clit I moaned loudly and uncontrollably.

"Keith!" I whimpered.

He stopped, peeking up at me. "What's my name?"

"Keith," I answered him.

"Remember that," he ordered.

He returned to me, to kissing, to nibbling, to tasting me without abandon. My fingers fisted his comforter as I arched my back and became undone.

For all the things he couldn't do to my mouth with his, he kissed me intensely, passionately, deeply between my thighs. My eyes crossed and my mouth remained open, and my soul slipped through.

A wave of molten pleasure overtook me and I rode it out as a peaceful bliss brought me back to shore.

"How do you like it?"

I opened my eyes and angled my head, catching Keith licking his lips and watching me.

"Missionary," I said.

He studied me for a beat more before going and kissing my inner thigh. "Turn over."

He got up to collect a condom and I sat up on my haunches. I liked it on my back, but perhaps it was better this way, from behind, less intimate. Less close.

"Don't pull my hair," I warned as he came back to the bed and climbed on with me.

He tore open the condom and rolled it on. There was something about the look on his face I didn't like. As if he would do exactly that when caught up in the moment. I narrowed my eyes and got on all fours, staring ahead at his plush gray headboard.

In another moment he seized my waist and gradually entered me. He didn't stop until he was all the way inside of me.

"Shit." I closed my eyes and fisted the comforter. I'd forgotten how big he was. How consuming.

The first stroke sent me forward until I was face down into a pillow. There was no time to adjust and prepare for the second.

Keith wasn't using his hands, but his wonderful hips to control and dominate me. And it felt so fucking good. He was hitting all the right spots. Branding me with his sex and leaving me unglued at the seams.

He was very big. Too much. So overwhelming. I had never felt this level of pleasure. This level of delicious pressure.

I tapped out.

"I can't! I can't!" I whined into the pillow.

Keith gripped my hips possessively. "You can."

His deep thrusts had me clinging to my sanity as I cursed his name loudly.

I couldn't take any more as my body let loose an orgasm that sent me seeing stars until total blackness drenched over me.

The echoes of birds chirping startled me awake some time later. I was alone in the bed, but a chill on my skin and a glance over my shoulder found the patio door open. The smell of cigarette smoke wafted into the house and I knew where Keith was.

I wasn't sure how long I'd been out, but I felt well rested. I needed to get up and dressed, or I'd do the stupid thing like stay over.

Beside Keith's bed, on the nightstand, was a copy of a brand-new book. New, I could tell by the receipt he was using as a bookmark. The spine held the title, *Night Changes*. The cover was an image of a young-looking Black couple in an embrace.

Oh.

I didn't peg Keith as the romance-reading type.

Curiosity got the best of me as I grabbed the book and flipped it open to its first chapter, wondering what he was reading.

```
There was something about summer that
made me delirious. Made me needy. I
thought it was the heat, the unrelenting
rays sending me into a starved frenzy.

It was June. The luminous sun burned
over my bare legs as I lay out on my
bedroom balcony, and I was aching. And
that's when it started.
```

The voice of the female character called to me, almost making me want to lay and read more. But I had to get a move on.

I swung my legs over the side of the bed and stood up.

Whoa.

My limbs were mush, nearly going out beneath me.

How could any woman get used to Keith's size and aggression?

I stumbled around the bed and picked up his discarded T-shirt. It felt like I was walking for the first time as I made it outside completely unsteady on my feet. Keith was leaning against the railing, smoking a cigarette in nothing but his low-slung joggers.

I slid up beside him and stole the source of nicotine right from his hand and brought it to my lips. With his gaze on me, on my mouth, I took a pull and blew out a stream of smoke.

Terrible.

I passed the cigarette back and leaned against the railing.

Keith brought the cigarette to his lips and hesitated for a second before taking a drag.

It was the closest we'd ever get to kissing.

"Why ask me how I like it if you're just going to take it from the back?" I wondered out loud.

Keith made a face as he regarded me. "I'm supposed to look down at your pretty ass face while I'm deep inside you and not kiss you?" He shook his head and looked off at his backyard beyond us. "I was tryin' to respect your boundaries."

Ah.

Keith observed me silently as he came back to me. "How's your father?"

I shook my head. "Don't make this personal, Keith."

"Well excuse the fuck out of me for being compassionate." He took a pull from his cigarette and I noticed the way his shoulders tensed up.

He was only being nice. A decent human being who'd remembered my father's illness. It was thoughtful to ask. To care. But that wasn't what this was about. Keith and I couldn't cross that line. He couldn't worry about me, and I couldn't fall for him. It would end badly.

"What are you thinking about?" I asked next.

Keith came back to me. "About how naked you are under my shirt."

The comment made me smile as my face heated up. I was naked. Just for him.

I chanced a step closer, nudging him in his ribs. "I had a good time. I've been kinda down this past week. I *needed* that release."

Keith was concerned again as he turned, facing me fully. "Are you still engaged?"

I peered down at my naked ring finger. "He's not letting me go."

Keith arched a thick brow. "How does that work?"

"He's not exactly a gentleman." Cain just dressed like one. Evil in disguise.

Keith shook his head. "And your father cool with this?"

I lifted and dropped my shoulder. "He hasn't seen the mask come off." Really, Cain didn't need to show his true colors for my father to know and do better. But that was another rant. Now wasn't about that. "Guess this is my rebellion."

Keith snorted, stubbing out his cigarette and bracing his arms against the railing. "I didn't think this would ever be serious no way."

We lived in two different worlds. A fleeting fling was the only thing we could have, and despite the risk, despite the red flags, I was interested.

I felt Keith's bicep, admiring his brawn and ink and how small it made my hand appear. "That works for me. I had a few no-strings-attached hookups in college. I know how this works."

"College girl," Keith quipped with a small smile.

I dipped my head. "I dropped out, actually."

Keith was quiet, drawing my attention back up. He wasn't judging me. "I didn't...finish high school. At least you made it that far."

"Can...can I ask why you didn't finish?" I asked cautiously.

Keith stared at me for the longest time, and I could tell this was a big issue for him.

"If it's too—"

"I was in a gang," he confessed. "It was real bad. My mom

pulled me out of school." His back was stiff as he looked off into the distance. "She saved my life." Once more he observed me. "Kinda personal, ain't it?"

"If you think I'm about to judge you, you're mistaken," I let him know. No one was perfect, but as long as Keith was trying that was all that mattered.

Still, it wasn't fair to shut him out and ask for more about him.

"I'm sorry I won't let you in," I said as I wrung my hands together. "I'd like to see you again, but only like..."

"*This*," Keith finished for me. "You want an escape from all the bullshit of obligation, suit and ties so you come here and climb into my bed, huh?"

"I'm here for you too if you ever want to just hook up and it not mean anything. No dinner. No movies. Just sex," I said, laying it out for him.

Keith was back studying me skeptically. "And you can handle all'at?"

As long as we kept it surface level, we were safe. "Yes."

Keith didn't seem convinced. "Are you *with* him like that?"

Even though my fiancé was attractive, I gagged at the idea of participating in any sort of sexual activity. "God no."

"So what's with the whole 'no kissing' thing?" Keith wanted to know.

I loved kissing. If I wasn't otherwise engaged, perhaps I would've gotten lost in Keith's nice-looking lips and engulfed in his strong arms. The idea, and want, was dangerous.

"It's stupid, I know, but maybe it's a little more anonymous without the kissing," I reasoned pitifully.

I didn't miss Keith rolling his eyes at that lousy excuse.

"If you want to kiss me, you can," I gave in. I gestured between the two of us for emphasis. "But this is all I can offer."

"Take it or leave it, right?"

"Unfortunately."

Keith scratched at his head, thinking over my offer. I could tell he was conflicted, not too eager to agree to a semi-friends-with-benefits setup. He blew out a breath and rested more against the railing. "I mean, there'd be some stipulations, but I'm not sure I'm ready for something real right now either."

"I get it," I said, accepting his need to lay out ground rules. "Let's hear it."

"Whatever you're not comfortable with sexually we can talk about, and vice versa," Keith reasoned.

"Agreed. Anything else?"

His sharp gaze cut to me. "If I'm fuckin' you, it's mine," he said with finality.

I forced myself to laugh, not wanting to give in to the tension, because it was clear he was deadly serious. "That's nice, but I belong to me. For now anyway."

Keith wasn't playing. He came close, picking me up and setting me on the railing. With his eyes on me, he repeated himself adamantly. "If I'm fuckin' you, it's. Mine."

Heat rushed between my thighs and I felt an ache so deep, it hurt. "A committed no-strings relationship?"

Keith wasn't amused by my sense of humor. "I'm an only child. I don't share well."

"Same," I admitted breathlessly. His determination to have me all to himself was a heady temptation I wasn't sure I could resist.

"This arrangement would work perfectly for a lot of men, but not me," Keith let me know. "I'm loyal to the soil. And I expect that in return. The moment you start feelin' ol' dude and givin' in, it's done—*I'm* done."

"I can only offer you sex. I can't love you, Keith," I insisted. "I won't."

He nodded. "Understood. But my point still stands."

Honestly, I couldn't have asked for a better agreement. He wasn't going to be out doing him while I was in Hampton Hills. He was free to date other people, but he wouldn't. To ask for my loyalty in return wasn't much. I kinda liked that he was willing to be faithful to me despite our not building anything real.

"Okay," I agreed. "No one touches me, but you."

"Only me," he repeated.

"Yes," I breathed out. The moment was soaked in a tension I couldn't wade from. All of my focus was locked on Keith. The feel of his hands on my body. His dark eyes staring back at me. The commanding tone of voice he was hypnotizing me under.

Keith came close, his eyes locked on my lips before gazing into mine and back. When I thought he'd kiss me, he didn't. Softly, he pressed his lips to my jaw and I felt my hands grip the railing.

Shit.

His hands gripped me harder, keeping me steady, keeping me sane.

"This is a terrible idea," he whispered in my ear. "We too grown for this."

I tipped my head back, loving his closeness, but knowing I should've moved away. "I know."

"So now what?" Keith asked as he reared back and stared at me, quirking a brow.

It was Sunday evening. My fiancé was out of town and I had no other responsibilities as far as I knew.

"I want you to take me back to bed," I told him.

Keith stared at me for half a beat before shaking his head and pulling me down to him. "Fuck it."

10

KEITH

I THOUGHT IT WAS A FLUKE. JUST A WILD ONE-OFF I'D think about from time to time. There was no way I'd see her again.

But then she called.

And here we were.

She lay there, naked, tangled in my sheets, wearing my baseball cap. Kennedy had put it on to be a pest, but I liked the sight of her in it, lying there. Her foot was poking out of the end of the sheets, exposing her white painted toenails.

I stood at the end of the bed, taking her in, completely mesmerized. If she were mine, I would've taken a picture to cement the memory.

But she didn't belong to me.

Kennedy told me she couldn't love me. It wasn't something I needed to hear. Especially after Leila. But for the time being, I could deal with a little no-strings-attached sex every now and then as I figured myself out.

There just had to be rules in place. A clear guideline to keep things organized and concise.

And right now, we were already breaking rules.

The day had winded down, the sun already having sunk in the sky. She'd wanted to come back to bed, and I'd indulged her.

As a true test to my willpower, I took her on her back, peering into her eyes as I buried myself deep inside her. The sensation of Kennedy made me weak on impact and it took great strength to hold it together. To accept that something in life could feel *that* fucking good. Watching her unravel for me, feeling her clench around me, hearing her sounds of pleasure, it all drove me to the edge. Before long, I brought her to the brink, until she was awash in waves of exhilaration, soon coming to shore behind her.

It definitely wasn't a fluke, and as long as we kept our emotions in check, I wouldn't mind keeping it going.

I was only wearing my joggers, an attempt to keep myself off her. Her smooth dark brown leg sticking out of my navy bedding called to me. The teasing smile on her full lips I'd yet to taste, irked me. The smell of her perfume soaking the air, made my nose twitch.

It had been too long since I'd had a woman over. Especially like this.

I shook my head. "See, this can't happen."

Kennedy fingered my sheets. "Are you kicking me out, Keith?"

I opened my mouth, but the sound of her stomach growling cut in.

Kennedy frowned, pressing her palm to her middle as she sat up. "Guess I *should* be going."

She said dinner wasn't necessary, but I couldn't let her go like this. "Nah, stay. I can whip somethin' up for you real quick."

Kennedy bit her lip, a habit I noticed she held. A distracting habit. "No, it's okay."

"Let me feed you," I insisted.

Kennedy wasn't sure. I watched her weigh the idea in her head, ultimately coming to the conclusion it was a bad choice as she shook her head in refusal. "I'm fine."

Her stomach protested that remark by making a sound once more.

I folded my arms, standing my ground. Okay, I could do the whole "friends-with-benefits" thing, but I wasn't an asshole. She was clearly hungry and I wasn't about to just throw her out. Discard her as if she were trash.

"Listen," I began, getting straight to the point. "I'm nice in the kitchen, but I promise if I feed you, you're not gonna fall in love with me, baby girl."

Kennedy peered over at me and I didn't back down. "Okay, but I don't eat meat. Just fish."

That proposed an issue. "I don't have anything thawed out." I grabbed my cell phone from my dresser and peeped the time. "And it's a little too late to order takeout on a Sunday." I lifted my head as I devised a plan. "I'll run to the store real quick and get something fresh. Finnegan's is still open."

"Oh, Keith, you don't have to go through all the trouble." Kennedy sat up some more and clutched my sheets to her breasts.

Not to be deterred, I pressed on as I grabbed a fresh pair of socks from my drawer and put them on. "What kind of fish do you like?"

Kennedy sighed. "I love skinless salmon, but any white or mild fish will do."

I nodded, mentally penciling it down. I chanced a look at her over my shoulder, catching the vulnerability on her face. She had a lot going on: forced engagement, sick father, and who knew what else. "You wanna ride with me?"

Kennedy smiled and relaxed, and the sight of her calming down brought me peace. "Yeah, but I don't feel like getting dressed. Hand me my purse. I'll pay for my fish."

I shook my head and stepped into my shoes. "Gotchu."

After grabbing a shirt and pulling it on, I went and sat beside her. The action caused her to shrink. That shy side of her coming forth.

I didn't trust myself to touch her, so I didn't.

"Can I have my hat back?" I asked politely.

Kennedy blushed, shaking her head. "Uh-uh. You gave me a bad hair day, and now I'm going to wear this hat until I leave."

Despite the fact she was being a brat, I smiled. "Okay."

Kennedy looked at me in a way only she could. Curiously. Innocently. Thoroughly. "You have a nice smile."

I rubbed at my jaw, looking away. "Do I?"

"Yeah, it's handsome," Kennedy replied.

Some thought of me as scary, intense—someone to avoid. At the shop, all it took was one look to get my coworkers out of my face when they were incompetent or annoying the shit out of me.

"Hey." Kennedy poked my arm, briefly fingering a tattoo. "Why didn't you kiss me?"

My gaze immediately went to her mouth. "Because you don't want me to."

Kennedy shrugged. "I said you could."

I declined. "I'll kiss you when you want it."

There was nothing worse than a lazy kiss, lazy head, or a lazy fuck. I wanted energy. Desire. And unless Kennedy was feeling it, I'd back off.

Kennedy pouted and that was way too tempting. "Now you're holding out."

I leaned in, closing the gap between us. Taking her chin in my hand, I lifted her face up and peered down at her. I stared at her as she stared up at me.

Shit, that face was too pretty.

"I'll be back," I said in the end.

She scoffed. "Fine, maybe I don't want your cigarette breath on me anyway."

Perking a brow, I questioned her. She shot me a sassy look in response.

Brat.

To settle the score, quickly, I leaned down and nipped her bottom lip with my teeth. The contact sent a brief jolt to my chest.

Kennedy's tongue snaked out and swiped my lip before I could pull away. A rush of blood shot straight to my dick.

"Careful," I said as I reared back and licked my lips.

Kennedy appeared playful as her hooded gaze lingered on me. "Or what? You'll punish me?"

I forced myself to stand up and get away from her. "You want anything sweet? They have a nice bakery." I grabbed my keys from my dresser and looked over at Kennedy again, awaiting her reply.

She shook her head. "No thanks."

I went to leave, but as I passed by the kitchen on the way out, something caught my eye.

Leila's grocery list.

I crossed over to it, going and reading it over like I didn't know it by heart after so much time.

Eggs
Bacon
Rice
Bread
Baby Spinach
...smile because I love you

My hand fell upon the old slip of paper.

It had been over a year since we parted ways. She'd moved on, found herself a good time under the spotlight and with a new partner. Me, I guessed I'd finally moved on as well. If only as a fuck buddy—someone to call whenever Kennedy needed some dick. Nothing deep. Nothing real. Nothing true.

"*You not goin' nowhere.*" Leila's words echoed in my ears and I felt a piece of me chip off.

This arrangement was another testament to her words.

The whole thing was ridiculous really. Kennedy had a Chanel bag, an expensive ride, and designer clothes on her back. The epitome of "Black girl luxury." This was just supposed to be sex, and it would only work that way. I wasn't sure I'd ever not feel dirty for touching her. Hampton Hills's princess.

"Keith?" Kennedy suddenly called out to me. "If you can, bring me back a brownie? I'll do whatever you want if it's frosted."

The sweetness she'd dipped her tone into managed to turn my mood around, causing me to smile.

She was a spoiled brat, but looking at her, I couldn't blame a guy for falling on his knee to give her what she wanted.

Despite our class differences, it wasn't hard to miss that Kennedy wasn't that experienced. Especially in the bedroom. I could tell by the way she reacted when I touched her. The way her body responded to mine. The feel of her coming around me.

Maybe all I could ever amount to was offering her sex. But at least it was good sex.

I avoided Leila's list and saw myself out of the house. I had some shopping to do.

Finnegan's was fairly busy when I parked my Tahoe in the half-full parking lot. As I got out, right away I spotted Dominique in a lime reflective safety vest pushing carts back into the store. The kid was still holding on to this job, a sight that gave me a sense of pride. I wasn't the best role model to follow after, but if I could steer Dom right, I'd feel worth a damn.

He had his earbuds in when I caught up to him at the east entrance. I had to tap his arm to gain his attention.

Ready to fight, Dominique spun around and glared at me. Up close, I could see he wasn't in the best of moods, something instantly putting me on alert.

"'Sup?" I held my hand out and he reluctantly slapped his against mine before coming in for a quick hug.

Dom shrugged his shoulders and frowned at the ground. "Not much."

Like me, he wasn't one to be smiling and glowing with an approach-me aura, but something about his vibe was off. Wary.

"What's going on? You don't look so hot," I said.

Dominique moved out of the way as a man with a few of his kids came into the store. He grabbed a cart and placed a toddler in the seat before leading two more other children into the store.

I led Dominique outside and stood with him, wanting to get to the bottom of his mood.

"This ain't enough, Keith, man," Dominique said, gesturing around us, emphasizing his job. "They don't pay me enough for this shit."

"Language," I corrected, earning an eye roll. "I know it's hard, but stick to it. Now, you're doin' carts, maybe in time you can get promoted to do something in the store and get a raise."

Dom hung his head, shaking it. "It's just me, my mom, and my sister, man. My mom not workin' as much as she used to. Her back be hurtin'."

Shit.

Being where we were from, having money issues, often led down a very bad path.

When I was fifteen, I'd joined a local gang. Getting jumped in proved to be a painful feat, but I'd done it, under the guise that it was worth it. To belong. At a chance to make money if needed. I'd never sold—much to my mother's relief—but I'd avoided the hard path for an easy way out.

Dominique would be better than me.

"And?" I pressed, wanting to know what he was thinking.

Dom sucked his teeth, looking off into the distance as he still had a good amount of carts to collect. "My boy got some work for me. He been talkin' about me linkin' with 'im to get some extra money."

I closed my eyes and bit my tongue, stopping myself from lashing out. Nobody when they're young likes being told what to do.

I scrubbed my hand down my face. "I'm here. If you need a

little extra money for help around the house, you got my number, you know how to reach me."

Dominique's eyes cut to me, the pride in them prominent. "And beg for a handout?"

"I'd rather give you my last than let you do something that's gonna potentially fuck you up for life," I told him.

I never wanted for much. I was damn near living paycheck-to-paycheck before Uncle Rod let me start using the garage to do side jobs as far as painting and customizing went. But I meant what I said. I'd rather zero out my entire bank account than let this kid start movin' illegal.

Dominique frowned, refusing to look at me. "Keith."

Tentatively, I reached out, placing my hand on his shoulder. In Bedford Heights, sometimes the city was counted out as a whole. But there was light here, good people with good intentions, and I'd do whatever it took to keep Dominique from falling by the wayside. To becoming another statistic.

"I got you," I let him know firmly. "Do yourself a favor and stick with this job. You're a minor now, but when the time comes, with school, you can elevate. Finnegan's got a reputation for handin' out scholarships for its employees. So, don't act like followin' your boys is the only way."

Dominique issued out a lopsided smile as he slowly bobbed his head.

I pulled him closer and gave him a quick hug. Not wanting to be too mushy since his energy was still hostile. "Keep your head up."

I let Dominique get back to work as I went back inside and collected a shopping basket.

The fresh smell of fish greeted me as I headed over to the seafood section of the store. The department was still open, and as I browsed their selections I was elated to see that they had skinless salmon like Kennedy liked. I ordered a couple filets before going over to the bakery and picking out a pack of chocolate frosted brownies.

I wouldn't make her *do* anything for them. It wasn't her thing to give head, but I was glad she'd enjoyed it when I felt her wetness on my fingers when I touched her. I wouldn't push, but I was hoping she'd do it again, on her own, unprovoked.

For now, she could have the brownies simply because she wanted them.

After checking out at the register I made a stop at the ATM and withdrew three hundred dollars. It wasn't much, but I hoped it showed I was someone Dominique could count on.

"Come on, man." Dominique's eyes got a little glassy as I met him outside and slid him the money. "I don't want that."

When he shook his head once more, I reached out and put the money into his hoodie's pouch. "Take it. I mean it, I'm here. So is Savon. You're not alone, Dom. We got you."

Misty eyed, he dapped me up and nodded. "Thank you."

I ruffled his plaits. "Always got you."

Because I didn't want to overwhelm him, and let the fish sit out for too long, I left him to finish his shift as I got back in my truck.

By the time I made it home I noticed Kennedy's car was gone. Inside, in my bedroom, I found a note and a fifty-dollar bill on my copy of *Night Changes*.

Family emergency. - Sorry, K.

Sighing, I went and put the fish in the freezer.

I wasn't disappointed. This was just a fling. Nothing more. Nothing less.

II

Kennedy

"So, what happened?" Jadyn asked me over the phone Wednesday afternoon.

I had just got in from my Pilates class and was munching on some grapes as I lay out on my sofa.

Jadyn's question sprang forth a vivid memory of what had gone down during my impromptu visit to Keith's that past Sunday.

Not that I would tell anyone, but I found myself to be incredibly limber these days.

It had been a while since Gaius, and sex was like a new awakening all over again.

Just the thought of Keith taking me on my back, my legs on his shoulders, made my middle burn. Every inch of him was big, leaving my body to have to accommodate him. I wasn't sure I'd ever get used to sex with him. He only fucked me, and I couldn't stop myself from wondering what it was like to have him go slow, to make love to my body, and be gentle.

I liked Keith's sex, but I was curious.

Then, I supposed, candles and sensuality were probably a bad mix for what we were doing. To be tender. To be affectionate. It would cross a line, and I feared I'd slip and tumble down that rabbit hole.

The no-strings thing was easier in college. Now that I was a little bit older, and dated seriously, there was a piece of me that missed romance. A connection.

I just had to accept that I couldn't have it all.

"K?" Jadyn pressed on, bringing me out of my thoughts. "Don't leave me in the dark."

"Right, sorry," I apologized. "I went over to his house and we hooked up."

"And...?"

And I decided to be stupid and jump into a committed non-relationship with him. "I fucked up."

"Oh no," Jadyn responded, sounding worried.

"We had sex and I fell asleep. When I woke up, I should've left, but I didn't," I said. "He was outside smoking and I went out to see him. I told him I wanted to see him again, but only like that." I rubbed at my neck, remembering Keith's reaction. "And he said if he's sleeping with me, no one else can."

Jadyn sucked in a breath. "Well, shit."

"I know."

"You down for that?"

"I mean, we're basically in a committed no-strings relationship," I pointed out. "But, I guess I can deal with that. At least I know he won't stray."

"What are the chances of you getting *two* men who want fidelity from you?" Jadyn joked. "And neither mean a thing."

Keith wasn't supposed to mean anything, and Cain never would. He was more so my warden.

"Tell me about it. I haven't kissed Keith, so there's that," I said.

Jadyn snorted. "Lame."

"I know."

"So what did y'all do?"

Guilt washed over me at how I left things. "He tried to feed me."

"What an asshole," Jadyn responded dryly.

I managed to loosen up and laugh. "Stop."

"So, he offers you loyalty, dick, *and* food? Besides your psycho fiancé, not seeing the problem here."

Cain being in the picture was the biggest problem. And beyond that, this thing with Keith was a recipe for disaster. "He could break my heart."

"Take that risk, girl, that's what glue is for."

I rolled my eyes. Jadyn was no help. "I feel bad. He went out shopping because he didn't have any fish thawed out, and I bailed while he was gone."

"Kennedy!" Jadyn chastised.

"I know." I cringed. "I didn't do it on purpose. There was a false alarm with my dad."

At once, Jadyn understood. "I'm sorry, K. Is he doing any better?"

On Sunday, my father had experienced some muscle cramps in his thighs, causing my mother to panic and take him to the hospital. I couldn't blame her for the dramatics. This whole ordeal had us all on edge as we had no agency over my father's health. It was an uncomfortable feeling, sitting around, watching, waiting, hoping for some sort of miracle that would make my father's condition bearable at the most.

He was in and out of the hospital, with some prescribed pain meds for the cramps. Being there in the thick of it, I could see what Cain had alluded to. My father was prideful, insisting that he was fine and my mother was overreacting. But I could see him wincing as he was helped back into bed from his wheelchair. I could see his gritted teeth. I could feel his rage.

He hadn't asked, but right then I conceded, allowing myself to stop fighting this marriage to make one part of my father's life easier. A sacrifice if you will. It was pathetic, but seeing with my own eyes how my father tried to fight defeat was a blow I couldn't recover from.

"He's adjusting," was all I could say on the matter.

"I hate this for him and you," Jadyn said. "Especially you, because you must feel obligated to help in anyway."

She knew me too well.

"How are things with the script?" I pushed for a subject change, if only to spare myself from dwelling on my predicament.

Over on her end, Jadyn groaned. "I was trying to go romance-less, but now I'm thinking my girl deserves a little love in her story. I mean, it's not like coming-of-age stories with guys don't feature love stories."

"Love *is* nice, Jay."

"I wouldn't know. It's been a while over here. Twisted or not, you're the one swimming in prospects."

Prospects. Right.

My only true prospect was Cain. With Keith, somehow, I had to manage to keep a wall up while sleeping with him. A task he seemed intent on making a challenge.

He asked about my father. Something small, humane, but left me feeling antsy.

I hadn't called or texted him to explain my abandoning him further, and he hadn't called or texted me to ask for an explanation. This was how it would work. No emotional ties. No questions. Just a phone call or text when either of us was horny.

"I'm trapped, Jay," I said softly. "It can only be sex with Keith, because if I fall for him, it'll only end badly."

There was a knock at my door, drawing my attention across the room.

"If you want to cut off ties now, I get it," Jadyn replied. "Whenever you want to escape the stress of Cain and your dad's situation, I'm here. Whatever you want, I support you."

I was entirely overwhelmed with what was going on. Sinking on a raft with no way to land. Having at least one hand reaching out to help me lifted some weight from my shoulders.

"Thank you, Jay. I mean it, you've been my rock since this whole thing started." I got up from the couch and went to answer the door.

"Of course, what are friends for?" Jadyn reasoned. "I don't want you to feel alone when you have me."

I opened my mouth to thank her again, but the words never came out.

Cain was on the other side of the door when I opened it. His men weren't too far behind him keeping lookout.

"J-Jay? I gotta go," I let her know before I hung up.

I was still in my sports bra and yoga pants, but Cain held the grace to look me in the eye.

"Cain," I said as I leaned into my door. "You're back."

He nodded. "I was in the neighborhood."

Somehow, I doubted that. "Okay."

There was no use in fighting him, so I let him into my suite and shut the door behind him. He made no move to remove his jacket or get comfortable. Instead, he stood in the foyer, staring back at me.

"Do you have any plans?" he wanted to know.

"Not particularly, why?"

"I'd like to take you out on a date. Somewhere...special to me," Cain answered. His eyes ran down my current state of dress before returning to mine. "You'd have to change of course."

I could've stood my ground, asked him to leave, but what was the point?

"What should I wear?" I gave in.

Cain's eyes returned to my figure. They were empty and impassive. If he lusted after me, he didn't let it show. "A dress."

Classy. Got it.

"I'm going to go shower and get ready. Please wait outside." I opened my door and Cain put up no fight as he began making his way by me. It caught me by surprise he didn't insist on waiting in my living room. "Wait."

Cain paused just as he'd made it back into the hallway. "Yes, Kennedy?"

"You can wait in front of the TV," I offered.

For the briefest second, Cain smiled at the change of plans, but still, he went over to his men and left me to be alone in my suite.

Who knew the Devil could be a gentleman?

Cain was in a fitted black suit. I preferred white, but I had just the black Balmain dress in my closet for the occasion. After all, this was my funeral.

Forty minutes later I was in the back of a town car sitting beside Cain as we rode over to his surprise date. Like a dutiful fiancée, I wore my ring as my only accessory. My hair was back in a bun, I'd only applied mascara and eyeliner for makeup, and my Balmain mini dress had caught the eye of Cain and one of his men. Beans had the decency not to be affected by the sight of me.

When the car came to a stop, I discovered we were downtown at some hole-in-the-wall spot I didn't recognize. The marquee out front glowed brightly with the venue's name. *Lucky's Blues Lounge*.

I faced Cain for an explanation, but he merely got out of the car and came and helped me out of my side.

"Come, they reserved us good seats," he instructed. With his hand on the small of my back, he led me inside and I didn't miss the fact that Beans and the other man were following us.

Lucky's Blues Lounge was like a step into the past. Once inside I felt as if I'd been immersed into the '40s with its dim lights, soul music, and classy attire. There were booths and tables, food being brought to patrons who wished to dine. The live singer on stage was singing a rendition of some old-school song I couldn't quite place, and I was in awe of the environment. It was something like an old-school juke joint.

Whoa.

"It's Etta James," Cain clued me in of the young woman on stage singing a cover. "'Trust in Me.'"

The lounge wasn't bustling with people, but there were enough in the room to let me know Lucky's was an exclusive spot. The crowd in the surrounding tables and booths were a mix of what looked like Black twenty-somethings, along with an ample amount of people in their thirties and forties.

Cain didn't take a moment to study the atmosphere like me, nor did he wait to be seated. He took the lead and led me over to a booth on the lefthand corner of the room, with a terrific view of the stage, as well as the door.

His men didn't join our table. They took a circular one a few feet away and focused on the menus on the tabletop.

I slid into the booth first, and Cain joined me.

All of the staff of Lucky's wore black trousers, button-down shirts, or dresses for the female members or skirts. They too looked like they'd stepped right out of the '40s—when men were "dapper," and the women were "dames."

Our hostess, a young woman in a black A-line skirt and white polo, came to our table with a chipper smile on her face. She procured a pad of paper to take our order before sweeping her attention between Cain and me. "Good evening, welcome to Lucky's. My name is Blair. How can I help you folks tonight?"

"We'll start off with some waters before we order," Cain spoke up. He glanced my way. "Is that okay?"

I could only manage a nod as I reached out and collected a menu from the table. The smell of beef filled the air, and I noticed a couple nearby eating steaks.

Blair went off to grab our waters and suddenly Cain and I were alone.

I took the time to examine the room. The young woman on stage was doing another cover, her angelic voice putting the entire first floor in a trance. The balcony area held patrons leaning over the railing to get a good view of her. Next to the smell of steak, cigar smoke wafted down from the second floor.

"They can smoke in here?" I voiced my surprise as I came back to Cain.

His eyes lifted to the balcony as he nodded. "If it bothers you, I'll have them put it out."

"You can't do that." It wasn't a big deal. The scent only served to remind me of Keith. Of sharing his rancid cigarette with him after sex.

"I can do what I want." Cain returned his attention to me. "I own this place."

That took me by surprise. A man of Cain's age and position, I would've guessed he would own a nightclub before something niche like a blues lounge.

"You like this style of music?" It was a silly question, seeing how here we were.

Cain hummed. "Blues, jazz, doo wop—most of my favorites are older. Think the last newest voice I would say who caught my ear would be Adele."

"Adele hive," I joked.

Cain glanced my way, and I could see him almost smiling. "What do you like, Kennedy?"

"R&B, and some pop. Mariah, Brandy, Janet, and Sevyn Streeter," I listed. "Just to name a few."

The style of music Lucky's presented wasn't bad. It reminded me of older movies I'd grown up seeing with my mother.

"Hungry?" Cain asked as he reached out and tapped my menu.

While I was happy that they offered several fish entrées, I wasn't in the mood to eat. "Too nervous."

"Don't be, it's just us," Cain insisted. "Then again, every man in here is looking at you, and I'm not sure I'm a fan."

"Oh please." I brushed him off and tucked a strand of hair behind my ear, suddenly anxious.

Had people noticed me? Or were they eyeing the owner? Something about Cain demanded attention. When he walked into a room, you knew he was a somebody, someone with power and prestige.

Whether he earned it or not.

Cain made himself comfortable as he went and removed his suit jacket. Right away I spotted the shoulder holster he was wearing beneath it. On the side closest to me, he had a gun tucked away. I'd never seen one before, and the sight made me uneasy.

Cain noticed.

"Safety's on," he assured as he removed the gun and held it in his hand. The proximity had me sitting up straight. "You ever use one of these before?"

"N-No."

Cain accepted this. "We'll have to fix that."

When he put the gun on his lap, I calmed down. If only a little.

"You trust me with a gun around you?" I found myself teasing.

Cain wasn't fazed as Blair came and deposited our glasses of water. He held his finger out to her, asking for more time to decide on what he wanted to eat. It was only when she was out of earshot that he replied. "If it's my time, it's my time."

He sounded so nonchalant, as if the idea of a violent death didn't scare him. Bastard or not, I didn't like that.

Cain chuckled at my frown.

"Everybody wants to be a gangster, until it's time to be a gangster," Cain quipped as he took a sip of his water.

Gangster. The moniker fit him to a T when I thought about it. There was nothing clean-cut about Cain Carter. "Now that we're engaged to be married, will people be out to hurt me?"

My father was a businessman and even he hadn't ever walked around with security like Cain did.

Cain regarded me, a serious expression on his face. "You'll always be safe and looked after when you're with me. You never have to question that."

I barely knew Cain, but I could just tell he was a man of his word. If he said something, he meant it. If he promised something, he saw it through.

"Still," I went on as I stole a peek at where Beans was ordering food with a waiter and the other man was scouring his menu. "Do you *have* to have your men follow you everywhere you go?"

Cain glanced at his men and came back to me. "Precaution."

"*Precaution,*" I repeated. "Sure."

Cain tapped his finger on the table, once more looking over at his men. "Vino's the only person you want watching your back. And Beans..." Cain's gaze fell to the tabletop. "He's the closest thing to family I've ever known."

"Really?" I didn't miss the way Cain's face fell, the sense of vulnerability in the air.

"We...met in foster care," Cain admitted.

At once I turned, giving him my complete attention. "*Foster care?*"

Cain stiffened a little beside me, letting me know this was a hard topic for him. "My mother...she died suddenly when I was twelve. With no father coming forward, that left me a ward of the state."

Despite it all, I reached out and placed a hand on his. "I'm sorry, Cain."

He regarded my soft palm on his. He gave a shrug, as if it didn't matter, but I called bullshit. "So, anyway, that's how I met Beans. He was...*different* from the other kids, and that made him a target. I stuck my neck out for him, and he's been loyal to a fault ever since."

Suddenly, I felt bad for Beans, being bullied after being placed in the system. "You know, with a little cleaning up, maybe I can set him up with a girl I know."

Cain almost seemed to smile. "That won't be necessary."

I got back to their relationship. "So, he owes you."

Cain was quick to shake his head. "He doesn't owe me a thing, but I respect his loyalty. I trust it."

"Trust seems like it's hard for you."

He frowned. "You have no idea."

"Could you...trust me?"

"If you give me a reason to trust you, Kennedy, I'll trust you one hundred percent."

I grabbed my glass of water and took a hearty sip, half paying attention to the Bill Withers song playing through the speakers in Lucky's.

We were engaged, and I was having an affair. I wasn't selfish enough to ask him to trust me.

Sitting so close, I saw it. There, on Cain's bottom lip, was a scar. About a few inches long, faded, but there.

"What happened there?" I wanted to know.

Cain thumbed at it and looked off. "Lost battle."

Somehow, my mind pieced together his time in foster care, his connection to Beans, and this telltale scar. Against all that I felt for him, my heart softened.

Cain peeked at me and snickered surprisingly. "Jesus, to think pity would've been a good route in winning you over."

I only halfheartedly rolled my eyes. "Can't help it that I have a heart. There's still time for *you* to grow one."

Cain glanced down at his glass. "In another life, perhaps, I would've had a chance." He observed me limply. "Guess we'll never know."

I didn't know his entire life story, but it was clear that Cain wasn't born this way. Rather, he was made.

His mother died young and suddenly. He had no father or other family to raise and nurture him. And then the foster care system had been cruel to what was left of the impressionable little boy.

I wanted to touch his scar, but I kept my hands in my lap instead.

I chewed on my cheek, feeling conflicted. "And when you said you wouldn't cheat, you meant it?"

He nodded. "You never have to question your trust in me. I

took a pay cut for you, to do that and fuck up by being weak would be foolish."

"Pay cut?" I questioned.

Cain ran his finger along the rim of his glass. "Damon wasn't going fifty/fifty after I proposed adding you to my end."

Shit.

Cain *wanted* me. There was something off about him, but then there was something nice, too.

Blair swooped back by, and this time, to distract myself, I ordered a Sprite and forced myself to get a Mediterranean salad with salmon. Cain ordered wine and a lamb chop meal, and once more we were alone as Blair went to turn our orders into the cook.

Another song by Etta James was playing and around me I could see some men and women swaying to the melody and giving their lovers the eye.

Cain undid his cuffs and pushed his sleeves up, revealing naked skin. Aside from that thorny-stemmed rose tattoo on his hand, his skin was bare of ink. Tattoos didn't quite seem his style anyway.

Blair came and handed me my Sprite and Cain his glass of red wine before going on to her other table.

"Can I ask you something?" I grew the courage to speak up. "I-I pretty much know the answer, but I gotta ask. Would you really do it? Would you kill someone who touched me?"

Cain didn't even look at me as he answered. "In a second. I wouldn't recommend testing that theory."

My heart dropped. "I wouldn't... I don't think I'm worth it. The hassle of doing all this."

"What's mine is mine," Cain declared. "I don't like people touching what belongs to me."

I belong to me. "How do you know I won't go to the police?"

Fear didn't register on Cain's face. "Guess I *do* trust you."

Either that or he was arrogant.

"I am going to have my hands full in the coming weeks and

months," Cain said. "I'm aiming to open The Residence at Cartier next year."

Next year? Most of my father's hotels took more than a couple of years to go from designs to opening day.

"That can't be done," I commented.

"It can when you light a fire," Cain responded. "I also think we should speed up the wedding, maybe do it in December."

"Cain—"

"It's just for appearance, mainly your father. I don't want to push it and he not *be* here in the end. We won't have to consummate it or anything."

A lump lodged in my throat at the possibility of my father passing before I said *I do*. "We wouldn't have to do anything?"

Cain shook his head. "You have my word. Not until you're ready."

I smirked, grabbing my Sprite and forcing down a mouthful. "What if I'm *never* ready?"

Cain chuckled, appearing handsome and young. "I'd like to think I can be somewhat charming."

Charming, sure.

According to my father, I only needed to last three years in our marriage before I could receive my inheritance. Could I go three long years in a sexless marriage?

"But if I don't want to?" I pressed, needing to hear him say it again.

Cain gave a stiff nod. "Do I want to wait until after we're married? Not at all. It's not up to me, ultimately. I don't intend to touch you until you want me to touch you."

I turned, facing him, giving him a better view of me. "And if I say yes, you can touch me?"

Not breaking eye contact, Cain responded, "I'd very much like to fuck you in that dress."

So he was attracted to me.

Swallowing thickly, I remained calm. "But since I'm saying no?"

He shrugged simply. "Then I'll wait."

"No crushing pills or ripping IUDs?"

The frown that took his face let me know he regretted those words. "I'd never do that, Kennedy. I'm a lot of things, but not a monster."

It was mid-February. If we got married in December, that would only speed up my countdown until I was truly free of this arrangement. Worst came to worst? He wouldn't let me go and allow us to divorce. Odd-case scenario? I got to know Cain and fell in love with him.

A sense of panic overcame me at that thought.

Really, in the end, I didn't have a choice. Prolonging the inevitable would only lengthen the time frame of this whole nightmare. I told myself I was doing this for the greater good. For my father.

I buried my discomfort as I raised my Sprite in the air for a toast. "I guess we're getting married in December, Dice."

Cain studied me. He ran his thumb along his bottom lip as he tilted his head, shaking it slightly. "*Cain*. I don't want to be 'Dice' with you."

"To a December wedding, Cain?" I reiterated, still holding my glass out.

Cain went and clinked his wine against my soda. "To a December wedding, Wife."

I took a sip of my Sprite, gulping it down as my hand shook, hoping he wouldn't notice.

12

KEITH

It was my day off, but there was no place else I would've rather been than the shop. I told myself I wasn't working Friday morning as I stepped into the garage to just take inventory and the atmosphere. I had a couple of people requesting paint jobs and rim placements, but other than that, I was free to go anytime I pleased.

Not that that was going to happen any time soon. I lived for this life, the hustle, the buzzing sound of a drill, the people from the neighborhood who only came to Rod's because they trusted us before anyone else, the feel of grease and metal in my hands—the garage was home to me.

Chatter filled the garage of Rod's Repair as mechanics were working away on clients' vehicles. I stood off to the side with Armin, an old classmate of mine who'd bought a restored Chevy Nova. The rusted body was in need of something fresh, something vivid to make it really stand out like the beauty she was.

Armin scrolled through his phone's image library, showing me several paint jobs he'd Googled to see which I liked the best for his ride.

"Whatchu think about the red, Keith?" Armin asked as he tapped the screen of his phone.

Red was a staple for some classic cars, and the Nova would look nice in that finish. Although, I was leaning elsewhere as I rubbed at my jaw. "It's nice, but that black is clean."

Armin whistled. "Shit, that's where my head is at. My girl was thinkin' the navy-blue, and that's cool too."

He went back to search for the navy-blue paint job.

"*Dayum,*" I heard one of the mechanics snap in the background.

My attention drew across the room, to the store entrance to the garage. Standing in the doorway, looking around, was Kennedy.

Nearly all the men in the room had their eyes on her, and I couldn't blame them.

My eyes traveled from her black lace-up stilettos, up her oiled legs, past her white lace summer dress, to her pretty lost face. Her hair was wavy today, there was a gold necklace with some pendant on it around her neck, and I couldn't take my eyes off where her dress ended and her thighs began.

One thing about Kennedy I'd grown to notice, she had a thing for wearing white- or cream-shaded clothing, and it worked for her.

I hadn't heard from her all week, and despite *her* rules, a part of me was worried. At least about her father. Seeing her now, and the way that white dress complemented her smooth, deep brown skin tone and hugged her body, was a hell of a distraction.

And it wasn't just me.

I didn't run the garage, Uncle Rod did, but even I knew he wouldn't like the sight of his men staring at the woman in the doorway rather than the vehicles in front of them. *I* sure as hell didn't.

Blinking, I caught myself and focused back on Armin if only to excuse myself. "I like the black, but the navy is cool, too. Think it over and get back to me."

I walked away before Armin could respond. Kennedy noticed me as I made my way over. She lit up, blushing it seemed, as she bit her lip and offered a timid smile and a small wave. She could feel my coworkers' eyes on her, see their tongues practically hanging out, but it was only when she looked at me did she appear nervous.

I came to a stop in front of her, towering over her, instantly awash in that sweet-smelling perfume of hers. I wasn't sure if I believed in Heaven or anything, but if it had a scent, it was this. Flowery rose, smooth vanilla, and an undercurrent of cedar. The essence of soft.

"Hi," Kennedy squeaked out.

"Of course she's here for Keith," one of my coworkers, Ian, grumbled out before sucking his teeth.

Too aware that we held an audience, I took Kennedy by the hand and steered her back into the shop, up the back hallway into the main area. As we passed the front desk, I managed to shoot Jake a glare for allowing Kennedy out into the grit and grime of the garage, before taking her back into Rod's office. Thank God he was out on a late breakfast run.

I closed and locked the door. There was a couch in the room, but I opted to go and stand against Rod's desk. It wasn't lost on me we'd returned to the scene of the crime.

Something told me Kennedy realized this too. She looked around, that blush growing, her eyes bouncing from here and there.

"Haven't heard from you," I spoke up.

Kennedy's attention returned to me. "I know, I'm sorry. Shit got complicated."

I nodded, knowing her situation was a mess. "How's your dad?"

The wall went up and Kennedy shook her head as she came closer. "This isn't about that."

I perked a brow, studying her closeness. "It's not?"

"Uh-uh." Her voice dripped in suggestion as she slowly sank to her knees before me. With her eyes on me, her hands reached out for my jeans.

The contact made me stand straight up.

I loved me some head, but fuck if the brain up top wasn't leading me in the moment.

"What are you doing?" I peered down at Kennedy, trying to keep my blood from rushing south.

"I wanna make it up to you for ditching you Sunday," she said.

This was one hell of a view and I cursed myself for not going with the flow. My hands shot out before I could second-guess myself. I grabbed Kennedy's wrists and helped her to her feet. "It's whatever."

Kennedy's hands were on my zipper once again as her eyes remained locked on mine. "I came here to do something, and I'm not leaving until I do it."

Shit.

It would take only a second to shove everything off the desk and lay her across it. Porn scenario or not, I was losing my resolve.

My fists curled at my sides. "I'm trying so hard not to fuck you right now."

Kennedy leaned up on her toes, going and pressing a torturous kiss to my neck, making a trail to my ear. "The only thing that needs to be *hard* right now is—"

"Keith?"

Fuck.

Uncle Rod was coming up the hallway toward his office, looking for me.

I moved in front of Kennedy at the first sign of her fear. With my back to her, I went and unlocked and opened the door just as Uncle Rod was reaching for the knob.

Confusion covered my uncle's face as he took in the previously closed door and then me. "Everything okay?"

The smell of sausage and eggs wafted from his grease-stained brown paper bag. He'd more than likely hit up Sonny's Kitchen, a local diner that served breakfast all day. Rod was a stickler for routine. His day wasn't complete without his sausage, eggs, cheese, and bacon sandwich combo from Sonny's. The steaming cup of coffee in his hand was another testament to the fact.

I took a step back and made room for him to enter his office, still making sure Kennedy's presence was covered as much as possible.

Of course, Uncle Rod still noticed the feminine energy in the room.

"Is that Leila?" he asked, keeping his eyes on me curiously.

Loyal to a fault, no one in my family was rooting for me to reconcile with my ex. Not after the state of darkness I'd fallen in after our breakup.

What I "had" with Kennedy wasn't real, but Sunday as I came to realize I was alone, I headed into the kitchen and put away my groceries. I peeled the Band-Aid from my heart and finally threw away Leila's grocery list. It was time to move on.

"No," I said firmly.

Rod leaned over, stealing a peek at Kennedy. I watched the surprise take his face. He was impressed, I could tell.

Uncle Rod came back to me, a proud dad-like smile on his face. "It's your day off."

I rolled my eyes. He wasn't getting rid of me that easily. "I'll take a lunch." I extended a hand behind me. "Kennedy?"

Her soft palm met mine and I squeezed my hand shut around it. Rod let us pass him by on the way out, managing to smile and nod at Kennedy's shy wave.

I wasn't hungry, but I wanted to talk to Kennedy. About some ground rules. About her father's health. About ridiculous boundaries.

I didn't know where she was parked, but it didn't matter as I took her over to my Tahoe.

"If we're going to your house, let me get my car," Kennedy

said as she let my hand go and gestured across the lot where her Lexus was parked.

My house was tempting, but I needed to focus. "We're getting lunch."

Kennedy stood her ground. "What I'm hungry for isn't on the menu."

Ignoring her, I did a mental skim of what Sonny's offered. "You eat eggs? Sonny's has the best breakfast in the city."

Kennedy's lip curled up. "Are you for real?"

Little Miss Princess was used to having her way, I could tell. "Very."

She huffed, but put up no fight as she went over to my passenger door.

I could've just fucked her. Given no care to the world about whatever was going on in her life. It wasn't truly *my* concern, but beneath her giddiness to see me, I could spot desperation in her eyes. The sadness. Something was up.

I wasn't dressed for work. Instead, I was casual in my T-shirt and jeans, making going out for lunch easier.

Sonny's Kitchen wasn't that far from Rod's Repair. We were there in less than five minutes. Maybe it was me being protective, or maybe it was an old customary habit, but once I was out of my truck I rounded it and met Kennedy on her side and was quick to take and hold her hand as I led her into the building. The action caused Kennedy to relax into me, and for some reason, I liked that.

Sonny's wasn't busy as we entered the small diner, but I kept Kennedy close anyway.

Sonny's Kitchen was an old-school, family-owned Black diner. They mostly stuck to the same radio station. As hits from the '80s, '90s, and early '00s from Black artists would play throughout the establishment.

Luther Vandross could be heard singing "Never Too Much" as we made it up to the front counter. The classic record had Kennedy swaying a little against me along to the beat.

Kennedy ordered first, going and getting buttermilk pancakes with strawberry syrup. I wasn't that hungry, so I piggybacked off Kennedy and ordered the same, except with blueberry syrup. Kennedy opted for the house's famous mango peach lemonade, while I settled with a glass of water. When she tried to pay, I stepped in, sliding her that fifty-dollar bill she'd left on my copy of *Night Changes*, before paying for our meals.

Kennedy rolled her eyes as she held the money in her hands and leaned back against the front counter. "I felt bad for making you go out and not being able to eat the fish you bought."

"Don't worry about it," I told her.

Kennedy folded the bill and eyed the pocket of my jeans. She didn't attempt to give the money back as she simply put it in her purse and tapped her straw against the counter until it sprang free for her to place in her cup.

I scanned the diner, wanting a place for privacy. Sonny's wasn't full, but people were spread out enough to where we wouldn't be alone in any section. No one I recognized was around, and no one was paying us any special attention. Taking a chance, I grabbed a booth in the back corner by the hallway near the restrooms. I sat on the side against the wall, allowing me to have a proper view of those in the room behind Kennedy.

"Do you always come here for your lunch break?" Kennedy wondered as she took in the décor of the restaurant. Red vinyl booths and matching stools at the front counter, marble tabletops, black tiled floor, and pictures of famous celebrities who'd eaten at Sonny's over the years littered the walls here and there. My favorite was the photo of the late actor John Witherspoon standing side by side with the owner, Sonny Calhoun.

I shook my head, thinking of the sandwich I'd left in the mini fridge in Rod's office. "I usually pack my lunch."

"Aww." Kennedy gushed. "Lunch-pail-carrying worker man."

A corner of my mouth curled up at her taunting. I was blue-collar after all.

"I hope I didn't get you in trouble." Kennedy suddenly frowned as she stabbed her straw into her drink.

I watched the way her shoulders sagged and how genuinely worried she was about her arrival at the shop. Knowing Rod, he was probably just happy I was *with* another woman finally.

Outside of Kennedy's visit, I was a model employee. Never late, often stayed over just to help out, and I never complained. I was sure I could afford a little leniency, not to mention, it was my day off.

"You're fine," I assured her. "It's my day off anyway."

Her gaze flickered to mine. "Good."

I started to ask about her father, but couldn't decide on how to go about it.

A young brunette came over balancing a large serving tray on her shoulder effortlessly. She leaned down and deposited Kennedy's plate in front of her before setting mine in front of me. Butter and blueberry syrup was drizzled atop of my three-stack high pancakes, leaving everything drenched in a thick blueness.

"Thank you," I told the young girl whose name tag read *Hannah*.

"Yes," Kennedy was quick to echo. "That was super fast."

Hannah looked at our two plates and bobbed her head with pride. "Sonny's has the best pancakes in the state. Our cooks *have* to keep making them on rotation."

The front doorbell went off as a couple entered the building.

I hadn't paid too much attention to the other patrons in Sonny's, but I did spot a couple plates of Sonny's famous pancakes on a table or two.

Hannah went to greet the newest guests.

"Wait!"

Kennedy grabbed her purse and dug out that fifty-dollar bill and slipped it into Hannah's hand with a kind smile.

Hannah's cheeks turned a tint of pink and she mouthed a grateful *thank you* before hurrying back to her station.

The benevolence wasn't an act as Kennedy kept her smile and demeanor as she returned to her pancakes.

She wasn't my type. Bratty. Entitled. Prissy. But then she wasn't some stuck-up snob either like some people could be from Hampton Hills. She didn't even seem judgmental. At her worst, her most vexing moment so far was her not wanting to get into my tow truck for the sake of her "Valentino" dress. Considering her love for whites and creams, I didn't blame her for being careful.

Kennedy cut neatly into her pancakes and ate a bite. "Hmm." She ate another bite and the smile broadened across her face.

I realized I was staring when she looked up, as if aware of my stare, and ran her tongue over her lips. My eyes followed the movement, entranced.

Focus. Focus. Focus.

There were more important matters at hand than the idea of her on her knees.

Kennedy placed her fork in her mouth and slowly pulled it out. Her eyes were on me. "Not quite what I wanted, but it'll do. I guess."

I knew the answer, but I wanted to hear her say it. "What did you want?"

"You."

I scratched at my neck, keeping my composure. "Thought it wasn't your thing?"

Kennedy gave an innocent shrug. "Guess you can say I developed a taste for it."

Just for me. "Good to know."

"You should've let me do it," Kennedy continued, bringing up her offer at the shop.

While I liked that she was willing and wanted to do it, ironically, my head wasn't there.

"Next time," I insisted.

Kennedy smirked. "'Next time.'"

She took a glimpse over her shoulder, looking around at the

front of the room and those behind her. When she came back to me, I couldn't read the smile on her face. The mischief in her eyes. But I could *feel* her energy.

One moment she leaned on her right side, and then her left, doing a little shimmy. Next, she bent forward, reaching under the table and coming back up.

Before I could question what she was doing, she was handing me something over the table balled in her fist. On instinct I knew it was her panties.

I froze as I accepted them in my hand, finding them wet.

Kennedy stood from the table, stopping at my side and whispering in my ear, "Maybe you'll change your mind."

She walked off toward the restrooms without a look behind her.

I caught a man a few tables over watching her walk away, checking out her ass. He noticed me and tipped his head, and I scowled at him. He quickly went back to his meal.

As if I needed a sign from the universe, Fabolous and Tamia's "Into You" came on. The melody ringing in my ears like a bell.

I studied the mesh lavender panties in my hand for a moment more before springing up and going after Kennedy.

Inside the women's restroom she was leaning against the sink, waiting with a cheeky grin on her face. "Took you long enough."

There was no sense of self-control left in me. I was too hard to think straight or reason about the risk of what I was about to do. I *needed* to be inside her.

My hand on her throat took Kennedy by surprise as her mouth fell open. I backed her against the door, my eyes zeroing in on those lips.

Click.

She still had sense left to lock the door.

I leaned close, nipping her bottom lip with my teeth.

"Ugh." Kennedy groaned and caved against the door.

She'd poked a bear and I hated the time frame we held. I couldn't take my time, not with a diner sparsely full of people on the other side of the door. Quickies weren't my style. "Panties to the side" was only cute to hear about in music. Otherwise, I craved skin-on-skin contact. Mostly, I liked it slow. But that was a bad combination with Kennedy. I could just tell.

Kennedy hastily reached out, unbuckling my jeans and digging inside. The feel of her soft palm wrapping around me, pumping me up and down, was enough to make me almost lose it.

I pressed my forehead to hers, peering into her eyes, meeting her hand movement with my hips. Kennedy stared up at me, her breathing heavy, her strawberry breath fanning my face.

"You like fuckin' in public?" I got out in a gruff voice.

Kennedy could only shake her head.

"Never?"

Again, she shook her head.

So she was a good girl.

I stepped back, reaching into my pocket and grabbing my wallet. I dug a condom out and pushed my jeans and boxers the rest of the way down.

"You only do this for me," I told her as I rolled it on.

Desire coated her eyes as Kennedy nodded. "Only you."

I lost it.

Picking her up, I entered her wetness until she was seated on me entirely.

"Fuck!" I'd had her before, but I could still not get used to this feeling. This paradise.

With her back against the door I thrust into her some more.

"Yes, yes, yes," Kennedy whimpered.

As much as I loved hearing her moan for me, I covered her mouth with my hand to stifle the sound.

Another stroke had me hiding my own moan into her neck.

Kennedy clawed at my shirt and I reveled in the fact that I was growing an affinity for fucking her in dresses.

Her strangled muffles against my palm was music to my ears as the feeling of her around me had my head in the clouds.

My heart beat violently in my chest at the adrenaline of it all.

I took her deep and hard, until a whirlwind of euphoria took us both under.

Chest to chest, breath for breath, we mirrored each other's motions as we came down together. My eyes never left hers and I never let her go.

If it could only be like this, perhaps maybe, that was enough.

13

Kennedy

I didn't think I would do it. Be like this. Bold and reckless.

After spending the week miserable and walking on eggshells, I decided to break free. I turned off my phone and headed for Bedford Heights. My father, Cain, and Phil were immersed in business talks and planning, and my mother was shoving bridal magazines in my face.

The sight of actual wedding dresses gave me a panic attack. The shooting pain in my chest, the nausea in my throat, the sinking feeling I couldn't shake—it was all too much.

Now here I was, in the Heights without a care in the world.

My head was still spinning, my legs were unsteady, and my heart was racing as I came down from my orgasm.

Sweat. Cologne. The unmistakable scent of motor oil. Keith.

Being engulfed in his strong arms as he held me up and fucked me was my new favorite thing.

He set me down and offered to clean me up, a gesture that left me speechless as I declined.

I was frozen in place as he went about discarding his condom and adjusting himself.

I didn't want to move or walk, but suddenly I was starved. All of me just wanted to lay and eat.

Keith didn't listen as he swooped me up and carried me over to the counter. He set me down and turned on the sink, soon gathering a couple of paper towels and wetting them. I said nothing as he parted my thighs and gently wiped me down.

Tender.

It was a side of Keith I admired. One look at him and I would've never seen him being so gentle and attentive. Especially not on the night we met when one glimpse at his face sent me recoiling. He'd looked so angry and mean then. A paradox to who he really was, or what I knew of him so far.

Either way, I liked watching Keith work.

He looked over at me, catching me staring. He smiled and went back to what he was doing and I bit down on my lip to contain my glee.

It was dangerous how much I was attracted to him. How much I could *like him*-like him. How much I wished he'd kiss me already. I wanted to feel his lips on mine while he was inside me. Wanted to feel connected in every way.

Keith finished with his task and threw away the paper towels. When he faced me, offering his hand to help me down from the counter so we could do a little walk of shame out of the restroom, I shook my head.

I needed to get ahold of my bearings. "Give me a minute."

Keith left me alone and I sank into my position on the counter.

God.

We'd just done that. Public sex in the restroom of a diner. Scratch that, *amazing* public sex in the restroom of a diner. I'd never forget this for as long as I lived. I was completely another person out there when I took off my panties—panties I wished I had currently—and passed them to Keith. My Darling Nikki took over and I commanded Keith's attention until he was chasing after me into the women's restroom.

I was living on the edge, young and wild, and I loved it.

At least, I would until I said *I do*. When I would leave behind this affair and become a dutiful wife. Till death do us apart and all that.

My mood dampened just a little at the thought of my impending nuptials. Cain was interesting, but he wasn't what I wanted, no matter how much of a polite effort he put in. When I was with him, it felt like I stepped into an old black and white world where women had no rights and waited for their men to give them orders.

I hated it.

Before I could depress myself, I washed my hands, fixed my dress, and put on a fake smile. One that no one could see through as I exited the restroom and greeted a few people on my way back to my table.

Keith was placing our food in to-go boxes when I got back to the table. The sight made me frown.

I wanted to eat.

"What's going on?" I asked as I came around him.

Keith kept at what he was doing. When he spoke, his voice was low. "We're leaving because you got sick in the bathroom."

Immediately my hand came down to my abdomen. I stole a glance at the counter, catching a few people in Sonny's Kitchen peeking in our direction. I wondered if they knew. As if there was a neon sign above our heads reading out, WE HAD SEX IN THE BATHROOM! This was so out of character for me, but I didn't care.

Keith placed our boxes in plastic bags and then took the lead out of the building with me following behind. I'd just managed to take a big sip of my mango-peach lemonade before having to abandon it. Paranoia had me believing I could feel everyone's eyes on me as we made it out of the diner.

Once we were outside, I could finally breathe and relax.

"I can't believe we just did that!" I waited until we were near Keith's truck to properly freak out.

He used his key fob to unlock the doors, smirking as he looked my way. "You're crazy, you know that?"

All I could do was smile as we got back into his truck and buckled in. Keith handed me the food and I felt a jolt of energy straight to my heart when his skin brushed against mine.

If he felt it to, he didn't let it show as he focused on starting up the Tahoe and pulling out of his spot.

I couldn't wait to get home and talk to Jadyn. She would be all for this latest escapade of ours. Really, I had no idea what had gotten into me.

Keith parked a couple of spots away from my Lexus when we made it back to Rod's Repair.

I gathered my bag of food and left Keith's bag on the seat before getting out of the truck. Keith got out as well. Ever the gentleman, he walked with me over to my car, making sure the coast was clear at the shop.

"Well, guess I'll see you next time," I said as I went and placed my bag on the back seat floor.

Keith appeared quizzical. "Where you think you goin'?"

"Home?" I said, confused.

He angled his head. "You got something to do?"

"No...?"

He gestured with his head back toward his Tahoe. "Come back to my spot with me. We can chill."

"Chill" as in, hanging out casually.

"Isn't that against the rules?" I challenged.

Keith advanced on me. "You and my uncle decided to disrupt my workday, so I've got the time."

"And what do you do for fun?" I took a step back, and he took a step forward. It was like a dance.

"Work," he countered. "Occasionally I volunteer at the community center."

Aww.

"To steer kids down a different path than you took?" I guessed.

Keith nodded solemnly, as if ashamed of his past.

That touched my heart, and halted my retreat. Keith took a hold of me, pulling my body into his. "Besides, maybe I don't want to see you go just yet."

"No?" Being jobless, I had an open schedule most people would envy. The luxury to do whatever I wanted, whenever I wanted. These days, post engagement, I preferred sulking in my penthouse. And even that was becoming more depressing, because I didn't even know if I would live there come next year. If Cain was moving *in*, or if I was moving *out*.

I blocked all that out as I focused on the man in front of me, the man holding me to him.

"I still got the brownies," he said, attempting to convince me.

It worked like a charm as I lit up. Without even thinking, I jumped on him, going and wrapping my legs around his waist. Keith caught me effortlessly, not even flinching with my added weight. "You bought the brownies?"

He chuckled. "You wanted them."

It was a simple request, one he'd obliged.

"Maybe I want you to kiss me now," I said as I locked my arms around his neck.

Keith shook his head. "Bad idea."

It was. But like a pyromaniac, I was growing to be completely in love with playing with fire. "Why?"

He leaned close, his forehead against mine. "Because I'm afraid once I start, I'll never stop."

A tremor ran through me and I shuddered. Definitely a thin line we were treading.

"I'm a terrible kisser," I lied.

Keith gazed at my mouth. "So, you're good at everything else, but kissing is where it stops?"

"Uh-huh."

He shook his head once more. "I don't believe you."

It was a bad idea, no matter how tempting it was. I *wanted* to kiss Keith. But the trouble was, I couldn't afford to *want* him. Sex was already pretty damn personal. Getting all emotional and kissing him over kind gestures would only lead to my downfall.

He set me down and I smoothed out my dress, calming myself down and pulling myself together.

No kissing.

"Okay, I guess we can hang out for a little while," I said.

I got in my Lexus and buckled in, easing out an easy breath, trying to steady my nerves. I should've driven home, but I didn't. I followed Keith over to his house and didn't hesitate to enter his home with him.

The last time I'd been here, I'd only gotten to see his bedroom and back patio. There wasn't time for a proper tour with where our heads were. Now, Keith wasn't interested in more sex as he took my pancakes along with his and went and set them on the counter in his kitchen. I found my way to his living room, with its polished amber wooden floors and clean white walls. There was a gray area rug underneath his glass coffee table and beige sofa. On a love seat across from the sofa was a pile of decorative pillows—something that piqued my interest because it said there was an attempt to find some sort of style.

It was fascinating how men didn't require too much for taste or decoration. Keith was clearly satiated with the simple things, as he had his large TV mounted on the wall in front of the sofa and coffee table, a blue throw blanket neatly folded on the back of the sofa in case he got tired, and then there were a few movies on a nearby bookcase that went along with his Blu-ray player.

Men didn't need knickknacks or trinkets because "it was cute."

Even if the minimalist thing worked for Keith, I still was curious about him adding a touch of pizzazz in his home.

On the TV stand beneath the TV was an Alexa. I went and turned her on as Keith entered the room, going and making himself comfortable on the couch.

"What do you like to listen to? Oh yeah," I suddenly remembered, "violence."

Keith was rolling his eyes when I looked back at him. "Enlighten me. What do *you* listen to?"

I leaned against the TV stand and pondered over what to request Alexa to play.

"Alexa, play R&B," I said.

Alexa indulged me, and soon we were hearing a classic song that had me turning and grinning at Keith.

"Naughty Girl" by Beyoncé came through Keith's speakers and he chuckled as he eased back into his seat on the sofa. He had a toothpick in his mouth as his eyes were locked on me.

A dark eyebrow arched upward. "You gonna do a little striptease?"

Now I was rolling my eyes. There was no way *that* was happening. "That reminds me, I'm going to need my panties back."

Keith sank back, manspreading comfortably. "Come get 'em."

The thinly veiled threat sent something lurching beneath my belly.

"Dance with me?" I asked.

Keith shook his head.

"Lame."

The Beyoncé song was too infectious to stand still. While I wasn't confident enough to do an actual striptease, I did feel silly enough to want to dance for Keith.

I restarted the song and turned around and set my gaze on where Keith was watching me.

On the top shelf of the TV stand was a red baseball cap. I picked it up and put it on, causing Keith to grin.

I began to move, not having the best rhythm, but deciding not to take myself too seriously. I swayed my body to the melody and played with the hem of my dress, daring to bring it close to exposing myself to him. But that was a part of the act.

Keith's attention was glued to me as I got down low and rocked on my heels, moving my hips from side to side. Keith was entranced and I loved the feeling of his eyes on me.

Slowly, I rose to my feet, continuing to whine my body. Deciding that the hat was too MJ, I took it off and tossed it to the side.

Keith laughed, his handsome face lighting up as he sat up.

I rolled my neck, played in my hair, getting more into my dip into Beyoncé—of course, there could only be one Bey.

I dropped down low once more, beginning to crawl on the floor in my best attempt to be a sexy lioness. I leaned low, arched my back, and kept my eyes on Keith. I didn't feel an ounce of the confidence I was oozing, but I was faking it until I made it as I shook my ass to the beat.

I danced for Keith until the song ended, going and collapsing back on the floor with my chest heaving as I let loose a small grin.

Jay-Z better have worshiped the ground Bey walked on. Dancing was a workout.

In my past relationships or experiences, I'd never done something like this. I'd barely known this man for two weeks, and already I was doing things I never did. Hampton Hills's Kennedy Nichols kept in line, never broke any rules, and was a perpetual sweetheart. With Keith, in Bedford Heights, I felt free.

A Ne-Yo song was playing now as I sat up on my haunches. Keith was still watching me, serious now.

"Come here," he said.

I got out of my heels and padded over to him. Keith wasted no time in wrapping me in his arms and bringing me to his chest. He planted a kiss on my jaw that sent me sighing deeply.

"Your silly ass is sexy, you know that?" he whispered in my ear.

Something jumped in my chest and I couldn't contain my smile.

Reluctantly, I sat up away from Keith's warm, inviting body. "Got any water?"

"Yeah, in the kitchen," Keith said as he nodded off out the room.

He started to get up, but I stood instead. "I can get it."

I hummed along to "When You're Mad" as I stepped out of

the room and made my way to his kitchen. Clean. Organized. Vacant. Perhaps what Keith needed was a woman's touch to add some *oomph* to his home.

In his cabinet by the sink, he had mason jars to drink out of and I liked that. I grabbed one and went over to the fridge to use the water dispenser on the door. It was when I did this, that it hit me.

Back at the garage his uncle had asked if I was someone else. Another woman. One named *Leila*. I hadn't missed the way Keith's back had stiffened slightly. The way he'd seemed distant then. As if he'd been caught in more than the act.

Huh.

I grabbed my water and went back out to the living room and sat on the sofa. On the end furthest from Keith.

He noticed.

He reached out, grabbing my foot to drag me closer.

"Who's Leila?" I brought up.

Instantly, he dropped his grasp on me. "What?"

Ugh. I hated when men did this. Respond to a clear question with a *huh?* or a *what?*

"Leila," I repeated before taking a sip of my water. "Your uncle thought I was a woman named Leila. Who is she?"

Keith's energy went from playful and warm, to cold and sterile. "Don't worry about it."

We weren't supposed to get too deep or personal, but still, I didn't like being in the dark. Was she someone else in his orbit? I didn't want to step on another woman's toes, and I didn't want to play second fiddle either. Ironic considering my engagement.

"Kennedy," Keith's voice danced on irritated.

I shrugged. "It's fine."

He sighed, going and running a hand over his waves. "Look, I don't even know the name of your fiancé—and I don't want to know. You're the one who didn't want to get personal, remember?"

I didn't. "I do. But if there's someone else…"

Keith made a face, a muscle in his jaw flexing. Leila was tough territory for him. "She's my ex. She's not around. It's been done for over a year."

Judging from his body language, I knew I was right in my guess of, "*She* ended things."

Keith nodded. "Wasn't good enough for her."

I felt the prick of rejection teeming from him. "*You?*"

Once more he nodded. "Me."

There, in his dark eyes, I saw pain. "Keith."

He moved away from me, forcing himself to shrug, I could tell. "I'm sensitive. I'd rather not talk about it."

I didn't know Leila, but right then I *hated* her for making him feel this way.

I knew men liked to bottle up their emotions, and it was probably for the best that we didn't exchange a heart to heart, but still I pushed against our limits as I set my water on the coffee table and went closer. I sat on Keith's lap, resting my chin on his chest as I peered up at him. He didn't look sad or anything, just empty and alone.

Touching a tattoo on his bicep, I focused there as I began to talk. "She was wrong about you."

"Think so?"

I followed the length of a stream of smoke with my finger. "Uh-huh." I drew my gaze up to his. "When you were younger you joined a gang for whatever reason, made some mistakes I'm sure, but you turned your life around when your mom got ahold of you. You didn't rebel, you didn't fight—you changed. And now you're here, strong, resilient, helping young boys who may feel like you did, and showing them the way. It seems to me, that you're more than good enough of a man, Keith."

Keith stared down at me, his forehead adopting a crease as he appeared lost in thought. He came closer and kissed my forehead and brought me more into him. "Thank you."

The lines blurred and I didn't care. I wanted him to know

that his ex was wrong about him. That he was good enough. That he mattered and was making a difference.

Keith reeled back, pushing some hair behind my ear. "Why are you a pescetarian?"

A smile washed across my face at a distant memory of a much younger me. "My father, actually. Outside of the whole corporate thing, he's a big hunter. One time, when I was like six or something, he, my mom, and me were on a trip—I forget where we went, but I just knew we were getting deer. The whole trip I sat in the back seat talking about how I was going to keep my deer as a pet and name him. I kept going on and on, and they let me."

Slowly, Keith began to smile, coming back to me. "They did, huh?"

I nodded. "Yeah, and I was so excited."

"And what happened?"

I frowned, remembering little bits of what happened next. "We got to this place, this meat market, and there's no deer. Just packs of butcher paper wrapped meat. That's when I realized I wasn't getting a deer, that they were all dead."

Keith didn't laugh at me like my parents sometimes did when I told this story. Instead, as if to protect me from the vivid memory, he held me.

"I stopped eating meat shortly after that. My dad used to fish, but I didn't mind that as much as the furry animals," I said.

"I get it," Keith said. "I don't mess with animals like deer, rabbit, or lamb no way. I just stick to the basics, chicken, pork, and beef. I do love seafood, though."

"Once in a while I may eat chicken when Jadyn gets some, but I try to stick to my diet," I said. "After I quit meat, my dad never fussed with me. He and my mom were good about making sure I had fish if they were eating meat."

My heart hurt just then, thinking of my family.

"How's your father?" Keith's question didn't come as a surprise. It wasn't his concern, but I did admire that he cared to ask.

I shook my head. "Keith."

Keith didn't back down as he sat up. "Who do you talk to about what's going on with your dad's health? With him playing a hand in your engagement? Mentally, it's not okay to just repress this shit," he reasoned. "I'm not an asshole to ignore you got real problems, and just keep fuckin' you."

I blinked to stop myself from being dramatic and crying. Truth was, I felt a *lot* when it came to my father. Didn't know how to unload it all or where. I wanted to be strong and not overwhelm Jadyn. And I didn't want to be a burden when there was already so much going on with my father's condition.

But shit, did it hurt.

"He was having a muscle spasm on Sunday and my mom panicked. He's stable now. The doctor gave him some meds to handle it," I explained. "Thank you for asking."

Keith stroked my cheek gently. "I'm happy to hear that."

My body relaxed into his and I lay my head on his strong chest, breathing him in.

Cologne. Cigarettes. Keith. My lover.

Sometime later he turned on his TV and I got to eat my brownies. He wasn't prepared for me to be around, so he ordered a large cheese pizza to accommodate for dinner. We found a movie on some streaming service and it wasn't long before my eyelids became too heavy and I fought with myself to stay up and follow along to the thriller we'd stumbled upon.

I didn't realize I'd fallen asleep until I woke up in Keith's bed. A splash of his neighbor's flood light leaked in through his bedroom window, but otherwise, the house from what I could see was dark. I was alone in bed I came to discover as I looked over and found no one beside me.

Without worrying about the time or my phone, I went out in search of Keith. He was on the sofa, under his throw, sleeping with the TV on. An old rerun of *Malcolm in the Middle*.

He'd given me his bed while he opted to sleep on the couch.

Go home, Kennedy, my subconscious ordered me.

Recklessly, I didn't listen.

I went and squeezed on the sofa next to Keith, going and covering myself with his throw.

In another moment, his arm came around me and held me close.

"If I crush you, it's your fault," his sleepy voice said to me.

I snuggled back against him. "Okay."

There was no thinking it over or questioning the consequences. I simply closed my eyes and went to sleep.

14

KEITH

Something smelled good. Sweet, yet salty and buttery too. An aroma too thick to be a part of my dream.

My eyes fluttered open and I realized someone was in my house, *cooking*.

The only person with a key was my mother, but she wouldn't drop by like this. Unannounced to cook me breakfast.

As I sat up on my couch, it hit me.

Kennedy.

She hadn't left.

Still, in disbelief, I got up and crept down the hall to the kitchen. I wasn't prepared to see what was waiting for me when I got there.

Her hair was in a messy bun. Slightly disheveled from going to bed without a scarf. Standing at my stove barefoot, Kennedy was only wearing a T-shirt. *My* T-shirt. It hung heavy on her, but she didn't seem to mind as she kept at whatever she was doing.

I watched Kennedy at work for a moment longer before slipping away to get ready for the garage.

In my master bath, I discovered she'd found a new toothbrush I'd had stowed away in my medicine cabinet. She'd gone through my clothes, stolen a T-shirt, and had washed up here in my bathroom before going about preparing something in the kitchen.

I tried not to focus on the feminine intrusion in my home and went ahead with my morning routine. Thanks to Kennedy's cooking, I was running ahead of schedule, up earlier than my alarm for once, giving me a good forty minutes before I was due at work.

She was still there when I came out of my bedroom dressed to go in. I found her in the kitchen, sitting with her legs folded underneath her as she read from my copy of *Night Changes*. There was something so homey about the scene. Kennedy, undone, at my kitchen table, reading a book and drinking a glass of milk. Before her, was her leftover pancakes from Sonny's Kitchen. And across from her...

Kennedy had made me breakfast.

"Looks like someone just made themselves at home," I said as I made my presence known.

Startled, Kennedy looked up from her reading and offered me a timid smile. "Morning."

I inched closer, setting eyes on a plate of my pancakes from Sonny's as well as what looked like grilled cheese. I arched a brow, questioning Kennedy silently.

She shrugged. "Didn't want to leave without saying goodbye this time."

"So you cooked for me?" I pressed.

She blushed, gnawing on that lip of hers. "It's just grilled cheese."

"Just nothin', it's a thoughtful thing to do," I argued. "Thank you."

Kennedy eyed the grilled cheese absentmindedly. "I'd make a horrible wife. I can't really cook."

That brought me out of my fantasy, sling-shotting me right back into the reality of the situation.

I couldn't help but roll my eyes as I took the seat across from her. "Fuck all that, you should be able to cook to sustain *yourself*."

"Well, I can't," Kennedy said with a lazy shrug.

"I'll teach you," I offered as I grabbed the grilled sandwich. "You never know what the future may bring. It's important you can fend for yourself."

Kennedy propped her elbow on the table, going and resting her chin on her fist. "Okay."

I bit into my grilled cheese and bestowed Kennedy's watchful gaze with a thumbs-up. You couldn't mess up grilled cheese, but the sandwich was good. For added flair, she'd put mayonnaise on it as well. A thin layer where it wasn't overpowering the cheesy taste. I liked it.

Usually, I didn't eat breakfast at home. I often opted to grab a doughnut from the faithful box Jake would get in the mornings.

"Dixie and Darius are quite the pair," Kennedy noted of my paperback a while into our meal.

I wasn't one to read or watch romance all like that. Reading about the main character's, Dixie Pete, longing and pining after the male lead wasn't my thing.

"They're something," I said as I finished eating.

Kennedy set the book aside, her eyes on me. "What made you get it?"

I thought of Eden, the look on her face as she spoke of the story and the joy she'd expressed as she read its pages. "Curiosity. It was recommended to me."

Kennedy appeared thoughtful, but she said nothing as she stood from her place at the table and went over to the fridge. She'd definitely gotten comfortable in the few hours she'd spent here with me.

"Before I forget, I made you a lunch," Kennedy said as she reached into my refrigerator and pulled out a brown paper bag. I'd kept a supply just for the occasions I made my own lunch, which was typically a sandwich, a bag of chips, and maybe a snack cake if I was in the mood.

I stood from the table and collected our plates before bringing them to the sink to rinse. "You made me lunch?"

A proud gleam hung in Kennedy's eye as she spun around and nodded. "Uh-huh. Turkey, ham, Swiss, mayo on wheat. And some grapes on the side. I used to make my dad lunch when I was little. And, uh, I just figured it's the least I could do since you bought me brunch *and* dinner yesterday."

She didn't have to cook me breakfast and make me a lunch for work. The gesture wasn't lost on me. I abandoned the dishes in the sink and gathered Kennedy into my arms. She was bare beneath my T-shirt. The sight of her erect nipples and the hint of her figure through the material of the shirt drove my appetite elsewhere. The way she was looking at me, I knew I could've had her on my counter, legs spread open as I ate my fill of her.

But I wasn't into rushing. I preferred taking my time, and time wasn't on our side.

"Can you squeeze in a quickie?" Kennedy wanted to know.

I shook my head regrettably. "Nah, it's too tempting to get carried away. Besides, the next time we're together I want *you* on top."

Briefly, Kennedy frowned.

"What?" I asked.

"It's...not my thing," she confessed.

She didn't like giving head, being on top, and she preferred missionary. "What are you? A pillow princess?"

Kennedy hung her head. "I...I don't think I'm that good at it, is all. I'm insecure, okay?"

Now I felt like an asshole.

Grabbing her chin, I tipped her head back until she was looking me in the eye. "I'd never judge you for what you're not confident about sexually, Kennedy."

Slowly, she loosened up. "Will you show me how you like it?"

"You naked on top of me is all I need," I insisted. I couldn't get enough of her naked body, or the feel of myself inside of her.

A playful smile had Kennedy beaming up at me as she tickled my chest. "Can I wear your baseball cap when I ride you?"

My dick was having a field day and my brain was warring with it. Could I do what I wanted to do in about...ten minutes?

Doubt it.

For the sake of my sanity, I took a step back and grabbed my lunch. "What are you getting into today?"

"My friend Jadyn's off from work. I'm going to head over there as soon as I get dressed and hang out with her for a bit," Kennedy responded.

She wasn't supposed to do this. Spend the night and make me food, but I didn't mind it. And it didn't seem like she did either.

"Thanks again for the food," I said. "It's never a problem having you here, just let me know ahead next time so I can have some fish ready for you."

Kennedy looked away from me, making herself busy pushing our chairs in at the table instead of replying.

The lust in the air dissolved at once and I could feel her coldness.

"What?" I asked.

She shook her head. "Nothing."

It was there. That sadness. That distant look in her eye.

I scratched at my head. "You might as well tell me. I can tell something's up. You've been anxious since yesterday."

Kennedy glared at me just then. "You don't know me to know when I'm anxious, Keith."

Truthfully, I didn't. But I knew what I saw when I looked at her. Knew she was troubled since the day I met her. Something was weighing on her and I couldn't leave well enough alone.

"Kennedy," I urged.

Her forehead creased as she shook her head again. "We...we have a deadline, Keith."

"A *deadline*?" I repeated, confused.

She looked up at me with sorrow in her dark eyes. "Cain, my fiancé, and I agreed to get married in December. This thing between you and me, it will end then."

All at once my mood dropped. "What brought this on?"

Kennedy shrugged, going and cupping her cheeks as she peered down at the floor. "He's worried my dad might not make it if we prolong it."

I didn't understand her father's illness. Part of me thought of this as a manipulation tactic, but there was the possibility that her father was borrowing time.

"So, that's it, huh?" I asked. "Throw the rice and all that?"

"It's not like that," Kennedy said helplessly. "Cain said I wouldn't have to consummate it."

I deadpanned. "Sure."

Oddly, Kennedy looked like she believed him. "He said he would wait until I was ready. That the wedding would just be for show. So my dad can see me be married before..."

Before he passed.

It was a fucked-up situation, one that made me disgusted with all the players involved, and annoyed for their pawn.

"And what happens if you don't marry the guy? If you put your foot down?" I wanted to know.

Kennedy frowned. "I lose my family. My home. Every cent I own—*everything*."

It wouldn't be the end of the world, but I could understand her wanting to keep her family intact.

Talk about million-dollar pressure.

"So, this ends in December?" I repeated with finality.

Kennedy nodded solemnly. "I'll understand if you want to walk away before then."

I knew the setup from jump. She warned me she couldn't love me and that this would only be physical. It was an honor to touch little miss rich girl. In the end, she was only slumming it with me before she went off to become someone's bride.

Fuck it.

This meant nothing and was just something to pass the time. It wasn't my business to get caught up in Kennedy's world and problems. If she wanted to be some weirdo's wife, so be it.

I didn't allow myself to care. So, I didn't.

"This is just sex, right?" I said with a lazy shrug. "I'm cool with it."

I watched her lips tremble and winced inside. "Okay."

With my bag in hand, I took off down the hall. "Do me a favor and lock up when you leave."

Kennedy stood back as I reached for the door and pulled it open. "When are you free again?"

I needed to get my head on straight and hit the gym. Kick back with Savon. Visit my mother and Betty Jean. Not get too wrapped up in this woman. "I think Wednesday. I gotta get in my yard, though."

"Can I watch?" She sounded hopeful and curious.

I looked back at her. "You tryna help?"

Kennedy thought about it for all of a second before bobbing her head, her mood lifting. "That sounds like fun."

That I'd like to see. "A'ight, cool. I'll, uh, text you if that's what I'm doing."

"Please do. I'm going to go shopping and get the perfect outfit."

Despite my loss of serotonin, I managed to smile at that. "Most people wear their ratty old clothes to do housework."

Kennedy examined my T-shirt she was wearing. "Ah."

She was so serious in her fancy clothes, her high heels, and her prim image, I *wanted* to see her in jeans and an old T-shirt getting down and dirty.

"I'll text you," I said as I felt the smile slip from my face.

I went out to my Tahoe and got in behind the wheel, reveling in the space now wedged between us.

Mobb Deep was playing as I drove in to work. A much-needed distraction from my overall disappointment.

As expected, Uncle Rod was lingering around when I made it in. On an ordinary day, he'd be in his office doing paperwork, while I worked the garage with a few other mechanics.

Today wasn't one of those days.

"'Sup, Keith," Uncle Rod greeted me as he leaned against the front counter, giving me his full attention.

Jake was on the other end, digging in a pink pastry box. He grabbed a cream stick and turned, eyes and ears eager to hear our conversation.

Not happening.

Ignoring my uncle, I breezed by the front room and stepped out into the garage. The smell of gasoline and oil swept around me, clogging my senses, ridding me of a certain perfume. Now if only an engine or tire could get the image of a silly little dance out of my head.

Whistling sounded at my back and I knew my uncle had followed me out here.

I grabbed a clipboard hanging from the wall and checked the day's itinerary. One of the cars amid the lineup was a Ford Fusion in need of fresh brake pads. Simple.

"She sure was pretty," Uncle Rod marveled as he came around me.

On second thought, it was best to store my lunch in the mini fridge in Rod's office first.

Naturally, he was on my heels as I took off in that direction.

"Drop it," I barked out as we passed Jake's stance at the front counter.

The sound of chuckling let me know my uncle didn't take orders from me. With everyone else in the shop, all it took was one look and they went scattering.

In his office, Uncle Rod was quick to lean against the doorpost, studying me as I tossed my lunch in the fridge next to the one I hadn't eaten the day before.

"What's gotten you in a foul mood, boy?" he asked.

I stood tall, facing my uncle and blocking out all bullshit from the past twenty-four hours. "Nothing. I'm just ready to work."

"Uh-huh." He wasn't convinced.

Fuck, I needed a cigarette and I really was trying to quit.

I sighed. "I got stuff I gotta sort out, that's all."

"Wouldn't happen to do with that pretty little thing that was in here yesterday, would it?" Uncle Rod went on.

"It's nothing."

"You know, you're not gettin' any younger, Keith," Uncle Rod tried to say. "'Bout time you found you someone nice and settled down, started a family or somethin'."

This was rich coming from a bachelor. Not that Rod hadn't ever been around with a woman before. Currently, he was in between partners, and he liked it that way. Or so he said. "Less complicated, less pressure," he'd argued.

The fact that he thought *I* should be with a woman when he found solitude peaceful was humorous.

He was right though. As was Savon. I wasn't getting any younger.

Trouble was, the first person I entertained post Leila was all things unavailable.

It was enjoyable, whatever the fuck this was with Kennedy, but I also missed the intimacy of sex. Of being truly close. Or maybe I'd aged out of flings and wanted something more. Something serious.

It definitely was a wakeup call to get back out there.

Kennedy had problems and I didn't need that drama in my life. I was only interested in a good time, nothing else.

I made up my mind I wouldn't see this through until December. That I would dead this before things got too tangled. That it was a bad idea to get my heart mixed in with someone who belonged to someone else.

Going forward, rules would go into place. No more spending the night. No more asking about her father. No more exchanging stories from our past. This started and would end just sex.

"Yeah, yeah," I said as I got back to my uncle and went past him out of the room. "I'll worry about my love life on *my* time. For now, let's get to it."

15

Kennedy

Since my father's trip to the emergency room, I made it a point to be more present in my parents' home. I couldn't afford to be two cities away in case something serious went down the next time.

So, I made myself readily available Sunday afternoon as I headed over to their estate. Though, by the luxury vehicle in the circular drive, I knew my father had company over. Deciding to wait it out, I got comfortable as I sat in my family's living room skimming a woman's magazine. I was flipping through the pages aimlessly when I stumbled upon an article advertising "The Best Sex Tips." There were a few illustrations in various positions and I found myself looking around to see if the coast was clear.

I thought of myself as good in bed, but there was no denying I could always better up my skill. Keith came to mind and I couldn't stop myself from smiling, from feeling warm inside. I'd never been confident about getting on top during sex. I didn't trust my stamina or my rhythm enough to truly drive my partner crazy. Gaius had never minded, but it was nice to know that Keith wasn't one to judge on this area. That he was patient enough to guide me through it.

I hardly knew him, but I was beginning to feel safe with him.

The first sex tip was to "Spend Time Kissing." A craving I was fighting off each time I was with Keith. I missed kissing. It was the best part of sex. Of being with a man intimately. It was ridiculous that we weren't kissing. As if not kissing would spare us from developing feelings more than our full-blown sex.

I'm afraid once I start, I'll never stop, Keith had said to me.

Threats like that kept me in check. Kept the line in place. But just once, I wanted to know what his lips felt like. What type of kisser he was.

Probably passionate, hungry, intense like his sex.

I shivered at the thought.

"Cold?" My mother entered the room and was looking at me worriedly.

I tossed my magazine aside. "Uh, no. I'm okay."

Before I would have to explain myself further, Irene, my father's part-time caregiver, entered the room and flopped down with a paperback on the other end of the sofa I was sitting on. Irene wasn't that much older than me. I thought she said her age was twenty-six. What I'd seen of her work so far, was that she was incredibly gentle and patient, something needed for my father's stubbornness and pride.

My mother shifted her attention to Irene, lifting a questioning brow.

Irene immediately sat up. "Business talk. They wanted privacy." She glanced at me nervously before returning to my mother. "The scary one didn't mind taking over when Mr. Nichols kicked me out."

I couldn't help but snort. I knew exactly who was here. My dreaded fiancé.

"He has a name, Irene," my mother chastised. "*Mr. Carter.*"

Irene shrank under my mother's scrutiny, ducking her head. "Right, sorry. *Mr. Carter* is taking over."

Feeling bad for her, I stepped in to get my mother's attention. "So, Cain's the one who's been up there?"

"Phil was here earlier, going over some paperwork, but Cain

and your father are still in a meeting, yes," my mother said casually as she held out her hand and examined her manicure. "Maybe you and Cain should get out for a while. He's been working nonstop. I don't think your father understands that Cain's whole life can't be about work. He's too young for that kind of commitment."

Her attempt at sympathy was lost on me. Cain could work all he wanted, so long as I was free to do what *I* wanted.

"He seems to like it," I pointed out.

My mother wasn't impressed. "I know, why don't you two head over to The Sheridan? That'd be nice."

Internally, I cringed. The Sheridan was Hampton Hills's premiere restaurant. Being that Hampton Hills was what many deemed "the Black Beverly Hills," it was only right that our best restaurant in the city was owned by a Black chef who studied abroad in France, spent time in Italy, and took notes in the Caribbean. Chef Jabari Peters could cook any dish he set his mind to. His esteemed restaurant was awarded three Michelin stars. It was because of this, The Sheridan was a known paparazzi hot spot. Many celebrities were often in attendance grabbing a meal, making the likes of TMZ and other nosy journalists and bloggers always on the hunt to snap a good photo or capture a juicy moment.

It was good publicity, if you *wanted* to be seen—which I didn't.

"Oh, Mom, that place is always swarming with cameramen," I whined.

My mother's eyes found me, indifferent to the idea. "So? You should be drumming up some press for your relationship. This engagement came out of nowhere, people are curious, it's time to make another public appearance. Especially since you flaked on the engagement party."

She said it as if I wasn't blindsided by this whole ordeal. Like I'd carried a secret relationship with Cain and had only let her in on it at the last minute. That was the story the world was getting, but it wasn't the truth. I wasn't even sure if we had chemistry enough to fake it for the cameras. I didn't get Cain's angle even more with the thought of the world watching us.

I was a socialite. Just that morning, I'd been bored and posted a picture of myself out by the pool. An hour later I'd already gathered fifty thousand likes on the image. Cain didn't even have a social media account. Being attached to me came with fame and influence in the Hills. Something that didn't seem his style considering his previous relationships. Was Cain ready for that type of exposure?

The society pages were already fantasizing about what we'd name our children. Truthfully, if we ended up procreating and having a boy, I was leaning toward *Damien*. If a girl, perhaps *Lucifena*. Maybe I'd even wrangle *Spawn* as a middle name for either.

Not feeling like arguing further with my mother, I stood from the sofa and went up to the second floor.

The door to my father's room was ajar, and instead of knocking, I found myself hanging outside to eavesdrop, to see my father and Cain together, to better understand their business relationship.

"You're ambitious," my father was saying. A peek inside and I saw him shaking his head. "You think you can get this up and going in a *year*?"

Cain was standing beside his bed. Posture strong and erect as he had his hands in his suit pockets. "Instead of completely building from scratch, I think it would be best to add an addition to The Residence and remodel the current hotel to *be* The Residence at Cartier. It's still a pricy and lengthy endeavor, but my men are drafting up the best model for you as we speak. This goes well, maybe I'll hear you out about Vegas and Canada."

My father chuckled at Cain's nonchalance and veiled arrogance. At least, he started to chuckle until he was full-on coughing. Once he started, he couldn't stop, and it sounded hard, as if a lung was launching itself up his throat.

I went to make myself known, but before I could enter the

room, Cain quietly grabbed the bottled water from the side table and went closer to my father. He leaned down just a little to help my father reach the straw in the bottle and drink from it.

My father was struggling, and Cain...was so caring. No judgment covered his face as he held the water bottle and watched my father drink thirstily.

"Ah." My father lay back and engulfed some air. "Thank you."

Cain simply nodded and returned the water to the table. "Perhaps you should get some fresh air. It would be better for you to get out of this room and see some new scenery."

Pain marred my father's face as he shook his head. "This...is where I've chosen to die."

A muscle in Cain's jaw ticked as he blinked. "Don't go out pathetic, Damon. It's unbecoming."

My father fisted his comforter and scowled. "I don't deserve this."

To that, Cain agreed with a bob of his head. "Sometimes, unfortunately, the worst things happen to the best people."

"Why her? Why my daughter?" my father suddenly asked after a moment's pause.

I crept closer, needing to hear Cain's answer.

He was gazing at the floor, lost in thought. "A few years ago, there was some fundraiser in the city, some charity for kids. I was dropping by to donate and that's when I saw her. She was playing with the kids, smiling, having fun—just radiating this glow, this light." Cain came back to my father. "I thought it'd be nice if I could have a little light in my life."

My father took in this information, sitting with it for a second before asking, "What if she never loves you?"

Cain didn't flinch. "Wasn't banking on it. But who knows, maybe she'll like me."

My father shook his head. "You could do a lot more for yourself." He made a gesture, requesting more water and Cain was quick to grab the bottle.

Even though my life, my freedom, was in the hands of these

two men, I couldn't stop my heart from warming at the scene before me. A monster being kind to my sick father was a sight I never imagined seeing.

"We have to include an infidelity clause somewhere," my father spoke up as he rested back once again. "You cheat on my baby girl and you're done, Carter. She's free."

Cain wasn't intimidated by the threat. He merely looked off, taking in my father's navy-blue room. "I'm a bastard, Damon."

"Noted," my father responded. "But my word still stands."

Cain's lips curled up a little as he returned to my father. "Let's get one thing straight: I'm a better man than my father," he stated adamantly. "You wanna talk about honesty? Integrity? Why don't you ask the late Mrs. James Carter how it felt to discover *I* existed?

"'I never lie because I don't fear anyone. You only lie when you're afraid.' John Gotti said that, and I couldn't agree more. I was raised on the outside, with a mother who never recovered from a broken heart, and a father who never acknowledged me when I needed him. I'm from the very bottom where you learn early that fairy tales are fictitious for a reason. I'm a lot of things, but not a cheat. Loyalty's the most important thing to me, and I would never step out on your daughter."

My father eyed Cain and the two men stared at each other for the longest time. In the end, my father held his hand out and Cain regarded it for a moment before shaking it. "You're a fucking devil, but I like you." My father soon snorted, shaking his head at something. "James left Dorothy nothing after thirty-something years of marriage. I knew you were decent when I heard you gave the widow a hefty settlement."

Cain shrugged. "For some women, fertility is linked to their ego. To not be able to bear a child for her husband was probably a lot to take in. To see that he had an heir on his own, one who looks just like him, had to be a blow she'll never recover from."

"Probably so," my father agreed. "Hence why I don't want my daughter going through the same thing. I think we've come to a clear understanding on that, haven't we?"

Cain reached out and patted my father's shoulder. "Yes, we have."

I decided to make my entrance just then, unable to hear any more.

At once, Cain's eyes cut to me.

"Father. Warden," I observed them both before going and kissing my father's cheek and giving him a gentle hug.

Cain came around the bed, coming and joining me on my side.

"Be nice," my father whispered in my ear as he released me.

I stood and faced Cain, just in time as my mother came into the room.

"Enough work already. Please. Damon, let the kids get out for a while." My mother came and placed a hand on Cain's shoulder and her other on mine. "I called The Sheridan. Our treat."

Of course she did.

Cain looked at me. "Is that what you want?"

Feeling the weight of my parents' eyes on me, I didn't put up a front as I exited the room. "Doesn't matter, does it?"

"Kennedy!" my mother gasped from behind me.

I didn't miss that Cain was following me out of the room as I made my way over to my old bedroom. Even though I'd moved out when I was twenty, I still held a good portion of a wardrobe here in my parents' house.

I went into my room and mentally decided on what I would wear to The Sheridan as I approached my closet.

Cain hung back in the doorway of my walk-in, watching me. "We don't have to go there."

"She already made the reservation," I replied with a shrug.

"You don't have to change, I'm sure," Cain tried to say next of my current state in a white blouse with black trousers.

I scoffed as I glanced at him. "It's The Sheridan. This won't do."

There were still two full racks of dresses to choose from, and in the end, I picked up a black Givenchy dress.

I'd showered after my little dip in the pool, and because I hadn't gotten my hair wet, there was time saved.

Cain obviously wasn't going anywhere. Deciding to not make a big deal of it, I undid my pants and let them pool at my feet before stepping out of them. I removed my shirt a second later. In my dreamy blue balconette bra and matching cheeky panties, I felt Cain's complete attention before I looked over and founding him watching.

His hands were in his pockets, his posture serious and straight, and his dark gaze was locked on me.

"It's rude to stare," I let him know.

His heavy gaze trailed up my body until he was staring me in the eye. "It's rude to tease."

I turned, giving him a full view of me in my underwear. "When I want you to have me, you'll have me. And not a second sooner. Now shoo."

Like a good boy, Cain did as told and left my room.

I dressed quickly before placing my hair in an updo, and lining my eyes and applying mascara. It was passable for The Sheridan, so it would do. You never knew who you would run into, or how you'd look if one of the paps snapped a picture of you. It was just always best to be on your game.

Out in the hall I discovered Cain was with my parents and Irene in my father's room. My mother was fussing with the pillows behind my father, and he was fussing with her.

"I'm okay, Ange, I'm okay," my father tried to tell her.

My mother gave up and planted her hands on her hips. "I just want to make sure you're comfortable."

My father turned to where Cain was seated beside his bed. "You sure you wanna get married?"

My mother was quick to swat the back of my father's head. "Dame!"

Cain almost smiled. "She just cares, Damon. Humor her."

My father stopped his fight and pulled my mother to his side.

Sometimes, lately, she was afraid to snuggle with him, and I could tell he missed the genuine affection.

Sensing the tenderness of the moment, I cleared my throat so Cain and I could leave and let them be alone.

"We'll be going now," I announced.

Cain stood and met me in the doorway.

My father squeezed my mother's hip and offered us a nod of approval.

"Have fun," my mother said.

Yeah, right.

We stepped out of the room and Cain was in my ear as he wrapped an arm around my waist. "You look beautiful, Wife."

I gave him a tight-lipped smile. "Thank you, Cain."

He held on to my waist all the way down the steps and out the front door. Beans was on the front walk, phone in hand while Vino was leaning against the waiting Maybach.

Cain let me go as we approached Beans. Cain eyed him and the phone clutched in his hand. "What's the word? How is Frank doing on his vacation?"

Beans glanced at me. Sensing the attention Cain was unloading on him, he got back to his boss. "Great. He found the keys to that mansion you were looking at."

Cain hummed, bobbing his head. "Good."

He'd already bought us a house? "A *mansion*?"

Cain regarded me impassively. "Just a brick mansion off the coast in Colombia." He looked at his close friend. "I may end up selling it now that I think about it. Wouldn't want to be too far from my roots."

"*Sell*?" I repeated, confused.

Beans considered this and agreed. "Colombian origin and hasn't been stepped in? You could easily flip it for a couple mil, more than you paid for it."

Cain grinned. "Perfect."

Their business talk sent my head spinning. I let it go as Cain steered me over to the Maybach. He let me inside first as Vino opened the back door for us.

I made myself comfortable as Cain came and sat beside me. I told myself to get used to this. My life surrounded by these men, because it would be my future in the coming year post December. As we rode away from my parents' estate, I tried not to let a panic attack seize me.

I faced Cain. "My mother's going to be insufferable with this wedding, you know."

He wasn't fazed. "Let her. This is a big moment for mothers."

I rolled my eyes. Maybe it wouldn't be so bad had I been marrying a man I loved. My father came to mind and I buried my discomfort and unease. Once more, I turned to Cain, now serious. "Can't you and Phil do your business at the office and leave my father out of it?"

Cain frowned. "Damon doesn't *want* to be left out. To sit by while his company is run by other people would kill him." He looked out the window, at the passing scenery. "Until he's physically unable to communicate and run things on his own, then he's still very much calling the shots."

That sounded like my father's wishes. To keep working until the death of him.

I reached out and ran my hand down Cain's chest, something that caught him by surprise until I was fisting the material of his undershirt and grabbing a hold of him. His curious eyes met my angry ones. "You let him overexert himself, and I will *never* forgive you."

Cain's hand came down on mine, taking and entwining our fingers as he nodded. "I won't."

For the rest of the ride, we were silent, but he never let me go.

Just as I'd feared, The Sheridan was surrounded by paparazzi when Vino pulled into the valet lane. Someone big and important was dining tonight and that had the paps crowding the entrance.

Shit.

Cain grimaced at the cameramen. "We could go somewhere else."

The idea was tempting, but I was too hungry to go elsewhere at this point.

"Let's just make it quick," I suggested.

Cain got out first and extended his hand for me to help me out next. At once, the lights were flashing and the spectacle began.

"*Kennedy!*" a man was heard shouting my name as I rushed to conceal my face with my clutch.

"*Kennedy, congrats on the engagement!*" another called next.

"*Kennedy, have you been in contact with Gaius? Do you think this news will knock him off his game?*" a female photographer yelled.

Just as we'd made it to the front door that last remark caused me to turn back, gutted. Guy and I, we'd talked about a marriage a few times after our first year. I hadn't been ready at the time. Thinking of his text, I knew this news was probably taking a toll on him. If he were single and hadn't moved on.

Tugging on my arm had me facing forward and ducking inside the restaurant with Cain.

"Good evening, welcome to The Sheridan. What's the name?" A hostess approached us as we neared her podium. She had on matte magenta lipstick, the color complementing her smile as she greeted us with bright eyes and a politeness that reminded me of how positive Jadyn could be.

"Carter," Cain responded. He leaned close to the woman whose name tag read *Draya* and dropped his voice. "Is there anywhere private we can sit, away from the swine?"

Draya craned her neck and looked past us, out the front door where the paps were waiting and some still snapping away. She returned to Cain and nodded vigorously. "Our enclosed rooftop dining area is the perfect spot."

"Perfect." Cain looked over at Beans, who had gotten out with us. "Text Vino where we'll be."

Beans did as instructed as another host began leading us away from the hostess station.

I stole a glance in the main dining room as we walked the corridor. There were a few famous faces in the room, some rappers, some ball players, and a few singer/actresses. I even spotted that up-and-coming pop girl group Souletté seated around a large table with who was probably their manager and team. They were young, probably still teenagers, but the lone Black girl in the group, Jehlani, was already my favorite from the glimpses I'd seen of her performing on social media.

We boarded the elevator and rode it up to the rooftop dining area.

It was another world compared to the main floor of The Sheridan. The view of the city at night and LA in the distance took my breath away as soon as we stepped off the elevator and were immersed in the atmosphere. More famous faces jumped out at me as our host continued guiding us to a table. The stars were out tonight, no, not in the sky above, but in the mix around me. People were coming to and from the outside balcony to sneak cigarettes or truly take in the night air and sky. Strings of lights were wrapped around beams overhead creating an ambiance, and the sound of chatter littered the air amongst the mid-tempo Beyoncé song that was playing from the DJ booth.

"Okay, I'm also a Beyoncé fan," I had to note as we settled down at a table in the corner of the roof. Immediately, I noticed that was Cain's way. Quiet corners, eyes on the entire scene, and a bodyguard nearby covering him and me, always. Something told me he was a chess player.

Cain took in my comment with a small smile. "Beautiful woman."

"Can I start you off with something to drink?" the young man asked as he deposited menus before us. Beans had taken a small table across from us.

"Your best bottle of red, please," Cain said before he looked to me for my order.

"A glass of water." I was feeling too antsy to anticipate eating as it was.

"Coming right up. My good friend Donald will be your server this evening and he will be right over with your wine and water." The young man bestowed the same hospitality as Draya had before he walked away to turn in our drink orders.

An awkward silence befell the table. Goose bumps covered my arms and I ran my hands down them to try to gather warmth from the sudden chill I felt.

Cain sat up straight and undid his suit jacket and draped it over my shoulders. His cologne and dark scent enveloped me with his heat.

"Thank you," I spoke up.

"If I ask you to put my gun in your purse, will you freak out?" he seemed to be joking as he was left in his dress shirt and dress pants. No one was watching as he undid his holster and tucked his gun onto his lap.

If he folded up his holster, everything would fit into my Chanel.

The thought of holding his gun *for* him made me blink and squirm.

Cain shook his head. "Thought so."

He left his gun on his lap and didn't push the issue as we began to scour the menu.

"The baked cod in white wine sauce sounds amazing," Cain said as he pointed out the item on his menu.

The dish did sound good, but I already had my eyes set on another entrée. "It does, but I'm going to get the pizza with the smoked salmon."

Cain found the pizza on his menu and I watched as intrigue peppered his face. "Salmon on pizza? Huh."

"It's good," I swore.

"I'll let you taste my cod if you let me have some of the pizza," Cain bargained.

"You eat fish?" I was surprised. The last two times we'd dined together, he'd gotten meat.

Cain nodded as if it were nothing. "Once in a while. Tonight seemed as good a time as any."

I knew what he was doing, and I refused to let it work.

"Fine," I decided as I shut my menu and sat back. "One slice."

Cain shut his menu as well. "Fine by me."

Donald came with our drinks and I was quick to take a big gulp of my water, needing to cool down my body suddenly. Cain's proximity was too overbearing.

"You could've gotten whatever you wanted," I said as soon as we were alone after giving Donald our orders.

"The cod sounded good, so I got it."

"Just like that?" I challenged.

"Maybe I'm just a hopeless romantic aspiring to sweep you off your feet," Cain said with an easy shrug.

I couldn't imagine a man like him being romantic, soft, sweet —he didn't have the demeanor for it. And frankly, I wasn't trying to get to know if he was capable.

Truthfully, I didn't think I was that interesting for his pursuit. Some gossip blogs liked to mock me for being too boring, even going as far as to say that was the reason Gaius and I had split.

I jumped.

Cain's hand was suddenly on my thigh.

"You don't have to be afraid of me," Cain insisted as he pulled his hand away.

I wiped at my lap, ducking my head to focus on the task. "I'm not."

He was closer. Near my ear. "If I don't lie to you, you don't lie to me."

It sounded like an order, one that sent me bobbing my head in agreement.

"So," I began, desperately trying to start a conversation that wouldn't go south. "What's your favorite movie?"

"*Scarface*," Cain answered matter-of-factly as he settled away from me.

"Really?" I hadn't seen it, but I knew of its iconic film poster. "Isn't there a gangster movie called *Casino*?"

Cain appeared thoughtful. "That's top five. A close second would be *Menace II Society*."

I knew the movie in title only through Jadyn. I made a mental note to sit and watch it for further reference.

Cain reached out, moving a lock of hair out of my face. His finger grazed my cheek and the softness of the action took me by surprise. "And you?"

"*Crazy Rich Asians*. It's so gorgeous cinematically and I love the story," I confessed. If I had to think of a close second, it would've been *Coming to America*. It had always comforted me with its humor and tone. At a time, it was a favorite movie I'd shared with my parents.

"I'll have to find time to watch it. Or maybe we can do it together," Cain suggested.

I didn't want to, but I agreed for the sake of moving this arrangement along. "Okay."

Vino arrived and joined Beans at their table. I almost felt tempted to wave them over to ours so I could disappear while the men talked about whatever they usually did when I wasn't around. Anything but sit and talk with Cain.

But, for the sake of trying, I put in an effort to get to know him a little more. He was uncapping his bottle of wine, that tattoo of his directly in my line of vision.

"Is that your only tattoo?" I asked.

Cain poured his wine. "Yes."

I liked the color of his skin and didn't mind at all suddenly that he bore no more ink. "Why no more?"

"In my world, it's best to blend in," Cain told me. "To go unseen or unnoticed."

I supposed he was right, in some ways. At least, for the corporate business world it made sense.

"Do you want children?" I asked next.

Cain arched a brow and really thought about his answer as he sat back in his seat. "No."

Considering his previous threat, I wasn't expecting that answer. "No?"

Cain thumbed at his lip. "No."

He wasn't going to expand on his reasoning and I didn't want to upset him. Something told me his wrath wasn't something I would ever be ready to face. His cool, collected, and calm façade when he was saying something menacing alluded to so much.

"Kennedy!" Screeching drew my attention across the roof toward the balcony exit.

Stephanie and Elyse were here. Elyse was waving spiritedly while Stephanie was busy ogling Cain.

"Go," Cain said. "Have a quick chat before the food comes. I'll text you when it's ready."

The enclosed roof was surrounded by glass, leaving no room for privacy when out on the balcony. The roof was crowded, but I just knew no matter where I went, Cain would still see me.

Still, it was an escape I welcomed.

I stood and removed his jacket, passing it back to him as he let me by. "Be right back."

Stephanie and Elyse weren't my favorite people, but I couldn't have made it over to them any faster than I had.

"God, I still can't believe you're marrying *that*," Stephanie whispered in my ear, slight jealousy in her tone.

We stepped out onto the balcony area, the music faint out in the night. Couples and groups were seated at tables and the first empty table we came to was next to a group of men. They were smoking cigarettes, causing Stephanie to wave her hand and wrinkle her nose as we sat down.

Cigarettes.

Keith.

"Hey, can I have one of those?" I tapped the man closest to me and asked for a cigarette, throwing caution to the wind. They were terrible, but the tobacco would only serve as a reminder, to keep me grounded, to let me know there was another man I was sleeping with to escape from it all out there.

The man, a blond, was all too eager to slip me a cigarette and light me up. He and his friends were all clad in suits, wore big white teeth smiles, and had proper haircuts and fancy watches. Accountants. Brokers. Pencil pushers. I could smell it on them after so much time in the Hills.

"Thanks." I turned back around and committed to sitting out on the balcony with the intrusive twosome to get away from Cain.

Elyse and Stephanie were sipping on drinks and I'd forgotten my water inside.

I wasn't going back for it.

"So, what's he like?" Stephanie wanted to know as she gestured with her head back toward the table Cain was at. "You know, in bed? Tell me you're ridin' that like he stole something."

The thought made me gag.

One look inside and I caught Cain talking to Vino and Beans, busy, distracted.

"We're waiting," I said as I came back to the girls.

Elyse frowned. "For what?"

I took a drag from my cigarette and blew out a stream of smoke. *Gross.* "I just haven't been ready."

Stephanie shook her head. "Shout out to your willpower."

"You know," Elyse began, appearing thoughtful as she took a glance over at Cain's table. "He sorta reminds me of Mister."

I furrowed my brows as Stephanie blatantly snorted, nearly spitting out some of her cocktail. "Oh, shut the fuck up."

"What?" Elyse looked at the two of us helplessly. "He does! Sexy, mysterious, powerful—there's something about him."

I took another pull from my cigarette and considered this. The idea that Cain was reminiscent of the male lead in the steamy and erotic *Mister* trilogy, Isaiah Keller. A successful Black businessman who sets his eyes on an ingénue who disrupts life as he knows it. The books, *Mister, Mister Undone,* and *Mister in*

Love, were mega bestsellers. Although, I hadn't read any, not being much of a reader. Jadyn had read all three and gushed over Isaiah's character, citing that although she didn't like alpha males usually, there was something about the domineering and hypnotic Isaiah that hooked her on the books.

Domineering definitely fit Cain through and through.

The thought of reading brought me back to Keith's house, and that romance he'd been reading. *Night Changes*. I should've read more, and that book *was* interesting. I kinda wanted to lay up under him and get his take on the book.

Thinking of him only drove me to grab my phone and snap a quick selfie, cigarette in mouth, and send it to him.

ME

Look what bad habit I've picked up

AUTO REPAIR

I can think of another habit that's better for you…

I read between the lines and couldn't believe how much I was into the act of getting on my knees for this man. I sent him a tongue emoji to play along.

AUTO REPAIR

Put it out

ME

Make me…

He didn't respond after that and I tried not to let it bum me out.

"Since when do you smoke?" Elyse asked as she took in the cigarette resting between my fingers.

"Since I'm getting married," I decided to say. Since my life wasn't mine. Since I realized I needed to think of Keith to get through this night.

"*This* is why you should be fucking that delicious fiancé of yours," Stephanie snapped, waving her hand to disperse the smell of my cigarette.

"Before someone else does," Elyse warned.

Stephanie gasped and was quick to elbow Elyse.

"Doubt that'll happen," I responded dryly as I took another drag.

Elyse eyed me skeptically. "You think this act of keeping it from him will work in your favor?"

I thought I was getting the hang of smoking. Inhale. Satiate the nicotine flavor. Exhale. "My fiancé wants to fuck *me*. Even if some other woman was desperate enough to give it to him because I won't, it wouldn't compare to what he's not getting from me." I gave a limp shrug. "And if he steps out, he loses me, and he can't have that." I was nice enough not to blow smoke at her. "I'm the prize here."

Elyse arched a brow as Stephanie laughed and slapped my arm. "Amen, girl!"

Oh fuck it.

This wasn't worth it.

"Excuse me." I stood up and bid them farewell before going back inside and joining Cain at our table.

My cigarette was still lit and I took one last pull. One last dose of peace.

"You don't like those women," Cain leaned close to say.

"You're observant," I said as I stubbed out my cigarette on the cement floor.

He tracked my movement, curious. "Thought smoking bothered you."

"It's something to do."

Cain's finger tapped along the tabletop. "Find something better to do to pass the time."

I never intended to smoke again after tonight, but after that order, I was tempted to buy a whole carton of cigarettes.

"Anything else, Husband?" I put on a perky smile as I faced him.

Cain glanced back at my public friends and returned to me. "Why do you associate with them if you don't like them?"

"It comes with the territory. Their parents know my parents. It's just the way it is. I only hang out with them when I have to make appearances. My only true friend is my friend Jadyn."

Cain was intrigued. "What makes her any different than those two?"

"She's not from around here. She's *real*," I pointed out.

Cain hummed. "*You're* from around here. Are you real?"

I snorted, leaning close, teasing. "No, I'm as fake as they come."

Cain's dark eyes very boldly ran down my figure, lingering in places he could only dream to touch. "Nah, there's a lot real about you from what I see."

Seeing wasn't believing. "You know, I have access to a lot of people."

"Yeah?" Cain said.

"Yeah," I began, an angle in mind. "What if I set you up with another woman?"

Cain scratched at his brow. "Didn't picture you as the threesome type."

My throat tightened. I wasn't. I was too greedy and jealous to ever share.

It shouldn't have surprised me Cain had probably experienced a ménage à trois before. I'd heard my share of women gushing over the man in passing too many times to count. I thought of that SZA song and could see someone being so lovestruck they didn't mind having him if only on weekends.

"I want what I want," Cain went on.

"Did you propose to those other women you dated?"

Cain shook his head. "They weren't what I needed."

"And I am?"

"We'll see," he said with a gleam in his eye. "What are you doing this weekend?"

Thinking quickly, I threw out, "Getting a wax."

"Great, I'll come along."

My upper lip curled up. "Why?"

"So I can see how you take pain."

He was being playful. So I drove my elbow into his side. He took it with a chuckle.

"Play in traffic, don't play in my face," I warned.

Cain's laugh was deep, musical, a side of him that felt rare. "Playing is the last thing I want to do with your face." To be a pest, he tugged on my cheek.

I bit at his hand and he was quick to remove it.

"I imagine it's small." I gaped at his crotch. "I mean, why else would a man force marriage on a woman?"

Cain didn't react at all to my comment. He took my hand and massaged it, his eyes lingering on my fingers. "What did I tell you about not wearing the ring?"

Caught. *Shit*. "I'm just not used to—"

He brought my hand between his legs, to his thigh, where *he* was resting against it.

My eyes enlarged as I snatched my hand back. Definitely. Not. Small.

Quickly, I grabbed my water and took a sip. "Well, *that'll* be fun."

"You'll get used to it," he said simply, as if this was a regular reoccurrence for him with women having to adjust to his length.

Oh God.

Slowly, Cain's hand ascended up my inner thigh, and I did my best to keep my face even, to not squirm, to not push him away.

"Would it really be so bad to get to know me?" Cain asked into my ear.

His hand felt poisonous on my body. Smooth and soft unlike the rough, strong touch I'd become accustomed to.

It was strange how I missed him. Deep voice, angry face,

rough hands, demanding sex...Keith Avery was giving me a schoolyard crush. How dangerous.

I couldn't be loyal to him, but still, it felt all things wrong to have my fiancé touch me in territory I'd left open for Keith.

Shutting my legs, I sat up straight and pushed the skirt of my dress down, ridding myself of Cain's hand. "Guess we'll have to see."

He snickered and leaned away. "Don't start something you don't intend to finish, Wife."

Noted.

"The next time we're together, I'd like to do it alone in my home," Cain said. "No Beans. No Vino."

Alone. In his home.

"Will...will we be living there when we get married? Do I have to leave my penthouse?" The idea made my heart drop. As if I'd be leaving the freedom of my home to go to my new prison.

"We can cross that bridge when we get to it," Cain said with a shrug. "I live in a high-rise, so it's nothing to swap."

Donald came carrying a large serving tray on his shoulder. He bent down before setting my plate of pizza in front of me and Cain's cod with the side of penne pasta.

I wasn't hungry. I wasn't comfortable. I wasn't okay.

But as I looked at my fiancé who stared at me with a warmth I didn't deserve, I put on a fake smile and adjusted.

16

KEITH

My workday was finished, and for the first time in a while, I wasn't interested in hanging around the garage.

"Spend you some time with that pretty little thing you had in here," Uncle Rod had suggested as I crossed the garage floor for the shop entrance upon clocking out.

Kennedy.

I was trying not to think about her in my free time. Of course, everywhere I went now was stained with the evidence of her. Rod's office, my home, and now Sonny's Kitchen. Still, I tried to ignore the idea of her as I let my uncle's words go in one ear and out the other.

In another moment, it was an easy feat as I set eyes on a familiar face.

Eden.

She noticed me as I noticed her. I was cool with a nod of my head in greeting as I was on my way out, but Eden cut into my path leaving me coming to a stop in front of her. Now that she was on her feet this time, I didn't miss that I easily had a foot on her.

She was standing there in jean shorts, a yellow tube top, and a gold chain around her slim waist. On her feet were a pair of yellow fur slides. Half of her hair was up in a ponytail, secured by big white hairballs. It all only served to add more to her youthful appearance.

Eden smiled up at me after taking me in. "Yeah, this fits you."

"Hey, what's up?" I greeted her.

Jake was at the counter, doing his best to steal glances at Eden on the low.

Couldn't exactly blame the guy, she was incredibly pretty, and her outfit only gave way to her curves.

I brought my attention back to the girl in front of me, the girl oblivious to my coworker's wanton gaze.

"I was ridin' with a girl from my job and her car started actin' funny." Eden gave an indifferent shrug. "So, she pulled in here and they're checkin' it out."

In the background I spotted another woman, one wearing a purple T-shirt as a dress with sneakers. She was on her cell phone, and judging by the tone of her voice, the way she was moving her hand as she talked, I could tell she was chewing some poor guy out.

I got back to Eden and bobbed my head. "Hope it works out."

She looked over her shoulder, frowning briefly as she watched her friend continue to argue. "Yeah, thank God I brought a book."

The gesture almost made me smile. It was cute she was a reader. "Hopefully something better than that other one."

Eden focused back on me, scowling. "Excuse me?"

"Nothing."

Eden narrowed her eyes, and then she grinned. "Wait. Did you get a copy?"

I scratched at my neck. "Unfortunately, I did."

She lit up and bounced a little. "Oh my God, what do you think? Are you finished?"

"Dixie's incredibly naïve," I said. "The world isn't all sunshine and rainbows."

"It could be," Eden chirped up.

I shook my head. She was young. "You're in for a rude awakening."

Eden clicked her tongue. "You're such a Darius."

I did relate to the male lead just a little. "He's pretty solid."

Eden rolled her eyes. "So, how far did you get?"

"A little over halfway."

Eden clutched her chest, her eyes enlarging. "You didn't freak out when Dixie was about to fall off the roof and Darius saved her?"

I shrugged. "It's the decent thing to do."

Eden deadpanned and very boldly reached out and shoved me. "God. It was beyond human decency. That's when he realized he cared about her, that he had a heart. His mind didn't just panic, but his heart froze. His heart, Keith! Like his world would stop if she wasn't there."

I'd read that scene, and admittedly was on my toes thinking ol' girl was about to bite it before the end of the book. Eden was right though, there was no missing the visceral reaction Darius had had when Dixie had slipped on that roof after they'd argued.

"Romance just isn't my thing, but it's good you enjoy it," I said in the end.

Eden held her hand up. "You gotta really pay attention when you read it. Let your mind go and just get sucked in."

"It's not realistic."

Her upper lip curled up. "I don't read for realism, I read for escapism."

"Enjoy your fairy tales then."

She pouted and I felt bad just then. I didn't know her story, but in her large dark eyes I could see something like experience, trials and errors, but unlike me, unlike Dominique, I saw no anger.

There was something about Eden, something bright and hopeful the more I talked to her. It was for this reason alone I didn't dump on her book too much.

Fuck, I was too jaded these days.

"Sorry," I apologized sincerely. "I don't know. He comes from nothing and she's got everything, and somehow, I'm supposed to believe she really looks at him and sees something?"

"Yes," Eden responded.

"Why?"

"Because love isn't material. Love isn't black and white—it's gray. Love isn't letting a class difference define what matters. Love isn't easy, but it's worth the fight." Eden's eyes fell to her slides as she kicked at the ground. "At least, that's what I get out of reading these books." She looked up at me and gave a little shrug. "I get hope. And hope makes the world go 'round. Hope makes you believe in the impossible, and for some people, love isn't realistic until they meet that person who redefines what it is."

She sounded just as naïve and idealistic as Dixie's character.

"You ever been in a relationship?" I asked curiously.

A sudden sadness washed over Eden as she nodded. "Not any good ones. But, you know, I still have faith. You can't write off the world, not when you gotta live in it."

I envied her just then, her drive to push forward despite any battle she'd faced.

"How old are you?" I had to know.

She loosened up, moving some hair out of her face. "Twenty-three."

Not a chance.

The lie made me chuckle as I finally walked around her. As I made it to the front door, I faced her once more. "Maybe aim a little lower next time."

Eden frowned. "Twenty?"

I laughed, that sounded more believable yet still too old. "See you around, Eden."

Love is gray.

To be young and full of optimism.

When I got home, despite the hour, I cracked open a beer and stood in my living room, racking my brain on my next move.

The sound of my phone ringing caught my attention and I welcomed the distraction of a phone call from my mother.

"Hey, Mom," I said as I picked up her call.

"Hey, baby," my mother responded. "Listen, when's your next day off?"

"Wednesday, why?"

"Perfect. Momma and I were thinking of having you over for dinner. So, how about it?"

Dinner sounded good, but then...

The image of Kennedy came to mind, of her in just my T-shirt, ever too eager to come do yard work with me. I couldn't wrap my head around why she would want to, or why *I* wanted to see her do it. I couldn't imagine Little Miss Priss willingly getting down and dirty to work. I should've blown her off, this wasn't a part of our arrangement, but fuck it if curiosity wasn't guiding me into pure stupidity.

"Uh," I let out as I got back to my mother. "I actually got plans to do some stuff around the house and get my yard work done. I'll probably be too tired to come through, but we definitely can pin down a dinner at some point."

"Ah, well, okay," my mother sounded disappointed. "Let me know the next time you're free. It's been too long, Keith."

I ran my hand over my waves, hanging my head in shame. "I know, I know. I'm sorry. We'll get together, I promise."

We hung up and I set my beer down on the coaster on my coffee table.

I needed not to think of a certain woman. "Alexa, play hip-hop and R&B."

A chime went off and Alexa obliged me by playing some music.

The instrumental was foreign to me, but before long I didn't have to guess whose song was playing when I heard her voice.

Beyoncé.

Grimacing, I barked out. "Play hip-hop."

Jadakiss filled the room as a new song came on.

Needing a distraction, I went and gathered laundry and brought it out to my living room to sort for the wash. I got lost in the task as hip-hop played around me.

Vince Staples was rapping about his coming up in Long Beach when I grabbed a pair of jeans from the basket. It was when I checked their pockets that I found them. A mesh pair of lavender panties she hadn't collected when we'd parted that day.

The thin, delicate material slipped from my fingers as I let them fall to my couch. The memory of her in the diner had me smiling.

"*I'm usually so boring,*" she'd confessed to me later as she lay on my chest back at my house.

Same, I thought of my existence of home and work and back.

I couldn't be like Eden, or Dixie, and have hope, but as I sat preparing laundry, regrettably thinking of Kennedy, I decided maybe it wasn't so bad to dream.

17

Kennedy

He called me Wednesday.

After three weeks of being engaged, Cain was finally reaching out to me by phone instead of just barging into my world.

I almost didn't answer. I was in the middle of getting dressed to leave, but I thought better of ignoring Cain's call. It was better to speak now, than risk him coming over while I was out.

I was lying too much these days and I needed to get ahold of it.

Still, that didn't mean I had to be nice.

"What?" I snapped into my phone as I picked up the call.

A sharp whistle greeted my ear, prompting me to pull the device away for a moment. "You're mighty bold over the phone."

Cain.

Even though we'd had a few encounters where we spoke to each other, there was something more intimate about a phone call. About his voice in my ear. Privately.

Cain's voice was melodic, calm, and confident. It was rich and young, smooth and pleasant—a grave stark contrast to who he was as a person. But then, it wasn't. I thought of Cain: tall, lean, blemish-free dark brown skin, handsome in the classic kind of way, and then there was that voice. In all honesty, he was the perfect honey trap.

Only, I wasn't taking the bait.

"Yeah, well, what can I say, you bring it out of me," I replied.

I could hear the smile in his voice as he asked, "Busy?"

I sat down on my ottoman at the foot of my bed and pulled on the garden shoes I'd bought for the day's task. I hadn't a clue on what I was doing as far as manual labor went, but I was dressed for the occasion. "Yes."

"And this weekend," Cain went on. "You're getting a wax?"

That had been a sarcastic throwaway comment. I didn't really wax. Laser hair removal was my go-to method for unwanted hair. It lasted longer and left my skin silky as a result.

Because I was trying to cut back on the lying, I decided to throw Cain a bone. "No, I was only joking."

"So, you're free? I want to get together and have a night in with you," Cain said, sounding hopeful. "If it won't be any inconvenience."

Like this engagement? "I guess I can move some things around, just for you."

"Saturday night sound good?"

"Can't wait," I said dryly.

"Hmm." He hummed into my ear. "Starting to sound like I'm growing on you."

"I'm pretty sure I'll never like you, Cain," I let out.

He chuckled. "Never say never, Wife."

"Stop, you're giving me a wettie," I said sardonically.

Cain's response was a laugh. "I'll see you Saturday night."

We hung up and I shook away the shudders that came with the thought of alone time with that man.

I wasn't looking forward to it, but I decided it was best to put it on the backburner as I gathered myself together and exited my suite.

Along the way to Keith's I made a tiny pit stop at the grocery store for water since we'd be in the sun all day. It was only sixty-five out, but it was better safe than sorry.

While I'd never really worked a day in my life, I was excited for this venture. It was only partly bittersweet when I considered those times in my youth when I'd walk barefoot in our backyard and along my father's garden holding his hand. He was a white-collar man, but I'd always admired his hobbies of gardening, and even hunting. His *need* to get his hands dirty.

I'd never felt more like his daughter than I did when I pulled into Keith's driveway beside his Tahoe.

Keith was out front when I pulled in, doing work in the plants by his front step. The sight of him gave me butterflies. To compose myself, I got out of my Lexus and quicky got busy digging in my back seat for my shopping bags. Anything other than obsess over Keith in a white tee and camo pants. The T-shirt did nothing but hug his broad chest and back and emphasize his toned arms littered in ink. The absence of a baseball cap only brought attention to his handsome yet angry scowl.

Music was playing from a wireless speaker I noticed as I got out of my car and grew courage to face Keith. Something told me it was old school by the rapper's cadence and the beat.

I bobbed my head to the melody, liking what I was hearing. "Who is this?"

It was as if my words had fallen upon deaf ears. Keith was kneeling there, squinting up me, his dark eyes taking me in slow. What more, he stood and came closer, silently appraising me even more.

Swallowing, I stood back and watched him assess me, feeling squirmy under his scrutiny.

It wasn't lost on me that my outfit of choice made me standout, as I had when I'd gone and purchased a couple of waters from the store. For the day's task, I wore a pair of dark gray overalls, a cream-colored long-sleeved thermal, garden shoes, and I topped it off with a floppy sun hat.

"I...I wanted to look the part," I confessed.

Keith bobbed his head, and I hated not knowing what he was thinking the longer he looked at me. Not knowing if I looked ridiculous. Not knowing *why* I cared if he thought I did.

I lifted my arm and the grocery bag that was dangling on it. "I brought water...and gloves."

Keith's gaze landed on the blue plastic bag in my possession. "I have water."

"But not Waiakea water. It's my favorite." I went and pulled out a greenish-blue bottle and held it up. "It's Hawaiian volcanic water. *So* good."

Keith accepted my water and mumbled a *thank you*, all the while stealing peeks at my outfit, and my hat.

"So..." I smiled shyly. "...who is this?"

Keith shook his head. "You don't know Heavy D?"

The name sounded a little familiar, but I couldn't place a face. "Guess not."

Keith turned, looking over at his speaker that was set up on his front step. "It's a station dedicated to old hip-hop and R&B." He came back to me. "Shouldn't be too much violence."

"Good," I said. I dug into my bag and pulled out my gray and blue gardening gloves I'd bought. "Shall we?"

Keith peeled his attention from me and glanced at his house. "I just finished with the front, let's head on to the back."

Even though Keith's house wasn't large or massive, he still held an expansive backyard to take care of.

I stood beside him and wiggled my fingers into my gloves, something that made him snort.

"What?" I asked.

Keith eyed my hands. "Smart move on the gloves."

"I set a nail and hair appointment tomorrow," I let him know. "Just in case."

"Of course," he muttered.

Keith took our waters and set them inside to stay cool while we worked up a thirst.

First up, he was insistent on teaching me how to mow a lawn.

A task that seemed daunting. Perhaps I was overthinking, but I couldn't help imagining how many toes or entire feet were lost in lawn-mowing related injuries a year.

I liked to think I had pretty feet.

Wiggling my toes in my shoes, I faced Keith apprehensively. "Yeah?"

"It's nothing to it," Keith assured as he guided me in front of the bright green mower. Unlike at my parents' house, his yard wasn't for a riding mower, but a push mower. "Some people use gas mowers, and some use electric. This is a gas powered one. Kinda old school, but it gets the job done best."

Mentally, I penciled this information down. *If ever I purchase a home, get a gas running lawn mower.*

Keith went and instructed me on each individual part, the control bar, the engine start lever, the recoil start and so on. It all sounded simple enough, until he wanted me to go and power on the mower.

I followed the steps from his brief tutorial, except when I went to pull the cord, the lawn mower didn't come to life. I yanked again. And again. And again, nearly ripping my arm out of the socket.

I groaned. "Dammit."

Tapping at my hip whirled me around as Keith came and helped me. With ease, he pulled the cord and the lawn mower started. He stepped back, out of the way, allowing me to take over.

Tentatively, I stepped up to the machine and gulped. This whole thing was to teach me to fend for myself, in case of emergencies—but surely if I ever did hit rock bottom I could scrape up a few coins enough to pay someone to handle my yard, right?

Better yet, I would just live in an apartment. Problem solved.

My hands shook as I put them on the bar. Suddenly, Keith's much larger hands were on either side of mine as his chest brushed against my back. All at once my anxiety slipped away at the sense of his nearness. His hands were on mine as he walked with me, helping me mow my first patch of grass. The lawn mower vibrated in my palms and it was a little heavy for a beginner like me, but it otherwise wasn't so arduous.

Still, I faked uncertainty, just to have Keith close, just to feel him against me, teaching me.

Together we mowed a line from his house to the back fence.

"Try to get all straight lines," Keith said into my ear before releasing me to do another row on my own.

Internally, I pouted at his absence, but I faced the task head-on. I wanted to make him proud, and most of all, I wanted to accomplish this to prove to myself that I could.

Even still, Keith only let me mow so much of his yard before he swooped in to finish. He did his lines with precision and expertise. It was okay, though, because he didn't go over my work. My lines were fine and even, making me proud.

Next, he taught me to immediately empty the bag, so that the next time I went to mow my lawn I wouldn't encounter a full bag and potentially have to stop and empty it while I was mowing. From there he taught me how to trim hedges, when to water the grass, when to fertilize, and then we got down to weed by his poinsettias arranged by his back patio.

Keith weeded on one end of the patch of flowers while I worked on the other. His wireless speaker sat on the back porch, playing more old school hip-hop and R&B. A Case song was playing, its melancholy content ruining my mood. "Missing You" was always such an emotional ballad.

To ignore the song playing, I began talking, anything to block out those lyrics. "So, have you lived here your whole life?"

Silence met my question for a moment and I briefly realized we were breaking another rule. We weren't supposed to get to know each other. Then again, we weren't supposed to do lawn work either, but here we were, thanks to me.

I looked over, finding Keith running his hand over his right arm, where that *BH* landscape tattoo was embedded in his skin. A declaration of love for his city. "Yeah. It's tough as shit at times, but ain't no place I'd rather be. I love the Heights."

His words echoed Jadyn's through and through. It was another driving force in why she wanted to write films about Black women in the hood existing and experiencing life, because she loved the world of Bedford Heights so much.

"I love it here, too," I whispered.

"You do?" Of course Keith had heard me.

"Things are so low key here. I can go out for lunch without someone snapping a photo or hounding me about my personal life. When I'm home, I always have to watch my back," I said. "Being my father's daughter comes with somewhat of a spotlight, but when I dated my ex, Guy, that's when I really rose to social media fame."

"*Guy*?" Keith repeated curiously.

"Yeah. It's short for Gaius." I nodded bitterly. "He's, uh, a player for the Long Beach Sharks, actually."

Keith paused and I felt him look at me. "An NFL player, huh? Your dad like him?"

"My parents loved Guy, and his liked me, too. We were together for two years, so it was a pretty close relationship."

"And before him?"

I shrugged. "In high school I dated some kids of my dad's friends, and in college I hooked up a little before I got with Gaius. Guy was my first *real* relationship. I, uh, got lucky, I guess."

"How so? Because he was a big shot?"

I wrinkled my nose. Gaius's being a rookie to the NFL didn't faze me. Money didn't matter to me, as privileged as it sounded. Cain was incredibly wealthy after inheriting his father's casino, and who knew what lay ahead come this venture with Nichols & Wagner. But Cain himself wasn't it for me. I didn't like feeling owned. I didn't like living in fear around him. "Because he was good to me. My best friend has had her share of assholes and losers, and I guess I'm fortunate to not have had a heartbreak."

My voice shook and I blinked to conceal the tears that were forming in my eyes.

I heard the moment Keith stopped pulling weeds and completely focused on me.

Now *so* wasn't the time to get in my feelings.

"Kennedy?" he pressed gently.

I shook my head, squeezing my eyes shut to will those ugly thoughts and tears away. The guilt had crept up on me ever so slowly until it was staring me in the face. Maybe...maybe I *deserved* what was happening with Cain.

"Do...do you want to get married? Someday?" I voiced instead.

Keith's eyes narrowed, slight agitation rolling off him just then at my topic switch. I hadn't fooled him one bit. He looked elsewhere, scratching at his neck. "I wanted to marry my ex. That didn't work out so well."

Just like that, disgust settled in my mouth. I was sure Keith wasn't perfect, but still, I loathed his ex for making him feel worthless. Like he wasn't good enough. Nobody deserved that.

Pot, kettle, Kennedy?

"She missed out," I said as I struggled to clear my voice. I lazily pulled at nearby weeds and focused on the chore. "My ex talked about marriage. I did love him, but I was twenty-two with what felt like the whole world watching me and I just wasn't sure. So, I let him down gently and fast forward to now and I guess I got what was coming.

"I had a man I loved and I broke his heart, and now I'm stuck with a man who treats me like an acquisition." I let out a pitiful laugh. "And the crazy thing is, I'm not even worth it. Like at all."

"You're too hard on yourself," Keith spoke up. He almost sounded annoyed at my self-deprecating.

"Think so?" I asked as I pulled myself together.

"Know so. That weird ass fiancé of yours doesn't deserve you. Besides, that situation with your ex was two years ago," Keith pointed out. "You're twenty-four now. Do you know what you want?"

Honestly, I didn't. Before, I'd always been fine with my schedule of yoga, hanging out with Jay, and spending time with my family. I admired that Jadyn aspired to be a fierce woman behind a camera, but I was okay with not doing anything as highbrow with my life. "Not really. You're twenty-nine, know what you want?"

Keith peered over at me, straight into my eyes, right into my soul as he spoke. "A family."

"You want kids?" I probed further.

Keith shrugged. "I'm not too sure about that. A family could be just me and the right woman. That's enough for me. I'm never going to be a white-collar type of guy. I'm not going to be big time. I'm okay with this, where I'm at and what I have. I love my job, I love my family, and I love my friends. It'd be nice, you know, to just have a woman. A house is not a home without one. I can live alone, but I'd rather share my life with someone."

A strange prickling bubbled inside of me at the thought of him getting that. Of him meeting another woman. Of him wrapping her in his strong arms. Of him breaking that angry face just to smile at her and laugh.

I hated the idea.

"See, your ex was wrong about you. You're a good man. But me?" I shook my head, trying to shake the feelings of inadequacy away. "Do you think I'm worth this much effort, Keith?"

"That's not a fair question," Keith responded. "You won't let me in." He ran his arm across his forehead to rid it of sweat before getting back to his work. "On the surface, you've got this prim and proper look about you, but then you're silly, nice, and you're not judgmental. If you would've asked me the night we met if I ever saw Little Miss 'This is Valentino' willingly getting down to weed, I would've laughed. Yet, you're out here, willing to learn, willing to do some work, and I'm impressed.

"What I *do* know, is that you're worth the chase, worth an

effort of getting to know. You're carrying the weight of the world on your shoulders with this bogus deal you got goin' on, but you're doin' it with a smile. And as pretty as that smile is, it doesn't compare to the one where you let your guard down, when you're carefree."

I forgot how to breathe as his words wrapped me in a blanket of solace.

He was right, but he was wrong, too.

I didn't truly know him, but what I saw so far, I liked...a lot.

Keith was angry and quiet, but then the closer I got, I marveled at his gentle side, at his strength, at the way he loved his city enough to give back.

I wouldn't tell him, but I liked the way he didn't apologize when he was standing up to me. Calling me out on my brattiness.

It was ridiculously absurd to think about not being with a gentleman, but I liked that Keith didn't sweep me off my feet and pamper me too much.

Fragile. To everyone else, I'd always been treated and seen as a princess. Handled with care and a delicateness as if I'd break. Not Keith.

"Thank you," I told him, feeling myself smile and calm down. "Weeding isn't so bad actually. I wish you had more flowers."

Keith settled down as well. "Yeah?"

And then, because we'd already blurred that line, I spoke about my childhood. "When I was little, and my father had the time, he used to tend to his tulip garden. I used to hold his hand and walk beside him whenever he was taking a stroll for inspection." Tears threatened to fall as I thought of the future. "Even though I'm so mad at him, someday, I'd like to have a house of my own and plant tulips in his honor."

Keith was closer now, using his knuckle to catch a fallen tear. "What's your favorite color of tulips?"

"White," I confessed.

Somehow, Keith smiled a little. "Of course."

I didn't get it, but I didn't care. I was just happy he was near.

I sniffled. Because I didn't want everything to be about me, I asked, "Did you always like cars?"

The question triggered a soft smile to cross Keith's face. He shook his head. "Not always." He nodded off toward his flowerbed before us. "In a way, it's like gardening. I got into gardening because my grandmother told me using my hands would better benefit me than resulting to anger. With cars, it's sort of the same. I started helping out my uncle at his shop and it kept me busy and focused. And gradually I grew in love with the process of restoring cars, of bringing beauty to damaged goods. The patience it takes to get it there."

All I could do was watch him with a smile, soaking in all his words and imagining him younger and angrier and finding himself as he went to work for his uncle and helped his grandmother with her garden.

Thank God for his family setting him straight and keeping him grounded.

"So," he began, squinting at me curiously. "When does this get boring for you?"

A loud laugh bubbled out of me. I nudged him. "I could ask *you* the same thing. When do you see yourself getting sick of me?"

Keith snorted. "Never." His eyes fell to my outfit once more. "Every time I'm around you it's an adventure."

He liked my clothes.

The realization made me blush. "Same."

Keith lifted his gaze to meet mine. "Most boring relationship?"

That was easy. "In college. He was a stockbroker. Very 'yes, sir,' and 'yes, ma'am.' Real polite."

"Polite is boring?" Keith challenged.

I shrugged. "It can be."

I couldn't explain it, but Keith was polite and respectful with me, but then at times, he called me out, was more aggressive—and I loved it.

I cleared my throat and went back to weeding and needing to know more about him. "What's your favorite football team?"

"Honestly? It's the—"

"Keith?"

A woman's voice sounded out beside us, drawing our attention to the left. An older woman was standing there, carrying a large casserole dish with some Tupperware on top. Her graying braids were pulled back out of her face, leaving the curious expression on it to be seen. She was staring at me, as if I were a foreign concept at Keith's home.

By some instinct, I knew. This was Keith's mother.

"Shit." He mumbled beside me before shooting up and going over to the woman. He ushered her more toward the driveway, away from me.

I couldn't be mad at him. There was no way to really introduce me. Was it socially acceptable to introduce your parents to your fuck buddy?

My own mother would have a conniption and my father would want to wring Keith's neck out. They would like him, though. I was sure. If Cain wasn't in the picture, I was positive my parents would like Keith. Manners, protective, honest, and hardworking.

At least, that's how I always perceived my parents before my father made it clear he wanted me to be well-off even after he was gone. As if my inheritance wasn't enough.

Keith quietly spoke with the woman who he looked nothing like. Her complexion was closer to my own than his soft brown skin, her gentle but serious face was so different from Keith's often angry one, and where her son towered over her with his six-foot-three height, she was a good five-seven at the most.

Still, there was no missing the love between them. Her, a concerned parent, and Keith, an adoring son. They hugged after she handed over the food. Despite no introductions, the woman offered me a tight-lipped smile and a wave before disappearing down the driveway.

Keith came over carrying the food and one good whiff of it had me realizing I was starving.

"I'll finish the rest of this later," Keith said.

I didn't want to leave him hanging. "You sure?"

"Yeah, it's not much left. You did good today."

I had worked hard and I felt it in my sore arms. "Thank you, for showing me the way."

"Never a problem." Keith gestured with his head toward his house. "Let's get cleaned up. I'll fix the fish I took out for you."

I bit my lip. He was always going out of his way for me. "You didn't have to do that."

Keith made a face. "I wanted to."

A fuzzy sensation buzzed inside of me as I stood up. "Okay."

"I was planning on grilling, but I'm not passin' on my mom's cooking," Keith said as he led us up the back patio steps. He passed me the keys to let us in as he carefully leaned down and turned off the speaker, abruptly putting an end to Jill Scott.

I unlocked his backdoor and stepped into his bedroom, the smell of him hitting me at once. *Cozy.* That's how Keith smelled.

I set my hat down on his dresser beside one of his baseball caps. A nearby mirror illustrated my hat hair, but I was too worn out to care about my appearance.

Keith came past me and I followed him out to his kitchen.

"That food smells amazing," I said as I watched him set it on the island.

He glanced at me with pride. "My mom's famous Marry Me Chicken, with a side of angel hair pasta."

It was too ironic of a name not to laugh. "Gonna share?"

Keith frowned. "I don't wanna put you out. I got some grouper."

I did love grouper, but that chicken smelled delicious. "I want the chicken. It smells good. It's been a while since I've had any. Besides, if you told me you were grilling, I would've brought over some salmon hot dogs."

All at once Keith's face fell. "Salmon *what*?"

I chuckled. That was exactly Jadyn's reaction when I discovered the food. "You heard me. Salmon hot dogs. They're good."

Keith wrinkled his nose as he came past me for the sink. He grabbed the bar of soap and began lathering his hands. "Shit sounds nasty."

I went up beside him, poking him in his ribs. "You would've tried them."

Keith was quick to shake his head. "Hell no."

Pouting, I gave him the puppy dog eyes. "For me?"

Once more, he made a face and rolled his eyes, before giving in. But not without slapping my butt. "Fine."

The goofiest smile crept across my face and I said nothing further.

We got cleaned up before settling down in his dining room and helping ourselves to his mother's prepared meal. Sundried tomatoes in a thick and creamy parmesan sauce, the Marry Me Chicken was to die for. I ate like I hadn't eaten in years and I wasn't ashamed. I had to try this with fish.

"Okay, this is the first recipe you have to teach me," I declared as I ate another serving of pasta.

Keith forked at his chicken. "I change my mind about that."

I paused. "What do you mean?"

"You can take a cooking class," he said simply. "Besides, I could replicate this meal, but my mom's the master at it."

He didn't want to teach me to cook anymore. He was right about me taking a class, where I could learn to create all kinds of dishes, but the stab of his refusal sank deep.

"Okay," I responded. I let it go and moved on. "Still, did she teach you how to cook?"

Keith took a swig of his water and nodded. "Yeah, her and my grandma."

"Was it just you three growing up?"

"Yeah, my grandfather died when I was a kid. Complications from cancer, if I'm remembering right," Keith went on. "My foundation and my roots are definitely my mom, my grandmother, and my uncle Rod."

I all but abandoned my food as he began telling me about some mishap from his youth that involved him eating all of his grandmother's ham and her teaching him how to make it to replace it.

I liked hearing Keith talk. The steady timbre of his deep voice telling me story after story never got old.

Before long, though, my eyelids grew heavy and I couldn't stop myself from letting out a few yawns.

"I should get going," I said as I covered my mouth on my fifth yawn.

Keith stood and collected our plates. "You should stay the night. You're tired."

"It's not that long of a drive," I assured him.

"I'm not letting you take that risk," Keith said adamantly.

I fingered the condensation on my glass of water. "Don't boss me around."

His hand was in my hair, his fingers grazing my scalp as he tilted my head back. Peering into his eyes, I knew then I didn't *want* to leave. "Please stay? I don't know what I'd do if you fell asleep at the wheel and got hurt."

How could I ever go just then? "Okay."

"I'll sleep on the couch. You can shower and take my bed. I'll even wash those clothes for you." Keith was out of the room taking our dishes to the sink before I could respond.

One minute he was close, and the next he was distant. I didn't like it. It was probably for our own good. To sleep separately, but I didn't want it.

Keith was right, though. As I dragged myself to his bedroom, I found it hard to keep my eyes open. The idea of stripping down and showering even sounded like too much work. His bed was all too inviting, but my clothes were dirty and I was sweaty. I didn't want to soil his sheets.

So I did the next best thing, I got down on the floor, folded my arms and rested, prepared for sleep.

I had barely drifted off when I heard his heavy footsteps entering the room.

"What are you doing on the floor, Kenny?" His tone was amused, yet it was doused in a sleepiness that sent warmth below my belly. Something like syrup came to mind of just how sticky his voice was to the ear.

Kenny. He'd called me Kenny in such a way I wasn't surprised at the goose bumps sprouting across my skin.

"I didn't want to get your bed dirty," I reasoned.

"So you get my floor dirty instead?"

Peeking one eye open, I nodded at him. "Uh-huh."

He tried to hide his smile, but failed. In another moment, he was crouching down, flipping me over onto my back and taking off my shoes and socks. Next, he was undoing my overall straps. He pulled them from my body before reaching out and picking me up as if I weighed nothing. I didn't mind at all as he carried me over to his attached bathroom.

Inside he set me on the counter and tapped my arm, indicating for me to raise my arms so he could remove my thermal. I did as instructed and when I thought he'd take off my bra next, he moved on to a drawer under his counter. He procured a brush, and then a beige bandana.

"Don't quite have a shower cap for your hair or a scarf. Unless you want a durag?" Keith asked.

I shook my head.

Keith accepted my response and quietly he began brushing back my hair, gently getting my edges and making sure every strand along the way was accounted for. He worked meticulously, and I admired him as he did so, especially when he secured my hair into a neat bun at the back of my head before tying down the bandana.

It was the most intimate thing, putting yet another crack in our fling.

When he was done with my hair, his eyes settled on mine. So serious. So mature. So...Keith.

Boldly, I reached out, running my fingers down his lips. "I like seeing you smile."

Keith bit my fingers gently. "What else do you like about me?"

A dark fog soaked the air between us.

"Everything," I breathed out.

"Everything?"

"Uh-huh." I nodded. "The sound of your voice makes me wet. Being in your arms makes me feel protected. Having you teach me makes me feel smarter."

Keith's eyes drifted to my lips as I spoke and mine trailed to his.

I wanted to taste his mouth. Badly.

Deep in my belly I knew it'd be addictive. Almost as addictive as it was being around him, learning him. This blue-collar man's-man who was entirely different from what I was used to.

There on the counter in just my green lace panties and bra, I was ready to surrender my body to him.

"Teach me how to cook, please?" I blurted out.

Those arms of his trapped me as his hands came down on either side of me. He leaned in, shaking his head. "*You* make all these rules, and you're steady breaking every one."

I was horrible and I couldn't deny it. I had no sense of self-control with Keith.

"I'll pay you," I offered.

Keith smirked. "No thanks."

Reaching behind myself, I unclasped my bra and let it slide to the floor. Resting back on my hands, feeling my chest rise and fall with Keith's total attention, I licked my lips. "I don't want to take a class. I want you."

Keith barely gazed at my breasts before his hard stare focused on mine.

"I'll teach you everything you want to know and should know," he said in the end.

Greedily, I perked up and grinned. "Teach me how to kiss, I'm awful."

A lazy haze coasted in Keith's eyes and I felt the atmosphere shift.

His rough palm cupped my jaw as he ran his thumb across my lips. His dark eyes were glued to the movement, lost in concentration. In another moment, he dipped his thumb into my mouth. Instinctively, I sucked on it, slow, feeling my thighs clench when he pulled it out.

Keith watched his thumb escape my mouth, but not before I flicked my tongue across it first. He removed his thumb and ran it across my lip again.

His eyes found mine.

"I want to, you know," I said.

"I know," he said.

Keith stepped closer, holding on to my waist as he leaned down and pressed his lips to my shoulder.

Oof.

Tender. His lips grazed my skin and his five-o'clock shadow scrubbed the surface next.

Aching. I was aching for this man. I wanted it all. His touch. His kiss. His feel. Everything.

But he gave me nothing as he reeled back and stepped away. "I'll kiss you when it's time to say goodbye."

A sadness formed in my belly at the idea. A bittersweet kiss that would be.

"Okay," I said. "Let's hop in the shower."

Keith backed off as he picked up my shirt and bra. "You go first. I'll clean up and wait my turn."

"Really?"

He held his hand out for my remaining articles of clothing. "Too tempting, and I'm not a fan of condoms and water."

I almost wanted to tell him one wouldn't be necessary since I was on the pill, but that was a level of closeness we didn't need. One that would destroy what little line we had left.

I let it go and shimmied out of my panties and handed them over.

There was a ticking clock above our heads and there was nothing neither of us could do about it. With or without that gaudy ring on my finger, I was marked for another man whether I liked it or not.

Keith knew it, and so did I.

But that didn't mean we couldn't get our fill of each other before the end.

"I know I'm cuddly, but I promise if we go to bed together you won't fall in love with me," I teased.

A ghost of a smile had a corner of Keith's mouth twitching. "You stay on your side and I'll stay on mine."

"Deal!" I jumped at the opportunity.

Keith snickered as he took my clothes and left me alone to shower.

I went into his standing shower and closed the door behind me. Alone with my thoughts. Just me, myself, and I.

That Case song came to mind, making me sad. I never wanted to miss him. I wasn't prepared for the day that I would. For the day we would inevitably say goodbye.

18

KEITH

She didn't listen.

I only agreed to go to bed with Kennedy if we stuck to our sides. I even lingered in the living room after her shower, going and taking my time to do her laundry. By the time I'd run the dryer, smoked a cigarette out back, and took my own shower after cleaning the kitchen, she was still up. As tired as she was, Kennedy waited for me to come to bed.

She greeted me with a tired smile from behind my copy of *Night Changes*. The little thief was in one of my white T-shirts—a fair compromise because I wasn't strong enough to go to bed beside her naked body.

I got in on my side and laid back, exhausted. Before long, I was asleep.

At some point, in the middle of the night, I woke up to her body against mine, and one of her legs was tangled around one of mine.

She didn't listen.

But I wasn't complaining.

When I woke up again in the morning, I got up to brush my teeth and wash my face. I wasn't due at the garage until noon, so sleeping in a little longer was my initial plan. Until Kennedy.

She was up when I came back to bed. She'd used the half bath out in the hall, and as I went to get back under my comforter, she slipped by to no doubt brush her teeth.

Closing my eyes, I prepared to get a little moment of sleep.

"Hey."

She was back in the room now, her soft voice intruding in on my sleep.

"Hmm?" I didn't bother opening my eyes, sometimes looking at her was too much. Those pure eyes of hers. The shyness that took over, revealing how inexperienced she was. The way she seemed to trust me completely.

"What time do you gotta go in to work?" she asked.

"Noon."

"Ah." Soon, I felt her on the bed, standing. "So we got a little time."

My eyes opened and found her standing between my legs, grinning down at me. My shirt hung like a dress on her. She was the tallest woman I'd ever messed around with, and I loved the sight of her bare legs.

Reaching out, I ran my hands up her calves and pulled her down to me. She caught herself before she could fall. Her hands shot out and landed on either side of my head. She was in my face, giggling, and my eyes soaked in her mouth, her plump lips. She came down and straddled me and I got lost in her eyes. In her attention.

"Can we...have a little fun before you go in?" she asked in a shy voice.

I liked her shy side.

"Fun you say?" I played dumb.

Kennedy nodded, licking her lips and slowly sliding down my body. Before I could question what she was up to, I got the idea loud and clear when her fingers curled around the waistband of my sweats and tugged. I wasn't wearing anything underneath, giving her complete access to me. One touch and she lit the flame.

She took me into her hand, staring at me with wonder and

want. Her hungry eyes caused me to become even harder. Hard, because of what she was about to do. Hard, because she'd said she didn't like giving head, but it was clear, she liked giving *me* head. Hard, because in this moment, she was mine and I was all hers.

She took me into her mouth and my head hit the pillow as I released a groan. *Fuck.*

This act wasn't her thing, but she sure as hell knew what she was doing. She had my head spinning when she licked it slow. I felt my toes curling as she took me in deeper.

"Teach me how to make breakfast like you like?" she suddenly asked me.

Honestly, she could ask for the world and while my dick was in her hand, I'd give it to her.

"Yes," I let out.

She was back at it, and I felt my heart racing at what was building up inside me.

"Stop," I managed to get out.

She didn't listen, instead, she kissed a path along my shaft before popping me back in her mouth.

"Kenne— Fuck!"

She'd bitten me.

I sat up and found her perking a brow, daring me to say something.

"*I'm* in control, Keith," she let it be known.

This side of her, all assertive and dominating, was enough to finish me off.

"It's like that?" I asked.

"Yeah, it's like that," she shot back as she soon sat up on her haunches and pulled my shirt off.

Entranced by her attitude and body, I laid back, letting her win.

"Bet you're happy you're not kissing me after that, huh?" Kennedy taunted as she wiped at her mouth.

Some guys I knew weren't into it after the act. "I can be nasty."

"Yeah?"

Hell yeah, but not with her.

I fumbled as I reached out beside me, going and pulling open my nightstand drawer for a condom. Lost in a lust-filled haze or not, I wasn't a dummy.

Kennedy wasn't experienced enough to put it on for me, so I tore it open and managed to loosen up and smile a little as she watched the process of me putting it on. Her eager eyes and curiosity were adorable.

But then it was back to business. She knew what I wanted, and even if she kept with her bossy persona, she was a little hesitant as she climbed on top of me. When I met her, I considered her a snobby little uptight brat, but the more I got to know her, the more I saw her willing to try new things and learn, the more I was elated to see I was wrong about her. A woman's experience in life, or in the bedroom, didn't too much matter to me, as long as she was willing to try.

"Oh." She whined and shook as she sank down on me and I began to fill her.

I inhaled sharply, trying to maintain my sanity because fuck this felt good.

Kennedy let out a small cry when she was completely on me. Her nails dug into my shoulders as she bit into her lip. She took her time finding her groove as she began to roll her hips in small circles. She wasn't confident on top. I could tell as she let down her walls and gazed down at me for confirmation. With my eyes on hers, I nodded, letting her know this felt right, good, amazing.

"I want it slow," she breathed out.

Slow.

I loved it slow and sensual, but with her it would be torture. I put up no fight, though, as I held on to her waist and accepted her pace.

"Oh Keith." She moaned as she bounced on me, eliciting a groan from me.

Kennedy threw her head back, her diamond earrings

glistening in the morning light, her breasts jiggling with the movement, and her svelte middle swaying as she rocked some more. I couldn't think of a better view.

Before long, I sat up, holding her closer, needing her.

Kennedy leaned down, trailing her tongue over the Patience tattoo on my left shoulder blade before planting a kiss on it. She went and did the same to my Progress tattoo on my right side. She kissed my chest, nipping my skin with her teeth, all the while she was riding me slow.

My hands danced up and down her spine, mesmerized by her soft, smooth skin. I took her right breast into my mouth, tugging on her nipple, teasing her.

She cradled my head in her hands as she began to speed up her strides.

That's what I need.

Kennedy's moans and cries filled my bedroom walls, challenging the morning birds outside. Skin against skin, her eyes peering down into mine, a slow and steady rhythm overtaking us, nothing else mattered.

"Was I any good?" Kennedy's voice greeted my ear as we winded down. She was resting on top of me. Her tone was partly teasing, but mostly genuine.

I ran my hand down her back. "You were perfect."

"Can we have a cigarette?" she asked me next.

I was trying to quit. I wouldn't be responsible for her picking up the bad habit, no matter how much I craved a fix right then. "No."

Kennedy huffed and rolled off me, leaving me cold. "I know you have a stash hidden somewhere."

I heard her pull open my nightstand drawer on the other side of my bed. Soon, she gasped, jumping back.

Her head whipped around, facing me. "You have a gun?"

Going and leaning over her, I shut the drawer. "Curiosity

killed the cat, Kenny." I went and laid back down. "A couple of summers ago, shit was getting tense around here. There were a lot of break-ins happening. You can never be too careful."

Kennedy calmed down a little as she came and laid against me. "I remember Jadyn mentioning that. Have...have you ever used it?"

I shook my head. "A few times at the gun range, but never on a person. Hoping I never have to."

"Me neither," Kennedy said.

She lived in Hampton Hills, where everyone had gated estates and security on the premises. Life for her was different, simple.

"Guess you won't be movin' to the Heights any time soon," I said, joking as I stroked her cheek.

Kennedy rested her chin on my chest, staring over at me. "If I didn't love my penthouse so much, I wouldn't mind being roommates with Jay."

Kennedy living in Bedford Heights, that I would've liked to see.

We lay there, naked, her against me, talking about nothing for a little while before we got up to shower and get dressed for the day. There was just enough time for a quick tutorial on breakfast before I had to go in.

"What do you usually get for breakfast at the hotel?" I asked as I raided my fridge for ideas.

"Avocado toast, eggs, and sometimes oatmeal, other times meatless sausage," Kennedy answered as she stood beside the fridge back in that T-shirt of mine. One rule I was considering adding to our arrangement? If she spent the night, she had to wear my T-shirts. She looked better in them than I did.

"I gotta get into avocados more," I said as I grabbed a carton of eggs and a stick of butter.

"And fruit," she noted as she looked around and came up empty on fruit in my home.

I scratched along my neck as I went over to the counter. "Maybe I'll grab some from the store tomorrow or something."

A ping went off in my pocket, alerting me to a text message. A look at the clock on my microwave found that I wasn't running late for work, so I doubted it was Uncle Rod.

I pulled my phone from my pocket to see that Savon had texted me.

SAVON

This weekend we linkin up with Kai n Gav, NO staying in

I didn't miss the lack of asking, but I didn't put up a fight as I texted him back that I was down. Makai and Gavin were old friends of ours from around the way. Makai was now married, and I'd hardly seen him before I went ghost.

"Your boss want you in early or something?" Kennedy wondered as she watched me text Savon back.

"Nah, that was my boy Savon. I've been summoned out this weekend." I looked up from my phone. "You got any plans?"

At once she shrank and my back stiffened. "I have a hot date with my fiancé."

I shouldn't have asked. I didn't even know this guy and I wanted to beat his ass. "What's this guy like?"

Kennedy pursed her lips. "Cain is...cold. Clinical. Emotionless. He just gives me the heebie-jeebies."

"Grotesque?" That would also explain his *needing* to force a marriage on a woman.

Kennedy was quick to shake her head. "He's attractive, but... He's just so dark." She shivered, doing her best to let it all go, I could tell. "So, anyway, what are you guys doing this weekend since you've been summoned?"

She had this way of changing the subject that I didn't like, but I didn't push. "A bar. Or more than likely, a strip club, it's where we do all our male bonding."

Kennedy rolled her eyes. "Strip club, huh?"

The green was hard to miss on her skin. *Possessive.* She wasn't the type of woman cool with her man going to a strip club.

Interesting. "Just something to do." I gave a lazy shrug as I grabbed a pan from under my stove. "Maybe you could hire someone to seduce your boy at his bachelor party."

She frowned. "He won't cheat on me. I don't know him that well, but I can tell he's a man of his word."

A faithful semi-abusive asshole? Huh.

I went about gathering items to make for our breakfast. Eggs, grits, toast, and some bacon for me.

"What's grits like?" Kennedy wanted to know.

"It's a Southern thing. My grandmother spent some time in the South. They're really good, I promise. Some people eat them with shrimp even," I said. "I like mine with butter, a little sugar, and shredded cheese."

"Okay," Kennedy said. "And your eggs?"

"I only really need salt and pepper for that," I admitted.

"Ah, you're one of those," Kennedy teased, earning a slap to her ass. She loved it, I could tell as she grinned and poked her ass out a little for more.

My mother seasoned her eggs more than I did, but some things for me were just fine with salt and pepper. Grits being another one.

I heated the stove and showed Kennedy how I liked my eggs, mostly over easy. How I liked to make bacon, sometimes in the oven, but the air fryer was quicker. And how to make a serving of grits.

Kennedy was like a sponge, soaking up my every word, even stepping in when it was time to flip the eggs. Whenever I was at the stove, she was close by. Even more, she had to touch me.

Her arms were around me, her cheek on my back, and it all felt so homey and right.

I stepped away to put space between us, only she followed.

Kennedy would be the death of me.

She was extra clingy, lingering on me like a second skin. And I didn't mind it as I covered where her arms locked with my hand.

"I should make you lunch," Kennedy said after we'd eaten breakfast.

I was at the sink, washing dishes. "No."

"Oh come on, it's the least I can do," Kennedy insisted. She was wiping down the table and focusing on the task.

A brewing headache ticked in my temple. I paused what I was doing, going and looking at her head-on. "We should talk."

Kennedy stopped cleaning and faced me. "Okay."

I shook my head. This had to be said. I had to put *me* first. I was the only one being burned in the end. "You said you wouldn't love me, but I never said I wouldn't love you. Don't leave your mark on me, it's not fair," I told her. Being vulnerable and honest was the only way to get my point across. "Staying the night, cuddling, making me lunch for work—it's too much."

"Should I go?" Her voice was small, and it crushed something in my chest.

"Fuck. No, just...try not to be too cute, okay?" I loosened up, tossing her a smile.

Kennedy padded over to me, her worried eyes looking up into mine. "I can't help but hug you. You feel good, Keith. I wish...I wish I could've met you sooner, to give you a fair shot. To not burden you by stringing you along."

But she hadn't met me sooner. She'd met me on the night she was running away from her fiancé and her engagement party. Oddly, Eden came to mind. She and her love of fairy tales. If this thing with Kennedy was written down, she'd be the princess and I'd be some guy in the background. *Star-crossed* was what they were teaching us before I'd dropped out.

Pessimism was hard to shake, but as I looked on at Kennedy, knowing and seeing that she meant her words, I allowed that dreamer's spirit to manifest some more. Who knew what the future could bring if fate existed.

I finished cleaning my kitchen and grabbed Kennedy's clothes from the dryer. She got dressed and upon seeing that it was chilly out that morning as we stepped out on the front step, I immediately came back inside and found a baby blue hoodie of mine in my closet and gave it to her. She removed that silly hat and pulled it on, smiling as she smelled my scent on the material.

And then, because she was still a brat, she came close, lulling her head back to gape up at me with a corny smile. "Goodbye, Keith."

Despite myself, I felt a corner of my mouth curl up. She thought she was slick. To get her back, quickly, I leaned down and caught her off guard as I gave her a fast peck on the lips. It hadn't been a second, but it was enough to send a jolt of electricity through my veins.

Kennedy's eyes widen. She'd felt it too.

"'Bye, Kenny," I said as I stepped back, needing her to leave first.

Her fingers brushed her lips. "'Bye, Keith."

She put her hat back on and went over to her Lexus. There was no missing the daze in her eyes as she got in behind the wheel. She shook it off, waving to me before she started up her car and backed out.

As her car disappeared down the street, I went over to my truck and got in. I could still feel her, smell her, and hear her as I drove for the garage. Images of her in my sheets, smiling over at me, reaching out for me, crossed my mind as I clocked in.

I had it bad and I already missed her.

19

Kennedy

Saturday came too quickly. All I wanted to do was stay in bed, cloaked under Keith's hoodie, but deep down, I knew I couldn't renege on my plans with Cain. He wanted a night in, and I knew he wasn't about to let me go back on my word.

Just because I wasn't putting up a fight, didn't mean I was going all in. No, to squash any semblance of my being interested in Cain, I went into my walk-in closet and found a black velour tracksuit by Shallow. After my shower, I slipped into the tracksuit and pulled my hair up into a ponytail. I doused myself with a little perfume and avoided any makeup beyond gliding lip balm across my lips.

And then the jitters set in, an icky sensation I couldn't shake. What if this was a trap? A lure to get me to his home where he wouldn't let me go? I already knew I'd never step foot in Vegas with him, because I was sure I'd never leave *un*married.

"You're overthinking," I told myself as I began to pace in front of my TV. No amount of coaching would stop my hands from shaking, however.

Ugh.

This man would send me into an anxiety-induced heart attack before we even said *I do*.

Knocking at my door startled me. It was five thirty. I guessed it was time to go.

I swallowed slowly as I advanced toward my door, unable to calm down even the slightest as I wrapped my hand around the knob. I unlocked the door with the other and pulled it open, at once breathing a sigh of relief at the sight of Beans on the other side.

One look at the large man in the way too big suit made me frown in pity. Someone needed to help him on the fashion side of things. It was odd, seeing how well-dressed Cain kept himself.

I poked my head out of my suite, scoping the background for signs of the man and his other bodyguard, Vino. Neither seemed to be in the vicinity, so I came back to Beans.

"Something wrong?" I asked.

Beans shook his head, his bored eyes peering down into mine. "Dice— *Cain* is putting some finishing touches on a project. I'll drive you to his spot."

My lips trembled and settled into a scowl. He couldn't even get me himself? For *his* date? "No thanks, tell him I'm sick."

Beans rolled his eyes, shaking his head. "You're not sick, and I never lie to D."

I folded my arms, attempting to take a stance. "Then what's his address? I'll drive myself."

Beans wasn't amused by this idea. "*I* am to escort you to Cain. You're not staying, and you're not driving. Don't make this any harder for yourself, Miss Nichols."

Cain didn't trust that I would bring myself to him? It was probably for good measure, because it was tempting to not go.

Curiosity got the better of me as I looked over at Beans. "You never lie, huh? What do you think of this arrangement?"

Beans shrugged indifferently. "He can do better."

My shoulders dropped along with my mood. "Yeah, forget I asked."

"He asked you out twice before and you shot him down," Beans went on. "I don't see the point in pushing the issue. Then again, Dice has a problem with rejection. He's been rejected his whole life, and I guess this is his way of fighting back."

I scoffed. *Someone play the tiniest violin.* "By forcing women into relationships? You're right, he could do better."

Beans scratched at his neck. "Don't disagree, but I don't work for you. Now, are you ready?"

There was no way out of this, was there? I went back into my suite and grabbed my Louis Vuitton and slipped it over my shoulder.

"All right, fine, if you insist," I huffed as I marched back over to the door.

Beans took a long look at me. "That's *all* you're taking? You don't want to pack an overnight bag?"

"I'm not staying the night," I let it be known as I stepped out into the hall and shut my door behind myself.

Beans made a face but didn't respond. "Suit yourself."

Ten reluctant minutes later, we were in his Charger driving toward wherever Cain lived. I gazed out the window at my home and city of Hampton Hills, taking in all that I'd ever known. With a population of over fifty thousand, many believed the Hills was a tranquil city. But how peaceful could it be if the likes of Cain lived here?

If you listened to propaganda, sometimes the media liked to paint cities like Bedford Heights as crime-ridden and dangerous, but I knew better. There were *good* people in bad neighborhoods, the same way there were *bad* people in good neighborhoods.

Turning to Beans, I sized him up, deciding he was loyal, but harmless. "So, he's just 'Dice' to you?"

Beans kept his eyes on the road as he responded. "He's been carrying those dice around since we were kids. Used to make all kinda stupid dares and bets with 'em."

"He's like a brother to you?" I wondered.

The car suddenly came to a stop. We were downtown, in front of a high-rise building that could easily stretch out of the stratosphere. The building was composed almost entirely of glass and metal. Its corners so sharp, I imagined bleeding if I dared to touch the surface.

"He *is* a brother to me," Beans said, drawing my attention back to him. "If I had to die for anything, I'd die for him."

Cain said he didn't have family, but Beans was the closest thing he'd ever known. I suddenly admired their bond, willing to stick their necks out for each other.

Valet came and Beans passed his keys over as another man helped me out of my side. People were entering and exiting Cain's apartment building, heading in for the night or out to enjoy it. A balloon full of anxiety blossomed in the pit of my belly as we stepped into the high-rise and soon boarded an elevator. I feared it would burst as we reached the top floor where of course Cain resided.

Like he did it all the time, Beans stepped off the elevator and headed over to Cain's door and unlocked it with a key. He pushed the door open and stepped to the side, making way for me to enter.

I set one foot in and gazed over at Beans. "So, he'll call you when I'm ready to go?"

Beans didn't hide his amusement as he headed back for the elevator. "Good night, Miss Nichols."

I didn't like the sound of that. I didn't like the implication that this would be a sleepover.

Having no choice, I faced Cain's home head-on.

I was standing in a foyer, hearing the faint sounds of jazz playing from deeper into the penthouse. The lights were dim, but I could just make my way inside as I closed the door behind me. Dark wooden floors were beneath my feet as I crept more into his home.

Black lacquer steps off the foyer led up to a second level. As curious as I was, I didn't take them but kept going to see the first floor itself. Something smelled good and delicious, and I suddenly wondered if Cain could cook.

Floor-to-ceiling windows surrounded me as I reached the

middle of the open space. To the right, was an entertainment area complete with a black sofa, matching chairs, a glass coffee table, all over a gray and black area rug. The sun was sinking in the sky outside. The buildings around Cain's were lit up with lights from homeowners. There was a bar beyond the sofa, made up of glass and offering the finest liquors and wine I was sure. The large TV was off, and underneath it I found the source of the music playing from a wireless speaker. An intricate gold light fixture hung overhead and I marveled at its beauty.

Taking a look to the left of the room, I immediately gasped. The next room housed a large kitchen and dining area. Cain was there, at the expansive island, straightening up a stack of plates. In front of him was an array of food.

As if feeling my stare, he looked up and spotted me. His eyes took in my clothing before settling on my gaze.

"Right on time," he said.

It was just the two of us. Scary. Intimate. Totally wrong.

Cain angled his head, gesturing to the food before him. "Come on, it just got here."

Grudgingly, I went closer, going and stepping up to the island and setting eyes on all the mouthwatering food spread out.

There was a tray of sushi, some California rolls and what looked like spicy tuna with spicy mayo on top. A large tray of shrimp pasta. Lobster. Oysters. Filets of salmon. And it wasn't entirely pescatarian. There was chicken, too. Something about the sight of it made me relax and warm up. I liked that he wasn't going to eat fish just for me. That he wasn't trying too hard.

"You ordered this, huh?" I asked as I dragged my eyes from the spread to Cain.

He came around the island, coming and standing next to me. His mere nearness unnerved me. His presence a heady cocktail of darkness and cold. He wasn't wearing a jacket, but still he was dressed in a fine white dress shirt and dress pants. His tie had been removed and a top button undone, giving me a peek at his chest.

Cain regarded the food and frowned, almost in a shy way. "I can't cook."

"Neither can I. You're not getting much of a wife from me, you know," I said.

Cain wasn't fazed as he moved along. "Not sure how I feel about gender roles, but I can deal with the whole no-cooking thing."

"Yeah?" I challenged, perking a brow.

"I've never had a homecooked meal before, so takeout is all I know," Cain admitted sheepishly.

"Really? Not even before your mom..." I stopped, letting the rest hang in the air.

He thumbed at his bottom lip. "Maybe, don't remember. She was kinda having a hard time."

I went back to the food. Despite myself, I was hungry. "Well, maybe you should learn someday. You never know what can happen."

Cain chuckled. "Not that you're wrong, but I always keep something in the ceiling. Just in case."

Just in case, whatever that meant.

Cain opened his arms out, gesturing toward his spread. "How'd I do?" There was a rare light on face, giving him youth.

"It doesn't completely suck," I managed to say.

He grinned, his perfect white teeth showing, as well as a dimple in each cheek. Young. Happy. And fresh. It was so weird he had a side like this.

"Let's eat," Cain instructed.

Eating provided a distraction, so I was quick to gather a plate and try some of the shrimp pasta and another of sushi. It was while grabbing the sushi that I noticed it.

There was a champagne flute filled with rose-gold liquid waiting for me at the table. I faced Cain. "What's in the flute?"

He eyed the dining room table where he set up a place for me and one for him. "White cranberry-peach juice."

"And how did you know I liked that? *And* the spicy tuna roll with spicy mayo?" I demanded to know.

My questions only served to humor Cain as he breezed by me and continued making his own plate.

He lifted and dropped his shoulder lazily. "I cheated, if that's what you want to hear. I asked Damon, and he provided me with some details of your favorite things to eat and drink."

Of course.

Annoyed, I grabbed my plates and walked them over to the table. It was cute how he set himself up on the end and my place adjacent, as if I wanted to enjoy a meal that close to him. I took and scooted my placemat down two spots.

"Don't." The authority in his tone sent my blood freezing in my veins.

I put the placemat back and sat down.

The sound of smooth jazz took over as we began eating. Whether I hated Cain or not, I couldn't deny that the food was good. The lemon garlic shrimp pasta was filling enough, but like a glutton I couldn't stop myself from enjoying the fresh sushi.

"Everything good?" Cain wanted to know.

"Mm-hmm." I hummed. "You ordered too much, though. It's all so tempting."

"Nah," Cain disagreed. "You can take some home, I can give some to my men, and I'll have food for the week."

He really did live on takeout. He must've religiously gone to the gym to keep his build.

There was only so much eating I could do, and because I was curious about his past, I turned and faced Cain eagerly. "So, I have some questions."

"I'm sure you do," he responded.

"Where'd you grow up?" I asked first.

Cain gathered his glass of wine and took a sip. "No place like this."

I looked around the area, noting the luxury and cleanliness.

Black was the overall theme of Cain's home. A cavern of gloom. It shouldn't have surprised me that he chose to live in the shadows.

"You *do* have a lovely home," I spoke up.

Cain bobbed his head. "My realtor all but begged me to never have children so they wouldn't fuck it up."

I almost laughed, but then I was curious again.

"Cain? How do you know James Carter was your father?" His mother died and he was placed in foster care. It didn't exactly add up.

Cain set his fork down, and all at once his expression went blank. "My mother was open with me on my paternity when I asked. Doesn't hurt that I look like the guy."

I would have to Google the late James Carter to confirm this.

"So when you were a kid you never met your father before...all this?" *Before he died and left you everything?*

Cain's finger tapped on the table momentarily. He caught the tick and reached up, swiping at his bottom lip. At his scar. "Once."

"Once?" I repeated.

Cain's posture tensed as he flickered his gaze over to me. "I don't have nice stories to tell."

I placed my hand over his. "It's okay."

Cain studied me thoughtfully before looking away and beginning his story. "So, I was about six, and we lived in this small house. My mother and I. I remember she was heating something up and I was playing under the kitchen table, and there was a knock at the door. She went to answer it and this angry voice started talking. It was him. He was yelling at her, telling her to stop calling his phone, to stop making things harder on herself. She was crying and telling him she was going to go tell his wife."

Cain didn't go on. He seemed lost in the memory. Lost and angry.

"Cain?" I pressed, wanting to know what happened next.

Slowly, he looked at me and a chill raced through me. In his empty eyes only blackness could be found. No regret. No emotion. Nothing. Just a hollowness that left me wondering if he had a soul.

He blinked and looked off, at nothing in particular. "The next thing I remember hearing is a loud slap and a squeak. I was still under the table, but I could see from their movement that he had her, was shaking her. He shook her real good and said his wife didn't talk to whores. He told her if she ever called him again he'd kill her.

"Right before he left, I poked my head out, to see him. He only took one look at me and snarled, asking me what I was looking at, before he stomped out of the house and slammed the screen door shut behind him."

Cain ran a hand down his face and shook his head, ridding himself of the past.

Of course he wasn't that simple.

The villain with the sad backstory.

James Carter had been an asshole. A cruel man who had cheated on his wife, abused his mistress, and abandoned his only heir, his son. Leaving his empire to Cain didn't make up for any of it, but I was sure it helped.

"You said you were in foster care. Were you able to keep anything of your mother's?" Being twelve, I couldn't imagine him having the sense to take what he could of hers. To always have a reminder.

Cain gave a stiff nod. "A few things. Others were...lost along the way."

Stolen.

Poor kid.

"Had my father been a man, perhaps I would've had a much different upbringing, a chance at something different," Cain said. "But I doubt I would've ever fit in."

No, not being born to a woman who wasn't James's wife. Other wives and girlfriends wouldn't have accepted Cain's mother, and there was the chance their kids would've picked up on it and taunted him.

"You don't belong in this world," I mumbled.

"I've never belonged," he said in a whisper, almost in defeat. But then he looked up at me, in a *what can you do* manner and let it go. "The side effect of being a bastard. I've paid for the sins of my father tenfold, and it's never enough."

It wasn't fair, but life often wasn't.

He hadn't wormed his way into my heart, but I could be nice after hearing a story like that.

I raised my flute of juice, offering a small smile. "Well, here's to making your own future and community."

Cain softened, smiling a little as he clinked his wineglass against my flute.

We finished dinner in a comfortable silence. We even managed to work as a team as we gathered the dishes to bring to the sink. Cain rinsed them before setting them in the dishwasher while I stood at the island closing containers and covering all the food.

"Geez." Cain's back was to me and I suddenly noticed he had a gun tucked behind himself.

He turned, catching my stare and putting together what made me uneasy. "You've gotta get used to it."

"Right, because it's my future," I said bitterly.

Cain grabbed a towel and dried his hands. He came over to me and I sucked in a breath, unsure what his motive was.

With his eyes on me, he reached back and grabbed his gun, going and holding it up in front of me. "I want you to hold it. Get used to the feel of it. We're going to teach you how to shoot one eventually."

I took a step back. "No."

Cain took a step forward. "Yes."

"Cain—"

In seconds, he removed the clip and released the bullet in the chamber with expert ease. Against my wishes, he came and placed the gun in my hand, turning me so that my back was to his front as he enclosed my hand around the handle.

The cold chrome in my hand made me shiver. This wasn't me. I never wanted to own a gun, much less shoot one.

"You have to be able to defend yourself," he whispered into my ear.

Across the room, our reflection could be seen in the large windows. The scene playing out was so foreign to me.

I whirled around, the barrel of the gun digging into Cain's chest. "Am...am I going to have to shoot at your enemies?"

Slowly, a smile washed across his face. His hand wrapped around his gun and he took it back, setting it on the counter beside us. Another step and he was right in my face, right against me.

His hand cupped my jaw and he tilted my head back. Soon, he was caressing my cheek, studying me as he ran his thumb over my lips.

Soft. His hand was incredibly soft. But I wasn't fooled. At any moment he could snuff the life out of me. The only thing keeping me from closing my eyes was the part of me that wanted him to see me, peer into my eyes as he stole more from me.

He didn't, though.

He stroked my lips with his thumb. "You don't have to be afraid, Wife. You'll always be safe with me."

I shook off his grasp and took a step back. "But I'm afraid of *you*."

I could never love Cain. Could never trust him either. Could never feel safe.

My thoughts must've radiated on my face, because Cain took a step back and buried his hands in his pockets. "I can live with that."

Bastard. "You'd rather be feared than loved."

He shrugged. "One's more useful anyway."

What kind of logic was that? "Have you ever loved a woman, Cain?"

He took another step away from me. "Despite it all, I loved my mother."

That was a given. "You didn't love those other women you dated?"

He shook his head.

"Did those women before me love you?"

As if this entire line of conversation was boring to him, he picked at a piece of lint on his arm. "They loved what I could do for them. How I fucked them."

It was clear, beneath the surface, he was longing for companionship. To be close.

"Have...have you ever been loved?" I wondered next.

Cain took a deep breath, his chest rising. "Doubtful."

"And you think *I* could love you?"

For a moment, he stared at me, straight into my soul. "No."

"But then—"

"At least we could give it an honest effort."

Against my better judgment, a part of my hate for him dissolved. "Ever consider therapy?"

Cain appeared thoughtful. "Therapy? Isn't that confidential? Whatever I say would stay between me and the good doctor?"

"Not unless you're considering harming yourself, or someone else," I clarified.

Cain *tsk-tsked* with a shake of his head. "Guess that won't work."

My spine stiffened. "So...you're planning on hurting someone?"

Cain almost smiled. "Running a casino is tough business, Kennedy."

"I can't fix you." It was true. I felt sorry for him, I did, but I wasn't enough for him. Whatever anguish he felt inside and pain he was running from couldn't be fixed by forcing my hand in marriage.

"I'm not aiming to be fixed," Cain stated with a hint of venom in his tone. "I'm not broken or cracked. I am who I am, and that's it."

We were getting nowhere. I hung my head and accepted it. "Okay."

"My turn." He was closer now, taking my hand and running his thumb across my knuckles. "You just refuse to wear your ring."

I snatched my hand back. "Why not make it a collar, since that's how it feels."

Cain dipped his head by my ear, saying in a low voice, "If I put a collar on you, Wife, you'd love it."

Gross. I shoved him back. "Never."

He grinned and stood straight. "When was the last time you had sex?"

Disgust had me moving further from him. I busied myself with pouring another flute of juice. "That's none of your business."

Cain whistled. "Actually, it is. Answer the question."

I took a swig of my juice and it went down heavy as the memory of riding Keith a few days ago enveloped me in a hot comfort I wanted to burrow in. Being on top was intense. He was so big and I had never felt so full.

"My sex life is none of your business, Cain," I shot back.

"I'm just curious. You broke up with the athlete two years ago. That was your last known relationship," Cain pointed out.

Glowering at him, I couldn't stop myself from spitting out, "What? Do you want to compare notes? Get ideas on how to please me?"

"When I fuck you, Kennedy, no one will ever compare," Cain said matter-of-factly.

A lump lodged in my throat and I struggled to swallow under his scrutiny.

"Easy." I forced myself to chuckle. "I still have a *choice* in that."

"Of course," Cain agreed.

"Besides, when was the last time *you* had sex?"

"It's been a while. For the sake of open communication, I've never had condomless sex and I've gone to the doctor and all is clear."

How responsible of him.

"Are you going to have strippers at your bachelor party?" I wondered.

"I'm not particularly interested in strippers," Cain admitted.

"Aren't there burlesque shows at the Cartier?"

"Yes, but it's not for me."

"Good to know." I took another swallow of my flute, keeping my face as even as possible. "It's been a while for me too."

"I hope you're not lying," Cain warned. "You don't seem like the type of person who could live with a man's blood on your hands. I don't think you have a conscience built for that." He let the message sink in before moving along. "But, humor me, what *do* you like in a man?"

Rough hands. Tattoos. Cigarettes. Eyes as angry as a wicked storm. "Respect."

"Respect is a two-way street that must be earned, but I hear you. Tonight, though, isn't going to end in a fairy tale. We've gotta build a foundation," Cain said as he grabbed some of the takeout containers and began storing them in his fridge. "I've been running around planning this construction project, in and out of meetings with your father and investors, and I'd really just like to relax."

I hated that my father was insisting on working still instead of leaving it all to Phil. "How's he doing?"

"Damon?"

I nodded.

"It can be tough for him to acknowledge his limitations, but he's good, determined. I don't like people, but I like your father. Phil's pretty okay, too," Cain admitted.

I narrowed my eyes. "Why? Why do you like my father?"

Cain shrugged. "His passion for this business is inspiring. The way he talks and plans things out, it's pretty nice. Not to mention, *how* he does business. There's a lot of cutthroat shit in the business world, but not Damon. He's good on pay and equal treatment. He's like a professor and I'm soaking it all in. Learning new tricks of the trade."

"I'd be impressed if he didn't stab me in the chest," I said dryly.

Cain's gaze cut to me. "It wasn't an easy choice. I wasn't interested in a joint venture or expanding beyond Vegas, but Damon and Phil were insistent. They *kept* coming to me. I was bullshitting when I threw out I'd consider the offer if he set me up with you—"

I held my hand up, stopping his soliloquy. "Please, spare me the story of your little pissing contest with my father over *my* future and life."

Cain let it go as he put the last tray into his fridge. He glanced at the time and then the TV in the next room before coming back to me. "*Crazy Rich Asians*, right?"

No. "How about *Scarface*? It's your favorite, isn't it?"

Cain came around the island and met up with me. "It's ultra-violent."

Even better. I wasn't interested in watching romance with him of all people. "That's okay, if it's your favorite, we can watch it."

Cain thought about it for a moment, and then he held his hand out for me to take. As much as I wanted to turn and run, I didn't. There was no escaping this man and the fate set out before me. So I placed my hand in his and went with him over to his sofa. The material was soft and cozy, inviting sleep almost instantly. I barely made it ten minutes into the movie before my eyes fell shut and I drifted away.

20

KEITH

The Cigar Room was located in downtown Bedford Heights. It was an exclusive men's only lounge on Sundays, akin to its sister bar The Lipstick Hub who hosted ladies' night on Fridays.

Sunday night I gathered around a black lacquer round table as I sat comfortably in a leather armchair talking amongst my boys I'd known since we was kids.

The room was dim as groups of men hung around other tables and booths. Some sat up at the bar, shooting the shit with the bartender or texting on their phones. In private rooms, other groups could be found holding exclusive poker games.

TVs hung up on nearly every wall in the large main space of The Cigar Room. Some were playing football highlights, and others were playing recaps of the latest NBA game.

I pulled my attention from the grueling defeat of the night's Lakers versus Pelicans match and shook my head.

The Lakers were letting me down this season.

At my table, Makai and Savon were engrossed in whatever Gavin had been saying. Makai was shaking his head and Savon was doing his best not to humor Gav—which let me know Gavin was on one.

"Look, all I'm saying is, if you're going to suck my dick in the morning, brush your teeth first," Gavin declared.

I managed a snort as the others let loose and laughed a little.

"Bruh, be happy any woman wants to go near that thing," Makai joked.

Gavin held his arms out, scrunching up his face. "So, I'm a bad guy because I want fresh breath on my shit? Nah, y'all just nasty."

Makai flipped Gavin the bird and Gav shrugged it off before taking a pull from his cigar.

Nights at The Cigar Room used to be a casual thing for our group. One person paid for the cigars and another person paid for the drinks and food. We rotated each trip to the lounge.

Tonight, Makai was sponsoring our cigars while I copped the drinks, D'Ussé for the guys and a beer for me.

At one point, our group had been bigger, with the added body of our friend DreSean. He'd gotten married and had a baby girl, and could only break free once in a blue moon. Whenever he could get out of the house, DreSean chose to do so with his wife for *date night*. Didn't blame him, he seemed content. I was happy for D.

Men's only night or not, that didn't mean the female staff of The Cigar Room didn't get to work. Our waitress came over and checked on our table as she issued out a round of smiles at all of us. When her gaze landed on me and lingered, I took the time to appraise her silently. Big beautiful natural coils, smooth butter pecan skin, and a cute smile as she gave me all of her attention.

"Can I get you anything?" she asked the table, but her eyes were on me.

Gavin picked up his Brandy snifter and swirled around its contents. "Nah, I'm good over here."

Makai waved her off as well. "I gotta work in the a.m., can't have too much fun."

"Heard you," Savon agreed as he raised his remaining D'Ussé in a toast.

On her perky cleavage, our waitress's name badge could be found. *Trish.*

I tipped my head toward her, letting her know I was good as well.

"Well, if you need anything, just give me a holler," she said before she walked away.

I took a pull from my medium-bodied cigar that was a pleasant mixture of spices, nuts, and cedar. As much as I wanted to quit smoking, I *needed* this. A certain someone was on my mind and they shouldn't have been.

The silence caused me to look up, finding my boys staring at me.

"What?"

Gavin smirked, looking past me at something in the room and coming back. "She was givin' you the signal."

Chancing a look over my shoulder, I spotted Trish at the bar collecting drinks for her other tables and sneaking a peek my way. When our gazes collided, she grinned before turning back to the bartender.

I focused back on my table and shrugged. "So?"

"*So?*" Makai repeated in surprise. "She cute."

She was, but I wasn't biting.

It wasn't serious, but I found myself saying, "I'm sorta... *involved* with someone right now."

Gavin snorted. "Duh."

Confused, I angled my head. "What's that mean?"

Gavin looked around the table before coming back to me. "I mean, I figured you was knockin' down something new and she wasn't lettin' you out."

"That's how April's ass had me in the beginning. She was on some vampire shit, had me all the way drained," Makai said with a shake of his head.

"So you married her?" Savon challenged.

"Oh, most definitely," Makai was quick to agree. He turned to me and pointed with his cigar. "We ain't seen you since you and Leila broke up. Now you got this new one."

I scratched at my jaw, debating over being open with them about my regression after my split. "I won't lie, I was heavy in my feelings over her."

Gavin sympathized with me, reaching out and squeezing my shoulder. "Y'all was locked in for a minute. Sometimes it takes time to get back to you and recalibrate after that."

"Exactly," Makai said in support.

"It took a minute to let it go," I didn't deny. "This new situation isn't serious, but she cool."

A nasty taste coated my tongue at *that* description of Kennedy.

"Ain't nothing wrong with a little fun," Gavin said.

I was past that stage of my life where I was fucking women because I could. Stability and closeness were what I was after. Something that mattered. A bond.

"I don't know," I admitted. "I think I'm too old for this shit. I wanna...buy her flowers, go for a walk, and *talk* to her, see how she's dealing with her family issues." I took a swig of my beer. "But I can't. I'm just the guy she calls when she wants some dick."

Gav looked at Makai who looked at him. Gavin swung back my way as if I were being stupid. "So, you're living the dream?"

The group burst into laughter and I loosened up and chuckled.

If only it was that simple. The sex was good. I loved the way Kennedy had her reservations, but was willing to drop them when I pushed just right. How she was letting her guard down and becoming comfortable with me.

That silly little dance of hers lived rent-free in my head some nights.

"It's...complicated," I said carefully.

A knowing gleam passed through Makai's eyes. "She got a man?"

Savon quietly watched me, and I felt an itch I couldn't scratch.

I sat up and took another pull from my cigar, needing that rush of nicotine in my veins.

All eyes were on me, the music in The Cigar Room all but forgotten as well as the scene around us.

Blowing out some smoke, I nodded. "She's spoken for."

Gavin snorted and shook his head. "Even better."

"She's not happy," I went on.

Gav was doubtful. "You fumblin' the play, man." He faced our friends in disappointment. "Next thing you know he gon' be listenin' to that moody, depressed R&B shit. Be out here singin' side-nigga blues," he joked, causing the table to roar with laughter. "Sick Wit' it Records."

Even I could laugh at myself with how pathetic I sounded moping over Kennedy. Still, something bitter lingered at the back of my throat, not going away the more I spoke these words out loud.

"Whatchu think, Von?" Makai asked, noting that Savon hadn't said much since the topic had switched to my love life.

Savon knew me most, was my closest friend. If anyone needed info on me, they'd hit him up first.

Savon shrugged, tossing back the rest of his D'Ussé. "He ain't even tell you the killin' part."

Both Makai and Gavin faced me, wanting to know the missing piece to the puzzle.

I sat back and rolled my eyes. "Her dad's got a lot of money. He set her up with this guy and once they get married, they'll probably be the blogs' new favorite power couple or some shit."

Makai's brows furrowed in confusion. "What's her name?"

I shook my head, not wanting to expose Kennedy.

"She's got a *big* name," Savon added.

Intrigue covered Gavin's face. "So, you can Google her?"

I nodded. Though, I hadn't done so. Wasn't sure I wanted to

see the face of the guy she was tethered to. Didn't want to make it realer than it already was.

"How big we talking?" Makai asked next.

I kept my face even, not wanting to react to the facts as they were highlighted before me. "A billionaire's daughter."

Makai and Gavin made matching stank faces as they whistled. In Bedford Heights, situations like this never happened. Not everyone was poor or struggling, but no one was a millionaire, let alone *billion*aire.

"So, she's legit, and all she wants from you is to pipe her down?" Gavin grabbed his snifter and raised it in appreciation. "Shit, that's the goal."

Again, maybe when I was younger. Now, I didn't think with my dick so much.

Makai yawned and checked his smartwatch. "I need to head in. It's past my bedtime."

"You mean it's past your *curfew*," Gavin teased as he downed the rest of his liquor. "You know April don't let you out after the streetlights turn on."

At that we were laughing once more.

I dapped up Gav and Kai and promised to link up again with them sometime in the future. In the parking lot, I saw them off as they climbed into their separate rides and pulled out of The Cigar Room's lot.

I hung back with Savon as he stood at his Bronco. Unlike Gavin and Makai, he wasn't about to mock me. As he studied me from behind his lens, I saw nothing but sympathy and understanding.

"Do you think you're fucked?" Von wanted to know sincerely.

Oh, I was, but I wasn't ready to admit it just yet.

I'd wanted to kiss her—not because she was half naked on my bathroom counter, not because she'd owned me when she went down on me, not because she rode me slow and stole my soul— but because of that fucking hat.

When I agreed to let her come through to do yardwork with me, I wasn't expecting her to show up in her usual conversative gear, but I didn't see the gardening outfit coming either. The hat may have been overkill, but it fit her. Made her look cuter than she was already beautiful.

It was non-sexual, and I wanted to kiss her, to wrap her in my arms, and crush her mouth with mine.

Suffice it to say, outside of the sex...I liked her.

I wasn't one of those people who got caught up in all that *soul-ties* talk, but there was something about Kennedy. Her inexperience. Her trust in me. How natural it felt when we were together.

My mind was flush with the image of her running her soft hands up my chest. Her kissing my tattoos. Her cradling my face in her palms as she came on top of me.

"*Keith!*" she'd whined for me, calling out my name as her body shook against mine. Wrapping her arms around me and holding me close for comfort as pleasure washed over her.

I thought about her slipping my T-shirt on, padding barefoot out to my kitchen to learn to cook breakfast the way *I* liked. She stole smiles at me the whole morning, blushing and radiating this glow. She'd looked so proud when she properly flipped her eggs for over easy. She'd never had grits before, or apple butter. Thursday morning in my kitchen she greedily ate slice after slice of toast covered in apple butter after realizing she liked it. Even more, she decided she liked her grits the same way I liked mine after eating from my bowl.

Only when she got dressed to go did she come down from cloud nine and lose her spirit.

Outside of the sex, I caught myself slipping and wanting to kiss her for other things.

I wanted to teach her everything under the sun. Be her only source of knowledge. But that wasn't enough. *I* wanted to learn her just as well. Learn her body, every curve, every pulse, every spot. Learn what made her laugh, smile, scowl—learn what made Kennedy tick and operate the way she did.

It was pathetic. I knew what it tasted like between her legs, yet I wouldn't kiss her. Maybe I was punishing both her and myself for this ridiculous agreement we had.

"Careful, man," Savon seemed to warn. "I don't want you getting caught up and she just be using you for a taste of the wild side."

I quickly shot that down. "It doesn't seem like that with her. She's not some stuck-up rich girl trying to have a little rebellion. The way she looks at me...it's like she sees the world."

Savon clasped my shoulder. "You better leave her now, because once you're in it then you're gone."

He was right. We couldn't get in it—at least *I* couldn't afford to.

"Heard you." I slapped my palm against his before reeling him in close for a hug goodbye.

My phone began ringing as I walked over to my Tahoe. As late as it was, a tremor of panic ran through me. Phone calls in the middle of the night were never any good.

My panic dissolved when I pulled my phone from my pocket to see that it was Kennedy calling.

It was almost midnight. She could only want one thing. As tired as I was, I might've been willing to give it to her.

I answered her call before she hung up. "Yeah?"

"Keith?" She sounded nervous. Uncertain. Shy.

"Is this a booty call?" I asked as I leaned against my truck and rested on the hood.

"No!" Kennedy was quick to say. "This...is me breaking the rules."

That was all we'd done from the beginning. "What do you need, Kenny?"

"God, your voice," she breathed out. "What are you doing?"

"Leaving a bar."

"And getting into a Lyft, right?"

I chuckled. "I'm not drunk."

"Keith."

"I just had a couple of beers. Nothing too heavy."

"Keith."

Damn she was bratty. "I'm not. Can't risk losing the one appendage you care about."

She scoffed on her end. "I care about you, too, you oaf!"

A corner of my mouth threatened to curl up. "Why I gotta be all that?"

"Keith... Just, drive slow, okay?"

I groaned. "You not my girl to be telling me what to do, you know."

"If I'm fucking you, you're mine, remember?"

Wasn't my exact words, but whatever. "Uh-huh."

"Please." She was begging now, her soft tone giving way to how worried she was over me. Just like I'd been at the thought of her driving home to Hampton Hills sleepy.

I stopped being an ass and sighed. "I'll drive slow, for you, okay?"

"Call me when you get in," Kennedy instructed.

We hung up and I got in behind the wheel. Almost immediately I found myself yawning and squeezing my eyes shut to let the feeling pass through me. Thankfully, it was a quick five-minute trip back to my crib.

Instead of calling Kennedy back right away, I went and took a quick shower first. I didn't have to work until noon Monday, and I was planning on enjoying every bit of sleeping in.

But I always kept my word, so as I lay back on my bed, I pressed the button on Kennedy's contact for a FaceTime call. We'd never done this, but I was fucked enough to admit I didn't just want to talk to her, but I wanted to *see* her, too.

She answered me and I got a glimpse into her world as I spotted her sitting on her bed as well. She had a plush beige-colored headboard and cream-colored silk sheets. She herself was wearing a low-cut royal blue nightgown with a matching satin scarf on her head. The curves of her breasts were visible, and I loved the way the blue complemented her skin.

Kennedy took one look at me and smiled. "You made it in safe."

I bobbed my head, feeling a blanket of sleep approaching. "I did."

Kennedy went and laid on her side, propping her head up with her arm. "So, a bar instead of the strip club?"

"Maybe next time," I said lazily.

She narrowed her eyes at me. "Next time, huh?"

"*You* won't strip for me."

Kennedy chewed on her lip, taunting me. "Is that what you want?"

Maybe at some point, but my mind wasn't entirely interested at the moment. "We'll see," I said as I rolled on my side and got more comfortable to look at her. "How was it with your boy?"

Kennedy frowned and shrugged. "It was okay. He's kinda sad, you know? His whole life story is pretty sad. I just hope he can come to realize I can't make anything better for him. That he deserves something real and someone better."

There wasn't a thing wrong with Kennedy. I couldn't imagine this guy topping her in the *better* department, but I didn't bother voicing it. "How was your day?"

Kennedy looked up toward her ceiling as she began describing her morning and afternoon. "Well, I fell asleep at his place. This morning we had breakfast and I had lobster and eggs, which was to die for. And then I went home and did some yoga. I talked to my dad for a little, and then I spent the day browsing recipes I wanna try to make. I actually want to go out and—"

"You look beautiful," I cut off her rambling and let her know.

She stopped talking and blushed, a glow in her eyes as she again bit her lip. "Thank you."

"So, when do you want to get together to learn these recipes?" I asked.

All at once Kennedy's mood sank as she lost her smile. "Actually, I...I think we should cool it for a while."

I didn't let her rejection faze me. "Okay, what's a while?"

"Maybe just a week," Kennedy said nervously.

She seemed off. As if a switch had been flipped. "What's up?"

She looked down at her sheets, refusing to look at me. "I haven't been...entirely truthful with you, Keith."

"I'm listening." And I was. Wide awake now.

Her sad eyes flickered to me onscreen. "That day after we met, I went home and had lunch with my fiancé."

"Uh-huh," I said when she didn't go on.

"H-He made some threats." Her voice was unsteady. "He said if I ever slept with another man, he'd kill him."

I squinted, wondering just who the fuck she was dealing with. Because that was a huge red flag. "And what did he say about you?"

Kennedy looked at me incredulously. "He's not going to hurt *me*. I'm worried about going out too much and establishing a pattern."

I wasn't convinced. It was nothing to brush off her fiancé's threat toward me. What bothered me was the fact that Kennedy didn't seem to see the bigger picture. That she must've trusted him, too, as if he'd only be a problem for me and not her.

"What did he say to you, Kennedy?" I demanded to know.

She shrank. "He'd keep me barefoot and pregnant so I would be too busy to stray."

What the fuck?

I gritted my teeth and squeezed my fist shut. "And this is what you want to deal with?"

"No!" She was quick to say.

"Your pops cool with a dude talkin' to his daughter like this?" I went on.

I could see tears welling in Kennedy's eyes and I knew I'd pushed too far. She looked away and wiped at a tear that had slid down her cheek. "I was upset with Cain after that. He actually apologized the next time he saw me and said he'd never do it. But he meant it about killing anyone I stepped out on him with. I just... I want to keep you safe."

"I'm already ready to beat his ass."

"He has a gun."

"So do I."

Kennedy's fear and unease was palpable.

Her martyrdom only served to annoy me. She was in a fucked-up situation and she was only worried about my safety.

My chest tightened at the reality and my rage lessened a degree.

Fuck, I couldn't get in it again. Not with this woman. She'd never be mine.

I forced out a sigh. "A week, huh?"

Pitifully, Kennedy nodded. "Just a week or so."

Or so. "Okay."

"I'll miss you," her soft voice swore.

I needed to just let her go. Tell her I was through with this. Let her go off and meet someone else.

But the thought of someone else having her, touching her, *teaching* her, made my stomach hurt.

This situation was both maddening and sickening, and I should've walked away for my own good.

I did no such thing.

"Yeah," I said before I ended the FaceTime call.

Feeling restless and stressed, I climbed out of bed and went out for a cigarette.

21

Kennedy

MY MOTHER WANTED TO GO OUT FOR LUNCH, JUST THE two of us girls. It had been a while since we'd gotten any alone time. The betrayal and engagement were a fresh wound, leaving us distant. But Tuesday afternoon when she called me up and asked to take me out I found myself indulging her.

This strife between my parents and me was hard to navigate. I loved my parents. Being on the outs with them felt foreign, especially given my father's health. As I sat across from my mother at our favorite brunch spot, the one on Townsend Boulevard where all the best shopping was located, I felt my heart throb at what was. They had never disappointed me as much as they had now with this marriage arrangement.

I thought if Cain wasn't so horrible, instead a well-meaning, awkward heir, then perhaps I could've seen the harmlessness in their insisting I marry the man. But no. Cain wasn't any of those things. Confident. Poised. Quiet. Enigmatic. Cain could only be summed up so succinctly.

My mother didn't share the same diet as I did, but for brunch at The Cabana Lounge, we shared a vegetarian Cobb salad. She limited herself to one mimosa since she was driving instead of having one of her and my father's drivers drive for us.

Mimosas were okay, but I opted for the Cabana's house fresh juice. A fruity blend of guava, pineapple, mango, and orange. It was delicious.

"Ugh." My mother suddenly breathed out as we continued to eat from our large salad. "I'm so glad we did this, you know? I *needed* this, Kenn."

I lifted my attention from poking at an avocado. My mother was opening up to me, peeling back a layer of her perfection to reveal her true state: exhausted, nervous—scared.

"It's been a long, lonnng, year," she went on as she looked off absentmindedly. "And your father..." She shook her head, her brows furrowing at the thought of my father. "He's a trooper, I'll give him that. I just wish he wouldn't fight me. I only want to help."

That sounded like my father. He was a man's man, from an era where men didn't show weakness and were taught to be resilient and strong. Allowing himself to be taken care of by health officials was hard enough, letting my mother see him wince and moan was another thing. I just wished he knew that we loved him and didn't think less of him in his condition. That we admired him for his strength and fight.

Strangely, just then, Keith came to mind. Something about him, reminded me of my father. He was a man's man, too, and I could imagine he wouldn't let me see him "weak" either.

I thought of the way he admitted he was sensitive and managed to smile. That took courage.

"It's good to get away," I said as I came back to my mother. "I think we've all been pretty consumed with Daddy's diagnosis and hoping for a miracle, that it's nice to step outside and breathe."

My mother was quick to agree. "I just feel like we're finally adjusted, you know? We've got a good team looking after him, he still can run his businesses with Phil, and Irene is great. I gotta get back on the ball. I'm so behind on the charity events around here. I've never been out of the loop on that. Never."

My mother was very philanthropic. One of her passions was

organizing charity events and donating money to noble causes. I liked to think that she was where I got my heart from. Some people in Hampton Hills were snobby, turning their noses up on anyone from a household that didn't bring in over a million a year. Not Angela Nichols. She hadn't come from a humble beginning, giving her a direct link to understanding the working class, but she was very much human.

"You've had your hands full. It's understandable," I reasoned.

"That I have," my mother said as she picked up her mimosa and took a sip. She didn't take time to reflect on her next few words. She said them as if they required little to no thought at all. "Sometimes I wish I could trade places with him."

My heart sank as tears threatened to pool in my eyes. "Mom."

She waved me off, smiling a little at my emotion. "I love that man. When we got married, we became one. I'm not sure I ever want to see a day where I'm just a *half*."

"You won't." My voice cracked and I blinked to get my vision straight.

My mother reached out and dabbed at my eyes. Her gentle touch was all I needed to feel okay and safe.

"Hey, we're not here to cry and ruin our faces," she joked.

We were out on the town, but I wasn't wearing makeup. My hair was even pulled up in a ponytail. But swollen red eyes was a look I wasn't going for.

I pulled myself together and ate another forkful of salad. "You're right. This salad is so good. I think I might order a soup for a side."

As I gave The Cabana Lounge's menu a quick browse, I was suddenly stumped between the salmon soup or...

"Do you like grits?" I couldn't keep the smile off my face as I asked my mother the silly question. "I had some recently, and I love them."

Keith had us make the pan of grits plain so that I could choose my own recipe for how I liked them. In the end, like a little kid following their older sibling, I copied how he made his bowl and decided that was how I liked mine as well. Salt and pepper, a dash of sugar, butter, and shredded cheddar cheese. Between the grits and his introduction to apple butter, I had true incentive to make breakfast at home now that I could cook *something*.

My mother peered down at her menu and shook her head. "Don't think I've ever had grits before." She glanced back at me. "Don't eat too much. Your father and I scheduled a cake tasting for later. We can go after we leave here. We just want to get everything squared away."

Just like that, my mood dropped.

I set my menu aside and focused back on the salad, barely tasting it now.

"He misses you," my mother said gently. "He really does, Kenn. This whole thing has been hard on all of us, and I won't lie, I was mad at first about this marriage, too. You're our only child, and we shouldn't put *this* on you."

"So don't," I spoke up.

We both knew there was no pulling the plug, even at this early stage in my journey down the aisle.

"I wish it could be that simple. I really do," my mother said. She sat back, defeated in her own way. "Don't get me started on Cain. When Damon first brought this up, I thought he'd lost his mind. That he was really trying to marry you off to some...*creep*. But then, as I come around Cain...I kinda feel sorry for him. His father—James was an awful, awful man."

That I couldn't deny, even if I didn't care for Cain himself. Hearing how he'd abused Cain's mother in front of him when he was a little boy was heartbreaking. Being raised in secret had to have been painful enough on its own.

My mother came back to the table and forked her salad. "I think he just wants a family. And I can't blame him. He has no mother or father."

"Why don't you and Daddy adopt him? I'd rather have a brother than a husband." I asked with a fake sincere smile on my face.

To that my mother managed to snort as she ate more of her salad. But then she was serious as she regarded me thoughtfully. "You're seeing someone else."

Four simple words sent my throat closing up on me. "E-Excuse me?"

My mother observed me thoroughly. "You were glowing. You looked beautiful—you *are* beautiful. The first thing I noticed when you got into the car was how radiant you looked. I thought you and Cain finally figured each other out, but just now when I mentioned the wedding your mood dropped."

I scoffed. "I can't be 'glowing' because I'm happy?"

My mother smirked, calling me out. She went back to her mimosa. "I won't say anything."

Her discretion caused me to lower my guard. "No?"

She shook her head, a sad smile on her face. "Make sure you end it before you get married."

Stiffly, I nodded, already having accepted my fate with Keith. "I know."

Her hand covered mine and squeezed. "I don't want this for you. I keep hoping Damon will come to his senses. You deserve to be happy and make your own choices with your love life. Whether we like Cain or not."

They liked Cain. He'd finagled his way into my parents' graces, despite our sham engagement.

I looked around the vicinity. We were seated on the outdoor veranda. A few older couples were nearby, as well as a lone businesswoman reading the newspaper, and a man tapping away on a MacBook. The world around us was going on and I had to get a move on to flow with it.

"Maybe...I'll learn to like Cain." I wouldn't. I wasn't a romantic. Never stressed having the proverbial "fairy tale," but I would never get over the way Cain came into my life. We would never be a love story. He *acquired* me. There was no prettying that up.

"Maybe we should get together with the girls and reach out to

LeChé. She's impossible to get a hold of in the winter, so it's best to book her now in advance," my mother brought up next.

LeChé Harris was a renown wedding dress designer. She had a shop in Hampton Hills, though she herself was often away on call. Only the best worked at LeChé's boutique, but if you wanted the signature LeChé wedding gown, you went to her directly.

Hampton Hills was full of places to shop, exclusive dining, esteemed businesses, and beyond all that capitalism could ever dream of, there were the pristine homes. It was a city that rarely slept. As everyone was constantly on the clock to keep up with their lifestyles. It wasn't a surprise LeChé was booked so far out. If I wanted to get my hands on the best dress for my wedding, I needed to get ahold of her *now*.

I'd always had a dream wedding dress in mind for the day I walked down the aisle. Something classic and royal. Off-the-shoulder with an extravagant cathedral train. Maybe off-white, or nude, instead of the traditional white.

It had been a dream of mine ever since I was a little girl and had the biggest collection of Black Barbie dolls.

Cain was the furthest thing I'd ever pictured for my groom.

"Yeah," I said bitterly. "We should get on that."

We finished most of our salad and then we only had to walk further up Townsend Boulevard to the bakery. Right away I felt my lunch threatening to come back up as I spotted the CLOSED FOR SPECIAL PARTY sign on the front door.

"Kennedy?"

A young voice reached my ear and turned me around to see a couple of teenage girls approaching me. By the Guess bags in their hands I could see they were on a shopping venture.

One girl with lavender box braids had her mouth open, exposing teeth covered in braces.

Her friend with Bantu knots managed to hold her composure as she shyly waved at me.

"Can I have a picture?" the one with the braids asked. "I follow you on Instagram. You're so pretty. Oh my God."

While I didn't think I was worthy of "fans," I never turned down a photo. When I'd done a brand deal with an up-and-coming urban cosmetics line, it had sold out in hours thanks to my loyal following. People were nice enough to support me, and the least I could do was smile for a camera to make someone's day.

My mother played photographer as I stood in between the two girls and pasted on a fake smile that said I was the luckiest girl in the world.

They bought it.

Only when they were long down the sidewalk did I let my mask slip and my true misery take over.

"Your father made sure we had the shop to ourselves as you picked out the flavor you wanted," my mother clued me in as we approached the front door to Piece of Cake!

Smart.

Going out with Cain was a nightmare when it came to the media. Thank God I didn't see any cameramen.

We entered the shop and right away the owner, Michele, greeted us with a warm smile.

"Hello! Party for Nichols, right?" Her cheery face made me feel terrible for my mood.

She'd made a thing of this event. On a series of tables were platters of cake wedges. Craning my neck, I could see cards placed before each plate to illustrate the flavor. There were colorful flowers arranged and set up, as well as a sign reading WELCOME, KENNEDY & CAIN!

I didn't think I could eat a bite.

Behind us, the shop's door opened and in walked my fiancé. More, he held the door open and my father was soon wheeling himself in on an electric wheelchair.

Daddy.

This was the first time I'd seen him outside of the house since walking became a challenge for him.

Immediately I rushed over to him at the same time my mother did.

"What are you doing?" I demanded to know as I shooed Cain away.

My father sat dressed in a fine suit, happy to see me and my mother. He used the chair's controller to wheel himself more into the shop. The grin on his face was such a rarity, I thought I'd cry.

"I was at the office. Wanted to see how things are going with the blueprints. Wanted to feel useful. Alive," my father stated simply. He turned the chair and eyed Cain. "And then I mentioned the cake tasting to Cain, and he insisted we come. Said I can't dedicate my life to hotels, not when an important moment is happening for my daughter."

My mother looked on at Cain, glassy eyed. He remained neutral as he stood back by the entrance. Outside, beyond him, I could see Beans and Vino keeping look out.

Thank you, my mother mouthed to Cain.

He tipped his head toward her and kept quiet. We'd been trying to get my father to leave his bed for months, and he seemed content on staying there. As much as I hated Cain, I was grateful for him in that moment.

"So, who's ready to eat some cake?" my father asked jubilantly.

My mother patted her middle. "None for me, I'm watching my figure."

"Hey!" my father snapped loudly in a commanding voice. "That's my job."

My mother laughed and shushed my father. He wheeled further into the bakery over to Michele to introduce our party and my mother wasn't far behind.

I kept back with Cain. Unable to process it all.

He turned so that his whole body was facing me, somehow managing to block out our surroundings entirely. "He needs this. To feel something other than his own pity."

Cain was right. It was important my father live his life. To leave the confines of his bedroom and be out in the world. He couldn't let ALS have him. He couldn't let the disease win.

To think, all it took was this heinous man to get him to see that.

I ducked my head. "Thank you for doing this, Cain."

"Don't mention it." Cain peered past us. "Well, let's eat some cake."

Michele came and greeted the two of us, shaking our hands and complimenting how "nice" we looked together. I played my part and smiled and clung close to Cain to appear as in love as the world thought we were.

My parents kept their distance as they settled at a table on the far side of the room and sampled different cakes while Cain and I sat together at a table browsing cake wedges. The spread was lovely, as Michele had model cakes set up to show her skills as a baker. I always admired gorgeous gourmet cake tiers, but at the same time, I always felt guilty for ruining such works of art.

To my surprise, Cain seemed to be enjoying the dessert as he tried a slice of several cakes.

"Sweet tooth?" I wondered.

He nodded, smiling a little. "Oh yeah. It's my one weakness."

"What's your favorite?"

My eyes were deceiving me, or Cain was...*blushing*. He peeked back at me. "Honeybuns."

Honeybuns. The name was familiar. "Not sure I've ever had one."

Cain shook his head and cut into a slice of vanilla bean cake with triple mousse icing. "Delicacy."

I was curious, but I said no more as I dug into my own cake. Lemon coconut cake with lemon curd and French vanilla filling. It was amazing. "Do you like the lemon coconut one?"

Cain wrinkled his nose and eyed my cake. "Not a fan of coconut."

"No?"

"Reminds me of fingernails," Cain said as he made a claw with his hand.

Interesting. At that, I perked up. "I think I found the cake I want for our wedding."

Cain met my grin with a raised brow. "Okay."

He wasn't going to put up a fight. Completely ruining my fun. "Which one do you like the most?"

Cain took his cloth and wiped at his mouth before taking a drink of water Michele provided for us in wineglasses. "The almond cake."

That was my second favorite. It had raspberry filling and French vanilla icing.

"What are we going to serve our guests to eat besides the cake?" I pressed next.

Cain sat up, turning and facing me. He tapped his finger on the table, thinking deeply. "Salmon alla Griglia for one entree option, and either grilled chicken or steak for the second."

It was like he had an answer for everything. I hated it. The thought of this wedding and marriage being very much real made me sick to my stomach.

I fingered the white tabletop before us. "All right."

Cain returned to his cake, and it really was a wonder watching him eat. He'd try a new flavor and smile to himself at the taste. Something that wasn't a big deal to me, was a lot to him. He'd never experienced a life of having an open channel for desserts before, making me question his foster parents and their approach to his diet. He sat beside me a tall and lean man, muscular, but not too much.

"Was your time in foster care all bad?" I asked.

Cain cut into a slice of red velvet cake, my least favorite due to how rich it often was. "Yes."

I wasn't a cruel person. I didn't have it in me to not feel horrible for how he'd grown up and what he'd gone through.

"The best home I stayed at was only for a night, and then the rest were different versions of hell." He suddenly shrugged as if it were not a big deal. "But don't feel bad. It motivated me in a lot of ways. I grew from the experience."

"I feel like you'd benefit if you talked to someone, expressed yourself openly and honestly," I said softly, trying to be gentle so he wouldn't lash out.

Cain's gaze cut to me. "Don't ask me questions if you're just going to analyze me."

I should've backed down, but I couldn't let him walk all over me. I couldn't let him win. "That's what marriage is, Cain. Knowing your spouse through and through. We're literally strangers to each other."

"You come from a castle, and I come from the very bottom," Cain pointed out. "You've never had to do the things I have to survive. Your parents loved and tucked you in. I was born in secret and treated like a mistake. You can't handle my truth, and I'd rather spare you the details than have your pity."

I didn't mean to pity him. His turnaround was legendary, overcoming his adversity and becoming one of the richest men in the West was a story of a champion. But there was no mistaking the fact that he wasn't happy. That something was missing behind his eyes. Whatever that was, *I* couldn't fill that void. He deserved true love, someone who wanted him, the good, the bad, and all the ugly. And that just wasn't me.

"Cain," I started, trying to stay calm and not have a panic attack. "What if...we didn't get married? What if we just became friends and got to know each other? Who knows, you might not even *like* me in the end."

Cain took my hand, going and adjusting his ring I was wearing. He lifted his eyes to mine. "If I say yes, then what?"

I couldn't believe he was considering it. That he'd give me an out. "Then we'll be friends. *Best* friends if you want."

A corner of his lips quirked up. But then he was shaking his head. "I say yes, and then you play along for who knows how long before you suddenly meet someone else? And then I'm left with nothing, but a *best* friend?

"I left my last ex because I found out she was trying to get pregnant. I lost trust." He ran his thumbs over my knuckles. His soft touch always such a paradox to who he was as a person. "I'd hate to lose my trust in you, Kennedy."

"Y-You trust me?" Surprise filled my voice at the revelation.

Cain nodded once. "Every day I don't receive a phone call from one of my friends at the HHPD, I'm a little more impressed with you. Do I know *every*thing about you? No, but I like what I see and know so far. I'm anticipating the rest." He scooted closer. "So stop trying to get out of this marriage, because it's happening, Wife."

The finality in his words let me know there was no escaping him. His admission to having friends at the local police station let me know there was no stopping his wrath. No calling for help. There was no way out.

Cain Carter really owned me.

He reached into his pocket and procured those familiar clear red dice. "Let's just see how the dice roll, okay?"

"Okay," I accepted.

For show, Cain released the dice onto the table with a subtle flick of his wrist.

He hadn't even tried and he'd rolled a seven.

22

KEITH

BOYS ALL AROUND THE GYM WERE EITHER SHOOTING hoops or studying. Except one.

Dominique was sitting on a bleacher by himself when I approached him. He was texting on his phone. The goofy grin on his face let me know he was more than likely talking to a girl.

"'Sup?" I asked as I took a seat next to him.

He jumped. His eyes enlarged as he whipped his head in my direction. "Come on, bro. Don't be doin' that."

Looking at Dominique head-on, I could see bags under his eyes from lack of sleep and an uneasiness about him.

Something was up, but I couldn't dive in just yet. I could tell by the way he was eyeing me that his guard was up and he wasn't about to come out and tell me he was in trouble.

"Shouldn't you be workin' on homework?" I brought up as I gestured to the guys who had their heads in their books.

Dom peered at the other kids around us and shrugged, not interested. In fact, I didn't even see his backpack in sight. "I'll do it tonight."

"Why can't you do it now?" I asked.

Dom faced me, a crooked grin on his face suddenly. "I'm talkin'."

"Oh yeah?"

He held his phone out, and on screen I caught a glimpse of his Instagram page. It was full of shots of him smoking weed, flashing the middle finger, holding money—all the juvenile shit kids thought was "cool." He pulled up a girl's page, some cute little thing who had a penchant for selfies and flipping the bird as well.

Kids.

"That's cool, but you should still hit the books," I suggested.

Dominique made a face and tucked his phone away. "Yeah, yeah."

I looked out at the floor, trying to come in casual. "So, what's up, D?"

Dominique leaned over, planting his elbows on his knees and huffing a sigh. "It's whatever."

"Mm-hmm." I hummed. "So why ain't you sleepin'?"

The frown that stretched across Dominique's face as he kept his gaze out on the gym floor made me tense up.

Something was wrong.

"I ran into some trouble." For once, Dom wasn't giving me the runaround. "My people...they wanted me to move some stuff for them. You know, do 'em a solid like how they looked out for me when I needed it." He hung his head, the muscles in his jaw flexing. "But I didn't think it was a good idea, because of the stuff you be tellin' me. They ain't like that I wasn't down. Almost had to square up with one of them."

Instinct had me wanting to reach out and touch him, but remembering what it was like to be in his shoes, I didn't.

"So now what?" I prompted when he didn't continue.

He shrugged, shaking his head. "Just been laying low. Whatever happens, happens."

A pain sizzled across my heart for the kid. He was just trying to do the right thing, and maybe it was already too late.

I scratched at my neck, peering down at my boots. "What are you thinkin', Dom? What do you need? I got you."

"I got heat, so I'll be okay if anybody want to roll up on me."

Closing my eyes, I shook my head. Seventeen with a gun and a few problems was a bad recipe.

I'd held my first piece when I was nine. Found it in the woods one day when I was on a walk with Savon and some guys. At the time, it had felt cool to hold such power in my tiny hands. We'd taken turns holding it, pointing it, and pretending to shoot each other and objects. It wasn't until I'd gotten jumped into the local gang that I realized shit wasn't so sweet.

I'd seen things I didn't want Dominique to see. Things that pushed me to be right where I was in this gymnasium trying to fix a problem that some men before me created.

"You don't want to do that," I warned gently. "Once you pull that trigger...ain't no turnin' back."

Not to mention what would happen to him if he ever ran into a cop holding a gun.

I scrubbed my hand down my face, watching the game going on absentmindedly. "I tried tellin' you about them people you hang with, Dom. The people that's really there for you, will look out for you, and don't expect anything in return. And by look out for you, they won't be trying to get you to do some shit that'll get you caught up."

For once, Dominique didn't fight me. "I know."

"The streets can seem like they welcomin' you with open arms, but take it from me, they don't love nobody. I've seen them take more than give," I said.

Dominique bobbed his head, quietly listening.

"It's too many of us losin' a war that should've never been started," I said further. "They say LA on a different type of time, but shit, it's *all* of southern California. You shoot at them kids and then they'll bust back, but they won't just stop at you, they'll get your mom and little sister because they won't give a fuck."

Dominique winced beside me and I knew I was getting through. He glanced at me, his eyes glassy. "What do I do?"

I'd just spent the weekend customizing a car for someone. I had money to spare and if Dom owed a debt, I was willing to help.

But in case it wasn't *that* easy, I was ready to offer more. "Let me have that gun, D. You need a place to lay low? You can stay at my crib. I got an extra room. You just go to school and come back, and most importantly, stay out of trouble."

Dom didn't like this offer too much. "I don't wanna look like a punk."

The male ego was such a fragile thing when you were young. "You wanna live to fight another day, or break your mom's heart by havin' her bury her son at only seventeen?"

Anger flashed in his eyes and his nostrils flared. "Man, watch that shit."

I slapped my hand on his back hard. "Yeah, the thought doesn't feel so good, does it?" I gestured to myself. "*I* was in a gang when I was your age. Shit had me gettin' pulled out of school by my mom, and contrary to what the movies show, I didn't have to get jumped out or fight anybody. I just stopped doing the shit I wasn't supposed to be doin' and it was done."

Dom narrowed his eyes. "*That's* it?"

"That's it." I was twenty-nine now, and of course things were different when I was a teen, but it wasn't a dramatic exit from my gang life like they showed in Hollywood.

Dominique snorted. "You tellin' me you can just leave the Bloods or Crips by just stop showin' up to work?"

His words caused me to laugh and he joined me. "A simple letter of resignation to the streets." I chuckled some more. "It was anticlimactic, but I'm fortunate to have gotten out and to have had my mom and grandma in my corner. I'm sure your mom is in yours, and you know you got me."

Dominique nodded and I was happy he wasn't too thickheaded. I knew a lot of the boys out playing basketball before us or reading textbooks scattered across the bleachers, but Dominique had always felt like a mirror of my younger self.

Besides that, I didn't want to see this young Black boy die.

The streets would chew you up and spit you out, and no one would bat an eye.

"You owe any money?" I asked, getting back on track.

Solemnly, Dominique nodded. "Just a stack, but I don't have it."

"Well, I do. You take it and you pay it back and let them know you're done. Do it publicly so that nothin' pops off."

"Thank you, Keith." He looked me in the eye, his gratitude prominent.

I held my hand out. "So, you comin' through my spot?"

Dom smirked, but he reached out and slapped his palm against mine. "You better have some good video games."

I stood up. "Nah, that's BYOS."

Dominique's brows furrowed. "Huh?"

"Bring Your Own Shit," I clarified. I'd never been into video games all like that. I'd mess around and play a game or two at Savon's if he was in the mood, but it wasn't my thing.

Dominique clicked his tongue, and before I could tease him further, I chanced a look at the gym floor and noticed my grandmother walking in. She'd spotted us and was making her way over and because she was alone that left me wary. She was eighty and active, but still, I worried about her.

Dominique came with me as I stepped down from the bleachers and met up with Betty Jean.

She was holding a couple of blue plastic bags carefully. "Hey, I came to give you a care package."

I was quick to scoop her in for a hug. Her familiar perfume of flowers and just her enveloped my senses.

I released her and introduced her to Dom. "This is Betty Jean, my grandmother—but really, once you get to know her, you see how she's everyone's grandmother."

Dominque was shy as he bobbed his head at Betty. "Hi."

"What you bring me, Betty?" I wanted to know, because it already smelled good.

She held out the bags and I took them from her, finding each to be a good weight. "Just some oxtails and rice, and a jar of some peppers I canned from my garden."

What a bounty. "For me? You too good to me."

Betty Jean and my mother knew how to throw down in the kitchen. Leila liked to say that I was a good cook, often spoiling her, but I knew I'd never measure up to my mother and Betty.

I handed the food over to Dominique. "Want some?"

His greedy ass didn't hesitate to snatch the bags and take off for the cafeteria. "Thank you, Miss Betty!"

Betty Jean beamed after him. She loved to feed people.

In a way, I owed my hobby for gardening and yard work to her.

After my mother had pulled me from school, I was still wound up, still angry, still raging. She hadn't known what to do with me. Betty, her approach had been simple.

One morning, she'd taken me out back and pointed to her vegetable garden. She pointed to her flowers next and looked at me.

"*Planting helps the environment,*" she'd said. "*Your anger, your wrath, destroys it, Big Man. Do something good. Create something, help it grow, nurture it and you'll find peace. I promise.*"

That day, we'd tended to her vegetables and then to her flowers, and in all the work, I found myself distracted, busy, losing some of my steam. At eighty, Betty still kept up with her beloved garden. Because of her, I kept my yard up too.

Dominique wouldn't like it at first, but maybe I'd get him out in the yard this weekend if he was still staying with me.

"What's up, Betty?" I asked as I steered her over to the bleachers for a seat.

She sat up, posture elite as she faced me. "I just wanted to stop by and see you, that's all. Your mother saw you a couple of weeks ago and it's been quiet ever since."

I really had to do better on that. Outside of work at the garage, I was caught up at the community center or doing side gigs with clients.

Still, I couldn't forget what my mother saw the last time I'd seen her, or, *who* she'd seen.

I scratched at my neck. "Yeah, I just been pretty busy. My fault."

Betty Jean smiled knowingly. "Your mother mentioned seeing a friend helping you in the yard."

Here we go. Kennedy wasn't even a friend to me, and now I had to lie to my grandmother about it. "Something like that."

"Your mother said she was dressed like a farmer," Betty pointed out next.

Against myself, I smiled, feeling a jolt in my chest. I wondered what Kennedy would wear when I taught her to cook.

"She's not used to doin' a little manual labor. She wanted to look the part, is all," I explained.

"Ah," Betty Jean responded. "She sounds cute."

My smile dimmed at the reality of how fucking beautiful Kennedy Nichols was. I was a hundred percent sure that was why her fiancé had pursued her. She was the type of beauty some men wanted to claim and show off, like a trophy after a well-fought challenge.

I liked how pretty Kennedy was, but I really liked how cute she was as a person, too. She wore white because she was heavenly, but she was humble as well. I was still reading *Night Changes* little by little, but I made sure not to lose her place in the book. She'd dog-eared her page, versus using a bookmark like I was with my receipt. A part of me wanted to know how Eden kept her place in her books and if she'd freak out over the corners of her pages being folded over.

"It's not like that, Betty," I confessed. "She's a temporary friend. Nothin' real or too serious."

Betty frowned, pouting for me. "Doesn't look like that's what you want."

I loved fucking Kennedy. In the bedroom she was submissive, which I liked, but assertive when she wanted it her way, and I liked that, too.

But I couldn't pretend anymore that this was just about sex.

I didn't *know* Kennedy to say that I wanted more, but I *wanted* to know her. Because I *liked* her.

After all this time by myself, caged off from everyone and everything, this woman slipped through the cracks and got in.

Deep down, I knew she'd never have to use any of what I was teaching her. She was going to marry a rich man in December. After that, she'd be set for life.

"Doesn't really matter, Betty," I admitted. "I never saw what happened with Leila coming, and it hurt. This thing, I know in advance." I tapped my temple. "It's smarter not to get too attached and wrapped up in it. It is what it is."

Betty reached out and patted my knee. "You know, tomorrow isn't exactly promised for people my age."

My fists balled up at the thought. "Don't talk like that Betty."

Her brows furrowed. "Why not? It's the truth. Don't let it hurt you. I don't wanna leave here and not see you happy, Big Man. And you don't need a woman for that, just yourself."

I hadn't seen Kennedy in over a week. That first week flew by without a peep and more than likely this one would too. Even if I never saw her again, I hoped things worked out and she didn't have to marry that weirdo. That she could go on and make decisions for herself.

Betty Jean's words hadn't fallen on deaf ears. I needed to be happy, with just myself before I could ever be happy with someone else. The crazy thing was, I hadn't spent my week sulking, or feeling sorry for myself, but instead, I'd caught up on things I'd needed to do around the house. Enjoyed a show or movie, and focused on work. I was whole.

I wasn't sure what the future would bring, but I knew that I was okay, that I was going to be fine, and for that, I was solid.

23

Kennedy

By some miracle my mother managed to get a hold of LeChé for a last-minute consultation before she was due to fly out to Paris for some heiress's wedding.

We had her studio to ourselves as she promised us exclusivity and her total attention. After all, *I* was West Coast royalty. It was "an honor," she'd claimed.

All around me as we sat in a private fitting room were rack upon rack of wedding dresses waiting for me. There were whites, off-whites, nudes, and a mysterious dusty rose one I couldn't help but crane my neck to peek at.

As I sat on a sofa in my vintage Baby Phat tracksuit, taking it all in, I couldn't bring myself to get into the groove of things.

Stephanie and Elyse were due any minute to join us for the pageantry of my trying on dresses and being measured, and I honestly couldn't muster up the energy to pretend to care. LeChé was off somewhere rummaging around for something she needed. It was just my mother and me as I tried my very best not to cry.

I did not want this.

My mother flicked her wrist out, eyeing the watch on it. "Everybody should be here by now. Did you give Jadyn the right address?"

I hung my head. "She's not coming."

At once I could feel my mother's gaze on me. "Well, then, she's certainly missing a lot of these events, isn't she?"

It wasn't that Jadyn was being an awful friend, it was just that I didn't want to put her through this. Her support meant everything, but she was too real to come around and "fake the funk" as she would say. One look at my empty eyes and she'd call out my parents *and* Cain—no matter how fine she thought he was. "It's not her, Mom, it's just...none of this *means* anything to me. She wants to be here, but *I* don't even want to be here."

My mother sympathized with me as she frowned. She was sitting across from me on a matching baby blue and white striped chesterfield. Between us was a clawfoot glass coffee table with complimentary glasses of champagne. I was sad enough to drink my troubles away, but I didn't trust myself with too much alcohol in my system. Being a nondrinker, I was a lightweight. Who knew if the stuff would act like truth serum and get every raging thought weighing me down out of my head.

"Does she know?" my mother asked gently, alluding to my affair.

I nodded.

My mother looked elsewhere, no judgment passing over her face. "Well, what's he like?"

My stomach lurched at the thought of disclosing information about Keith.

My mother snorted. "Oh, come on. At least let me know what this young man is like. Where did you meet him? Does *he* know about what's going on?"

My lips stayed closed and a visceral pain had my fingers clutching the material of the seat cushions.

My mother noticed. She calmed down her approach. "Kennedy. I haven't said a word to your father or anyone else. What you have going on is safe with me."

In my past relationship with Gaius, while I hadn't told her *every*thing, she'd still been up to date on us. She knew whenever he sent me flowers, whenever he wanted to take a trip, and whenever he was upset about a game. She was my mother. I could come to her for any and everything. She'd always welcomed me with open arms and all I wanted to do in that moment was fall into her and confess my sins, but I remained seated instead.

"Keith is good to me," I said in the end. "I, uh— When I left the engagement party that night I went to Bedford Heights and caught a flat tire. He came to help me and we just sorta happened. He's such an amazing guy. He's hardworking, honest, making a difference for his community, and he could do a lot better, but he doesn't see that yet."

My mother narrowed her eyes. "What makes you think *you're* not good enough for him?"

I knew what she was doing, but this wasn't about my self-esteem. I smiled bitterly. "His ex really did a number on his ego by making him feel like he wasn't good enough for her, and here I am telling him he's only good enough for a screw.

"I hate this for him, because I'm only holding him back. But I'm selfish because I want every bit of him and I know I can't have him, or give him more." I blinked back tears. Happy I'd forgone makeup for the day. "In a perfect world...I'd love for Daddy to meet him, because I know he'd love him. Keith teaches me things, and he's not impressed by all this."

Instead of watching me crumble, my mother stood and came over to me. She hugged me close, allowing me to bury my face into her chest and let out a long-earned sob. Thankfully, I didn't ugly cry and do the whole waterworks thing, but letting out the pain eased up the vise on my heart.

My mother pulled back and wiped away my tears. "Oh, baby, we gotta get this handled. I don't know what to do, but these men gotta leave you out of their business. Even if Keith isn't the one for you in the end, it should be up to you."

I sniffled, fixing myself together. I thought of my father, and I thought of Cain. Everything was gray as confusion set in.

Somewhere in the background a door shut loudly and I

snapped to as I rushed to look presentable. Tucking some hair behind my ears, I sat up straight and braced myself to face other people.

Footsteps echoed across the hardwood floor as Stephanie and Elyse entered the room from our left. Both looked ecstatic for the day's event. Elyse was even wielding a bottle of her own champagne.

"Oh, you're here!" I let out as I took in their arrival and wiped at my face in case a tear had leaked free.

"Right on time," Stephanie said with a wink.

Just as they entered the room, LeChé was coming in behind them appearing apologetic. "Sorry for the wait, I got caught up on the phone with my assistant." She glanced at my superficial friends and brightened up. "Ah, welcome, bridal party."

Elyse squealed as she came rushing over to me to hand over the champagne. Stephanie was not far behind bearing an equally big cheesy grin on her face. Together they surrounded me as I stood up, and hugged me.

"Oh my God, Kenn, this is really happening," Stephanie gushed.

"Have you decided where you're honeymooning?" Elyse wanted to know next as she ran her fingers through my hair.

A honeymoon with Cain? Suddenly I felt like Persephone about to endure her winters with Hades.

I racked my brain for cliché honeymoon spots and came up empty. I hadn't given it much thought at all. "So much is going on, I can hardly focus as it is. Maybe Bali?"

Elyse's eyes enlarged as she gaped at Stephanie before turning to me. "Looove it. Take *lots* of pictures when you go." She nudged me on the sly. "And don't come back empty, either."

I almost threw up in my mouth.

"Bali sounds good," LeChé agreed as she came close to our group. She took a hold of my hand and did a once-over of my body. "You are going to be a beautiful bride, Kennedy."

With all eyes on me I did my best to fight my nausea. I was

used to being the center of attention. Now I felt like some type of public sacrifice.

LeChé clasped her hands together loudly. "Now, let's find your dream dress!"

"Yeah!" the girls cheered and my mother was nice enough to play the part and smile along.

Not me, though.

"Do you have a particular look you have in mind?" LeChé started out asking as she eyed her rack of dresses. "I'm happy to create anything you desire from scratch if you can't find anything here. Most modern brides tend to gravitate to the A-line or ball gown style, but everyone's different."

"It doesn't have to be this big production," I insisted. "In fact, anything that fits will do."

My mother gulped on her champagne as Elyse and Stephanie frowned.

I was breaking character, but this whole thing was depressing.

"Oh-kay, have you set a date? I think your mom mentioned December?" LeChé glanced to my mother, eager for her to join in on the conversation.

"December fourth," I said lazily as I stepped around the women and helped myself to examining the first rack of gowns.

"Ah, okay, any special meaning to that day?" LeChé asked.

I shrugged as I browsed a sequined strapless dress. "It's Jay-Z's birthday."

This trivial piece of information I only knew from being a Beyoncé fan and because Jadyn loved *The Black Album*.

Sensing I was being a bitch, I spun around and pasted on a convincing smile as I slipped into my role. "My fiancé is a big fan and he sorta reminds me of Jay in that old soul kind of way. I know it's corny and trite, but when he proposed to me he was so happy he sang a rather *bad* rendition of 'Love on Top,' and it just felt cosmic to pick the fourth for our December wedding."

My lie caused the awkwardness to cease as laughter filled the room at the idea of Cain Carter singing one of Beyoncé's most popular songs.

That was all that was needed to start the torture of finding "the dress." LeChé was gifted in the creative department, a true mastermind of designing dream gowns. I hated to waste my one opportunity to work with her on a fluke.

After trying on five dresses and earning approval on each one, I settled on a long-sleeved sequined sheath wedding gown. It wasn't my taste, but I didn't care to look beautiful on what would be the worst day of my life. I tried it on and of course the damn thing fit me like a glove.

"Oh, Kennedy." Despite the circumstances, my mother had bawled at the sight of me in the dress of my choosing. Stephanie and Elyse were quick to comfort her and agree that the dress was the one.

Even I couldn't make an ugly dress lose its splendor.

Go figure.

I hadn't seen my father in over a week and no amount of animosity could stop the fact that I missed him. After finalizing the dress and making plans for December, I got back with my mother and together we made a pit stop at the nearest McDonald's before coming back to the house.

At a time, I could just snuggle up with either parent and watch our beloved *Coming to America* and all would be right with the world. I told myself as I got out of the car and carried my bag from McDonald's with me that things would be better if I got lost in nostalgia with my father.

I was so caught up in my hopes that I missed the sign of Cain's presence until I spotted him coming down the steps as we entered the front door.

"Cain!" my mother greeted the man briefly before facing me. "I'll go check on your father."

Cain was caught up admiring an old family photo of my parents and me. I was a young girl, probably seven or eight, and together my family and I were in Canada as my father had been opening up another international hotel.

I set my McDonald's on the table near the steps and went over to Cain. "We went dress shopping today." I gathered my phone and brought up the picture my mother had taken of me in the dress and showed Cain my screen. "What do you think?"

Cain brought his attention from my younger self to the picture of me on my phone. He angled his head before bringing those dark eyes of his over to me. "Isn't it bad luck for the groom to see the bride in her wedding dress before the wedding?"

"Is it?" I played dumb. "Why don't we roll the dice and see?"

As if to call my bluff, Cain reached inside his suit jacket and procured those clear red dice.

I scoffed. "Those things are probably rigged."

Arching a brow, he handed them over. The brush of his skin against my palm sent a chill down my spine.

The dice were light in my hand, giving no tell if they were loaded or not. I didn't know much about gambling or dice, but I thought I knew rolling sevens and elevens were good.

I shook the dice in my hand, only to have Cain's hover over it.

I looked up to find him shaking his head. "Blow on them."

Opening my palm, I glanced at the dice. "You don't blow."

"I tend to have a stroke of luck without it," he said simply.

That sounded like bullshit. So, I ignored his suggestion and tossed the dice onto the table where I'd set my McDonald's bag. They tumbled and rolled until they landed.

One was a three, and the other was a two.

They weren't loaded.

Cain said nothing as he thumbed at his bottom lip.

I collected the dice and handed them back, playfully nudging him to get the resentment out. "Anyway, what did *you* look like as a kid?"

Cain tucked his dice away and took another glance at my younger image. "Scrawny."

"You'll have to show me some time," I said. I wondered if even younger him sported horns.

Cain studied me for a beat before going back into his jacket and coming up with his wallet.

"You carry an old photo in your wallet?" I teased.

"As I told you, a lot of my memories were lost along the way. What mattered I learned to keep close," Cain was saying as he opened up the black leather wallet. In it, were two photos, one he was pulling out, and the other he managed to quickly shield from me.

Cain held out an old picture of a much younger him sitting on a park bench with a basketball beneath his skinny legs. In the photo he was sitting next to who I was assuming was Beans. They were laughing, Cain had a little fro, bright eyes, and a big toothy smile.

"You kept that," I mumbled, unable to pretend I wasn't touched.

Cain nodded as he put the picture back. "I've never had anyone, outside of my mother. Forming that friendship with Beans was lifesaving in a way. I moved from home to home, sometimes too far from him, but I kept the picture so that I wouldn't forget what it was like to have a friend."

No, Cain wasn't so black and white, but gray.

"And what's the other picture?" I wondered.

Cain took a step back. "Nothing."

"Cain—"

"I can handle your jabs, but I won't have you talk about her," he warned with a firm shake of his head.

The other photo was of his mother.

I wasn't the nicest to Cain, but even I knew there was a line. "I'd never..."

A chime went off between us.

Cain pulled his phone out and placed it back into his pocket. He looked over at my McDonald's. "What's with the food?"

"It's, uh, a tradition. My dad and I eat McDonald's whenever we watch *Coming to America*. He gets a Big Mac meal and I eat fries with a Sprite. I haven't seen my father and I figured it'd be nice."

Cain reached out, his smooth hand caressing my cheek. "He'd like that, Kennedy." He ran his thumb across my skin momentarily before stepping around me and taking off for the door. "I have to go. I'm having a piano delivered to my place."

"You play?" My parents owned a piano in their living room, but it was more for show than actual use.

Cain shrugged indifferently. "Whenever I get in the mood."

He liked jazz and could play the piano. Somehow, it fit him.

It wasn't until he'd pulled the front door open that I realized something. "Where's Beans and Vino?"

To that, Cain offered me a small smile. "I like your father. I don't need to watch my back with him." He tipped his head toward me. "Enjoy your movie, Wife."

He was out the door and gone.

His guard was down. He trusted my father. He trusted my home. He trusted me.

Something like guilt had me swiping up my McDonald's and heading up the steps. If I didn't think about it, I wouldn't second-guess myself. If I didn't second-guess myself, I wouldn't allow myself to feel sorry for Cain.

The door was open and my mother was inside my father's room, adjusting his pillows and suppressing a smile down at him. His hand was on her hip and by the gleam in his eyes, I knew they were flirting.

Moments like this warmed me inside. To feel and see some sense of normal. To know that they could still be happy. That my father could still have this with the love of his life.

I cleared my throat, not wanting to let the food get any colder. "Don't mean to interrupt."

My mother leaned down and kissed my father, sweet and romantic, before rising and excusing herself out of the room. We used to watch the movie as a trio, but I'd been avoiding my father, and this alone time was needed.

"McDonald's?" he appraised. "What's the occasion?"

I removed my shoes before I went and climbed onto the bed beside him. Testing his strength, I passed him the bag and sat cross-legged. "Haven't seen *Coming to America* in a while."

Today was a good day, as my father managed to fish out each drink and hand mine over before placing his on the nightstand beside his bed. He grabbed his Big Mac and smiled at the sight, knowing what this all meant.

I watched with blurry vision as he grabbed his remote to find the movie we both loved and brought us close.

Twenty years, let him be strong for twenty more years, I begged the universe. When his legs had gone weak on him, he'd all but given up on himself. Confining himself to this bed and refusing to be seen in public. There was nothing but excuses issued out whenever my mother and I made appearances at events and galas on why my father was missing in action. For so long, he'd been miserable, depressed over his plight.

Cain must've put a spell on my father, because he seemed the most jubilant I'd ever seen him since his diagnosis.

"So, what's the damage?" he asked as he took a bite out of his Big Mac.

I took a straw and stabbed it into my Sprite. "The dress? Not so much. I found one that was nice. It only cost you seven hundred dollars."

"I'm surprised you didn't break bank buying the most expensive dress you could find," my father joked.

"I'd rather wear a burlap sack than a pretty dress down the aisle to a man I don't love," I said bitterly.

My father lost his smile and I lost my appetite.

I forced a fry into my mouth anyway as he found the movie on a streaming service and put it on.

It was ironic how the movie I loved so much growing up now mirrored my life. It made our rewatch bittersweet.

When we got to the part where Akeem tried to beg his father to let him choose his own bride, I heaved a sigh. Even *his* father wasn't listening to a word he'd said.

"Neddy," my father began as he paused the movie. "I'm sorry."

I nodded quietly.

"Do you like Cain?" he asked me.

In the beginning, it was easy to hate the guy. He'd been nothing short of a monster. But the more I got to know him, the more it was easy to feel sorry for him instead. He'd gotten the short stick in life.

"Not like *that*, but he's not as bad as I thought," I said.

"I like him. He's a good kid, a hard worker, and most of all, he listens. A lot of these young brothers get a little money and don't wanna listen. But I can talk and break down the business and he'll listen and ask questions, take notes—study.

"James was a piece of shit for not being there for that boy, but in the end, Cain's more of a man without his influence." My father took a moment to gather his Coke and take a sip. His hand shook a little as he set it back down and he wrung his fingers. "I'm working him. Keeping him close, letting him know I respect his ideas and plans, and I'm working my way into convincing him to let this engagement go."

"Yeah?" I refused to get my hopes up. Cain was stubborn and set on having me as his bride.

My father nodded. "The Residence at Cartier should have nothing to do with you."

It shouldn't have, but it did. Forged on the birth of my impending marriage to Cain. If the money was enough, Cain would've never sought me out. Something told me it wouldn't be easy for my father or my mother to change his mind now.

And for that, I stuffed another fry into my mouth and looked back at the TV across the room.

We continued the movie, laughing at the antics of John Amos, singing along with all the passion to the Soul Glo commercials, and then when we got to the ending where Lisa and Akeem were waving to the crowd as they rode away after their wedding, I felt my heart break. Break at the fact that Akeem got his happy ending, but I never would.

24

KEITH

Friday afternoon I picked Dominique up from school. Something in my gut told me to handle his debt personally. Shit could go left before it ever went smooth.

Dominique had contacted his "friends" and told him he had the money. They wanted to meet up in the alley by Third and Maple, but I wasn't feeling that dynamic. On one hand, it was out of sight from authority should things look as shady as they were. On another, it was too much free rein for them to pull a caper. Too many times across news stations did I hear about some unfortunate soul who'd gotten robbed *and* killed. Taking the money wasn't enough for these guys. It was as if they *had* to take your life.

It wasn't goin' down like that for Dom.

So, I told him to tell his people he'd meet with them at Friedman Park. It was public and out in the open. Far better chances of survival.

Dominique rode shotgun as I drove us to the park and found a parking space in the back of the large lot, giving me a good view of the whole scene. For backup, Savon was nearby should I need reinforcements. I told myself these were kids I was dealin' with, but these days, that didn't mean much.

There was nothing like dudes on the come up. The ones who started smellin' themselves and thinkin' they were hot shit because they had a little paper in their pockets. Those were the ones who were often reckless. Desperate to prove their street cred or gain one.

Dominique wouldn't admit he was scared, but I could tell he was relieved to be staying with me as he had all week. I hadn't made it easy for him. I had him out in the yard with me to learn to make use of his hands, or in the kitchen, to learn to fend for himself. He complained, like the whiney kid he was, but he sucked it up and kept up with me.

I had an envelope filled with ten freshly printed hundred-dollar bills sitting in the cup console beside me. I kept the music on low as I scanned the playground and park for any signs of activity. My phone was out on my lap as well in case Savon spotted anybody.

Beside me, Dominique was nonchalant as his phone kept pinging every other minute.

"Havin' fun?" I asked on the fifty-eleventh notification.

Dominique smiled and looked my way. "Chill."

Another ping had him back in his phone.

I rolled my eyes and focused out the window before me. "How's work?"

Dominique lifted and dropped his shoulder. "It's cool. They hired some more people. They're sayin' if I want, I can move inside and become a stocker."

"More money?"

"Not really, but if I get more hours I can earn a raise they say," Dom went on. "I kinda like pushin' carts. I be in my own little world out there. Nobody faster than me at it."

I liked that he enjoyed that feat. That he had something he liked about workin' at Finnegan's. "Yeah, but if you move inside you could be the fastest stocker."

That got Dom to grin. One thing I noticed about the kid, was that if he put his mind to something, he wanted to be the *best* at it. Despite his shortcomings, Dominique was a good kid and a hard worker, and I was sure if he kept busy with his job he'd be on the fast track.

"So, what's up with you and your girl, man?" Dominique asked a minute later.

"*My girl*?" I questioned.

He smirked as he tapped away on his phone. "Yeah, I can tell you talkin' to someone. You not walkin' around as pissed-off as you used to. Like someone finally took that stick outta yo' ass."

Annoyance took over me as I deadpanned and faced the little shit.

Dominique laughed blatantly and shrugged. "I'm just sayin', Keith."

I made a face and shook away his ignorance. "I woke my ass up, that's what changed. I realized who and what I had left in my life." I glanced his way. "I couldn't fall back and let you down, my uncle, or my mom and Betty. I looked in the mirror and kicked my own ass."

"Word?" Dom asked.

"Word," I responded. "I mean, there is someone new in my life, but I can't base my joy on her, no matter how much I like her." I looked him in the eye as I spoke. "You can't be too caught up in these girls, man. It's important to be able to stand on your own two feet and be stable."

"I hear you," Dominique said with a bob of his head. He gave me a lopsided frown. "It would kinda suck if you dropped off the grid again."

I wouldn't.

Holding my hand out between the driver and passenger seat, I swore an oath. "I'ma be around. I promise. Okay?"

Dominique slapped his hand against mine and we shook on it.

I was about to ask him about college or a trade school when I spotted a group of individuals approaching the basketball court. I sat up and eyed the group, noticing at once they were holdin'.

"No matter what goes down, stay. In. The. Truck," I instructed sternly.

Dominique sank in his seat beside me, nodding. "I will."

I sent a Savon a quick text before grabbing the envelope and climbing out of my Tahoe.

Pulling the brim of my baseball cap down low, I made my way over to the bleachers where Dom's people were crowdin'.

They spotted me just as I stepped foot on the court. A shirtless, tattooed heavy-set man wearing a durag turned his back on me, exposin' the Beretta tucked into his waistband.

My piece was at home. An attempt to show Dominique you could move without it.

Some teenagers were shooting hoops on the court, girls and boys were playing jump rope on the sidewalks, and parents were pushing littler kids on the swing set. We were surrounded by witnesses, but some people just straight didn't give a fuck.

Didn't care, though. I wasn't letting this situation go on further for Dominique.

I lifted my chin at a tall skinny guy who was hanging back, staring at me. "I'm here for Dominique."

The heavy-set one stepped closer. "Ain't no Dom around here. You see 'im?"

I held my envelope with a firm grip. "Whatever he owes you is all in here."

His beady eyes zeroed in on my thick envelope and he switched his weight from one foot to the other.

Things got quiet around us as the game went on in the background. Some kid yelled "Foul!" and some parent at the benches nearby called for their daughter. Wind blew between us, inviting a scent of skunk weed to hit my senses.

I stood my ground. "Well?"

Skinny clicked his tongue and the heavier one backed off.

Most of the group looked to be late teens and early twenties. Low-level hustlers who hopefully weren't any serious threat to Dominique's well-being.

Skinny cut through the group and stepped up to me, sizing me up and peering into my eyes curiously. "Keith, right?"

I nodded.

"I seen you around the way. Whatchu doin' here in this shit?" he wanted to know.

I gestured to the side, as if to illustrate Dominique. "That's me."

Skinny shook his head. "I ain't know you was big brother."

I thought of the little nickname Dominique had slipped and called me during his stay with me. *Twin*. I wouldn't let it show in front of these guys, but it felt good to feel important to him. Like brothers.

I held up the envelope for emphasis. "Neither here nor there. He's done with you and all this."

Skinny smirked. "You think so?"

Stepping closer, I did my best to rein in my temper as I got in his face. "Know so."

Skinny stared at me as I stared at him. His group came closer, standing shoulder to shoulder with him, letting their presence be more known.

"Is there a problem?"

Savon.

He stepped up beside me and eyed the rest of the group, prepared for whatever was about to go down.

In Skinny's eyes, I could see he didn't want it to go that way. Not with the money so close to his grasp.

I held it out and he slowly took it.

"Nah," he said as he opened the envelope and leafed through the bills. "We straight." He lifted his gaze to mine. "Tell Dominique it's whatever."

"Stand on it," I let it be known. "Don't come around him no more."

Skinny shrugged as he waved me off dismissively. The debt was paid and he couldn't care less. It showed as he joined back up with his crew and they left in their herd.

I watched them leave down the street from the park until they were a safe distance away.

Slowly, I faced Savon. "I had it."

Savon chuckled. "Looked like you was about to get jumped by a group of middle schoolers."

They hadn't been big or intimidating at all. I managed to loosen up as I slapped Savon's arm.

Movement to my right caused me to look over and catch Dominique approaching. His hands were in his hoodie and his shoulders were hitched up.

"Everything okay?" he asked warily, looking around for any signs of his old friends.

"It's settled," I announced.

Savon reached out and jabbed Dom's shoulder. "Be smart next time, D. Don't go mixin' yourself up with stupidity like that. Some people are going up, and some are going south. You gotta surround yourself with people who only want to elevate you and see you do better."

Dominique nodded, a tiredness to his eyes. "I know, Von."

"If you ever find yourself in a jam again, you know you can call up me or Keith, right?" Savon pushed on. "I got a cot you can lay your head on, too."

Dom's lips trembled as he accepted Savon's hug and let him embrace him. We were out in the open, so it wasn't "cool" to show affection, but fuck it.

"We love you, man," I let it be known. "So the same way you don't want me disappearin', don't go doin' anything that's gonna have you missin'. Okay?"

Dominique nodded, scratching at his plaits. "I'ma be good, Keith. I swear."

Savon playfully swatted at the back of Dom's head. "Good, now stay yo' ass in school."

Dominique groaned as we crossed the lot for the parking area. "Here y'all go with this shit."

Savon looked at me as I looked at him. Together we smacked the back of Dom's head and chuckled when he called us out on it.

I was sure Dominique's future would be solid. After all, I planned to be around to see him through.

25

Kennedy

JADYN WAS AT HER LAPTOP TYPING AWAY AS OLD-school R&B played in the background. Candles were burning on the surfaces of her nearby bookcase, and a glass of wine was close enough for her to reach out and steal a sip.

I almost felt in the way of her creative zone, but we'd made plans that Saturday evening.

Truthfully, I felt a little antsy being back in Bedford Heights for the first time in three weeks. While I'd FaceTimed and called Jadyn regularly, I hadn't seen her in forever. Not to mention someone else I felt way too tempted to stop by and see.

Keith gave me my space and as much as I valued his respecting my need to keep a low profile, I missed him all the same. I almost felt pathetic wondering if *he* missed *me*. He was older than me, more mature and serious, and knew what he wanted. In reality, I was wasting his time, and I feared he'd realized that with all the time put between us.

"Ooh, turn that!" Without tearing her attention away from her screen, Jadyn waved her hand in my direction.

An all too familiar classic was now beginning to play and I felt my forehead crease in confusion. "What's wrong with this song?"

Jadyn swiveled around in her chair and shot me a pointed

look. "I need positive vibes only for this scene I'm writing." All of her hair was secured up in two big buns, making way for the stern expression on her face to shine through.

"Oh-kay?" I still didn't get it.

"'Don't Leave Me' by Blackstreet is total emotional manipulation. The whole song they're talking about 'going insane' and twisting some poor woman's arm to stay in a relationship. It's not romantic, it's psychotic...sorta like your fiancé."

I wrinkled my nose. "You totally ruined that song for me, thanks."

Jadyn grinned. "Oh, I'm still gon' let the song rock because it's fire, but did I lie?"

The lyrics of "Don't Leave Me" started jumping out at me as the song continued to play. They *were* threatening to go mental if a woman left. Cain *was* manipulative, getting the upper hand when my father was at his lowest. But he didn't want me to pity him. He'd never use that as a tactic to get me to be with him.

"I don't know, Jay," I admitted. "Cain doesn't seem... completely horrible?"

She pretended to gasp. "He's gotten to you?"

"God no. I'm sure he's a bad person, but at the same time, I don't think he's *all* bad."

"Forcing marriage on a girl sure constitutes as bad in my book, but what do I know? How's Keith?"

I blew out a breath and sank down on the chair across from her. "Complicated."

"How so?"

I looked around her office space, admiring her dedication to her craft. Jadyn was old school in the way she'd write out plot lines or character trees in notebooks before typing them up on her laptop. She even had a large whiteboard on one wall filled with little scribbles and ideas. Looking at her and all her talent and intellect, sometimes I wished I were good at something.

Getting back on track, I returned to my best friend and

opened up. "We've been taking a break, but, I can tell if he had it his way, we would be more than just friends with benefits."

Jadyn gave me a once-over. "You are a nice catch. Can't blame a guy for trying."

Keith wasn't trying to be more, at least, not outright. He drew a line in the sand the same way I had in the beginning, but it was me who kept crossing it. Me who spent the night. Me who wanted to learn to do yardwork. Me who wanted to learn how to cook by his hand alone.

Maybe we needed this time apart. To loosen up and not get too attached.

Yeah.

"So, anyway, I thought we were going out?" I changed the subject and gestured to where Jadyn was sitting cross-legged on her plush black chair at her desk.

Jadyn bit her lip and faced her screen. "I know, but I put my other script on pause—creative funk, ugh. And now I've been hit with something else, something juicy."

The passion in her eyes said it all. Jadyn was in love with this new project, enough so she had trouble getting away, even if only for a few hours while we hung out on the town.

"What's this one about?" I wondered.

A sneaky smile crossed Jadyn's face as she turned back to me. When she didn't say anything, a terrible idea popped into my head.

"You are *not* writing about this," I practically hissed at her.

Jadyn chuckled as she plucked up her wineglass. "I'm a writer. Anything you do or say can and will be used in a script."

"Jay."

Jadyn gave an innocent shrug as she looked at me over the rim of her glass. "I changed a few details to protect the innocent."

I narrowed my eyes. "Such as?"

"For starters, our heroine is based in Bedford Heights. I figured a story about a street-smart woman enamoring a bougie guy was more interesting."

That did sound intriguing for a plot.

I settled down. "What are you calling it?"

"*All I Need*," Jadyn said as she hit a few keys, seemingly saving her progress before shutting her laptop. "Now, we can go."

"I'm reading that script," I declared.

Jadyn lost her sense of humor. "Sure, you can read it here."

That was the thing about Jay. She always turned down my offers to get her scripts into the right hands. There were plenty of Hollywood elites who often passed through our local Residence Hotel, but Jadyn wanted to make it on her own, not by nepotism.

The thing was, Jadyn was good. I'd read four of her scripts and she was truly gifted with words. Everything was easy to follow, from her descriptions to her dialogue. I lived for her character descriptions and how she set her scenes.

I couldn't buy Jadyn's career. She could sell herself.

"All I can do is hand your script to a director or producer, it's up to you to sell it. Which you will because you're so good," I swore.

A sense of vulnerability tugged on Jadyn's features. "Maybe someday."

I didn't push as Jadyn got ready for us to leave. She swapped out her shorts for a skirt, making me feel extra covered in my ripped jeans.

We were going to a gastropub for a much-needed night out. Usually when I was in Bedford Heights, I only hung out at Jay's, but I was excited to be hitting the scene.

"Fuck your diet for the night," Jadyn announced as she drove for the downtown area. "This place has the best food."

My stomach grumbled in compliance. "Seafood?"

"The *best* beer battered shrimp you can ask for," Jadyn swore.

"All I need to hear."

Jadyn smiled my way, and then a look crossed her face. She reached down and lowered the volume on the Muni Long song that was playing. "So, I got a crazy idea."

Uh-oh. "Am I going to like this 'crazy idea'?"

My best friend smirked. "Considering your unyielding loyalty to your dad, no."

I wasn't going to like what she had to say. "So, let's hear it."

We reached a red light and Jadyn faced me. "What if...you married Keith?"

I waited for the punchline and it never came, but I forced myself to laugh anyway. "Excuse me?"

"Think about it," Jadyn went on with an easy shrug. "You can't get married, if you already are."

While it was both true and obvious, it wouldn't be that easy considering my father and Cain. My father would be upset and probably make good with his threat of snatching away my inheritance and funds, and Cain... Cain would probably retaliate, leaving me a widow before I was even out of the honeymoon phase.

It was too risky.

Then I thought about it from the angle purely involving Keith. I didn't know him any more than I knew Cain, but the idea of marrying him didn't terrify me nearly as much as marrying Cain.

"That's ridiculous, Jay," I told her as she began to drive as soon as the light hit green. "Marrying someone else would cause more problems than solve them."

"Such as?" Jadyn challenged.

"Such as my dad and Cain's deal. Cain would just back out and that would piss my dad off."

"It's not always about your dad, Kennedy. Besides, it's just an idea to keep in the back of your mind, or the *front*."

It was an idea. When I thought about it, I had some big decisions to make. And I wasn't sure if I were brave enough to face the consequences of any.

The car came to a stop and we'd arrived at On Tap. A neon blue sign illustrated that they were also a pool and billiards hall as well as a bar. It was the weekend, so the parking lot was pretty full, letting me know the inside would be packed. A sense of claustrophobia overtook me as I got out of Jadyn's Volkswagen.

Music was pumping and could be heard even from outside of the building. The faint sounds of classic Cam'ron echoed from On Tap as we headed up the front walk toward the entrance.

Once inside we were immersed in a lively room. A bar greeted us first, and seated on every other stool were patrons drinking beers or shots. Some were even eating and stealing glimpses at the TV mounted on the wall replaying some NBA highlights.

The pool area was in the back of the room and a few games were going, making me anxious and curious. I'd never been too active with sports, save for a few years playing tennis in high school.

"Hey, queen, can I buy you a drink?" some man at the bar shouted at Jadyn as we were just about to pass it.

Jadyn wrinkled her nose. "No thanks!"

The man made a face but backed down.

I couldn't help but snicker. "Easy, girl."

Jadyn was indignant. "First, they call you queen, and then they treat you like a peasant. You'll know the right approach when you see it."

I thought it didn't matter for me. Men were off-limits.

Jadyn ticked up a finger. "First things first, Jell-O shots!"

I frowned. "Jay, I can't."

Jadyn waved me off. "They're plant-based."

Well, that solved that.

One drink wouldn't hurt.

"One shot," I conceded.

That was all Jadyn needed as she tugged me over to the bar. "One shot, baby kidneys. And then you can switch to Sprite."

Being with my best friend after a month of stress was all I needed.

And yet, an ache singed in my chest. One I couldn't shake along with a feeling of longing.

Jadyn approached the bartender with a cool confidence I'd

always admired and respected. She held up two fingers and looked the man straight into his eyes. "Two vegan Jell-O shots. Make 'em cherry."

The man slid his gaze over to me, briefly eyeing my cleavage in my lace top, before tipping his head and going to grab our shots.

A nervous chill danced down my spine when he returned with two shot glasses filled with vegan cherry-flavored jel topped with whipped cream and a cherry for garnish.

My hand shook as I accepted a glass while Jadyn paid for them. One whiff of the shot and I realized it was *coconut* whipped cream. At least it smelled good.

Jadyn gathered her shot and held it in the air to signal a toast. "To women only, fuck these men."

I cracked a grin, feeling that message through and through. I clinked my shot glass against hers. "Hell yeah!"

We knocked back our shots after eating the cherries and I was elated to find that the alcohol in them wasn't strong or overpowering. I could almost go for another.

Jadyn set her glass on the bar and scanned the room. "We gotta touch the pool table, at least once. And I'm getting you a basket of beer battered shrimp. Be right back."

Jadyn took off to check the availability on the pool tables while I sat back at the bar and faced the room. Groups of men were scattered around in tables and booths, some women were here and there, either with a man or with other women. Most were caught up in their own worlds, enjoying food and drinks, while I looked on curiously.

A man with a sleeve of impressive tattoos could be seen seated on the right side of the room with a young woman who was practically up under him. He was in a T-shirt with jeans, and she was too. Her natural hair was up in a single puff and by the way he was staring at her face as they sat close, I could tell he was in love. When he reached out and caressed her cheek and she smiled at him, a knot formed in my stomach.

I whirled around on my stool and dug my phone out of my

purse. "Hey, can I have another shot?" I asked the bartender as my hand trembled around my phone. I'd need liquid courage to do what I was about to do.

He set another shot in front of me a moment later and when I reached into my purse to find my debit card, a hand covered my line of vision.

Beside me, a man was shaking his head. "I got it."

A twinkled glowed in his green eyes and his friendly handsome smile put me at ease. "Thank you."

He shrugged and faced the bartender. "Put it on my tab, Rick."

I raised my shot toward the man next to me. "To friendly people."

He tipped his beer my way and nodded. "To *beautiful* people."

I was happy when he didn't press for more conversation and allowed me to sneak and make my phone call.

Keith's line rang a few times before he picked up. "Hello?"

I hadn't heard his voice in almost a month and the sound of it made me melt, causing me to squirm on my stool. "Hey."

There was a pause and then he was back on the line. "Where are you? It's loud in the background."

Being coy, I lifted and dropped my shoulder, as if he could see me. "Nowhere special. Jadyn and I are out getting vegan Jell-O shots and enjoying the night."

Keith heaved a sigh. "Make sure you get an Uber home."

"They're not that strong." In fact, I could almost go for a third.

"Kenny," his tone was filled with a warning.

I loved it. "Well, there are some nice, *handsome*, strong young men here. Maybe one of them will give me a lift."

"Oh yeah?" Keith asked.

"Uh-huh." I hoped he could hear the grin in my voice.

Again, Keith sighed. "You're in *my* city, you don't think I know you're down at On Tap where they exclusively serve plant-based shots?"

Oh crap. "So?"

"I'll see you when I see you, Kennedy." He hung up and I was left looking at my phone screen.

Was that a threat?

A rush of heat settled between my legs as the ache in my chest intensified.

Usher was serenading the room with "Dot Com" by the time Jadyn made it back to me. She put in an order for two baskets of fries and shrimp and then we grabbed a private booth. Her with a Coke and me with a Sprite. *See, we were responsible.*

"Are you still getting hitched in December?" Jadyn asked. "It seems like things are happening way too fast."

"Tell me about it. I almost want to get married next week to just hurry up and start the countdown," I said.

Jadyn scowled and took a sip of her Coke. "I still can't believe you're actually willing to go through with this sham marriage."

"What choice do I have?"

"You shouldn't have to choose between being left out in the cold and going along with your dad's fucked-up deal."

I shouldn't have, but this was where we were.

"Order for Jones!" the bartender shouted at the bar.

Jadyn was quick to get up and collect our orders before returning with two baskets heaping with fries and beer battered shrimp. She hadn't lied. The shrimp was to die for. I was definitely going to need to hit Pilates hard in the coming week, maybe add in an hour on the elliptical for good measure as well.

When we were finished, we made a run to the women's restroom and cleaned up before hitting the first available pool table.

The pool cue wasn't heavy to hold, but I was still clueless on how to use it. I'd seen Gaius shoot pool a few times when we were together, but back then I'd always been caught up hanging out with the other WAGs to pay attention to the rules and methods.

Jadyn of course was a very hands-on woman, barely needing instructions because she picked up on things easily. Like pool. She racked the balls in the middle of the green felt before proceeding to circle the table to find where she wanted to make her first move.

Maybe I'd ask one of the men around us the best way to maneuver with the cue.

A gust of cologne washed over me. In seconds, two tattooed arms came down on either side of me where I stood on my end of the table. A step back had me brushing against a solid chest. Soon, lips were coming and grazing the crook of my neck and I shuddered and closed my eyes.

Keith.

The sound of clacking and balls scattering across the felt drove my eyes open.

Jadyn wasn't paying attention to where the balls went. Her eyes were fixed on Keith. "So..." She stood straight, clutching her cue like a warrior. "This must be Keith."

He came from behind me and stood beside me. He nodded his head in Jay's direction. "I am. You must be Jadyn."

Her eyes swept over him. "I am."

Keith came back to me and he didn't look the least bit happy to see me. He glanced at my outfit, his eyes measuring the way my lace spaghetti-stringed top hugged my curves and offered cleavage. "Know how to play?"

I didn't, but I wasn't interested in the game just then. Not when he was so close. His proximity had my palms sweating and my knees going weak.

"No," I confessed.

Keith was behind me again, his cologne filling my nose and wrapping me in a warm embrace. When his hands took me and positioned me over the table with my cue, I clumsily closed my eyes again and basked in the closeness.

It had been too long.

"Like this," his deep voice said into my ear as he showed me how to work the cue between my thumb and index finger. "You can't be too far or too close to the ball. You need just enough distance to be able to drive the cue like...this."

With Keith's help, I managed to hit the cue ball and send it flying toward a solid orange one.

Was I solids or stripes?

Didn't matter, I wasn't interested in playing anymore suddenly.

"Guess that game is a bust," Jadyn drawled as she came closer. "*I* was solids, K."

Of course she was. I needed to brush up on my skills outside of shopping.

Keith shook Jadyn's hand and she made no attempt to hide that she was appraising him.

"I feel like I seen you from around the way before," Jadyn noted.

Keith kept his cool. "I be around. My uncle run an auto body shop, so you could've seen me up in there."

Jadyn looked my way as she responded. "Could've." She set her cue stick back on the table, abandoning the game as well. "Well, I'll be back in the booth if you need me." Jadyn met Keith with a fierce look that sent a rattle to my bones. "Be good to her, or else."

"Yes, ma'am," Keith said as he let Jadyn pass us.

Jadyn hadn't been gone a second before Keith was crowding my space, causing me to back up into the pool table and panic when there was nowhere else to go.

Keith kept coming, not stopping until his hand was in my hair and he was steering my body into his. He held me close, burying his face in my neck, groaning. "Fuck, I missed you, Kenny."

My emotions seized me and I had to blink to conceal my blurry vision. He *missed* me. Just like I'd missed him.

I wrapped my arms around his neck and beckoned him closer, smelling his scent and reveling in his touch.

All too soon he let me go.

"Have fun?" he asked as he looked around the room.

Those shots were good and the food was delicious. Pool would take another go, but I did enjoy my time at On Tap enough to come back.

"Yeah," I said.

Keith's hand took mine and squeezed gently. "Good, because we're leaving now."

I should've held my ground and put up a fight, but after not seeing him for weeks, there was no place else I wanted to be.

"We have to stop by Jay's. I packed an overnight bag," I said.

"Of course you did."

I tilted my head back, grinning up at him. "Mad?"

Confused, Keith perked a brow. "Why would I be mad when I came to get you?"

Giddiness took over as I walked with him back to where Jadyn was in the booth.

"I'm heading out, Jay," I said as I patted Keith's bicep. "Sorry to abandon you."

Jadyn wasn't offended in the least. In fact, a wicked grin had me curious. "Oh, don't be. Just thought of a much-needed pool scene for my script."

Oh God. Here we go.

I trusted Jadyn more than anyone in my life these days, so I knew she was working on a masterpiece that I'd love by the time I got my hands on it.

"Let me guess, the male lead's name is *Kenneth*?" I quipped.

Jadyn chuckled as she stood from the booth and grabbed her purse. "Whaaat? Do I look like the type of person who would be so obvious?"

I deadpanned. She had named the bougie man Kenneth. Great.

"Do I want to know what's goin' on?" Keith asked.

Jadyn put on her best innocent act. "Nah, you don't."

Keith was still confused, and I couldn't help but laugh. I

hoped whatever Jadyn was writing ended with a happily ever after. Not all of us were so lucky.

After stopping by Jadyn's on the way to Keith's to get my bag, and deciding to leave my Lexus because of my two shots, Keith brought me to his house. My hormones were suddenly raging and one step in the front door and I was on him.

"What time you on?" Keith's husky chuckle liquified my insides, leaving me wet and horny.

"It's been forever," I whined as I stepped out of my heels.

I all but tugged him to his bedroom where I was ready to tear off his clothes with my teeth if I had to. I quickly undid my jeans and let them pool to the floor before I mounted Keith in my bodysuit.

Only, he wasn't matching my energy. He held me at a distance as I attempted to kiss my way from his neck to his mouth.

"We can't," he said as he sat back on the bed.

I reeled back, confused, needy, desperate. "Please?" I took his hand and let him cup me, showing him how much I wanted it.

Keith moved the seat of my suit to the side and brushed along my entrance. The tip of one of his fingers entered me and I bit my lip and felt myself sink down on his hand for more.

"So greedy," he mumbled as he removed his hand.

My eyes flew open and I pouted. I wanted it, anyway he wanted to give it to me.

Reading the frustration on my face, Keith came and laid me down, hovering over me. He stuck his finger into my mouth and watched as I sucked it dry.

He neared my ear and whispered three words that smothered my hormones. "We're not alone."

Immediately I bolted up, colliding against his chest. "What?"

The grin on his face was handsome enough to quell my panic. "Dom's in the spare bedroom asleep."

Dom. It must've been one of the kids he helped with at the community center. But then...

"Why bring me back here if you had a guest?" As if the boy could walk in at any moment, I hurried and slid underneath the comforter.

Keith's humor dissolved as a seriousness coated his face. "Because I missed you and having you here was enough."

Enough.

Such a heavy word passed between us. Because deep down, beneath the surface, I couldn't have agreed more. It wasn't the sex I missed with Keith. It was *him*. And it was clear he'd missed more than just the physical with me as well. We'd missed each other.

I laid back and sighed. "What do you want from me, Keith?"

His hand came down on my heart, causing it to beat hard. And then he slid it under my breast until it was beneath me altogether.

"Nothing," Keith said in the end. "As long as you're happy, I want nothing."

He wanted nothing when everyone else wanted *something*.

He came and lay beside me, bringing me to his chest and sending me to my doom. I was falling for this man and it wouldn't end well.

"Did you miss me, too?" he asked.

I hated that he had to question it. "I slept in your hoodie every night."

It was the only thing that kept me sane.

My confession earned me a kiss to my temple. "I hate this."

I took his hand and interlocked our fingers because I feared he'd slip away if I didn't get ahold of him. "Me too." Turning over, I faced the wall and snuggled back into Keith. "Would you run away with me if I took off?"

He snuzzled against my hair. "Where would we go?"

"I've always wanted to go to Greece," I admitted.

"Greece, huh?"

"Yeah, it looks so beautiful," I said.

"Greece might be out of my price range, Kenny."

Mine too if I really ran. "What if I paid?"

Keith squeezed where our hands were tangled and kissed my bare shoulder. "Only if we could take turns."

I liked that. That my money didn't intimidate him in the long run. "Okay."

"But what if they cut you off, because you ran? Then what?" Keith asked next.

More than likely, that would be the case if I did decide to flee and not marry Cain. My father would freeze all my assets and empty out my penthouse. "Would...would you want me if I were poor?"

Keith let my hand go only to turn me on my back and peer down at me. "Kennedy, I'd want you if you had nothing. Where you come from doesn't define you unless you let it. Your father's money doesn't mean anything to me. All I need is you."

All he needed was *me*, and all I wanted was *him*. That was the brutal thing about reality, though. We couldn't always get what we wanted or needed.

26

KEITH

In the morning, I woke up alone. The other side of my bed was empty and cold. Kennedy was long gone.

Or so I thought.

After stepping out of my bedroom upon freshening up, I heard the sound of the TV in my living room. Dominique had brought over some game system, and when he wasn't hittin' the books, he was on it raging at other online players. I'd tried to sit and play with him, but it didn't hold my interest.

Instead, I found myself browsing Bedford Heights's local florist's website.

As I passed by my kitchen I was hit with the smell of breakfast and soap. Food had been made and dishes had been set in the sink to be cleaned. There were *two* places at the table I noticed as I kept on walking, and when I made it to the living room I discovered why.

Sitting side by side, Kennedy and Dominique were caught up playing a video game. One that was very bright and colorful and required them to race cute animated characters. One of Dom's lesser violent games.

Kennedy was moving her joystick as she attempted to beat

Dom, who was coolly cruising around the lap they were racing on.

"Ooh, I'ma 'bout to make bank!" he hollered as he crossed the finish line and won.

Kennedy's shoulders sagged and I recognized the con all too well.

Folding my arms, I leaned against the post of the doorway. "Please tell me you're not in here hustlin' money from my girl."

My surprise arrival had them both whirling around and shooting up from the couch. Dominique was dressed in his Finnegan's T-shirt and a pair of khakis, while Kennedy had her satin wrap on along with a pair of cream-colored pajamas.

Kennedy bowed her head, but not without leaning toward Dominique. "Do you take checks?"

"Zelle would be quicker," he whispered back.

I narrowed my eyes. "How much did she lose?"

"Just five hundred, but I was starting to get the hang of it," Kennedy rushed to say.

I shook my head and entered the room some more. "She's not paying you, Dom."

He rolled his eyes. "Here you go." Dominique spun around and went about shutting off his system and collecting the controllers.

Kennedy padded over to me and wrapped her arms around my middle, hugging me close and resting her cheek on my chest.

I held her close and focused on Dominique. "You goin' in?"

He finished with his game and came around the couch, but kept his distance. "Yeah. And, uh, sorry about the dishes. I started to wash them but then we kinda got caught up in the game."

"*You* was about to wash dishes?" Ever since he'd been staying with me he was good about cleaning up after himself, but he never offered to clean the dishes after I'd cooked or ordered takeout.

Dominique gave a lazy shrug and gestured toward Kennedy.

"That's a woman, Keith. The least I could do after she cooked me breakfast was clean the dishes."

He was lucky he was too far to pop because I'd be damned if he started acting brand new for Kennedy's benefit.

But at least he was respectful.

"We were hungry," Kennedy explained as she lifted her head and peered up at me. The gleam in her eyes and the faint smile on her face? She couldn't be this content with being with me, could she?

I'd made plans to take a step back and be more loose and casual with her, but all it took was one phone call last night to shatter that plan. She'd been playing around when she mentioned other men at the bar taking her home, but the idea drove me to get dressed and shut down any possibility of that even happening. One look at her in that tight top and those jeans and I knew I was taking her home with me.

I didn't need the sex, but just the feel of her next to me was enough. I wanted to wake up beside her. Smell her expensive perfume, feel her softness, pretend to hate how she'd tangle herself in my legs—she wasn't the only one breaking rules.

Now here I was, wanting more, even though I knew I couldn't have it.

"You need a ride?" I asked Dominique.

He studied where Kennedy was clinging to me and shook his head. "Uh, nah. And tonight, I'ma head back to my mom's. She can only do so much and I *am* the man of the house, so you know how that goes."

Dominique was quick to go and grab his backpack before heading out the door, but not without dapping me up first and issuing Kennedy a goodbye.

And then we were alone.

"When do you go in?" Kennedy asked as she let me go and led the way back into the kitchen.

I missed the feel of her in my arms already. I didn't hesitate to scoop her back up and walk with her over to the kitchen table. "I'm off today."

Kennedy hummed and backed into me, teasing me with her ass as she went about making me a plate of the breakfast she'd made. Eggs over easy, bacon, and surprisingly, French toast.

Warmth spread through my chest as I took it all in. "What do you have planned for today?"

Kennedy looked around and shrugged. "Nothing. I'm supposed to be with Jadyn."

I scratched along the stubble on my jaw. "Feel like goin' on a run with me?"

At once Kennedy perked up, down for anything. "To do what?"

"I just housed a teenager for a week. I'm out of food," I joked. "I figure we can head to the grocery store and I can give you a clue on what to buy whenever you're cooking."

"You're going to teach me how to cook?" Kennedy lit up with excitement.

"Of course." I reached out, cradling her face in my hand and tilting her head back. Gazing down into her eyes, I'd never felt more tempted than I did just then to kiss her.

God willing, I held back.

27

Kennedy

"ARE YOU SURE THAT'S WHAT YOU WANT TO WEAR?" Keith asked me for the third time since I'd gotten dressed after my shower.

I took in my six-inch gladiator heels and my little white dress that was off the shoulder. Maybe to many it wasn't ideal to shop in, but it was all that I had packed.

Besides, I wanted to look cute.

"Yeah," I said as I turned away from my reflection. Keith was standing in the doorway as I finished prepping in the master bath.

"That's a lot of walking in heels," Keith pointed out.

It would be, but I could endure it. "I'm sure if I get tired someone will offer me a piggyback ride."

Keith stroked his jaw. "*Someone*, huh?"

"Mm-hmm, we'll be in public, so I'm sure there'll be some nice man willing to—"

Keith was on me, cornering me against the bathroom counter. A giggle escaped my lips as he lifted me up and set me on the counter.

He nipped my bottom lip and I released a pathetic moan. God, I was weak for this man.

"Before I'm through with you I'm going to fuck you all over this house," he swore.

I hoped he was never through.

I braced myself by grabbing onto his arms. If we got carried away, he'd have me all over his counter and mirror.

Keith grinned against the corner of my mouth. "Let's go."

He stepped back and helped me down from the counter.

We didn't have sex. We went out to his Tahoe and went to the grocery store.

I sat beside him giddy as ever as he drove comfortably with one hand on the wheel. His hip-hop was playing throughout the truck. Jadakiss and Styles P were rapping about "making it."

I was enjoying the song when Keith lowered the volume.

"Question," he began as he glanced my way. "Have you ever paid a bill?"

Instantly, I shrank. He wanted to talk about this *now*?

"Why?" I asked.

"I just wanna know, I'm curious," Keith said.

Still. "You'll just laugh."

Keith scrunched his face up. "I'm not gon' judge you. It's just us."

Us.

Such a simple word, yet it left behind a strong sense of yearning. We were only supposed to be strictly physical, but I liked the time we spent together *not* having sex. I liked the idea of *us*.

"The first and only bill I was responsible for is my cell phone bill," I confessed. My Lexus had been a sweet sixteen present, and by the time I went to college, I'd been gifted a newer model. "My family's accountant handles their affairs, and mine."

Keith appeared thoughtful as he kept his gaze on the road ahead. It was a nice March morning, making me think of the fact that spring was quickly approaching. "So, do you have your own bank account?"

I nodded. "Yeah."

"Have you ever earned your own money?" he went on.

The money I made from my brand deals weren't much to write home about. They certainly couldn't keep me up with my lifestyle if my father ever cut me off. "I've done some campaigns for makeup and lingerie before."

"Lingerie?" Keith's brows shot up as he snuck me a surprised look. I loved the expression on his face. He didn't seem like the type of person who ever got taken by surprise. Really, I was intrigued whenever something would break that angry scowl of his and he'd light up, even if only a little.

"Nothing too risqué, but I was offered a nice chunk of change for a year's worth of shots. It made dropping out of school at the time less shameful for me," I said.

Keith hummed, bobbing his head. "So, you have some money saved up in your account?"

"Yes."

"And if you wanted to, you could empty it out and buy you a nice little spot somewhere modest and start over?"

He was just asking a few questions, but the ability to breathe suddenly became a challenge as my lungs began to feel as if they were being squeezed.

I could empty out my bank account and take off, and start over when the money ran dry. But why did that feel so overwhelming? So huge of a step?

"You can always come down from that tower and live amongst us common folk," Keith teased, easing me away from my panic attack. "Just an idea."

The Tahoe came to a stop as he found a parking space in the parking lot in front of Finnegan's Supermarket.

I didn't rush to unbuckle myself as I fought to keep my anxiety at bay. "It's not so easy."

His rough hand slid onto my thigh and squeezed gently, sending a jolt of tranquility to my chest. "I know."

"I've always listened to my dad, Keith. He's always had a say, and looked out for me." I shook my head as I peered out the window, catching a woman ushering two kids to a van a few spots in front of us. "But this whole marriage thing...it's the first time I've seen him be selfish *with me.*"

"Kenny..." Keith paused, completely stopping whatever train of thought he'd had. He patted my thigh and let the idea go. "Let's just focus on shopping, okay?"

"Okay," I said softly.

We got out of the truck and when we met at the trunk, Keith immediately took my hand. I liked that about him. How he was such a man. He walked a few inches in front of me with me tucked close to him to keep me safe.

That's how I felt with Keith. Safe. Physically, and mentally. Deep down, I knew if I let go, I'd be emotionally sated as well.

"Hey, Keith," a man shouted as he was walking out on the other end of the store exit.

Keith recognized the man and lifted his chin in the man's direction.

Just as we were entering the store we spotted Dominique across the lot pushing carts. He tipped his head our way and we waved back. This morning when I stepped out of the bedroom and found him rummaging in Keith's cupboard, I wasn't sure how to react. But Dom had been polite, even if he was totally scamming me during our session playing that video game.

Once inside Keith grabbed a grocery cart and led the way onto the sales floor.

The first department we came across was the floral department. A wall of various bouquets greeted us and I marveled at the displays.

Keith abandoned me to go and pick up a white bundle of roses.

"For you," he said.

I set the roses in the seat of the cart and quickly kissed Keith's cheek.

He held me close against him, peering down at me with so much joy and light in his eyes it felt like my heart would burst from the attention. I loved that it was aimed at me. I loved that *I* got to see him this happy. This attentive. This wrapped up in *me*.

"I've been wanting to buy you flowers for a minute," he said. He glanced at where the bunch sat in the cart and came back to me. "I know I'm not supposed to make this personal, but fuck it, you know?"

I did. I really did.

We continued on, and just as we passed the checkout counter for the floral department, I spotted a NOW HIRING sign.

Keith noticed it too and nudged me. "Not a bad idea."

If I ever got a job, I knew I didn't want to work in the food industry. That was a level of patience I wasn't built for. I wholly commended those who managed to do their jobs with grace no matter how awful their clientele were.

But flowers? I loved them, they reminded me of my father, of his gentler side, of his garden and how I truly wanted one of my own someday. I could work with flowers. I could help men or women pick out the perfect arrangement for those they loved and cared about.

"It isn't," I agreed.

Directly across from floral was the produce department.

"Now, most people have jobs," Keith joked, flashing me a small smile. "So, they cut corners when they cook. Since you have time, you can work with making everything from scratch if you want."

"Is that how you cook?" I wondered. I didn't know his exact hours at the garage, but I was curious if Keith preferred everything homemade or if he was lenient with skipped steps.

He shrugged. "I love homemade mashed potatoes whenever my mom or Betty Jean cooks, but when it's just me at the crib I do cheat and buy a container of Bob Evans precooked mashed potatoes. I was apprehensive at first, but that shit's amazing."

Precooked mashed potatoes? "Frozen French fries or homemade?"

"I've never tried making homemade French fries," Keith admitted. "I guess that's my one cheat: potatoes."

I chuckled, finding the bashful expression on his face adorable. "So why am I going to you to learn how to cook again?"

Keith popped a brow before surveying our surroundings. "Okay."

The subtle threat made me clench my thighs together. *Relax.* "So, you cut corners on potatoes, anything else?"

"I prefer fresh vegetables." Keith showed a hand toward a wall housing bagged pre-cut vegetables. "Especially green beans, growing up I thought I hated them, but then I realized I didn't like them canned."

We went over to the pre-cut section and Keith grabbed a family-size bag of green beans and tossed them in the cart. He then grabbed a bag of broccoli florets and tossed them in next. He eyed the wall of bagged leafy greens and settled on a large bag of spinach to place in the cart.

I toyed the edge of that fine line between us and grabbed a bundle of asparagus and placed them in the cart as well.

Keith angled his head and nodded. "Asparagus is good."

Going even further, I pushed the cart over to the fruit section. Keith was fit and decadent, but he already had a nasty smoking habit. We couldn't let *all* of his health suffer. "Fruit is an important part of nutrition, Keith."

He didn't fight me as he came over and eyed the bags of apples, oranges, and mixed fruit. "Yeah? What's your favorite thing to munch on?"

I looked around and found the shelf of grapes and quickly made my way over. "Cotton candy grapes."

Keith made a face. "I don't like cotton candy."

"Me neither, but I love the grapes."

No one was watching. The produce worker was up front talking to the floral employee. I reached into the bag of cotton candy grapes and plucked one free. Along the wall of lettuce, the automatic mist was going off and I made sure to rinse the grape before going and shoving it in Keith's mouth.

With his eyes cast down at me, he sucked on my thumb slowly as I pulled it free, scraping his teeth across my skin.

He chewed on the grape and soon was bobbing his head. "Yeah, that's potent and works."

Happy, I grabbed the bag I'd stolen from and placed it in the cart. I added in a pack of blueberries, strawberries, and a bunch of bananas for good measure.

"Can I make your lunch for tomorrow?" I asked as we got ready to leave the produce section.

Keith's hands came down on either side of mine on the cart and he leaned in close to my ear to speak. "If you must."

I shivered, his proximity killing me.

"What up, Keith?" Another man spotted Keith as we were rounding the produce aisle and passing the beer and wine section of the store.

Keith broke away from me to go and greet the man. It wasn't just a simple dap, though, Keith full-on hugged the man. "Nice to know you're still around, Dre."

The man snorted. "Speak for yourself, I heard you was ghost for a minute."

Keith stepped back and frowned a little. "I was down for a little. Von definitely been on my ass about that. So, what you been on?"

Dre held his arms out, waving the pack of Pampers he was holding. "You already know. Charéal got us all wrapped around her finger. Louise sent me out to get some stuff." He looked at me and tossed Keith a knowing smile. "So, who is this?"

Not missing a beat, Keith wrapped an arm around my waist and tugged me close. "This is my girl, Kennedy. Kennedy, this is my friend, DreSean."

DreSean extended his hand and I was quick to shake it. "Nice to meet you."

"Likewise," he responded.

I didn't miss the impressive look he gave Keith.

They spoke some more while I stood back and reeled over five simple words. *This is my girl, Kennedy.*

It was the second time he'd called me "his girl." I didn't mind. It was far more appropriate than explaining to Dominique or anyone else that I was the woman he was casually sleeping with. I thought I'd be offended if he called me his *friend* as well.

Looking up at Keith as he laughed at something DreSean had said, I decided no matter what, I did not want to be his friend. If I couldn't have him at all, I didn't want to settle for friends. I was too selfish to ever stomach him being content with someone else.

"Actually, I just linked with Savon and them not too long ago. We definitely gotta make a routine of it. It's too easy to get caught up and lose track of people."

"Heard you," DreSean agreed. His phone began ringing loudly and he made a show to roll his eyes. "Listen, hit me up the next time y'all about to hit the Room, and I'll come through."

"Got you." Keith hugged him again and DreSean waved at me as he answered his call and took off.

"He got married and had a baby, so you know how that go," Keith said, by way of explanation.

Perhaps if I were a normal bride-to-be, I'd anticipate being so wrapped up in my future husband I'd miss out on spending time with my friends.

But the thought of spending uninterrupted time alone with Cain for days on end made me nauseous.

Three years. I'd only have to submit and be with him for three years minimum if we got married. He hadn't mentioned it, but hopefully my father hadn't stretched the truth on that little slip.

Still, that was a long time to be married to a man I didn't love.

I let it go and advanced forward as Keith pushed the cart onward.

We were near the bakery and the seafood section. An odd neighboring, which left the sweet smells of the cookies and cakes competing with the fishy scent of the nearby filets.

There was a cold wall with sheets of cakes and slices of what looked like cheesecake and cakes with filling. I'd never had much of a sweet tooth, but the baked goods called to me and I had to go browse with Keith in tow.

"Oh, so according to my nutritionist, we can have snacks?" Keith teased.

Being playful, I tugged on his tee. "You *are* a snack."

Keith smirked and I stuck my tongue out to taunt him further. One minute he was standing in front of me, and the next he was seizing my waist, leaning down and licking my tongue with his.

I snapped to attention and blinked rapidly.

Him.

I could taste him on my tongue. A novel flavor that had me in a daze. The small dose of him sent a violent shock to my system.

As if he wasn't fazed, Keith went on by me and grabbed a cold wedge of cheesecake with a cherry drizzle. "My one weakness."

I came to. "Love cheesecake." Though, I was a glutton for brownies. Finnegan's served a variety of options: fudge frosted, cream cheese frosted, German chocolate, and peanut butter iced. I relied on old faithful and grabbed the fudge frosted kind.

"Okay, time for fish. One of the recipes I looked up that I really want to try making is lobster mac and cheese—actually, mac and cheese is a dish I'd love to master regardless. Jadyn's great aunt makes the *best* soul food macaroni and cheese I've ever had," I said.

A tiny smile washed across Keith's face. "We can definitely teach you that."

There was a small line in front of the seafood counter. The right side of the case offered shrimp, from raw to cooked, as well as lobster tails, mussels, clams, and oysters. The middle of the case offered marinated filets of salmon, tilapia, as well as stuffed salmon and stuffed cod. And the left side of the case had all the filets Finnegan offered. Some of the fish was wild caught, and the rest was farm raised.

I went over to the lobster tails, noting that they were thirty-four ninety-nine a pound for four to five ounces, versus forty-nine ninety-nine for ten ounces. I tried to do quick mental math to see how much I'd need to make a pan of lobster mac and cheese and came up clueless.

"That's pretty pricey," Keith noted as he came up beside me. He went over to the freezer beside the case and opened the door and grabbed a bag of something and held it out. "That way is probably good, but why not try using langostinos since they're already bite-size?"

"Think I need three or four bags?" I asked.

Keith glanced at the price and appeared thoughtful. "Maybe three since they're only a pound each."

I stepped out of the way of the customers who were next in line and went over to the freezer. The langostinos were seventeen dollars a bag. "Geez, this stuff really adds up, huh?"

Keith nodded. "Rule one of grocery shopping: never do it when you're hungry."

Because my stuff was purely experimental, I went and tried to separate them in the cart. "I'll pay for mine."

"It's cool," Keith insisted.

"Your chivalry isn't going ignored, trust me, but I'm paying for my own food," I said.

He eyed the frozen lobster meat. "So, what's your game plan? You're going to drive all this back to Hampton Hills?"

He had a point, depending on traffic, it was a good forty-minute drive at least back home. That was a long time to be driving with frozen and fresh fish.

"Fifty bucks, and you can keep this at my house," Keith said in the end.

"A *hundred* bucks and deal," I agreed.

"Fine."

I returned my attention to the seafood case and another idea popped into my head. "You know what I really want to try? Catfish. I've never had it before."

Keith eyed the case as well. "Hmm. Okay, change of plans. We will definitely teach you how to cook, but that'll have to be for another day."

I pouted. "Why?"

"You in Bedford Heights talking about you've never had catfish before. It's mandatory for you go to Yvette's Kitchen. Best soul food in the city. You can get you some fried catfish, macaroni and cheese, and whatever else sound good to you."

Fried catfish sounded mouthwatering.

I put up no fight and agreed to cut our shopping for fish short. Keith gathered a few items from the meat department along with other household needs he held. When we got to the register, he was good on his word and we split the payment with my chipping in a hundred bucks and him paying for the rest. He pushed the cart out of the store and when we made it to his Tahoe, Dominique was around to help him stow the bags in the trunk.

Everything about the experience was so normal and homely, and I liked it. Discussing recipes as we shopped, giving each other ideas on what to buy, and feeling like a *real* couple.

This was more than just sex, and as bad as that was, I loved it.

Through the windshield, I could see two men leaning underneath a Toyota's hood, trying to see what was wrong with the vehicle.

"Are you going to teach me how to fix cars?" I asked as Keith got back into the driver's seat.

Keith spotted the men as well and shook his head. "No."

"No?" I teased.

Keith flashed me a smile. "That's *my* job."

I bit my lip, if only to smother the urge to kiss him.

Feeling overwhelmed by the moment, I reached up and unclasped my necklace. It was rose gold with a diamond-encrusted jasmine pendant. I held it out before Keith. "This is the first thing I bought with my own money. I know it's silly to buy jewelry instead of 'saving' money, but I was proud of myself. This necklace has always meant a lot to me, and I want you to have it."

Keith's thumb tapped against the steering wheel as his eyes focused on me. "Why?"

"No matter what happens, I want you to know that *you* mean a lot to me, Keith," I said.

Keith accepted my necklace and placed it on. When it was clasped together and hanging on his chest, he reached over, taking my face into his rough palm and stroking my cheek with his thumb. "Thank you." Leaning over, he whispered in my ear. "You mean a lot to me, too."

I kissed his palm and peered into his eyes as he reeled back.

This could end in the morning, and no matter what, I knew I would always look back on my time with Keith and know that I was happy.

Keith took us to Yvette's Kitchen. Almost as soon as we were out of the truck someone recognized Keith and shouted a greeting over to him.

Everyone knew Keith, and I liked that he wasn't bigheaded about it or walked around like he was the Man. His humbleness made me lean into him and smile.

When we stepped inside the restaurant Keith was quick to take me into his arms as we stood back from the other people waiting ahead of us. I rested into Keith and peered up at the menu, already planning on trying damn near the whole thing. It all sounded so good, especially the macaroni and cheese.

"Your eyes are bigger than your stomach," Keith warned me gently.

I didn't listen. When I went and ordered the catfish and fries snack, small catfish nugget, along with a small side of macaroni and cheese, greens, and coleslaw, Keith only chuckled at me. He'd kept it simple with his fried chicken, okra, and mashed potatoes.

The whole way back to his house the smell of the food sitting on my lap was too tempting.

"You can go in and eat," Keith told me as we got out of the car and he went to open the trunk of his truck. "I'll unload the groceries."

It was the best invitation, but I knew better. After he unlocked his front door I set the food inside on the dining room table and then I went out to help him with the rest of the stuff. We worked like a team, with Keith taking most of the load. As hungry as I was, I stayed with him and watched his process of putting away his groceries. When he was done, he saved all the blue bags by stuffing them into one and storing them in a cabinet under his sink.

Through my own exploring I knew a lot about Keith's kitchen. Where he stored his bread, where he kept his lunch bags, and where he kept his snacks. He'd bought fresh lunchmeat before we'd left Finnegan's and I was already planning on making him a ham sandwich for his lunch for Monday.

With the groceries all put away, and my flowers set in a vase with water and plant food, we washed our hands and settled in the dining room to finally dig into the food.

My first taste of catfish had me sitting back, closing my eyes, and moaning. *God*. I'd been missing out.

Keith's husky chuckle sent a blanket of warmth through me. "Glad you like it."

"*Like* is such a small word, Keith William. I am in love," I declared.

"Oh, we usin' middle names, Kennedy *Elizabeth*?" he taunted.

He'd remembered. A part of me wondered if when the time came and we went our separate ways, if he'd ever forget about me. This was the furthest thing from casual, from anonymous. Like a tattoo, he'd embedded himself within my skin and I hated the idea of letting him go.

"This food is so good. Why learn to cook when I can just eat this?" Realistically, I was only kidding. As delicious as it all was, I was going to hate myself for pigging out two days in a row come my workout routine Monday.

"Because eating out adds up," Keith remarked. "If you get good enough, you can make your own food that's better than this."

I doubted it, but I was hopeful. "When are you off next?"

"Wednesday," Keith answered as he grabbed his glass of water and took a sip. "Think about what you want to cook and we'll do it then."

I wanted to cook, and I wanted to do it with him, but hogging up all his free time? "You sure it won't be an inconvenience?"

Keith shrugged. "I'ma stop by the community center in the afternoon, but I'll have time to come and cook with you. I mean, I gotta eat, so it's whatever. I want to help you."

He wanted to help me. That was all I needed to hear.

I ate more of my food, and I hated to admit that Keith was right, that I'd been so hungry I'd overordered.

"So, what were you up to while I was on lockdown?" I joked.

Keith frowned in distaste at that statement. "Come on, you had to do more than that."

"Well, outside of sulking, I went to a cake testing with my parents and Cain. It was almost, kinda, nice? It was the first time my dad's been in public in a year, and we all just sorta had a decent time eating cake. We both liked the white almond cake with raspberry filling, so I guess that'll be 'the cake,'" I said. "And I also found my dress, which isn't my *dream* dress, but it'll do. My mom and the girls liked it."

Keith wasn't eating as he sat listening to me ramble. Gone was his earlier humor, replaced with a blank mask I couldn't decipher.

"So, how was your time?" I asked, trying to steer the conversation back to him.

"I slept with someone else," he said. There wasn't a hint of a joke or remorse on his face.

A lump got caught in my throat and I struggled to swallow and concentrate as those ugly words circled my brain.

He'd *slept* with someone else.

A burning stab pierced my heart as tears pooled in my eyes. I shot up from my chair and went for the door.

"Kennedy." Keith was behind me, but I wasn't interested in hearing any more that he had to say. He'd said enough.

Only, when I went to open the front door, his hand shot out and shut it.

"Stop." My voice was weak and I refused to cry over this.

"No," he said firmly. "How are you even goin' to get home when your car is at Jadyn's?"

"I'll walk," I said as I held my head up high.

"Kennedy." It was a plea.

Whirling around, I faced him, unable to look at him long without the fresh hurt surfacing. "What?"

"I lied," he admitted. "All I did in the past few weeks was some work around the house. I did some custom work for a guy, and I was lookin' out for Dominique. That's it."

I didn't understand. "Why would you lie like that?"

"Because it fucking hurts me to hear about your little perfect family, and how you and your boy found the perfect wedding cake," Keith snapped as he gestured to me. "That pain you feel in your chest right now is how it felt in there listenin' to you go on about cakes and dresses."

Relief and anger coalesced into one, and it gripped me fiercely.

"Fuck you and your ego!" I yelled at him before I turned and attempted to leave again.

"I think about you." Those four simple words halted my desire to leave, turning me around and allowing Keith to walk up on me until the tips of his boots brushed my heels. "When you not here, you're on my mind. I hate that you're gearing up to marry another man. I hate that this feels like it should be real and just us. I hate that this is bigger than me fucking you."

It was a confession, one that didn't excuse his rudeness, but explained the root of it.

"Don't treat me like shit because you're mad I'm stuck." I folded my arms and started to go back to the dining room. "I'm only staying because I like the food."

Keith seized me before I could get too far. His hands ran down my arms, setting my skin ablaze. "I'm sorry. I'm an asshole with an ego."

A smile threatened to disrupt my frown, but I kept my face in line. "You were *acting* like an asshole. You're not one."

"Your parents liked that NFL dude because he was a baller no doubt, and this new one is set for life too if he's got his own business and linkin' with your dad," Keith went on. "I can't compete with that. If I fuck up for some reason, I can't just hand you a credit card and let you go wild to make it up to you."

It was like he'd struck me. "Wow, is that how I come off? If I actually marry this guy, that's going to be *his* solution to any problem. I don't want that. I don't want to be bought. I *want* to be respected. Cain doesn't like *me*, he likes the idea of me."

Keith came closer until my back met the wall. "I know you're not like that, but that's how your parents want you set up."

He wasn't wrong. To my parents, my dislike for my marriage was easily dismissed when it came to the pros outweighing the cons.

"I'm sorry," Keith said gently. "It wasn't right to lash out."

It wasn't, not when the thought left me sick.

The realization of this drove my gaze up to his.

"This feels like more than just sex. The idea of you sleeping with someone else *hurts*. You're not mine, and I'm not yours, but I don't like the idea of someone else touching you," I said as I looked into his eyes.

Keith reached out and grabbed my arm, going and placing my hand to his chest, over his beating heart. "Now you see where I'm coming from?"

We'd crossed the line and hadn't looked back. Emotions were

involved and there was no escaping this without being hurt. Hearts were going to break, whether we planned it or not.

"You want me," I said.

Keith nodded and caressed my face. "I do."

"Then why don't you kiss me?" I had to know.

He came forward, resting his forehead to mine. "Because at least when you walk away, I can't say I had every piece of you."

It was settled. Keith Avery would be my undoing.

I went with him back to the table, where we had lunch, and then when I was too full to eat any more, we settled on the couch where I fell asleep in his arms. I had spent the night and next day with Keith, and we hadn't had sex, and yet I'd never felt more content.

28

I stopped by my parents' house Wednesday to see my father after he made a request to speak to me.

I had hoped it was good news. That he was summoning me over to tell me that the engagement was off, but there was no such luck.

In the doorway to his bedroom my hopes were crushed by the ever-present sight of Cain. My father had his reading glasses on and was skimming a stack of papers as Cain stood back waiting patiently.

There was business, and then there was harassment. Why couldn't Cain work with Phil while my father took a step down?

"Sit," my father ordered without taking his eyes off his reading.

Of course Phil couldn't just lead Nichols & Wagner. My father wouldn't step down if you paid him.

"Can't you say please?" I replied as I remained standing in the doorway.

My father lowered his glasses and gaped at me.

Cain said nothing as he stood coolly waiting for my father to finish whatever they were going over.

A beat went by as my father continued to stare at me. In the end, like always, I conceded.

I went and took a seat in the chair by his bed and waited my turn.

My father went back to Cain. "You wanna extend on my property, fine, but you're thinking small."

Cain took the criticism with ease. "Damon, a complete remodel would take far more time than an extension."

"Okay?" my father challenged. "I've got time. What, do you have something else more pressing at hand?"

Cain's gaze flickered to mine. "He's going to outlive us all."

Even if he were teasing, we could only hope.

My father held the papers out for Cain to take. "I still want the new structure in LA. The Residence at Cartier should be a completely new look and design. We're not cutting corners."

Cain accepted this with a nod of his head. "Yes, sir."

"Now, on to the next order of business." My father removed his glasses and sat up a little more, trying to get comfortable as he faced me.

"Should we be alone?" I wondered of Cain's presence.

My father made a face. "Up to him."

I watched as Cain's finger tapped the stack of papers in his hand as he looked from my father to me. Being polite, he decided to step out into the hall to give us privacy.

I waited until the door was shut behind him before giving my father my full attention. "Well?"

The grave expression on his face had me wary. "About the wedding," he began with a sigh. "It is tradition for a father to walk his daughter down the aisle to give her away. Have you been thinking about that?"

My wedding. He wanted to talk about the impending *worst* day of my life.

"No," I admitted. "I haven't."

"I don't know how I'll be by December," my father sounded vulnerable, unlike himself. "This thing can't be controlled or reasoned with. The most people live with this disease is three years and we're on year two."

I wanted to plug my ears, to stop him from talking about such a possibility of him not being here. Of him dying. I knew the statistics of ALS like the back of my hand after so much time. Only five percent went on to live twenty years, and ten percent lived ten. My father, he was a special man, a strong man, and a fully capable man of living *with* this diagnosis rather than succumbing to it.

Only a small few had ALS remit, and others had it burn out within them. On average, it wasn't stoppable or reversible, but I had hope my father could continue the fight. He seemed determined enough.

"You'll be the one," I spoke up clearly and concisely. "You've always been the strongest man I know. I'm positive you'll be the one who sees another year and then another and more."

A wry smile had my father's face briefly lighting up. "Your mother wants to plan something for January. A big charity event to bring awareness. There's only so long I can put this off. I thought about skipping the wedding, but then that wouldn't be fair to you."

The wedding itself wasn't fair to me, but I didn't have it in me to bring it up. "We could always not do a wedding, and just get married at a courthouse."

My father clicked his tongue. "I'd rather you move the wedding up than do that."

Move the wedding closer? I shuddered to think of my time being semi-single being cut short. Cain had given me his word we wouldn't have to consummate our marriage if we got married, but I wasn't willing to test that theory any time soon.

"Couldn't you just work *this* angle with Cain?" I pleaded. "Try to get him to see how absurd this whole thing is. Our family is going through a lot right now and who can think of planning a wedding and a marriage?"

"I talked to him, Neddy," my father said. "And he's certain he wants to go through with this. He's a little cold, but he's not so bad. What's wrong with him?"

"I don't want him!" I practically snapped. I had to stop and collect myself before I seriously broke down. "What about what *I* want, Daddy? You're making this about money. As if a man with a normal job couldn't make me just as happy."

"We'll never know now, will we?" My father was dismissing my train of thought and I knew better than to argue.

Instead, I stood from my chair and lifted my chin with dignity I didn't feel. "You better hope you do outlive us all, because otherwise you're willing to spend your last days ensuring my misery all while you and Phil land a deal *you* won't see through."

I didn't bother waiting for a response before seeing myself out of his room and down the stairs. I had to go and meet with Keith. Being with him was the only means of happiness I knew these days.

"Kennedy!" My mother was coming down the hall with Cain behind her. She was smiling and flagging me down. "Don't go, the food is on its way."

"Excuse me?" I asked.

"Well, I was thinking about how the official engagement party didn't go so well," my mother began as she glanced between me and my fiancé. "And, so, I figured it'd be nice to have a personal engagement dinner with the family. Your father's going to come down and we'll all eat at the table. I ordered catering."

Horror washed through me at the idea. "No."

At my mother's surprise and Cain's attention, I quickly went on. "I...I have plans."

My mother swallowed. "Well, I should've considered you were busy. I-I guess we could always reschedule—"

"Nonsense," Cain insisted as he came up beside me and placed a hand on my shoulder. "What Kennedy means is, thank you."

The finality in his words stunned me silent.

My mother frowned. "If Kennedy has plans it's all right to do this another time."

Cain regarded me. "What are your plans?"

Oh shit. "Jadyn and I—"

"Invite her over," Cain responded before I could finish. He faced my mother. "If that's all right with you? We've been engaged for over a month and I haven't even met Kennedy's closest friend."

My mother's eyes widened as she looked at me. She felt just as put on the spot as I did. "Well, if it's no trouble for Kennedy, it would be a treat to have Jadyn over."

I wanted to speak up, to say that it was an inconvenience to have this impromptu dinner, but I couldn't. Not when I wasn't going to see Jadyn, but Keith. "Sounds...good."

My mother rubbed behind her neck, forcing a smile on her face. "Well then, Irene and I will go and get your father." She looked toward Cain, studying him. "You can invite your men in. There'll be plenty of food. And, please, take off your jacket. Get comfortable."

The moment she stepped away I gathered my cell phone to send Keith a text.

Or so, I'd planned.

One second my phone was in my hand, and the next Cain had it.

"What are you doing?" I snapped.

"You heard her," Cain replied. "This is a night for family."

"I have to talk to Jadyn so she can come over," I said as calmly as possible.

Cain held my phone up. "Then call her. I'll wait."

Fuck.

"This is psychotic," I bit out as I snatched my phone.

Cain arched a brow, taking a curious stance. "How so?"

I couldn't call Keith. Not with Cain standing in front of me. So, reluctantly, I pressed the contact for Jadyn's number and called her as Cain watched me while my hand shook.

"I hate you," I uttered as the line rang.

"That's an interesting response," Cain marveled as he stuffed his hands into his pockets.

Hate was such a strong word. And I had every right to feel that way about Cain.

"Hello?" Jadyn picked on her end and I wished it were Keith I was talking to instead. Keith who was about to be stood up. Keith who didn't deserve to worry over why I didn't show up.

"Hey, listen, my mom's throwing me a private engagement dinner here at the house. She wants to invite you over," I explained. "My warden would like to meet you."

Jadyn snickered. "I really don't know what to say to that, K."

"Well, it's too late to vet the guy, but it would be *nice* for you to meet," I tried to make a joke of it but my mood wouldn't lift. My heart was pounding in my ears and I couldn't stop thinking about what I was giving up by staying and having dinner here.

"Got you. I'm on my way," Jadyn promised before hanging up.

With that squared away I had no choice but to relinquish my phone as Cain held his hand out expectantly.

"I'm not a child, you know," I said through gritted teeth.

Cain tucked my phone away. "This is a night for family, and friends. Why would you need to be on your phone?"

I glowered at him. "Because it's *mine*."

Really, I'd never been a violent person in my life, and all I wanted to do was strangle him with his stupid tie. And then I took in his Tom Ford jacket. My mother wanted it off so he'd be more at home.

Rolling my eyes, I held out my Saint Laurent open between us. "Your jacket. My mom said to take it off. I don't know about you, but it's not good dinner etiquette to have guns out at the table."

Cain thought about my offer for all of a moment before he slowly removed his jacket. He set it on the table near the stairs and then removed his gun and holster.

"Thank you," he said.

Cain gathered his jacket and slung it over his arm. "Try to have a good night, Wife."

With him and my parents holding me hostage? I wouldn't.

Jadyn arrived at the same time as the catering was delivered. My mother had ordered from The Sheridan, making me at least anticipate the food. Except, I was naturally expected to sit next to my fiancé instead of my best friend.

"Jay, this is my fiancé, Cain Carter. Cain, this is my best friend, Jadyn," I said by way of introduction of the two.

Cain reached out and shook hands with Jadyn, offering his version of a kind smile.

It worked. Jadyn had gushed over his photographs. In person she was doing a double take at Cain's good looks.

Perhaps I was an anomaly for not being affected by my fiancé.

"Very nice to meet you," Cain said smoothly. "I've heard great things."

Jadyn peeked at me. In her eyes I could see the question of, *Is he really that bad?*

Focus, my gaze said back.

"Likewise," Jadyn responded to Cain before going and taking her seat.

Jadyn had worn a cozy looking maroon sweater and jeans. I was only supposed to be stopping by, so I'd dressed in a hoodie and leggings. I felt out of place as I removed my baseball cap and settled in my seat next to Cain. Worse, I was antsy over Keith. I didn't know his number by heart to sneak and call him to let him know I wouldn't be coming. I hated to think he was at home waiting on me.

"Well, look who it is!" My father's voice boomed into the room as he came in on his electric wheelchair.

To further hide my father's condition, my parents had

installed a lift onto the back staircase, helping him be able to be transported from the first and second floor without being seen.

Jadyn took my father in for the first time since he'd been diagnosed and her face broke out into a smile as she rose from her chair. She went and hugged him close. Prior to recent events, my parents had always adored Jadyn.

"You're looking sharp," my father appraised Jay.

My best friend blinked back tears. "So are you. I've missed you, Damon. It's good to see you."

On Jadyn's side of the table, Vino and Beans had joined us reluctantly. Unlike Cain, they didn't remove their jackets. Down time or not, they were still carrying.

Irene helped my father get situated at the table and I could tell by the grimace on my mother's face she was anxious to step in.

"Now, everyone good?" my father asked.

Everyone murmured that they were.

"Good, let's eat," my father announced.

Around the table everyone began passing dishes. There were meatballs and pasta for the meat eaters, along with chicken marsala, a house salad, and tomato mozzarella bruschetta. My mother had gotten shrimp paesano for my benefit.

As good as it tasted, I could barely eat a bite. Not when I was supposed to be in Bedford making dinner with Keith.

"So, Cain, where are you from?" Jadyn asked. She had this innocent look to her, but I knew she was digging for me.

"Kinda feels like I'm from all over. I spent some time in Inglewood, Lindenwood—"

"And now you're in *this* neck of the woods," my father joked.

His corny dad joke gathered a round of light chuckles.

"Right." Cain offered a loose smile. "Where are you from, Jadyn?"

"Bedford Heights," Jadyn chirped up proudly. "BH all day."

Cain tipped his head. "Good area."

Jadyn agreed. "It's not too far from here, which I can handle when it comes to K." Her eyes drank me in and a sadness touched them. "Just promise me you two won't move to Vegas on me."

Cain ran his hand up and down my arm, a silk caress that left me startled and stiff. "I mostly run Cartier from here. I do fly out to do walk-throughs and make sure things are on the up-and-up, but I have no intention of moving Kennedy away from her family."

I forced a shrimp into my mouth and attempted to focus on the garlic goodness to keep my face even.

"How long have you and Kennedy been friends?" Cain asked next.

"We met freshman year at UCLA. We both tried the whole sorority thing and realized it wasn't for us," Jadyn confessed. "But *we* clicked, though, so we've been friends ever since."

"UCLA? What were you studying?"

"She's an aspiring filmmaker," my father spoke up thoughtfully. He'd always admired Jadyn's ambition as well. "She's going to be the next big thing."

"As soon as she lets us hand over a script," my mother teased.

Jadyn blushed and shrugged in Cain's direction. "My dream is to direct and write, and as much as I appreciate the Nicholses and their support, I kinda just want to make it on my own."

"Nothing wrong with a little help," Cain responded.

"We'll see," Jadyn said, non-committal. "So, what about you? What's it like running a casino?"

Cain regarded my father before turning back to Jadyn. "It's... an adjustment. The whole thing sorta just fell into my lap when my father passed."

"Sounds overwhelming," Jadyn noted.

Cain didn't disagree. "It was. I kept most of James's team since they know Cartier by hand, and I can say since working with Damon and Phil, I've learned a few pointers as well."

My father was touched by that remark as he smiled and ate some of his pasta.

Growing up, he had never been the type of man who stressed

about having a *boy*. He was comfortable and happy to have me as a daughter. In the weeks since the engagement, it was almost as if he'd adjusted to the idea of having a son as well. Especially one willing to learn the trade.

"So." Jadyn rested her chin on her fist as she peered at Cain intently. "What made you want to marry Kennedy?"

I smirked as I caught my mother coughing on her wine.

Cain wasn't fazed. "I saw her at a charity event and she just held the whole room's attention. She radiated grace, light, humility—she had everything I'd ever dreamed of in a woman."

"And you just had to have her?" Jadyn commented, her genuine interest showing.

Cain glanced my way. "So long as she's willing to have me."

It was a "cute" comment, one earning an *aww* from Irene and even Jadyn, though I was sure at least Jay was faking.

As expected, I lit up at Cain's words and played my part.

Dinner went on and I went on autopilot, smiling when needed, laughing when others did, and appearing interested even though my mind was miles away.

While I'd only gotten a portion of the shrimp paesano, I noticed Cain had a little of everything. He wasn't a picky eater I could see as he seemed to enjoy it all without complaint. It was while watching him try some of the bruschetta and smile to himself that it dawned on me. At some point, he had *starved*. I suddenly recollected all of the meals we'd shared together and I could see a pattern. He ate with appreciation and he was always gracious to our server. He was his most humane when eating, because it was a luxury he hadn't always had.

My appetite slipped away as the idea settled into my mind.

Before he was a villain, Cain Carter had been a victim, too.

When dinner was over, I hugged Jadyn close, wishing to take some of her confidence with me.

"Take care," she told me. Her vision slid to Cain and her

demeanor changed as the smile slipped from her face. "Let's cut the bullshit since her folks ain't around. This isn't a cute little romance—we *all* know that. You got my girl wrapped up in whatever the hell you're doin' with her dad and that's wack. She may feel trapped enough to go along with it, but just know..." Jadyn took a step closer to Cain, holding her finger out as she sized him up. "...you fuck with her, you're fuckin' with me, and I'm the *wrong* one."

Cain didn't crack a smile or try to find the humor in her threat. He simply nodded, staring Jadyn in her eyes. "I respect that." His attention flashed to me. "It's not my intention to ever harm Kennedy. If it takes forever, I'll be here to show her I'm not going to hurt her."

Jadyn wasn't impressed. *Good.* "Why won't you let her go and go about your business with Damon?"

"What can I say, when I know what I want, I go after it." Cain gave a small shrug.

Jadyn snorted. "No reciprocity at all, huh?"

I took it as my cue to cut in. I loved Jadyn down for coming to my defense, but it was hopeless. At least, it felt that way. "Jay... I can handle this, trust me."

My best friend sighed, coming and wrapping me in a tight hug and rocking me for a moment. "I know, but you shouldn't have to."

Jadyn let me go and faced Cain once more. "I mean it."

Cain stood beside me. "I know you do." He eyed Vino. "Walk her to her car."

Jadyn shook her head. "That won't be necessary."

Vino went ahead and opened the front door. "I insist."

"Who said chivalry was dead?" Jadyn managed to joke as she slid past Vino and walked out to the front step. He joined her outside before shutting the door behind them.

Vino was quiet and only spoke when spoken to. He was a tall man, muscular like an athlete, with smooth olive-brown skin and fine jet-black hair with the slightest curl. Vino was handsome, but like Cain, he had a coldness to him, a darkness to his coal-black eyes that just read *killer*.

What an appropriate person to hire as a bodyguard.

With Jadyn gone, and my mother and Irene helping my father back up to his room, I took Cain and brought him to my family's living room where we sat at the grand piano. We sat side by side on the cushioned bench, and for once, I didn't feel the need to scoot away.

"You said you just bought a piano," I brought up as I glanced Cain's way.

He nodded.

I gestured to my family's Steinway. "Play something."

Cain regarded the piano behind him and shook his head.

"No?" I questioned, partly bummed.

"I only play when I'm not in the best of moods," Cain explained.

I nudged him, almost smiling. "So, you're in a good mood?"

Cain peered into my eyes. "I'm moderate."

I couldn't help but chuckle. *I'm moderate.* Did he have to be so serious?

We were sitting so close, close enough to touch. So I did. I reached out, taking his hand into mine and entwining our fingers. I wondered if there was a part of Cain that had a heart.

"I wish we could be friends," I said.

Cain squeezed my hand in his. "Why can't we be both? Friends *and* lovers?" When I didn't answer, Cain let my hand go. "You hate me too much for that."

I didn't think I could ever love him, be attracted to him in that way, or *want* him. As I sat beside him, knowing he hadn't always been this way, but rather, was made, I realized that I couldn't hate him either.

Facing the piano, I went and pressed a cold key. A note sounded out. It was sad. Like the moment between us.

29

KEITH

She didn't call.

There wasn't a hint of Kennedy all day Wednesday. After I got in from the community center I sat and waited for a call or a text—some sign that she was coming through.

By the time the sun went down, I'd given up entirely.

I could've called her, and ordinarily, I would've, but then I thought about the possibility of her being around her family. Around *him*. She probably had me saved under an alias, but it was a chance I wasn't willing to take. To potentially get her in a sticky situation.

Looking at my blank lock screen, I shook my head and shoved my phone back into my pocket.

It would always be this way. Operating on *her* time. Something I'd known from the beginning and had so easily accepted.

The fact of the matter was, I was nothing more than a sidepiece. Convenient dick whenever Kennedy needed it. It was a bitter pill to swallow, but there was no other way to feel as I came to realize I'd be spending my Wednesday evening alone.

Fingering the pendant hanging from the necklace around my neck, I felt a slight sense of guilt overtake me as I wrote off whatever the fuck this was I had with Kennedy. I knew what I saw when she looked at me, and I knew what I felt when I was with her.

Maybe I was *more* than a booty call, but that didn't stop the irritation from stirring.

I still needed to cook, but I found myself grabbing my pack of Malboros and heading out to my back patio.

The first intake of nicotine calmed my nerves and curved my appetite. The second intake cleared my mind.

I was gearing up to jut out my second cigarette when I caught myself. Reluctantly I blew out a stream of smoke and stubbed out my cigarette before stuffing it back into the pack.

Enough.

I needed to make better choices in my life. No more getting wrapped up in women who weren't hundred percent available, and no more fucking up my lungs.

I gotta let these bad habits go.

The night air danced around me and cooled my mood, settling my decision even more.

Heaving a sigh, I tilted the pack and poured that half-finished cigarette into my palm and relit it. What the hell? What was one last taste before I gave it up for good?

30

Kennedy

"I'm so sorry, Kennedy," my mother was saying as we stood alone in my family's foyer. Cain and his men had left. He'd forked over my cell phone and I'd let him dig out his holster and gun from my Saint Laurent.

I was partially relieved to find that Keith hadn't called or texted me during dinner. Partly relieved, and partly disappointed.

I hoped he wasn't mad, even though he had every right to be.

"You're just trying," I mumbled as I placed my phone into my bag. "That's all you've *been* doing since Daddy got sick. Trying to make the most of things."

My mother's gentle hands came and held me against her. I pressed my face into her neck, inhaling some of her familiar perfume and homey scent. And then I gathered my keys and went home.

It was late, and I didn't know Keith's work schedule, but that didn't stop me from attempting to call to make things right as soon as I got into my door. The line rang and rang, until it reached his voicemail.

"This is Keith, you just missed me. If you leave your name and your number I'll hit you back," his deep voice greeted my ear in a lazy monotone.

A tone sounded out, indicating for me to leave a message. I didn't.

I hung up and called again. When the same fate fell upon me, I gave up calling altogether.

ME

I'm sorry I stood you up

He didn't text me back, and he didn't call.

In the morning, I awoke to no returned calls or texts. Just messages from Jadyn questioning my next move as far as Cain went.

I didn't want to think about Cain.

ME

Faking my death sounds good

JADYN

Being dramatic won't solve your problems

She was right. I was in a big mess.

My first priority was getting through to Keith.

This time when I called him, he answered.

"What's up, Kennedy?" He sounded dry, disinterested.

"Thank God," I breathed out. "I've been trying to get ahold of you."

"I see that."

So he'd ignored my calls and texts?

"Keith?" I questioned, unsure what this all meant.

He sighed on his end. "Listen, Kenny, it's been a fun little minute and all, but maybe it's—"

"No!" I rushed to say, immediately cutting off what sounded

suspiciously like a breakup speech. "Can you come by? We can talk, okay? It's not what it looks like, I promise."

He snorted on his end. "Actually, I have to get ready for work. My day off was *yesterday*."

I frowned. He *was* hurt. "Keith, please. Let me explain."

"I gotta go in. It's whatever," Keith said dismissively.

"Then come by when you're off," I suggested. "I'll text you my address and you can stop by."

He whistled. "Nice and late enough not to be seen, huh?"

"I can't meet you in the lobby—"

"'Course not," he responded coolly.

"I'm sorry."

"Don't be."

He was being way too casual about this and it made me antsy. I could feel my grip on him slipping and I couldn't lose him. Not my last thread of sanity.

"I would never leave you hanging. Just, please, come over and we can talk," I begged.

He was quiet on his end and I feared he'd hang up on me.

I stayed silent, not wanting to press him further. I wanted to believe I was strong enough to endure whatever he had to say next, but that wasn't true at all as I felt my heart crawl up my throat.

Another sigh came to my ear and he was back on the line. "Listen, text me your address and I'll think about it."

"Okay," I said, trying to keep the hopefulness out of my voice.

"All right then, Kennedy," Keith said.

"All right then."

We hung up and I sent him a text with my address and instructions to get to my suite. Then I hugged my knees to my chest as I sat there in my bed.

If I had any guts at all I'd take what money I had and run off to Greece. Running sounded cowardly, though, even if I planned to go to a beautiful island.

On the other hand, facing my problems head-on felt daunting all the same.

For the time being, I told myself if I settled things with Keith I could handle the rest. Just one thing at a time.

I busied myself with going to my Pilates class and grabbing lunch with Elyse and Stephanie, the latter I hadn't been in the mood for, but I welcomed the distraction.

"So, have you thought about bridesmaids and your maid of honor?" Stephanie asked as she doused her French fries in malt vinegar.

After my very unhealthy weekend in Bedford Heights, I kept it simple with a small ahi tuna niçoise salad. I put more interest in eating than conversing with the girls, but Stephanie had asked a legitimate question. One I couldn't tap dance around.

To be honest, I hadn't thought about my wedding in grave detail. I had a dress, but no color scheme. LeChé had even mentioned finding matching dresses for my bridal party when I'd picked out that plain dress. I couldn't have been bothered then, and I still very much felt the same way now.

Ideally, if I weren't marrying Cain and someone I loved instead, I'd have my dream dress, a champagne and cream-colored wedding theme, and of course Jadyn would be my maid of honor. For body count purposes, I'd have Elyse and Stephanie as bridesmaids.

But this marriage to Cain wasn't that, so I wasn't interested in ironing out the fine print.

Lazily, I lifted and dropped my shoulder as I chewed on some tuna. "Everything's been happening so fast I've barely had time to think."

Elyse glanced over at Stephanie who pointed a drenched French fry in my direction. "You should've just married Gaius."

Elyse's eyes bugged out. "Steph."

Stephanie went on indignantly. "Oh, come on, that way she would've easily had her wedding colors be blue and white."

Even I gagged at the thought. The Long Beach Sharks' colors

were capri blue, gray, and white. There were some WAGs who'd gone and used their fiancés' team colors for their weddings, but I didn't like the colors that much to ever do that. I also wasn't a *true* sports girl. I'd feel like a fraud.

Just like I did as I endured more of my lunch with the girls.

Elyse and Stephanie were about the aesthetic. As long as I looked good amongst my fellow upper crust in Hampton Hills, that was all that mattered.

I needed to cut them off. After the theatrics of my wedding, I would become "too busy" for them. The mere idea left me smiling and half paying attention to whatever it was that Stephanie was saying.

I stopped by the bookstore after lunch and bought copies of *Night Changes* and the first *Mister* book.

At home I curled up in a chair and began reading *Mister*. It was about Simone, a young woman who gets her first serious job being an assistant for successful entrepreneur Isaiah Keller. Unlike Dixie and Darius's lightly dramatic romance in *Night Changes*, something told me *Mister* would tug at my emotions with the dynamic of Simone and Isaiah.

I got caught up in my reading, focusing on page after page until well after night had fallen.

Knocking at my door pulled me away from my book, where I'd read my way to the middle, too engrossed to miss a second. I dog-eared my page and set the book aside as I stood and stretched before going and answering the door.

Keith.

He was standing there under a baseball cap slung low, a denim jacket, T-shirt, and jeans. Head to toe in blue.

My first thought was to jump on him and hug him, but then I thought better and politely stepped to the side so he could enter my suite.

Keith did so and looked around, his dark eyes lingering on every corner and piece of furniture I owned. I'd kept the color scheme the same, but I added a little touch of me to every room to make my suite a home.

"Make sure yourself comfortable," I insisted as I tried to take his jacket.

Keith moved away from me, shaking his head. "Can't stay too long, Kenny."

He was distant and I hated it.

Threading my fingers together, I got down to it. "My dad called and wanted me to stop over. So, I did. That didn't really go too well and when I was leaving my mother mentioned she'd ordered food. She wanted to have a nice family dinner to celebrate my engagement."

"Have fun?" Keith asked, arching a brow.

"No. Cain took my phone and refused to give it back. I had to lie and say I had plans with Jadyn to explain why I was so desperate to go, and then Cain invited her to our dinner," I said. "I got stuck there and I didn't know your number to sneak and call you."

Keith stood there, unaffected by anything I'd said.

"Keith, I would never stand you up," I swore.

He removed his baseball cap and ran his hand over his waves. "I know that. I figured something came up when you didn't show or get ahold of me."

"Okay then," I said. "Please don't take it out on me."

Keith fixed his gaze my way. "I'm not mad."

"You kinda iced me out earlier like you were."

"I'm just tired. This shit is a lot to deal with," Keith threw out.

Lowering my guard, I padded over to him and tugged on his jacket as I peered up into his eyes. "I know, and I'm sorry. You're my peace. The only thing keeping me together these days and I can't lose that. It'll never happen again, okay? I promise."

Keith shook his head. "You can't promise that."

"I won't let that happen again," I reiterated to make my stance clear. Going forward, there'd be no more family dinners to fake an image I wasn't interested in. They could drag me kicking and screaming down the aisle when the time came, but I wasn't about to *act* like I liked any of what was going on. I intended to be an icy bitch until the day I got the luxury to annul my father's decision.

Unless of course he came to his senses, but that wasn't looking too good.

With Keith silently looking down at me and my staring up at him, everything felt on the line. His handsome face was of anger and stone, and I wanted to make things right.

Very quickly, I stood on my toes and pressed my lips to his. Startled, he parted his lips and I dove in for more, loving the feel of finally kissing him.

Only, not too long into my triumph, Keith jerked back. "What was that?"

I shrugged in an *oops* manner. "I just...needed to know what that felt like."

His head tilted to the side. "Have you been curious about kissin' your boy?"

"Gross," I let out.

Keith released a breath through his nose. And then he took a dangerous step closer. One leaving me backing up. He tracked this movement and smirked, his hooded eyes locked on me. "You know, I've been very good about *your* boundaries. But you've never given a shit about mine."

Another step closer. And another step back.

I turned, wondering if I could outrun him for space—

My back was slapped against the wall of my living room and Keith's hands planted on the wall beside my head, caging me in.

Keith came close and pressed his lips to my ear. "You're a spoiled, *selfish*, fuckin' brat."

I reeled back. I had never been so insulted in my life. "I—"

Keith ate my words. His lips claimed mine, causing my knees to buckle as a deep moan traveled from the pit of my belly.

Shit.

Keith's body brushed against mine as he gave in and kissed

me. His lips. Fuck. His lips were so soft, strong, and skilled. Aggressive, possessive, and determined. I had no choice but to submit. Keith was in control and I loved every second of it.

But I needed more.

Hastily, I reached out between us and began undoing his belt buckle. I wanted to kiss him with him inside me. *Needed* to kiss him while feeling him everywhere.

Except Keith stepped back, leaning away from my hands and breaking our kiss. Leaving me wet and aching.

"What?" My chest was rising and falling.

"I don't have anything," he let it be known as he ran his hand down his face. His eyes softened and the Keith I knew and wanted came to the surface. "I didn't come here to dick you down, so I wasn't thinking about grabbing anything."

A condom. He didn't bring a freaking condom?

I shoved him, annoyed as I walked off. "It's...it's okay. I'm on the pill." Biting my lip, I began to search the area for a manila file folder I'd recently acquired. "I went to the doctor last week, and unfortunately for my fiancé I'm not carrying any contagious diseases. So, all is—"

He grabbed me by the waistband of my leggings and pulled me back. "I can get you my medical records." He looked into my eyes, appearing as serious as ever. "Are you sure about this?"

Slowly, I swallowed as I managed a nod. "Yes, I trust you."

"Good, because I'm tired of fuckin' playin' with you."

That was all he needed to hear. Gone was his patience as his hold of me became rough. In seconds he'd picked me up and was finding his way to my bedroom. I had never been so horny and needy in my life. I kissed all over the side of his face and his neck, causing his grip on my ass to harden.

Once we crossed the threshold of my bedroom Keith didn't stop until he reached my bed where he tossed me down onto it. I bounced momentarily as I watched Keith take off his jacket and sling it to the side. Next went his shirt and one look at that body and those tattooed arms and I helped myself to rushing out of my tank top.

I let out a squeak when a rough hand grabbed a hold of my ankle and yanked me down to the edge of the bed.

Keith's fingers curled around my waistband as he quickly ripped them down my legs.

"Don't let me hurt you," he said in a warning.

"You won't," was all I could manage to get out.

And he didn't.

Keith removed the last of my clothing before stripping nude. With renewed focus, he crawled onto the bed and kissed me again, leaving me just as wanton as I'd been out in my living room. He left my lips and traveled to my breasts, giving each equal attention. The kissing continued further south where he buried his head between my legs and kissed me tender and numb.

All of this was for me as his anger took a back seat and he handled me with a softness I couldn't get enough of. He brought me to the brink before coming back up and parting my thighs. He entered me slowly and at once let out this deep groan that sent my sex clenching around him.

"Fuck, Kennedy." He moaned into my ear and I felt so much closer.

Keith made love to me for the first time and it was the most intimate experience I'd ever had. His hands were all over me as he took me slow and gentle, patient for what was brewing inside of me. Not once did he stop kissing me. Not once did I want him to.

There wasn't a breath I took that didn't involve his. We were one. Entwined. Entangled. Endless.

He held me tight and close when I came and I clung to him, needing him like a second skin as I rode out the sensation.

And then, as if a switch had been flipped, the anger was back as Keith took hold of my hips and slammed his into mine.

"Keith!" I could only call out his name once before another harsh intrusion sent me silent.

God he was deep. So deep inside me he felt embedded into my system.

"So what's your plan?" he demanded to know as he peered down at me, irritation inflaming his dark eyes. "You're gonna marry this dude, and then come and sneak into my city to fuck me every now and then?"

Tears pooled into my eyes as one stroke sent me close to the edge again. "No!"

He perked a brow. "Oh?"

I shook my head, my tears falling. "I only want you. I'll never be his."

Keith stilled, staring down at me, reading between my words for any hidden meaning. "We'll see about that."

He dove deeper inside me and I cried out.

Gone was Keith's patience as he took what he wanted. He fucked me like he owned me. Like I was *his*. He stamped his name all over me. *Keith. Keith. Keith*. Claiming me. And I had never come harder in my life in the aftermath.

Cool air brushed over my naked skin as I lay on my side, facing Keith as he was facing me. A stupid smile on my face had me blushing into my pillow.

I was too sore to move, but I needed to get clean.

Keith's palm ran down the length of my body and he followed the movement with a contented look. That was most intense sex I'd ever had and I was hooked for more.

I already liked how he fucked, but I *loved* how he made love, how he focused on giving me pleasure, how gentle he was, and how in the moment he seemed.

I ran my finger down Keith's solid chest, wanting to trace it with my tongue but feeling too comfortable to make the move. "I like it soft and slow like that."

Keith took my hand and kissed the back of it. "Yeah?"

I nodded. "Didn't you?"

Keith bore a small half smile. "*Like* is a small word, Kennedy Elizabeth."

Inching closer, I pressed my hand to his heart. The feel of it beating hard made me rejoice. "I wish you could stay the night."

Keith's smile dimmed. "Yeah."

He probably had to work in the morning and there was no telling if Cain would stop by unannounced or not.

Tiredly, I sat up, noting how tender I was. "I'm going to get in the shower. I'd invite you...but I don't think I can last another round."

The proud smile on Keith's face made me shy.

We would totally have to change those sheets before he left.

Carefully, I got up and made my way to my en-suite bathroom where I quickly

hopped into the shower after wrapping my hair and putting on a shower cap.

After my shower I pulled on my favorite silk robe and stepped back into my bedroom only to find Keith tying his boots.

"What's the rush?" I joked as I noticed he seemed intent on leaving.

Keith stood up and regarded me. "I gotta go."

"So you were going to leave without telling me?" I asked with a forced smile.

He hung his head as he kept back. "Nah, I wouldn't do that." Slowly, he looked into my eyes. "I think it's time, Kennedy. I kissed you and now it's time to say goodbye."

My heart froze in my chest as I struggled to breathe. "What?"

"I'm done," he said more clearly.

"Why?" My voice came out small and weak.

"Because I'm tired," Keith explained. He gestured around us. "I can't stay because who knows if ol' boy might stop through? I've never been to Hampton Hills, and you can't even show me around because we might get seen by people who know you."

"Keith..." I didn't know what to say, because his frustration and complaints were true.

"You told me from day one you couldn't love me and what the deal was, so it's *my* fault for getting caught up. My fault for going along with this shit when I knew it wasn't for me," Keith went on. "I'm too old to be fucking with no feelings involved."

"I have feelings too." I hated that tears were lining my vision. I hated that I had no control over any part of my life, and the one small part that I did, was currently blowing up in my face.

Keith shook his head. "But your feelings don't mean anything. You wanna know why? Because what you say and what you're doing are two different things." He paused, as if stopping himself from going further.

"What?" I demanded. "Just say it."

Wounded, he looked at me and sliced me open further. "You *want* this marriage. You're willing to go through with it because you want to."

"No!" I cried out, unable to grasp how he could say such a ridiculous thing.

"Have you ever stopped to think if you grew a backbone and walked out of here with nothing but the clothes on your back, took the money you *earned* from your bank account, or none of it, and left—even while your father is at his lowest, that maybe, just fuckin' maybe, he'd take you seriously? But no, you're just complainin' and poutin' about marrying this weirdo.

"You haven't put your foot down once. You're willin' to marry him because that's what your father told you to do. You're not willin' to give *any* of this up," Keith accused as he gestured around us once more. "You don't have to marry Cain. You can walk away any time, and that could be all it takes to get your father to open his eyes and see what *he* put you through."

His words pierced my chest and I felt my shoulders sag at the weight of it all.

"I get it. You're twenty-four and you don't know the answers to everything, but here and now the only answer that matters is where do you want to be and what do you want?" Keith pressed on. He sighed and looked at me for what felt like the final time.

"I've never asked you for anything, but now I'm asking you to choose yourself."

There were no words that could form on my tongue to explain all that I was feeling.

Keith walked over to me and I was trembling, breaking down at this goodbye. At this closure.

He kissed me on the lips, long and chaste, before leaning away. "Goodbye, Kenny."

He walked out the door and took my heart with him.

31

Kennedy

WITH SWOLLEN EYES, I FUMBLED WITH MY PHONE Friday as I got ready to call Jadyn. I could barely speak, but I needed someone to talk to. The only person I had left.

"Hey," Jadyn picked up almost instantly.

"Hey." My voice was hoarse from all the crying. My throat was sore as well. One look in the mirror and I'd come to realize I looked like shit. I was in no shape to face housekeeping when they came to do their daily cleaning.

I'd locked myself in my spare bedroom where I'd been all night, too hurt and ashamed to sleep in my own bed.

"K? You don't sound so good. What's up?" Jadyn's concern caused the tears to well up in my eyes.

Just when I thought I couldn't cry anymore, I turned into a blubbering fool as I rambled on about what happened. At the end, when there were no words left to say, I let the tears take over.

And Jadyn listened, being the greatest friend she could be.

"K?" Jadyn asked softly when the line had gone quiet for a while on my end.

"Yes?"

"What do you want to do?" she asked. "I'm riding with you whether you want to go through with this or not."

I sniffled and wiped at my nose. I appreciated her genuine support, but I wanted her honesty. "What do you think about what...K-Keith said?"

Jadyn took a minute to gather her words while I waited on pins and needles. "I think that man cares about you. I think he fell for you. I think this took its toll on him and it wasn't fair to string him along. He said some real shit that ultimately you have to sit and think about.

"*I* understand where you're coming from, though. This is your dad. He's always been there and supportive of you. It's gotta be a lot of pressure to feel indebted to go through with this marriage so that he can get a casino out of it. But at the end of the day, is his legacy worth your happiness?"

It wasn't. "No."

"And Cain..." Jadyn groaned over on her end. "He has the charm and the looks, but have you tried getting to know him? He's infatuated by an idea, but has he gotten to know *you*? Not that you're not worth it—because you are, but jumping into marriage because you seem ethereal is wild."

I hadn't tried to get to know Cain. I'd rebelled against the whole idea of taking him and our relationship seriously from the start. While I loathed the idea of the man, there was no denying the part of me that felt sorry for him, that sympathized for his upbringing and all that he'd lost. He was cruel, there was no doubt about it when I considered his threats to kill any man who touched me. But then he was thoughtful too, when I thought about the way he treated me when we were together.

Wiping at my eyes, I thought about the possibility of trying to get to know him. Of trying to see where things could go if I gave in and gave him a chance.

Betrayal seized me at the idea of being with someone who wasn't Keith.

I had heavy choices to make, and there was only so long before I could put them off before a harsh reality awaited.

A long week went by without a word from Keith. It was really over and I didn't know what to feel beyond hurt.

I thought of my parents, the only family I'd ever known, and couldn't imagine walking away.

"It's just three years," I mumbled to myself.

I'd known from the beginning that I couldn't have Keith. I'd known the risk, and still I'd taken the chance.

Knocking sounded out at my front door and I stopped staring at my reflection from where I sat in front of my vanity mirror.

Uneasy breaths filled my lungs as I made my way to answer the door.

On the other side, Cain was standing alone. Out in the hall I spotted Vino at the elevator.

Cain's eyes went to what I was wearing, or lack thereof.

Before him, I was only wearing a cream-colored silk robe. Beneath it, I was nearly naked, something he could see as I hadn't tied the rope tightly to conceal this fact.

The two black voids of Cain's eyes drank me in slow before he managed to trail his vision up to mine. "What's all this?"

I blinked back the first urge to cry.

Here it was. A test. To see if I could do it. Be with this man and give him a try. To see that I'd made a mistake in running off that night.

"Did you mean it when you said we wouldn't have to consummate our marriage?" I asked in a steady voice that didn't feel like my own.

Cain nodded quietly.

I took a step back and pulled him into my suite. "That's a *big* risk. What if we're not compatible?"

Cain said nothing, making me go on.

"I have needs," I let it be known. I took his hand, hoping he didn't notice that mine was shaking, and pressed it to my cheek.

Cain eyed the connection and lifted a brow. "Needs, huh?"

I brought his hand into my robe, to my left breast. "Yes."

Cain didn't squeeze or grope me. His soft touch only lingered. Slowly, he undid my robe altogether, exposing him to a view of my bare breasts.

Please don't cry. Please don't cry. I sucked up the discomfort I felt with him looking at me, telling myself to keep going, to make this work.

"You told me you hated me, and now you're asking me to fuck you?" Cain questioned as he stood back.

He was making this too complicated. I went up to him and worked on his belt as I stood on my toes and brought my mouth to his. "That's what I said."

Tentatively, Cain kissed me back, lazily and slow. Almost as if he couldn't believe this was happening and I was finally giving in.

He reached up and held my face as he kissed me with more fervor, more desire, more want.

I stumbled back as he walked up on me and before I could run away from this, I grabbed his hand and pulled him to my bedroom.

Cain didn't let me take the lead for long. He pulled off my robe and threw it to the side before he laid me down. He hovered over me, staring down at me for just a second, before kissing me again. His hand fisted a bunch of my hair as he tilted my head back and as close as we were I could feel his erection brushing against my thighs.

Just the thought of it sent my vision blurry and I choked as anxiety hit.

Cain reeled back, leaning away to stare at the thong I was still wearing. He hooked his finger around the seat of my underwear and ran it up and down, the back of his finger brushing against my clit and sending a shiver to my core.

In another second, he yanked my panties to the side and got a good look at me as he angled his head. Squeezing my eyes shut, it was too late. Tears had fallen and I couldn't make them stop.

No.

This was wrong.

Cain wasn't the same. He kissed different, tasted different, touched different—he wasn't what I wanted.

"Very nice," he said, his voice gravelly and heavy. He let go of my thong and I felt his presence disappear. "But like I said, I'm not going to touch you until you *want* me to."

How could I ever want him to touch me when all I could think about was someone else?

His touch froze my heart and sent goose bumps all over my body. I clammed up at the thought of him seeing my sex, of him touching me there.

"I don't," I sobbed. "I don't want you. I can't."

"Hmm." Cain only hummed and said nothing further.

His footsteps retreated from my room and in the distance I could hear my front door open and close.

Turning on my side, I buried my face into my pillows and cried until nothing else came out of me.

32

KEITH

I had the garage to myself Saturday night after closing early. I'd taken a custom paint job and had been spending my evenings seeing it through. After spending three nights sanding down the 2012 Honda Civic, it was almost time to paint.

The owner wanted a deep purple color, and I was all for it, just to see the finish for myself. It had previously been black, but the paint had faded and peeled, and this new paint job would really make her shine. If there was one thing I lived for, it was working on cars.

I hadn't been in the best of moods since leaving things done with Kennedy, more than ever I was extra grateful for Uncle Rod for allowing me to use his space to do these side jobs. They kept me busy and my mind focused and distracted.

In my pocket, I felt my phone vibrate against my thigh.

Unlike before with Leila, I wasn't about to go ghost again. I stopped what I was doing and dug my phone from my pocket to see my mother calling.

"It's late," I pretended to chastise her as I picked up.

"I know, but I forgot to ask if you wanted to stop by for dinner tomorrow night," my mother said. She sounded tired, a warning not to stay on the line too long.

"Definitely," I agreed. "What we havin'?"

"Momma wanted to fry some pork chops, and I was craving some homemade scalloped potatoes," my mother explained.

My mouth watered at the two dishes and I realized I hadn't eaten a proper meal for the night. Nothing in the vending machine back in the shop was nearly as appealing as what my mother had painted.

"I'm there," I quickly agreed.

"Are you coming alone, or are you bringing a friend?" She'd done a good job of tiptoeing around Kennedy for weeks, and now here she was checking in on that situation.

I'd walked away, but there were no hard feelings. I still had love for Kennedy, would help her if she ever got in a jam and needed me. I just needed to step back and let my feelings drop.

No such luck yet.

I didn't miss the sex. I missed *her*. I'd made a grilled cheese sandwich the other day and found myself adding a thin layer of mayonnaise to each side before placing the cheese in the middle. I'd stopped reading *Night Changes* because it wasn't the same knowing her place in my book wouldn't ever change.

For lunch that day, I'd brought a sandwich bag of cotton candy grapes. I'd always preferred, and still did, red seedless grapes, but the cotton candy flavor was a new taste I was beginning to like as well.

It was the little things that made me think of Kennedy. The little things that stuck.

"Hell no," I decided to joke with my mother instead. "More food for me."

She snorted. "You're so bad. Are you doing good, Keith? Rodney said you've been quiet lately."

Uncle Rod wasn't one to press, but he also wasn't about to lie to his sister. "I'm straight. I'm in the middle of a job, so I've been caught up in that." I glanced at the analog clock on the wall and saw that it was nearing nine. "I actually need to eat right *now*. You sound sleepy, so I'ma let you go and get with you tomorrow."

"Okay, I love you," she said softly.

"I love you, too."

I hung up and decided it was time for a break.

After putting all my supplies away and cleaning up, I got into my truck and drove to the corner store, 7 Corners, up the street. There was a microwave in our break room at the shop, and depending on if I got a sandwich or a cup of noodles or not, I was planning on using it. It wouldn't quite be a full meal, but I needed something in my stomach before I attempted the first round of paint on the Civic.

The parking lot was empty, save for a couple of vehicles probably belonging to the store employees. I got out of my Tahoe and made my way inside, immediately tipping my head at the man behind the counter skimming a magazine.

I was the furthest thing from high maintenance, and as odd as it sounded, I had a thing for gas station or convenience store foods. This store had the best deli sandwiches. The first place I hit was the cold wall of burgers and sandwiches and swiped up an American sub.

Jackpot.

"Girl, hurry up, he ain't gon' catch you."

A woman's voice caught my ear and turned me around. In the aisle behind me, I could just make out two colored heads. One purple, and one red. The purple-haired one was tall enough so I could see her face. I recognized her from the shop, letting me know the one with red hair was Eden.

"I don't know." Yep, definitely Eden.

Purple Hair huffed. "Stop being lame and come on. He's not even watchin'."

Crumbling of a wrapper echoed through the air and I knew she was stealing.

Shaking my head, I went about collecting a bag of chips and a bottle of water from the fridge, telling myself to mind my own business.

When I made it over to the checkout counter, Purple Hair breezed by and quickly went for the door with Eden in tow.

"Hey! I saw that!" the cashier shouted as he looked in their direction. His hand went under the counter and I didn't like the odds of him pulling a weapon. Thief or no thief.

Fuck.

Purple Hair ran out of the store giggling and Eden froze. The goodness in her had her not making a move to flee.

"She's with me," I spoke up. My voice drove the cashier's attention my way, off of Eden.

"She shouldn't be stuffing shit in her pockets before I can ring it up." He was tired and no doubt working the third shift. I could understand his angst.

"What do you have?" I asked as I glanced at Eden.

She fidgeted from one foot to the other. "A bag of Reese's Pieces." She pulled out the neon orange pack and held it up.

"It's three seventy-nine for those." The cashier's nostrils flared and a redness tinted his pale cheeks.

"Got it," I told him.

He punched in the candy and scanned the rest of my stuff before telling me my total. I slid him a twenty and let him keep the change.

"Trust me, she won't be so reckless next time," I assured the cashier as I accepted my black plastic bag and headed for the exit.

Eden had waited around and walked with me out of the store into the night.

Under the bright lights of the parking lot, I saw her, *really* saw her. On her right cheek a bruise was fading, sending me on alert as my fist balled at my side.

"What happened?" My tone came out harder than I'd meant, causing her to flinch.

She turned so that I couldn't see the damage. "Nothing."

Bullshit. "Eden."

"It's nothing, okay! I'm just...clumsy."

Clumsy my ass. I knew a war wound when I saw one. Still, I

didn't push. I barely knew her, and as much as I wanted to put hands on whoever had hurt her, I knew forcing the issue wasn't the way.

"I oughta take that candy," I warned as we stood apart. There was no sign of her friend. She'd been ditched.

Eden's bottom lip trembled and I knew I couldn't do that to her. "I got money."

"Then why steal?" I challenged.

She shrugged. "It was just a stupid game."

"Playin' stupid games can get you stupid prizes," I warned.

"I won't do it again," Eden said earnestly.

"Don't," I told her. "And while you're at it, you should be making better friends."

Eden looked off, noting we were alone in 7 Corners's parking lot. Shit could've gone left and her friend had abandoned her.

It was late. Eden was only wearing a small tube top and shorts with a cardigan that was hanging off her. It was only sixty-something out, not quite chilly, but still.

"Need a ride?" I offered.

Eden smiled and shook her head. "No, there's a bus running nearby."

"A ride would be quicker," I pointed out.

"I like the bus," Eden countered.

I didn't push, unsure if she trusted me enough to be alone with me or not. "Okay."

"I'll, uh, make you some cookies with these Reese's Pieces and bring them by the shop since you saved my ass in there," Eden said.

"Oh, you cook?"

Eden lifted her chin, appearing proud. "I love to cook."

There was something wholesome about that, making me smile.

"All right then, I can get with that. You should add some chocolate chips, too," I suggested.

Eden grinned, catching a little attitude. "I didn't say I was taking requests, but I'll think about it."

"Stay safe," I said as I let her go. "And watch your back."

Eden didn't fight me on that last remark and bobbed her head in agreement. She took off down the parking lot and rounded the building, disappearing into the night.

Turning around, I prepared to get back into my truck.

At least, that's what I'd been about to do. Parked directly behind my Tahoe to where I couldn't back out of my space, was an all-black Rolls-Royce Phantom with tinted windows. It was a luxury vehicle and a sight to see, but whoever was behind the wheel needed to back up.

I raised my arms, in a what-are-you-doing gesture, trying to get the driver to read the room.

On the other side of the car, the driver's door opened. Stepping out of the Phantom was a large man in a suit. When he turned around, recollection hit me, leaving me to angle my head and squint.

"Beans?" I said it more as a question than a statement.

The large man driving the vehicle was a familiar face I recognized from back in the day. When shit was kinda wild for me. I was a few years older, but I was good with faces. *Beans* wasn't his real name, but a nickname he'd gotten from some kids around the way. He'd been called "Beans" so much, I'd forgotten what his *real* name was.

Beans said nothing as he propped an arm against the hood of the Phantom and merely stared at me.

And then the back door opened on my side and a shiny loafer stepped out. A suit clad leg was attached and I followed the leg until the person inside the Phantom came out.

"Dice."

It was like staring at a ghost, as another blast from my past was standing right in front of me.

His was one face I'd never forget. Even as a kid he held nothing behind his eyes, reminding me of the first time I'd ever seen *Halloween* with Michael Myers. Now, as an adult, not much had changed.

Kinda like Beans, I didn't know too much about Dice since he'd been younger. Though, I should've known Dice wasn't far, because if there was one thing I could remember vividly from my youth, was the time he'd slashed some kid's face open for making fun of Beans.

They both stayed in the neighborhood at a house that was a home for foster kids. Beans hadn't been a tough guy. Being "soft" made him an easy target in the street, until Dice stepped in to his defense. After that, they were never far from each other. Until Dice was relocated with another foster family.

Dice stared at me as I looked between him and Beans curiously. We'd never been friends, but rather stayed out of each other's way.

Something about the way his car was parked told me it was intentional. Something about the way both men were looking at me caused me to go on alert.

Dice heaved a sigh as he glanced back at Beans. "I hate surprises."

Surprises?

I opened my mouth to question what was going on, but no words ever made it out as all went black around me.

33

Kennedy

My phone was ringing again. Like I had the first time Cain had called me, I ignored it. I was partly embarrassed after the way we'd left things, but mostly just over it all.

I was done.

As I brought the last of my things out to my Lexus, I took one final glance at the place I'd called home since I was twenty. For so long, I'd loved living in my penthouse. It made me feel like a real princess, having my needs met and my own privacy away from my parents.

But it was time to say goodbye.

It wasn't about Keith. I wanted to be with him, I did, but for the first time I had to see the whole picture. Was my inheritance worth my freedom, even if only for three years? Was it worth the disregard for my personal feelings? The blatant disrespect? Was it worth my right as a human being? As a daughter?

What good was having everything you could ever ask for if you couldn't have what you wanted? If life was lived within the confines of a gilded cage?

I loved that Keith challenged me as much as Jadyn, but even if things didn't work out, I knew I was making the move for me. That I wouldn't go back for a second.

So, I cried like a baby as I made the hardest decision I ever had to make in my adult life: to walk away from my family.

It wasn't quite leaving with *just* the clothes on my back, but after stowing a few bags of my belongings into my Lexus, I climbed in behind the wheel, set to leave for good.

This was real. I was really doing this. I'd never committed to anything wholly in my life. I dropped out of my sorority before leaving college altogether. I ran from Gaius when he wanted to be more. I felt overwhelmed and nauseous at the thought of moving out and into my own space. It was all too easy to fall back and just accept what was happening to me.

But no more.

It was time to be a big girl and choose me.

"I'm doing this for me," I said to myself as I caught my reflection in my rearview mirror.

If my father wanted a casino more than he wanted my happiness, he would have to find another way to broker this deal. I was leaving, and thankfully, I had Jadyn to cling to. She'd been all too ready to take me in. What would happen next, I wasn't sure, but this step was the most important. The first major move I'd ever made in my life.

My cell phone rang again and I only answered it to properly tell Cain he could now go fuck himself.

"What?" I snapped into my phone.

His musical chuckle greeted my ear. "It's a very good thing you picked up this time, *Kennedy*."

I was so fucking done with this shit. "Look, Cain, this—"

"I'm having car trouble," Cain cut in casually. "I need you to pick me up."

I rolled my eyes. "Send one of your henchmen to do it."

"Nah, I want *you* for this. Hold on a minute, I'll send you the address."

Half a beat later my phone pinged with a notification from my Maps app. I clicked on it only for my heart to drop to my stomach.

He'd dropped a pin. He was currently at Rod's Repair.

"I...I don't understand," I let out.

"Do not play fucking stupid with me." It was a cool threat that sent terror dancing down my spine.

Cain knew. He fucking knew.

"O-Okay," I stammered.

"Do you remember the first lunch we ever had?" Cain asked.

"Yes."

"Do you remember what I told you I'd do if I caught you with someone else?"

My eyes squeezed shut at the memory. "Y-Yes."

"I'm about to test if Keith is bulletproof."

Oh God. Oh God.

My body began to shake at the possibility he'd really kill Keith. We'd parted ways, yet Cain was still intent to make me miserable. There was no way out of this. I was trying to leave, to put myself first, and here was Cain pulling me back.

"I was marrying you!" I cried.

"But you were fucking him," Cain responded dryly.

"Please!" I begged as my throat began to throb and I felt tears on the horizon.

"Better hurry up. My favorite way to relieve stress is by pulling triggers."

He said no more before hanging up, letting the warning hang in the air.

I let out the loudest scream as I began beating my steering wheel.

I was done. I was supposed to be done. It wasn't fair.

Tap. Tap. Tap.

Tapping on my window drove my attention over to find security peering into my car worriedly.

"You all right in there, Miss Nichols?" the security guard asked as he shined his flashlight at me.

I shielded my eyes as I nodded. "Yes!"

The guard didn't look too sure, but he let me go.

With everything I wanted to call the police, but after being told that Cain had friends with badges, I knew better.

I sent Jadyn a quick text, telling her something came up with Keith and I'd be late getting in. I couldn't drag her into this mess the same way I had done so with Keith. If Cain did anything to Keith—I refused to go there. He couldn't be so unhinged that he'd kill a man because *he* couldn't have me.

I drove like a bat out of hell to Bedford Heights, desperate to get there before Cain acted recklessly. By the time I pulled into Rod Repair's lot no other cars were around except Keith's. Leaning against it, smoking a cigarette, was Vino.

"Oh God," I whimpered as I slowly climbed out of my car.

Vino jerked his chin to the right. "Let's take a walk."

I shook my head. "Where is Cain?"

Vino made a face as he approached me and I backed against my Lexus. He went and patted me down, making sure I didn't bring any weapons, and as he peeked briefly into the sweatshirt I was wearing, I imagined he was also making sure I wasn't wearing a wire.

When he was certain I wasn't a threat, he took a firm grip of my arm and tugged me around the side of the building to the back where the garage was. On this side of Rod's Repair, I noticed a Rolls-Royce Phantom and knew Cain was near.

One of the three garage doors was pulled up and one step inside sent the tears flowing.

"Keith!" I wasn't able to get to him as Vino's strong arm wrapped around my middle, holding me back.

Among the distinct smell of motor oil, metal, and gas, bound to a chair, bleeding from his brow, was Keith. Beans stood behind him and Cain stood in front of them. All around the ground was plastic sheeting. The perfect setup...for *murder*.

My hand covered my mouth as I looked on at Cain in shock. His jacket was gone and his tie loosened.

"Nice of you to join us," he drawled.

"What is going on?" I asked.

Cain rolled his eyes. He went and flung a stack of papers at my feet. Vino let me go and closer inspection found them to be photographs. All in black and white. Of me...and Keith.

My eyes snapped over to Cain who wasn't hiding his anger. "You...you followed me?"

"Not at first. Didn't have a reason not to trust you. You seemed like a compliant woman," Cain spat venomously.

"How did you know?" The photographs were from my trip to On Tap, of me going home with Keith, of us shopping the next day and getting catfish at Yvette's Kitchen.

"You were right not to like those women," Cain said. "I got a little phone call and then a very interesting video of you." His gaze flickered over toward Beans. "Show her."

Beans stepped from behind Keith and brandished a cell phone. On the screen was a video of me sitting with my mother at LeChé's. The angle was low, from behind, but there was no missing us.

"*Keith is good to me,*" I was saying in the video. "*I, uh— When I left the engagement party that night I went to Bedford Heights and caught a flat tire. He came to help me and we just sorta happened. He's such an amazing guy, he's hardworking, honest—*"

Beans cut the video short as panic set in.

Betrayal. I'd been stabbed in the back. I was having a heart-to-heart with my mother, being vulnerable, only for it to be stolen and recorded to share with my enemy.

"Elyse?" I asked as I got back to Cain.

He shook his head. "Stephanie. She even offered to be here for me in case I was having a 'tough' time dealing with this." He chuckled and his face lit up. "Now, that's a social climber if I've ever seen one." He became serious again as his gaze fell to the photos at my feet. "I hired a private investigator after that to confirm there was a Keith. I gotta tell you, I'm more than a little disappointed there is. Especially now that I know what's under all those clothes."

Keith's eyes raced to me and I shook my head, trying to let him know nothing had happened.

"Please," I begged, getting back to Cain. "This is between me and you. Don't do this."

Cain pulled his gun from his holster. "Uh-uh. I want you to see this. Keith's death will be on *your* hands. I warned you, Kennedy, and you didn't listen."

"NO! NO! NO!" I didn't think. I fell in front of Keith on my knees, not above groveling. "Don't do this!"

Cain cocked the hammer, his eyes empty as he stared down at me. He was going to do it. He was going to pull the trigger and shoot Keith.

"Take me! Take me! I'm not worth it. I'm not," I pleaded desperately.

I couldn't let Keith die. Not when he meant so much to so many people. Not when he made a difference in his community. Not when he mattered.

Behind me I could hear Keith's muffled protests as he struggled with his bindings, scraping the chair across the ground.

"Take me," I begged tearfully as I peered past the barrel of Cain's gun into his eyes. "Please, take me."

"Move," Cain ordered.

Refusing, I shook my head. "I won't let you do it. Take me instead."

I closed my eyes as the tears kept coming, prepared to take a bullet if it meant sparing Keith's life.

Keith's mumbles persisted as well as his movement and I declined to open my eyes. Too afraid of what I'd see.

"Take her out of here," Cain's voice commanded coldly.

A strong hand seized my arm and pulled me to my feet. Vino had me and he was taking me away from Keith.

"NO!" I screamed as I struggled against Vino's hold.

It was no use. He was much stronger. He took me out of the garage and reached for the door. It hadn't even shut all the way before the gun went off.

34

KEITH

THE SOUND OF THE GUN GOING OFF WAS ALMOST deafening, Dice was so close.

Dice had shot into the wall, placing a bullet-sized hole in it.

With his eyes on me, he lowered his weapon.

"I needed that," he let out. "I fucking hate seeing women cry."

I couldn't see Kennedy when she'd broken down, but it tore my heart up hearing her beg and plead to die instead of me. Hearing how she was willing to take my place.

I'd sooner die *twice* than let that happen.

Dice—*Cain* came closer and kneeled down before me. His wrath hadn't lessened and his next move was questionable.

"I had her on her back, open for me," he said, holding his palm out for emphasis. "But she was crying for you." His eyes trailed to the necklace hanging around my neck. He took the tip of his Sig P226 and tapped the pendant. "That's when I knew I was going to kill you."

He was lucky I was tied to this chair, or else he'd be eating those words.

I had no choice but to keep my cool and bide my time as I glared into his eyes. One of his men had snuck me from behind at

7 Corners. When I'd come to, it was from a fierce blow to the head, courtesy of who Dice referred to as *Vino*.

I didn't recognize him.

Nothing made sense as I became coherent and found myself back at the garage with Dice pacing back and forth. Beans had been leaning against the trunk of the Civic. And I found that pretty looking son of a bitch eating *my* sandwich as he stood a few feet away. He'd even offered me some with a smirk I wanted to knock off.

"This shit is dry," Vino complained as he helped himself to another big ass bite.

Dice looked to me. "Got any condiments inside?"

Blinking, I began to nod.

Vino clicked his tongue. "See, now you say somethin'. Shoot 'im in the knee, D."

I had no clue what was going on, until Dice said her name.

Kennedy.

Never in a million years would I have drawn the connection from Kennedy's Cain to Dice. Fucked-up Dice from Bedford Heights. Emotionless, unremorseful, no-conscience-having Dice.

It still didn't make sense. Kennedy said Dice had business with her father, and if the rumors I'd heard about Dice were true, it wasn't adding up.

Dice sighed. "Ungag him."

Beans ripped the tape from my mouth, leaving behind a stinging sensation.

Fuuuck.

"Did you know about me?" Dice asked.

"I knew she was being *forced* to marry some weirdo," I answered.

Dice took this information and sat with it.

"I never knew your *real* name," I spoke up some more. "She said you had a business you inherited from your father and even that doesn't make sense from what I remember about you."

Dice peered at Beans before focusing back on me. "My late

father was a billionaire casino owner in Vegas. He was a 'happily married' man when he preyed on my young mother and I was conceived. Despite his immense wealth, he threw her a few scraps when she decided to keep me.

"When my mother's heart couldn't take the rejection and pain, and she died, I was left a ward of the state when daddy dearest didn't come to my rescue." A tight smile tugged on Dice's lips, but it didn't reach his eyes. "I won't bore you with the rest." He tapped my knee with his Sig. "That's not what this is about. Now, is it?"

My legs were tied to the chair as well, making me unable to kick this motherfucker in his face like I wanted.

"No, I guess not," I responded.

"I thought I recognized you from the pictures. Seeing you up close, that's when it really dawned on me," Dice said with a shake of his head. "I remember you from around the neighborhood. You never really bothered anyone. You seemed like a good guy."

He knew of me as I knew of him. The world was way too small, because I still couldn't believe he was the guy Kennedy was being forced to marry.

"Have anything to say for yourself?" Dice taunted, watching me.

"If you kill me, leave her alone. Walk away and don't bother her ever again," I wagered.

A smirk crossed Dice's face. "He's willing to die for her, and she's willing to die for him. What do you make of that, Beans?"

"How romantic," he said in a bored manner.

That remark got Dice to smile as he stared into my eyes. "Nah, don't knock it. Passion happens to the best of us. I'd never let a woman die for me, but I'd kill for that type of loyalty. That type of *devotion*."

He dug into his pocket and pulled out two clear red dice. He rolled them in his palm, causing them to clack against each other, before releasing them onto the floor. While I didn't see what came up, he angled his head to read the outcome.

"Huh." He collected his dice and put them back into his pocket.

My brows furrowed in confusion, trying to make sense of whatever was going on.

Dice stood up, towering over me in my position bound to my chair. "Untie him."

Beans did as told. He took a bowie knife and cut me free, first my legs, and finally my arms and hands. The weight of the ropes slipping away gave me a sense of freedom, but there was still one problem standing in front of me.

"What are you doing?" I asked.

"It's your lucky day, Keith. You get to live."

That seemed too easy. "Just like that?"

Dice shrugged, as if it were that simple. "I'm a man of principle. When I take a life, I look at a few simple things: will they be missed, if the world is a better place without them, and if they deserve to die. And as much as I'd love to put a bullet in you for fucking what was mine, you don't meet the criteria." He rattled the dice in his pocket. "They were in your favor."

It sounded like bullshit, but I'd go with it.

He was tucking his gun away, and that was all I needed as I took a step forward.

Dice regarded me, tracking my movement. "At best, you only get in a cheap shot. And then Beans gets in a *kill*shot."

I didn't like those odds, but fuck it.

I swung on him, punching him dead in his face, sending his head snapping to the side.

Dice chuckled, his shoulders shaking as he leaned over and spit blood onto the plastic sheeting on the floor. He wiped at his lip and peered past me. "A little late on the draw there, huh Beans?"

"You had that coming," Beans said as he kept his distance.

Dice made a face and came back to me. "If it's any consolation—"

"Fuck you," I said loud and clear.

Dice appeared amused by me. I'd never seen him like this and it made me that much more on my toes. "She's willing to die for *you*," he said, getting serious. "Never take that shit for granted."

I wouldn't, not for as long as I lived. Right after I shook some sense into her.

"What now?" I asked, needing confirmation on what Dice was up to.

He shrugged, standing back. "If you break her heart I'll kill you, Keith. Understood?"

In some sick twisted way, he was giving up, and letting Kennedy go.

We were not about to shake hands and go grab a beer. I wanted him gone, back to wherever the fuck he came from.

"Stay away from her," I warned.

Dice shook his head. "I'm going to be around. Not all ties will be cut."

Her father.

Feeling bold, I had to address a rumor I was beginning to believe was true. "Does her father know he was about to marry his daughter off to the biggest coke dealer in the West?"

Slowly, a broad smile stretched across Dice's face. "No, and I'd appreciate it if that stayed in this room. Matter of fact, I'd like it if you acted like we don't know each other."

So, word on the street had been true. He had gone off to become a well-connected coke dealer. I'd once heard this from either Gavin or DreSean in passing when I'd wondered whatever happened to Dice, but I never was too sure. When we were kids, he'd sold a dime bag here and there from what I could remember. Now, he'd apparently graduated to higher endeavors.

Kennedy had dodged a bullet.

I didn't too much like the idea of keeping the fact that I knew Dice, if barely, from her, but if it meant he'd stay away, I would. There was no going to the police about this. That wasn't how things worked in Bedford Heights. If he was as high level as I'd heard, he more than likely had a few contacts at the local precinct.

I took a step closer. "How much say do you have in Bedford Heights?"

Dice narrowed his eyes. "Enough."

"Do me a favor?"

"Because I'm in such a favor-giving mood," he said sardonically.

"Tell whoever you run, to leave Dominique Ferguson the fuck alone," I demanded. We'd squared away his debt, but you could never be too sure.

Dice smoothed out the arm of his dress shirt, uninspired to even reply. He walked over to the Honda Civic and grabbed his jacket he'd laid aside. He shrugged into it and once again wiped at his mouth.

Nothing had felt better than punching that fucker in the face.

Dice turned toward Beans. "Let her in."

I guessed we were done negotiating.

35

Kennedy

I sat on the ground in a catatonic state as Vino stood by keeping watch of me.

There had only been one gunshot, but it was probably enough to do the trick. My eyes watered and I made no move to wipe them.

All I could do was breathe and that was hard enough.

Behind me, I heard the garage door lift back up. I kept my vision out at the woods before me. I wasn't strong enough to see him like that, knowing that I had ruined his life.

"Time to go, princess," Vino said as he came closer.

Go? Where was there to go? I would rather Cain shoot me too than go back there.

"Don't touch her."

That voice. That timbre.

I whirled around and stumbled back.

Keith was still alive.

He was coming to me and before I knew it, he'd taken me into his arms and pulled me to my feet.

He wasn't bleeding and there didn't seem to be a wound. I didn't understand. "I heard a gunshot!"

Cain came past us. "Target practice."

Keith held me close and tight, ushering me behind his back.

Cain wasn't impressed. "I guess this is breaking up?"

What a sick little joke. A look closer and I could spot blood on his mouth. I hoped Keith got him good.

"Don't talk to her," Keith warned.

Cain rolled his eyes and peered straight at me. "This isn't over. Tomorrow morning at nine, no sooner, no later, we're going to have a chat with your father. Bring Keith."

"O-Okay," I stammered.

Keith stepped in front of me more, as if to keep Cain from seeing me for a second.

Impassive, Cain turned his attention to Beans and Vino. "Let's go. I'm hungry."

Together, the three of them got into the Phantom. It was idle for a second before it pulled away and rode off.

I only got to look at it for so long before everything got shaky.

Keith had a hold of me and was shaking me.

Roughly, he grabbed my face, hard and determined. "Don't you ever do some stupid shit like that again!"

Anger and delirium poured from him as he shook me once more for good measure.

"Was I supposed to let you die?" I cried.

"I'd rather you than me!" he snapped at me. He held me to his chest, nearly crushing me. "I can't lose you, Kenny. Fuck."

He reeled back to get a good look at me. There were unshed tears in his eyes, and it broke my heart. I'd never seen a man cry. Not even my father when he'd gotten his diagnosis. "Why would you ever try to die for me?"

"Because I'm falling in love with you." A world without me felt irrelevant, but a world without Keith? I couldn't fathom the thought. I saw the good in him, and I couldn't let Cain take that away. "I broke the rules when I decided to care about you. And I'm not sorry."

"I love you too much to ever let you do that for me." Some

tears fell as Keith brought me back into his chest and squeezed. "Don't ever do that again. You hear me?"

I nodded into the solid flesh of his chest and breathed in his scent, feeling safe, feeling at peace, feeling like I was home.

All I could do was shake and sob, unable to believe we made it. Keith was alive and I was finally free.

Bright and early Sunday morning Keith and I went to my parents' estate after leaving my penthouse. That morning when I woke up next to Keith I'd never been more thankful in my life.

After the night from hell, we'd gone to his house where he grabbed a change of clothes and I'd left most of my belongings. We only stayed at the penthouse because it beat time in the morning.

We arrived at my parents' house at the same time Cain was pulling up.

"Stick close to me," Keith instructed as he glanced at Vino and Beans making their way out of Cain's Phantom.

I thought Cain had too much respect for my father to do anything lethal.

Keith and I got out of the Tahoe and held hands as I led us to the front door. We didn't speak to Cain or his men outside of a nod of acknowledgment.

Instead of using my key, I rang the doorbell and waited beside Keith.

Priscilla came to the door and let us in.

My mother came down the hall and immediately paused at the sight of our large gathering. "What's going on?"

Cain stepped up and approached my mother. He went and kissed her cheek in greeting. "I've scheduled a meeting with Damon."

That got my mother's full attention as she scowled at Cain. "You've created a monster. He's actually in his office."

Cain grinned and I hated to see him so normal and humane. "Trust me, it's good for him, Angela."

Her gaze floated over to me, lingering where I was holding hands with Keith. "Who is this?"

Cain turned and gestured toward Keith. "Oh, that's Keith. He's a topic of our meeting. You're welcome to sit in. It's family friendly."

My mother blanched, running her hand to the column of her throat. "Oh."

"Which way to the office?" Cain probed, moving things along.

My mother came to and led us down the hall where we cut a corner and traveled to my father's home office. She knocked briefly before opening the door and leading us in.

Behind his desk, my father looked whole as he wore a dress shirt and was freshly shaven and groomed. He was on his desktop computer, but paused at the arrival of our group.

His eyes went to my mother, and then to Keith and me. "What's all this?"

Cain helped himself to a chair in front of my father's desk.

Keith took the one next to him, leaving him in between us as I sat next to him. My mother took the chesterfield along the back wall while Beans and Vinos stood at the door.

My father liked to start all of his meetings with a firm handshake. Cain was quick to lean over his massive executive desk and shake his hand. When my father looked at Keith, he merely remained seated and stared straight back at my father.

The lack of a greeting caused my father to truly study Keith. Him in his T-shirt and jeans, versus Cain in his suit and tie, and me in my blouse and trousers.

"Who is this?" my father asked impatiently. Time was money, and he didn't like to waste either.

Cain gestured to Keith with a tilt of his head. "That's Keith, the man your daughter was seeing behind my back."

My mother sucked in a sharp breath and my father amazingly held it together. He examined Keith again, squinting. "Did you beat him up?"

A squeeze came to my hand, evidence of Keith's attempt to rein it in.

Cain turned and looked at Keith, acting surprised at the state of Keith's patched brow. "What happened to you?"

Flaring his nostrils, Keith kept his gaze forward. "Either get to the point, or we're leaving, *Cain*."

Cain almost smiled and my father clasped his hands together. He glanced at the Rolex on his wrist and got back to us. "Yes, that sounds like a good idea. Mind telling me what is going on?"

Cain took the lead, going and beginning this meeting he'd called. "As I said, Kennedy has been seeing another man."

My father shrugged, showing he couldn't care less. He wasn't sympathetic or scornful. "Okay? She never wanted you, something we *all* knew. You just couldn't take no for an answer and forced this whole charade. Next time dial that ego down, son, there are plenty of fish in the sea."

"Be that as it may, as far as I'm concerned, *I* kept my end of our bargain. I've been very forthcoming with my team and the Cartier brand. She was your end, and that means *you* fell through on the deal."

My father breathed through his nose and I could see that angry scowl of his manifesting as his patience was being tested.

"Cain, if you try to fuck me with this deal—"

"Nah, that's not what this is about," Cain said coolly as he sat back comfortably in his chair. "We both know that *I* never cared for this partnership, but somewhere along the line, The Residence at Cartier became of interest to me. Kennedy was your bottom line, and I got cheated. So, consider this meeting a renegotiation of sorts."

"Stop talking about her like she's a piece of property and get to the fuckin' point," Keith snapped as he swung his gaze from Cain to my father.

My father eyed Keith, curious, but annoyed. "Son, if you want the right to speak in my business meetings, you at least owe me the respect of shaking my hand and introducing yourself."

Keith shook his head. "I don't respect men who treat their daughters like cattle."

My mouth fell agape as one of my father's brows rose. "I'm her father—"

"Then act like it," my mother's stern voice broke in. We all turned to catch her standing there with her arms folded, anger teeming loudly from her body as she glared at my father. "Keith is right, she's not a piece of property, she's your daughter. Act like it."

I'd never felt more vindicated than this moment.

Cain looked bored as he sat awaiting what would happen next.

My father peeled his gaze from my mother and focused back on Cain. "If you think you're getting a dime more out of me after *you* dragged my daughter into this and paraded around with her, you're mistaken."

Cain wrinkled his nose. "I'm not a greedy man, Damon. I'll take an even fifty/fifty split."

My father closed his eyes, composing himself as best as he could. All this stress couldn't be good for his heart. "Fine."

A corner of Cain's mouth curled up. "Pleasure doing business with you. I'll have my people redraw up the contract and I'll get with you and Phil on it, and then we can get back to work."

Cain stood from the chair and shook hands with my father for a final time, cementing their agreement.

He was about to leave, and something knotted in my gut didn't sit right with me.

"Cain? Wait." I stood to follow him out of the room, but Keith's hold kept me in place. I looked down at him, seeing unease in his eyes. "I'll be okay."

Cain held the door and I stepped out into the hall where he shut it behind us for privacy. His men took off down the hall, headed outside to wait.

One minute he was standing there in front of me, and the next, my hand was flying across his face.

For so long I'd wanted to smack the shit out of him and nothing felt better than accomplishing that goal.

Cain took my slap and remained standing, staring at me blankly.

"I won't apologize for that, or for Keith," I said as I squared my shoulders and stood my ground. "You...you have done a lot of horrible things in your life, I'm sure, but...I don't think you're a completely awful person." I couldn't. It wasn't in me, not even after last night. There was just something about Cain that didn't feel beyond redemption. I took his ring off my left hand and looked at it. "You may need a really good therapist, but you deserve to have someone love you for you, too."

Cain thumbed at his jaw. "'Fraid that's not in the cards for me."

"Everyone deserves love, Cain, even you," I said as I took his hand and put his engagement ring in it.

"Touched, Wife." He took a looming step closer, going and tugging on my cheek. "Don't ever try to sacrifice yourself for a man again. If Keith ever hurts you, he's a dead man. Understood?"

I snorted. "Go fuck yourself."

Cain briefly smiled before circling me to leave.

"Kennedy?" I turned, catching him watching me soberly. "I'm sorry."

Firmly, I nodded.

Cain turned and disappeared around the corner. In the background I heard the front door open and shut. Just like that, he was gone out of my life.

36

Kennedy

Stepping back into my father's office, I found him undone with a loosened tie. Keith was sitting back in his chair, no longer rigid, but somewhat relaxed. My mother was on the chesterfield, calm as well.

As much as I wanted to question what had gone on while I dealt with Cain, I thought better of it.

I went and scooped up my purse from my chair and eyed Keith. "Okay, let's go."

Keith stood and brought his hand to my waist, prepared to help me out of the house.

"Wait," my father spoke up just as we made it to the door.

My back stiffened as I turned and glanced at him. "Something you need?"

He frowned, looking to my mother and then to Keith. "Please...give me a moment alone with Kennedy."

Keith looked to me, needing confirmation that this was what I wanted. If I wanted to walk, he'd hold my hand all the way out to his car. I loved that about him. It wasn't about my father's word, but mine.

I nodded, needing to hear what my father had to say.

Keith and my mother stepped out into the hall and shut the door.

Instead of sitting across from my father again, I remained standing by the door.

Lifting my chin, I held my head high, keeping with my stance to go. "What do you want?"

My father sighed. "Look, let's not leave things like this."

"I took what mattered most to me and I left the penthouse. You can donate the rest of my things to charity or Goodwill. Either way, I have no use for them."

My father sank in his chair. "Don't do that. The engagement is done. Over. No need for the antics."

"*Antics*?" I repeated through gritted teeth. "Fuck you, Dad."

"Okay, hold up. Wait," my father pleaded as I made an attempt to leave. "I'm sorry, okay? I'm not mad about Keith. It needed to happen."

"I don't care if you are mad. It's *my* life."

"I thought I was doing something right by you," my father said.

"By holding my inheritance over my head? By making choices for me? By ignoring what *I* wanted?" I snapped.

"I just thought I had your best interest at heart, and I was wrong."

My best interest would never be marrying me off to some man I didn't know.

"For the first time in my life, I can't trust you," my voice cracked but I braved through it, needing to get my hurt off my chest. "I looked up to you like a hero, and you fell farther than your condition could ever allow. You *hurt* me, Daddy.

"You put me through the most traumatic experience I've *ever* gone through, and for what, to capitalize on a casino you don't even need?" I was so hurt at the betrayal I could've cried, but I refused to shed another tear. "I don't care that it's over, what you did will never sit right with me, and I'll never forget."

My father ran a hand down his face, guilt taking his eyes. "I...I didn't like it when he brought you into the deal. I wanted to wring his neck for even having the balls to bring you up, but then, I looked at it from an angle of him being a successful young man who didn't have any baggage. Cain seemed like a nice guy for you." He studied me, becoming serious. "What? Did he hit you?"

I scoffed. "We are not about to run down a list of things Cain didn't do to me when the most important thing is I didn't want him."

My father didn't have a quick response for that.

A silence fell between us, setting a tone for a defining moment in our relationship. I was ready to walk away if needed be, leaving him behind no matter the state of his health. It cut me deep to think of doing this, but it had to be done.

"I'm sorry, Neddy. I crossed a line and I should've respected your voice more," my father began. "You were hurting and I just ignored your cries, and I'm so sorry."

It wouldn't fix the past, but it was a start.

"Maybe with me in Bedford Heights and you here, it'll give you time to really think about what you did."

My father's gaze snapped to mine. "Excuse me?"

"It's important, to grow up, to move on and find myself. I'd like to own a house and make a home for myself," I said. "Throw myself into something like what Mom does with her charities."

"A house? In Bedford Heights? Never," my father stated adamantly.

"Dad," I said.

"You want a house of your own? Fine, I'll buy you a house. Here in Hampton Hills."

"Why? So, you can snatch it from me the next time I don't do as you say?" I challenged.

My father shook his head. "This will never happen again. You have my word. I'll write it out, sign a contract, whatever it takes for you to believe me. I just want to look out for you."

"I don't want to be bought," I said. "I feel like you weaponized my inheritance. I'd rather take what money I earned on my own and get something modest that I can feel safe in."

"Going forward, from this day on, my business is mine and Phil's alone," my father swore, looking me in the eye. "I'm not trying to win you over by this offer, I just simply want to do something for you. You want a house; you can have a house."

"In Bedford Heights," I clarified.

My father scowled. "Absolutely not."

I threw my hands up. "See! You're not even considering what I want."

He huffed. "Fine, we'll get you a house in a *nice* part of Bedford Heights, and we'll install a security gate, security cameras—"

I groaned. "That's dramatic."

"Fine, you pick the house, but you will call me every day. Those are my terms and conditions." My father wouldn't budge. He was going to be a dad no matter what. Bedford Heights didn't have the best reputation, and I admittedly was sheltered and not street smart.

His papa bear side tugged at my heart strings. I wanted my space and my own home, but first, I wanted my father more.

"You really hurt me," I said softly.

My father nodded, his eyes glistening as he looked away and wiped at them. "Keith said something to me that I can't shake. He said that most people when diagnosed with illnesses, whether terminal or not, make the choice to bond with their loved ones and cherish life more, not move on to the next merger. Nichols & Wagner has always been important to me, but it could never replace you and your mother.

"Whatever the next move you want to make, whether it's moving into a shoebox in Bedford Heights or finding a place here in the city, I'll support you. I just want my baby girl to stay in my life for whatever time I have left. I want to work on us, dedicate a day a week for us to move forward and just connect. I want to hear more about Keith. He seems like a great young man. I want *us* to be a priority. Would that be okay?"

He would support me whether I stayed or left, so long as we could still be father and daughter.

That was all I needed to hear before going and collapsing on his lap and smothering my face into the crook of his neck.

37

Kennedy

EIGHT MONTHS LATER

"WE JUST THINK YOU'D BE THE PERFECT MODEL FOR our brand," Ginette was saying as I video chatted with her in my living room. She was the creative director of an upcoming fashion boutique who'd contacted my agent about my modeling for their catalogue and ads. "What Slayed is all about is young, fun, sexy, women on the go, and you represent that completely. We love your style, and how it's totally unique and you. That's what we want to sell at Slayed."

I couldn't help but blush at the compliment and proposal. I'd been opening myself up to taking more brand deals, and this was one I was excited about. As my one major weakness in life was clothes.

My agent, Hans, wanted me to take some of the movie and TV roles filling my inbox, but that didn't seem authentic. That didn't seem *me*.

A glance at the clock on the wall told me I was running late.

"Listen, Ginette, it really means a lot that you guys are reaching out to me. Right now, I have a prior engagement, but I will definitely get with Hans and we will talk about it, and hopefully get on another call with you, because this sounds like a fun opportunity."

Ginette didn't sweat my needing to leave as she beamed at me on her end. "No worries, Kennedy. Please, let us know what you're thinking as soon as you can."

"I will, I promise," I swore.

We hung up and I was quick to slide into my heels, grab my sunglasses and bag, and rush out the door of my penthouse. Down in my Lexus, I almost burst into laughter when my phone rang, showing my father was calling.

I was still in my penthouse, still deciding whether I wanted to make a move to the Heights or stay in the Hills. My family was in Hampton Hills, and while I had a couple people who would make Bedford Heights home, too, I was still unsure where I wanted to be. But I was in no hurry, as things were better for me these days.

I felt more independent as I made my own money and helped out at the local florist in Bedford Heights whenever I was free. It was a bitch for my nails, but I loved building arrangements through and through.

"Hello, Father," I said as I picked up his call, trying not to laugh as I drove for the highway.

He was working with the best doctors, trying his hardest to live with his illness rather than succumb to it. My father had accepted that he'd never gain his mobility or strength to walk ever again, but he'd also learned to appreciate and respect the fact that he was fortunate enough to still have the ability to speak, to breathe, to move his arms and hands. That he was living.

These days, he was doing his best not to take on too much with Nichols & Wagner, and allowing Phil to lead most of the company. A feat I still couldn't believe.

I saw Cain a few times over the past few months, something that took getting used to. In a way, I admired his relationship with my father. Business or not, it was nice to see them interact. It was almost like my father had gained a son in the end.

Better a son than a husband as far as I was concerned.

"How'd the meeting go?" he asked right away.

I rolled my eyes. "At least you're not going to pretend to not know about it."

He chuckled, sounded healthy, sounding good, giving me hope. "What? Can't an old man be curious how things are going for his daughter?"

"You can quit sending jobs my way," I teased. "It sorta defeats the purpose of this whole independence journey I'm on."

Both my parents were in full support of me trying to branch out and do things my way, but that didn't mean they weren't going to pull strings for me. With enough nudging, they'd finally gotten Jadyn to hand over a script to one of their Hollywood friends. While the jury was still out on that for a response, my parents were sending little jobs my way.

I could get angry, but I loved that they were trying to help me in any way they could.

"You can be independent all you want, doesn't mean we can't help you," my father responded. "That's one of the biggest things I've learned from my physical therapist. There's nothing wrong with a little help."

My heart softened at his words. For so long he'd prided himself on being strong, and now here he was, okay with needing assistance.

"You're right, thank you," I said as I cleared my throat. "The meeting went great. She showed me a lot of cute pieces. I'm going to get with Hans and we'll decide what to do from here, but I'm really excited."

"You should be. My girl's about to be a model," my father said. "So, what are you about to get into now?"

I bit my cheek to keep from blushing. "I'm on my way to my next cooking lesson."

My father sighed. "Off to make another terrible dish of macaroni and cheese?"

I sucked my teeth, unable to believe he'd gone there. "Hey! I got the steps right! It was the measurements where I went wrong."

Jadyn had walked me through what I needed to make mac and cheese, and all had gone well until I cut into my first wedge upon pulling it from the oven and found the noodles bland. I'd used a whole box versus the measurements Jadyn had given me for half. The miscommunication resulted in a bad pan of mac and cheese that my father wasn't letting me live down. Him, and another one.

I was determined, though, to be able to make a soulful pan of the dish.

"Cooking isn't for everyone, Neddy," my father teased.

It wasn't, but I was doing pretty good in other areas. "I'm going to master it the next time I make it, and you'll love it."

"I'll love it because you made it," he said.

"So, you'll try it?" I asked as I got onto the highway.

"For you? Of course!"

That was all I needed to hear. After a rocky start to our year, it was nice to be here, to have this.

"Well, let me focus on driving. I'll call you when I get in, okay?" I said.

"Okay. I love you, Neddy," my father told me.

"And I love you."

We hung up and I drove onward to Bedford Heights, where thirty minutes later I was pulling into the driveway of a familiar home I'd grown to love as much as the owner himself.

I didn't have to knock. I had a key. A key I used to let myself in.

"Hey!" I let my presence be known as I removed my heels by the door where a shoe rack I'd bought was placed.

Keith poked his head out from down the hall, grinning when he saw me.

Butterflies filled my belly as I took him in and felt my heart race.

We'd taken a break after the whole ordeal with Cain, Keith to breathe, and me to just reflect. Without him I wanted to do all those things I'd set out to do when I'd faced off with my father, and with him, I knew I could do them with a strong support system.

When we made our way back to each other, I'd never been more sure of anything in my life. This was who I wanted. This was the life I wanted to live going forward.

Keith sized me up. "C'mere."

I was a sucker for his voice and the way he looked at me, but still, I made my way to join him in the kitchen slowly. Appearance's sake and all.

The smell of fresh fish greeted me as soon as I stepped into the room. Tonight, we were frying walleye and preparing a salad.

First, I went over to the sink to wash up. It wasn't long before two hands came and blocked me in against the counter.

His lips brushed against my ear. "How was your day?"

I turned, sucking in a breath as my breasts brushed against his chest and I was wrapped up in his cologne and scent. "Great. I was offered a modeling gig for a boutique."

Keith popped a brow. "Not lingerie, right?"

I pretended to put up a fight. "And if it is?"

His eyes ran down my figure, a sexy smirk taking his lips. "You only show that for me."

Reaching out, I patted his cheek. "Well, I belong to me and I'm showing off—"

His lips seized mine as I was mid-sass. I hoped I never stopped feeling weak in the knees when this man kissed me.

"Okay, I guess I can handle it," Keith taunted as he pretended to think it over. "Just as long as I get the first peek."

I threw my head back and laughed. Maybe I would stop by the store and find something cute, little, and lacy, for his eyes only.

After all, he loved me best.

COMING SOON

THE DARKEST REDEMPTION

Eden & Cain's story

ACKNOWLEDGMENTS

As always I have to thank Anaisja Henry for believing in me and encouraging my experimental ideas, and especially my going indie.

To all my readers who devoured this book and begged for more. Your love and support was immensely inspiring.

Cassie, for asking your Facebook group for premade ideas and delivering such a fantastic cover when I mentioned a Black couple. Thanks for supporting characters of color!

Bee, for the flawless discreet cover I loved as soon as I laid eyes on it.

Yenthe, for the STUNNING character art. I'm obsessed and can't wait to see what you do with Eden and Cain.

Erica, for making me feel like my writing is good enough. Like I have a place in adult romance. Your genuine excitement and cheering means the world to me.

Quirah Casey, forever thanks for the title. Previously this book was called *The Beautiful Ones*. Quirah had a set of premades in her Facebook group and one was entitled *The Sweetest Devotion* and I just fell in love with that title for Kennedy & Keith.

To everyone who enjoyed Kennedy & Keith's story and are waiting for what comes next ;)

Until my next release,

Britney

About the Author

Britney July is a dreamer from the Midwest who grew up camped out in her local library gorging on books. Now as an author, she endeavors to write fun and steamy edge-of-your-seat romances that leave you devouring page after page and emotionally undone.

When she's not writing, Britney can be found watching films, as her second love is cinema.